JAMES STODDARD
THE FALSE HOUSE

WARNER BOOKS

A Time Warner Company

WARNER BOOKS EDITION

Copyright © 2000 by James Stoddard
All rights reserved. No part of this book may be reproduced in any form or by any electronic or mechanical means, including information storage and retrieval systems, without permission in writing from the publisher, except by a reviewer who may quote brief passages in a review.

Cover design by Don Puckey
Cover illustration by Bob Eggleton
Hand lettering by Carl Dellacroce

Aspect® name and logo are registered trademarks of Warner Books.

Warner Books, Inc.
1271 Avenue of the Americas
New York, NY 10020

Visit our Web site at
www.twbookmark.com

Ⓦ A Time Warner Company

Printed in the United States of America

First Paperback Printing: January 2000

10 9 8 7 6 5 4 3 2 1

Acclaim for the fabulous world of Evenmere,
for author James Stoddard,
and for *The High House*—a *Locus*
Recommended Novel of the Year

"Stoddard tells a thrilling story . . . that features not
only a unique and powerful family but a magnificent
edifice filled with mysterious doors and passageways
that link kingdoms and unite the universe."
—*Publishers Weekly*

"Rich . . . filled with clever ideas and an elegance
lacking in much modern fantasy." —*Sci-Fi Universe*

"A high fantasy with intelligence and literary
power."   —*Realms of Fantasy*

"A real treasure. . . . Without question, *The High House*
is one of my favorite books of the year."
—**Charles DeLint,** *Magazine of Fantasy*
and Science Fiction

"For all connoisseurs of high fantasy and imagination."
—**Greg Bear, multiple award-winning author of**
Songs of Earth and Power

"Extraordinary . . . delightful, troubling, quirky."
—**Diane Duane, author of *The Book of Night***
with Moon* and *To Visit the Queen

"Intelligence and amazing literary power. Remarkable."
—**R. A. Salvatore, author of *The Demon Awakens***

more . . .

"A delightful secret passage of a book, quirky and exuberant."
— Sean Stewart, author of *Mockingbird* and *The Night Watch*

"This is what all fantasy should be: exciting, literate, intelligent."
— David Feintuch, author of *The Still*

"A very promising first novel."
— *Science Fiction Chronicle*

THE FALSE
HOUSE

The Crater

Carter Anderson, Master of Evenmere, stalked alone through the twilight corridors of the High House, where the flickering of the gas lamps, green-flamed, sent shadows twitching like seizured men, the hissing jets, their exhaled breath, the only sound amid the maze of gloaming stairs, drear avenues, cheerless cornices, glaring portraits, the staring statues in the brown-stone naves. In silence he went, Lightning Sword swinging jagged from his hip, Tawny Mantle shrouding his form, its chameleon powers merging him with the brown baseboards, the brown carpet, the brown buttercups on the tattered wallpaper of Innman Tor. In the gloom he could pass unseen inches away.

Three months had elapsed since his victory over the Bobby and the anarchists. The rebuilding of the White Circle had occupied his days, and even as he paced the passages, he chided himself, saying he had no time for this journey. Yet four nights before, at the witching hour, he had sat upright in his comfortable bed within the Inner

Chambers, awakened by a beckoning such as sometimes summons the Master of Evenmere, whose life and heart are attuned to the creaks and swayings of that ancient house. He had slept no more that night, but donning his travel garb and his soft leather boots, and taking up his mantle and his sword, had summoned his butler, William Hope, and informed him of his plan to depart at once to Innman Tor. And though he could have mustered a thousand soldiers as escort, it is the nature of the Master to travel alone.

He had avoided the Long Corridor, preferring more secluded reaches, and had passed through Naleewuath, and Keedin, and little Nyaset, thus seeing few other men, save some merchants traveling to Kitinthim, a pair of philosophers from Moomuth Kethorvian, and an ornithologist from High Gable, where the study of birds is considered the highest art. He had slept little and eaten only from the meager supplies in his pack.

Three hours before, he had crossed the border from Wainscot—a perfect country, faceted as a jewel, its every window a rose-stained glass—into the drab melancholy of Innman Tor. Combined with his own weariness, the tedium of halls made colorless by the anarchists' rule left him dispirited. Save for Fiffing, which lingered still in insurrection, Innman Tor had been his enemies' strongest foothold in the White Circle. There was much yet to be done.

Carter descended a spiral stair. Its hand-wrought banister, carved as leafy tendrils to imitate the branchings of a maple tree, with fanned leaves for the railing knobs, bespoke a time when the country had prospered. Still, with the expulsion of the anarchists, conditions were improv-

ing. Settlefrost, the old administrator, had resign
grace, and the people had elected Count Aegis, a man
known to be eccentric but forthright, as their First Factor.

Any other would have lost his way amid the myriad
twisting corridors, but it is not so with the Master. The
maps of the High House are within him, and Carter
moved easily between the shadows, sensing the vast heap
of wood and stone above him, the magnificent pile of
building. Each new vista brought an image to his mind,
and he could have mentally followed a single path unerr-
ingly for hours; indeed, he had done so many times the
last few weeks, sitting in his study beside the Book of
Forgotten Things, pursuing the winding of the corridors
as other men ponder a problem in chess.

He stepped through French doors and stood beneath a
night sky, moonless, but heavy with stars. Orion climbed
the eastern sky; red Mars stared piteously down. As often
occurred in the windowless halls, he had lost all perception of time, and to his surprise, his pocket watch marked
the approach of midnight. He had wanted to arrive in daylight, but he dared not tarry, and paused only long enough
to light the lantern from his pack.

Across wide fields he spied the lamps of the village of
Innman Tor. Despite the appearance of being outside the
house, he knew he stood in a vast courtyard, with Evenmere all around. As he trudged toward the squat houses,
the circle of his lantern light revealed young wheat standing defiant in scattered patches. The last time he had seen
the fields they had been brown with blight, and he gave a
grim smile.

He traversed the fields and doused his lantern as he
crossed the railroad tracks where the train slumbered, pale

yellow as a cat's eye, its locomotive scent pungent in the night air. A watch would be kept; having no desire to explain himself he kept near the buildings, trusting to his Tawny Mantle.

He crossed a barren course in the midst of the houses and came to the tattered edge of a crater in the very center of the town. It was a pit two hundred yards across and a hundred feet deep, where a tall hill—the Tor for which Innman was named—had once stood. In the darkness he discerned the monstrous crescent of the far side, the deep shadows of the descent. He stepped back warily, having forgotten its magnitude. Whether the anarchists had removed it through sorcery, science, or secret excavation, he did not know, but its demolition had been hidden by a false, skull-shaped Tor, an illusion substantial to the touch. He had dispelled this apparition three months before by speaking one of the Seven Words of Power, which only the Master may wield.

As he knelt to relight his lantern, his glance fell upon a peculiar mound, which he gradually perceived as the prone figure of a man. Silently, he drew his Lightning Sword, which emitted a soft, golden glow, and cautiously approached, sword tip aimed at the inert form. The man lay dead, his arms flung wide, a dark blot staining the front of his shirt. A rifle lay by his side. Reluctantly, Carter touched the corpse, to assure it was cold.

A light wind rose, startling him with the rustling of the tattered stalks of grain all around. He stepped back, sheathed his sword lest its rays reveal his position to any observers, and dropped to his knees to survey his surroundings. He saw nothing more in the uncertain light until he crawled to the edge of the crater and looked down upon a shrouded, bobbing lantern. He heard the dull stroke of shovels against earth.

He slid over the brink to the left, where the way was less steep. The bowl of the crater sloped gently down, and once he was no longer framed at the rim, he rose on his haunches and descended over red sandstone serrated beneath his hands where water had run. There had been hard rains during the rule of the anarchists, and the last reports had indicated a lake standing at the crater's core, though apparently it had finally seeped away.

As he drew near, he saw seven men in the gray coats of the anarchists, laboring with shovels and wheelbarrows while one with a rifle kept watch. Their faces were pale and grim beneath the lantern light; they worked in silence. At first Carter thought they were excavating, but quickly perceived they were instead filling a hole at the crater's center.

He considered his circumstance: eight men, all surely armed. Had they taken something from the crater, perhaps the legendary treasure of the Tor, or were they attempting to conceal a deed done long ago? As their work appeared far from concluded, he judged he had time to rouse Innman Tor and return with a party to arrest them.

He turned to depart, and found a ninth anarchist nearly upon him; he caught the gleam of upraised steel, heard the man's grunt of exertion as he strained to strike. Carter whipped his Lightning Sword from its scabbard and struck with an upward cut. The terraced blade erupted in a shower of sparks, almost cutting the man in two. Before the anarchist could even scream, Carter had already turned on his other foes.

He summoned a Word of Power as the sentry with the

rifle took aim. *Falan.* Even for the Master the Words are not easily employed, and invoked so quickly, the Word Which Manifests tore at his throat. The earth shook; a wave of force propelled outward from him, a golden, rippling circle, its light blinding in the darkness. As the surge struck the sentry, the rifle flew from his hands, and he fled, screaming in panic. The three anarchists standing nearest were knocked from their feet, the lantern falling with them; its glass shattered; its light failed.

Before any could recover, Carter drew his revolver. Two of the four men still standing dove into the unfilled hole, the third reached for his pistol, and the last stood frozen in fear. Carter fired twice at the one with the gun, who dropped it and fell backward, clutching his shoulder, even as the frightened man fled in terror.

As the brilliance of the Word faded and darkness closed, the two men in the hollow opened fire, their gun barrels spitting flame. Carter dove to earth, shooting blindly, and was rewarded by a cry of pain.

Hidden by the night, he crawled to a point left of his opponents, while bullets seared the earth where he had been. As the gunfire ceased, he grew still to avoid revealing his position.

Another man would have fled against such odds, yet an intuition of evil had summoned him to Innman; if he departed, the anarchists would slip away, leaving him to learn nothing. He could not retreat, and he was hardly helpless—in his excitement, having possessed his Tawny Mantle but a short time, he had forgotten its power. Once wrapped securely around him, it would grant him the appearance of his surroundings, a shadow among shades.

The first anarchist had spied him when he failed to keep it close.

"I have the lantern," someone hissed, not ten feet away. Carter raised himself on his haunches, ready to spring.

He leapt to his feet at the striking of the match. Distracted by the light, veiled from seeing by the Mantle's power, the two anarchists in the hollow did not sight Carter until he loomed above them, appearing as if from the ether, Tawny Mantle billowing, Lightning Sword in one hand, pistol in the other. He fired point-blank at one and slashed the other across the neck. The first screamed, the other groaned, and the light flickered out again.

Carter danced backward as two more pistols thundered, shells whistling past him on both sides. He slid to the left, a specter, until nearly behind his foes, where he crouched to consider his situation. By his reckoning, two of the nine had fled, and five were either dead or wounded, leaving two. His odds were greatly improved.

He approached stealthily, stopping often to listen. As his eyes reaccustomed themselves to the night he perceived two shadowy figures pressed against the earth, several feet apart. A third lay prone, groaning softly, his right arm thrown above his head. Carter searched the field but saw no one else.

He advanced silently, relying on his Mantle, and when quite close, thundered, "Make no move!"

The anarchist on the right whirled onto his back, and died there, shot twice through the chest. The other man threw his hands high and cried, "Don't shoot! I surrender! I surrender!"

Carter forced him to lie down again, hands and feet sprawled to the four quarters, then checked the groaning man and made him do the same. All the others had seemingly fled, and finding himself secure, Carter began to tremble. He had killed more men tonight than in his whole life before; he struggled to keep from being ill.

"I am the Master of the house," he said softly to the unwounded man. "What are you doing at Innman Tor? What did you steal?"

"We took nothing, my lord," the man said, voice quavering.

"Do you know the power of the Master?" Carter asked. "Answer truthfully or face my wrath."

"I implore you, my lord, do not abuse me. I am not a common lout, but a professor of history."

"You are far from your scholarly studies. A man becomes what he does. Why are you at Innman Tor?" Carter drew his Lightning Sword, and its glow made his features stark and cruel. He could not resort to torture, but to bluff and bluster.

"Mercy! I will tell. I will tell all! Mercy!"

Carter was never able to reconstruct what happened next, except he felt an enormous dread, as if a hand squeezed his heart. Simultaneously, the air trembled, and from the darkness coalesced an enormous face, illuminated with a light of its own, yet conferring no radiance on its surroundings, the visage of a man, shrouded in a hat and cloak. Malice emanated from it, a beating force that drove Carter to his knees. And beyond the countenance, another—the cold, white features of Lady Order—framed it.

Both faces rapidly shrank, and suddenly a figure twice human height, deepest jet, smooth as stone, a shadow among night shades, loomed above Carter and his captives, its hands the smooth claws of an eagle, perfect in their cruelty, descending to rend him.

Barely in time, Carter parried, hurling the Lightning Sword before him; a blinding charge erupted where blade and talon met; a burning wave like liquid fire beat against Carter's face. The assailant gave a shriek of pain and staggered backward, even as Carter's sword arm fell useless to his side, the blade dropping pale and cold from his hand.

Yet, as both adversaries stood benumbed, Carter summoned the Word Which Gives Strength, the only Word that leaves its Master stronger after being spoken, though it later takes its toll. *Sedhattee.* The earth shook; his arm grew hardy. He scooped up the sword and scrambled to his feet.

His enemy advanced again, towering above him, features suffused in rage. As Carter lifted his Lightning Sword in defiance, its star-light bloomed blinding radiance, brighter than before, causing the assailant to falter and cast his hands before his eyes. Carter struck without hesitation, slashing at his foe's left leg, ripping a cruel gash in the thigh. Not blood, but gray mist poured forth; the monster howled its rage and retreated toward the captured anarchists.

"Creature of Order!" Carter shouted, and at his words the monster paused. "You stand before the Master, who holds dominion over you. Fight no more, I command it, but return whence you came!"

It staggered as if struck. Then, with a baleful glare, it raised its hands above the anarchists; a dark whirlwind descended among them, only to dissipate just as quickly; and then the creature vanished.

Carter turned in a swift circle, heart pounding, seeking his foe. Seeing he was truly alone, he lit his lantern and examined the ground where the assailant's talons had torn the earth. As the light flickered over the captured anarchists, he gave a gasp at faces moon-pale, drained of life. A shiver raked his spine.

Before he could survey the excavation, he heard the whinny of a horse above the crater's edge. "The treasure!" he cried, and sprang away, his lantern light sending the shadows bobbing.

He sprawled over the crater's rim to the noise, diminishing in the distance, of fleeing hoofbeats and rattling wagon wheels. The tracks lay fresh in the loose soil, and he followed at a fast trot, stumbling over the furrows, thankful he kept himself in condition. Upon reaching the streets, he spied a wagon plunging along an avenue, carrying several men. Wasting no time in stealth, he ran after, and soon heard the cries of sentries at his back. When he disregarded the warnings, shots ricocheted on all sides; momentarily he feared being slain by his allies, but the pursuit soon fell behind.

At the outskirts of town, he followed the single road leading from Innman Tor. He maintained a strong, steady pace, while reserving a shard of strength for combat. At the end of a mile, beneath tall shadows of Corsican pines, rose the eaves of Evenmere.

He spied the wagon, standing beneath the gabled roofs, the light from a half-open doorway spilling onto a lathered, blowing horse. After a moment's indecision, he doused his lantern, slipped between the sheltering pines, and drew close enough to survey the house. He could not be certain whether any anarchists lurked there, but after careful observation, crept toward the rear of the wagon.

He found it empty; the thieves had indeed vanished. Drawing his pistol, he sprang to the half-open door and flung it wide. Pale yellow light flooded into the night. He stepped into a narrow foyer, then on through another door, finger on trigger, expecting an assault, but discovered only an empty corridor stretching into the distance. He pounded down its length; his quarry had several minutes advantage, but their use of the wagon suggested they carried a cumbersome prize. He came to an intersection, leading left and right, where he paused in uncertainty. Mentally, he followed the maps, tracing the branching corridors. The way to the left led to assorted rooms eventually returning to the courtyard surrounding Innman Tor, the way to the right, to other portions of the house. He took the latter, down the brown, lusterless halls, into unlighted passages. As he knelt to kindle his lamp, he thought he caught a distant flicker far down the corridor, but it faded too quickly, leaving him uncertain he had seen it at all.

He brought the lamp to a low burn, then mantled it, so its thin stream of escaping beams formed mock constellations on the walls. As he plunged at a trot into the shrouded way, objects seemed to leap before him, keeping him miserably apprehensive, the only sound his footfalls on the threadbare carpet, the pumping of lungs, the air flowing past, the hushed burning of the lamp.

He came to a spiral stair, with the corridor continuing beyond. If he followed the passage, it would soon lead to the fringes of Veth, where captured anarchists were usually hanged—if he chose the stair, the upper stories presented roads going either toward the Long Corridor or to the dark reaches of the south.

Wide-eyed, Carter ascended the stair, which ended at the next floor and opened onto a multitiered gallery. Gaslights sputtered in the hall below, luminating an intricately tiled floor. Tall windows stared down from the east; surely the room would be lovely in morning light. By this, he knew he had left drab Innman and passed into the ornate region of Lippenhost, one of its protectorates. He kept close to the banister rail, and had nearly traversed the gallery's length when he heard low voices and muffled footfalls above him. He doused his lantern at once and leaned over the railing to view the floor above.

A shrouded light passed directly overhead, but the railing hid the men from his sight, nor could he fathom their muttered words. Still, he was certain there were more than two, and their grunts and exhalations indicated they struggled with some burden.

He sought a route up, but having no rope, nor being able to reach the floor above by mounting the railing, raced toward the stair, guided only by the luminance below, certain he would meet no adversary. The mistake proved nearly fatal, as a shot rang out, not ten feet from him. He returned fire, and was answered by an agonized cry. He rushed to his assailant, knowing a wounded enemy to be most dangerous, but found the anarchist sprawled on his back behind a supporting pillar, dead. Carter could not comprehend how his life had been spared—until he recalled the power of his Tawny Mantle, for he had been running near the wall, concealed by his cloak. The man, seeing nothing, but hearing footfalls, had fired blindly.

He rushed through the gallery and clambered up the stair to the next floor, where he passed back through the hall, heart drumming, only to reach its end without meeting his foes. A rising panic overtook him, for they were approaching an area of many branchings, and he went as swiftly as stealth allowed, thinking he must be nearly upon them.

He entered a large, open area, knowing it so only by his maps, for with the lamps of the hall far behind, he went in utter darkness, listening, calming his breath lest he miss the breathing of others. Finally, he drew his Lightning Sword. Seven doors, outlined by its light, stood along the wall. By considering his maps, he eliminated all save two, of which either were likely. Both led by stairs in the same general direction, though they ended miles from one another. He chose based on hope alone.

The stair consisted of long runs and wide landings, red carpet soft as velvet, redwood railings, red-bird wallpaper running alongside—a comfortable place once, when it had been inhabited, made ghostly by the sword-light, the yellow eyes of the cardinals fiendish in its golden glow. Carter shivered and took the stair two steps at a time, but softly, to avoid coming unawares upon his foes. The top landing, like a red river, cascaded to crimson corridors, which flowed to more stairs, which coursed to corridors again, narrow passages like estuaries, with pictures of red roses hanging askew, flowers upon the banks. Yet always he knew his way, for only one exit in the upper stories could carry the anarchists beyond the wing.

When at last he reached that door, after a long hour of jittery corners, he found it irrevocably barred, nailed shut from his side, with metal plates strapped across it and screwed into the frame. Dismayed, he charged back the way he had come, dimly wondering what terror stood beyond that door for men to bolt it so fiercely.

With two hours lost, he reached bottom and began ascending the other way. Gambling against another assault, he abandoned caution for haste and finally exited onto a long passage. Although there are as many doorways in the High House as tunnels in a colony of ants, he now knew the anarchists would proceed toward the Long Corridor, thus avoiding the more populated region of the Downs of Gen. From there, he could not guess their final destination.

He followed throughout the night, and when the morning sun lit the panes and washed across the dancing motes, it found him following still through Querny. He welcomed the dawn, though it reminded him of his weariness, and he halted long enough to sit and breakfast on strips of dried meat from his pack.

Thereafter, because of fatigue, the way became arduous, and he went as in a dream. At midmorning, he met a man warming his feet before a fireplace, who offered him hot tea and reported seeing "four gentlemen, dressed in gray greatcoats, bearing a burden hidden in a burlap sack, carried between two poles as if it were the Ark of the Covenant."

Strengthened by the tea and the knowledge he had not lost the track, Carter pursued another three hours, eating lunch from his pack as he went. His enemies were surely as weary as he, yet showed no sign of flagging—desperate need, beyond the fear of pursuit, drove them. Afternoon gave way to evening, and still he did not overtake them.

At last, when the sunlight lay pale upon the lintels, he

attained a certain site he had sought, drew a ragged breath, gathered his strength, and summoned a Word of Power to mind. At first he could not bring it into focus— the Words are difficult to command, and his weariness strove against him—but finally it hung suspended within his thoughts, the letters burning with fire. He carried it to his lips, and spoke it with an effort. *Talheedin.* The Word of Secret Ways.

The corridor shook; the lamps trembled. A blue square of light, indicating the presence of a secret panel, arose from the doors of a wardrobe standing against one wall of the passage. He opened the wardrobe, reached into its depths, and pulled aside a row of fur coats to discover a hidden mechanism that caused the back to open onto a black corridor. He lit his lamp, entered, and shut the secret door behind.

The walls of the passage were bare and the corridor itself less than five feet tall, forcing him to stoop. The bare boards creaked beneath his boots, and part of the ceiling had collapsed to the floor, vanquished by the damp. According to the maps this passage provided a shortcut to the Long Corridor, which he hoped to use to outstrip his opponents.

Through two long hours he followed the dreary, changeless way. The use of the Word had drained him, and he stumbled as he went, but at last reached a hidden portal opening into the Long Corridor. A glimpse through a lensed spy-hole assured him no one was about, so he unlatched the door and exited.

He was far from those drab portions of the Long Corridor near the Gray Edge, and the wallpaper and carpet in the deserted passage glistened soft peach. He shut the door to the secret passage, a picture frame containing a rendering of Ilya of Murom riding in the pouch of the giant Svyatogor.

Doubt assailed him. He had hoped to arrive before his opponents, but could not be certain he had done so; they might be either before or behind him. Since he did not know their destination he might miss them either by dashing ahead or remaining behind. After brief consideration, he resolved to press on, hoping to encounter other travelers who had seen his foes. He soon met a pot-maker, dragging his creaking cart down the halls, who had followed the Long Corridor all the way from Naleewuath without glimpsing the anarchists. Now certain his enemies lay behind him, Carter turned back. He was tempted to conceal himself in one of the doorways and await their coming; midnight approached—his pursuit had lasted twenty-four hours, and had come after a long day of travel—yet he feared to lie down, lest they slip by while he dozed.

He walked dazed and dull for three hours, fighting to stay awake. At last, when he must either halt or sleep on his feet, he heard rustlings around the bend of the gently curving passage. He drew his pistol, hugged the wall, and crept forward.

The anarchists had raised a hidden door in the center of the corridor. Only three men were visible, the fourth having apparently already descended, one keeping watch while the others struggled to carry a burlap-wrapped burden into the opening. The sentry, expecting pursuit from behind, kept his attention there, giving Carter an opportunity to draw within a few feet.

"Halt where you are," he commanded, pistol aimed.

The sentry turned, gun flashing, but Carter downed him with a precise shot. The other two anarchists bolted down the stair, while a shout issued from the fourth below, who had apparently been struck by the full weight of the burden. One of the anarchists reached back up to shut the trapdoor; Carter fired to prevent it, but missed his target, and the door slammed shut, followed by the clatter of a bolt sliding into place.

Reaching the spot, he drew his Lightning Sword and struck a mighty blow; power exploded from it, disintegrating the carpet and leaving a burning stench, but the material beneath remained seared but otherwise unscathed. Carter stared in weary bewilderment, for the sword seldom failed to penetrate its target, yet apparently the Long Corridor was made of sterner stuff. He sheathed the blade and brought his maps to mind. The course the anarchists followed led through myriad turnings. Even with their burden, within twenty minutes they could reach passages too varied to trace.

"Faugh!" he cried aloud at his lack of foresight. Yet few of the secret ways are known by any save the Master; he had not considered his quarry using them.

Though he knew the cause lost, he refused to surrender. Despite his weariness, he made his way by a winding course into the passages the anarchists had taken, where he spent three hours vainly seeking their trail. Finally, foot-sore and defeated, he threw himself into a narrow alcove and tumbled into a slumber racked by dreams of corridors and flighty men.

He woke late the next morning. For a time, he considered returning to Innman Tor, for he wanted to investigate the crater by daylight, but he was almost as near to the

Inner Chambers now, and decided to send word to Count Aegis, ordering him to station a ring of sentries around the crater and await his coming. This time, he would not go alone.

The Flagstones

"The Master is coming! The new Master!"

Six days after Carter's pursuit of the anarchists, a young girl dashed down the streets of Innman Tor, shouting as she went beneath skies eloquent with the first warmth of spring.

The streets themselves were squalid; dust rose from the unpaved lanes at every footfall, lifting in a slow haze that covered the town, leaving it the dull brown of earth, from a distance indiscernible from the surrounding fields. There were no ornaments on the shutters or etchings on the doors, no carved eagles or bright banners. Everything was colorless—the window curtains, the wooden doors, even the clothing—for want of cloth most still wore the shapeless brown garments induced by the reign of the anarchists. Still, snatches of color were returning, as the inhabitants pieced together raiments from clothes hidden in trunks and musty closets. Lizbeth's own rebellion was an azure ribbon proudly tied round wisps of blond hair.

Amid the dreariness, she turned a corner and aimed to-ward a gaudy spectacle at the end of the street: Old Arny, guarding the gate to the Little Palace, standing stiff and proud beneath a withered oak, buttons straining on a scarlet uniform exhumed from a crate in his attic, a garment he had worn as a young man in the Yellow Room Wars. Though it was thread-worn and faded, Lizbeth thought it grand. He had served Count Aegis for decades.

His head rose at her approach, and though she tried to dodge, he intercepted her beside the gate, dropping his sword as he knelt to catch her in his arms, his red-feathered busby tumbling over his eyes.

"Arny, Arny, let me go! I have to tell Sarah the Master is coming!" She struggled in his arms, giggling.

Arny only grinned and held tighter. "And did you think she would not know, with the whole town assembled to see? But you're scuffing my shoes! Go ahead, Lizbeth, but slow yourself. We can't have you bowling the count off his feet."

She grinned back, all mischief in blue eyes, and dashed away as quickly as before. "Thank you, Arny."

The Little Palace was Count Aegis's home, and not a palace at all, but since the old palace had vanished with the Tor, and his was one of the few buildings with a stone fence and a gate to be guarded, it became the Little Palace immediately after his election two months before. It was not particularly large, but a two-story house of white wood and rough, ivory rock, with lambs carved in the lintels, stone faces peering from the four corners, doorknobs shaped like scarab beetles, and a gallery encircling the upper story with a honeycombed balustrade where a family of seven swallows had chosen to nest.

Lizbeth darted down the cobblestone path, scattering squawking chickens across the yard before her, and bounded up the steps onto the porch just as Sarah left the house in a silk dress, all soft pale gray, her midnight hair a striking contrast beneath a wide-brimmed hat trimmed with ribbons and feathers. She wore an amethyst brooch at her collar and pleated trim down the front to her wasp waist, which was encircled by a pleated belt and bow. Lace inserts jaunted the length of her long dress, ending in a border at the hem. She bore matching gloves and carried a long-handled umbrella. She was tall and fine-boned, which made her elegant, with cobalt eyes, blue and iron-gray intermixed in languid grace, though now looking slightly annoyed. "Lizbeth, I've been searching all over for you."

Lizbeth came to a halt before her, eyes agape. "Sarah, you look beautiful!"

Sarah's eyes softened, so Lizbeth knew she was not truly in trouble. "Thank you, little one, but it scarcely fits me at all. I've had it hidden away the last two years."

"Is it because of the Master?"

"And what else would it be? A pompous aristocrat, no doubt, full of stories about himself, come to Inman Tor to tell us everything we've done wrong and criticize Father, who has had little time to right the wrongs. But we have to follow ceremony, for the sake of the land."

"Is he not a good Master, then? My friends at school say he drove the anarchists away. I don't miss the soldiers. How cruel they were! And the children had to be very quiet and march in long lines, and follow all the rules and regulations. If the Master made them go away, he must be nice."

Sarah reached down and kissed her forehead. "You make the best of everything, my sweet, and shame me. But you shall ride with us to the station, to meet the new Master and judge for yourself."

"Could I? Truly, that would be wonderful!"

"Then you must hurry upstairs and put on your good dress."

Count Aegis stepped through the door onto the porch just then, clutching the bowler he wore only on state occasions, attired in his finest garb: a checkered Norfolk jacket, ten years old and frayed at the elbows, with a large bow tie dangling above his waistcoat. Upon his lapel he bore a red pin, the sole symbol of his office. His spectacles had shifted to the bridge of his nose.

"No time for dresses now," he said. "Dresses were an hour ago. Come as you are or come not at all."

Sarah reached up and adjusted his spectacles. "Are you nervous, Father?"

"Nothing to unnerve us. Lord Anderson is just a man. Puts his socks on one toe at a time, like the rest of us. But his train has come and we must meet him. Off to the carriage. March, march!"

"I put my socks on five toes at a time," Lizbeth said as Sarah guided her out the front gate.

"Then don't be surprised if you find one missing someday," Sarah said. "Friction, you know."

"Nuh uh," the child said.

"A scientific fact, like osmosis and steam engines."

The count helped Sarah into the worn carriage, and lifted Lizbeth up before climbing on himself, while Arny held the mare.

"Arny, where is Puddlesee?" Sarah asked.

"He went to find his best shoes, my lady."

"Shoes were ten minutes ago," she said. "Since he is not here, you must drive."

"Me, my lady? But who will guard the gate?"

"Arny, everything we own of value is now *in* the carriage."

"But Count Aegis likes to drive himself."

"If you wanted my father to drive his own carriage, you should never have elected him First Factor."

"I didn't, my lady. I voted against him."

"You voted against me?" the count asked, feigning shock.

"No offense, sir. You said you didn't want it."

"Arny, the carriage," Sarah said.

"Yes, my lady."

The streets were filled with those rushing to glimpse the new Master, and the mare, Judith, only two summers younger than Sarah's twenty-one, found it beneath her dignity to wade through the crowds, so Arny spent every moment coaxing her.

"Could have walked more quickly," Count Aegis said.

"Father, neither you nor I care one whit for formality, but today we must," Sarah said. "You must act the ruler, pomp and all."

Aegis glanced down the street at the houses, most still the dull brown the anarchists had painted them, and his eyes went bleak. "I will act the ruler when the people have bread and potatoes, pretty clothes for their daughters, and paint for their walls. What will the Master think of us?"

"And will we have root beer?" Lizbeth asked.

"Barrels of it," Aegis replied.

Lizbeth thought the count monstrously old, over forty surely, but she loved him dearly, with his spectacles always falling down, his walrus moustache turning gray, his shoes untied half the time, and his funny sayings, which she did not always understand. Sarah she idolized, thinking her the most beautiful, intelligent woman in all the world.

A brass band consisting of four tarnished trombones, one battered trumpet, and a booming drum played by a boy of nine struck up a ragged march as the carriage halted beside the train station. The pale yellow engine belched black smoke, the wind swirled dust to meet it, and for a moment the passenger car lay shrouded in grime. Out of this cloud of soot stepped a tall figure, wearing a top hat, a black frock coat and matching trousers, an upright collar with a knotted tie, and a peculiar, leopard-spotted cloak, nearly no color at all, across his shoulders. A sword jagged as lightning swung from his hip.

"We're just in time," Aegis said, hurrying Sarah and Lizbeth from the carriage. "Sarah, remember to be polite. Impertinence was only cute at seven."

"I'll be good, Father, so long as he treats you well."

They came quickly to the platform, for the crowds had stepped back, overawed.

The count strode to the fore and bowed at the waist. "Lord Anderson, Count Aegis."

The Master bowed as well, and then the two shook hands.

Lord Anderson looked nothing like Lizbeth had imagined, for she had expected him to be the most handsome, broad-shouldered of men, half a head taller than all others, part warrior, part saint. She had heard stories of how he drove the anarchists from Innman Tor and killed their leader with his bare hands. Standing on the train platform, save for his mantle and his sword, he might well have been a schoolmaster. His face was kind, not ferocious at all, though his eyes, the brightest of blues, looked sad.

"Lord Anderson, this is my daughter Sarah," Aegis said.

And then a strange thing happened as Sarah stepped up to the Master; Lizbeth remembered it quite clearly thereafter, for Lord Anderson's face went suddenly pale, and his eyes appeared odd, as if seeing something new. He did not speak for a moment, until he remembered himself and rasped out, "My pleasure." And Sarah, who Lizbeth knew feared nothing, and had not wanted to come at all, fell speechless as well, the resentment plunging from her face even as she dropped her eyes and executed a clumsy curtsy. And then they both stood, looking and not looking at one another at turns.

"Do you really own the whole house?" Lizbeth asked, seeing she was not to be introduced.

The Master turned to her eagerly and cleared his throat, "No, little miss, it is rather that the house owns me."

"How can a house own a person?"

"It is a very special house. And are you the count's daughter as well?"

"No, sir."

"Lizbeth came to live with us less than two years ago," Aegis said. "Her mother died when she was young. Her father, who joined the Anarchy Party after her death, vanished the night the Tor was transformed into the aspect of a skull. He was never seen again. We were in school together as boys; he was not a bad sort, though misguided by grief. We had known Lizbeth all her life, and she had nowhere to go."

Sarah stroked Lizbeth's hair. "Those were hard times."

"Yes, my brother and I were here toward the end," Lord Anderson said. "Which reminds me, I am forgetting myself."

He turned and waved back toward the train at a young, blond-haired man, a short, round-faced gentleman supervising the carrying of the luggage, and a swarthy ancient wearing the black curls of an Assyrian prince. A dozen ivory-mailed soldiers, members of the White Circle Guard, milled among the crowd, eyes alert for danger. The three men came quickly forward.

"This is my brother, Duskin Anderson," the Master said. "My Windkeep, Enoch, and my . . . butler . . . William Hope."

"Delighted," Mr. Hope said, removing his bowler and bowing to all.

"Peace upon your house," Enoch said, bowing as well.

Duskin's blond hair curled at the back of his cap; in the sunlight his eyes were even more pale than his brother's. He was dressed less formally than the Master, in a dark green lounge coat with checked trousers. When he was introduced to Lizbeth, she said, "Our hair is the same color."

He was but seventeen himself, and Lizbeth thought him wonderfully handsome. At her words, he smiled for the first time, bent down beside her, and held their hair together across his shoulder, comparing the color.

"Yours is more golden," he said.

"They're the same," she insisted, though he was correct.

"And have you always been beautiful?" he asked.

She giggled and socked his arm. And from that day she knew she loved him.

They supped at the Little Palace upon an oak table covered with white linen, just large enough to seat all seven. Sarah wanted Lizbeth to eat in the kitchen, but she would not, and Hope and Enoch insisted *they* should eat in the kitchen, which was only proper for servants, but the Master refused to allow it. They dined on braised goose with glazed vegetables, cucumbers in white sauce, truffles roasted in the embers, and Aylyrium cakes with coffee filling, a meal far more elegant than Lizbeth ever recalled before, so that she knew it would cost them their supplies for a week thereafter. She watched with interest as Sarah kept the pewter plates positioned so the holes in the linen would not show.

Carter Anderson proved a thoughtful man, with a quiet humor. Hope, more talkative, curious about everything, asked all sorts of questions, while Enoch told marvelous, ancient stories smelling of walled cities and pyramids. But Duskin seemed to enjoy Lizbeth better than he did the adults.

"You have done much in two months," Lord Anderson said to the count. "You have made wise use of the materials we sent."

"Honestly, my lord, it has been a cup of water to revive the desert," Aegis said. "We are grateful for everything you have done, but there is so much more to do, and little to do it with. When I took the reins from Settlefrost, the people thought we would find money and supplies hoarded in his coffers. We misunderstood his situation; the wealth of Innman Tor had been taken by train out of the country. If he was a weak ruler, he was more honest than we knew, a prisoner in his own palace. That is why he stepped down willingly. But as a result, we want for everything. And since the rain at the beginning of the summer delayed the planting, there will be little food for winter."

"We will find what you need," the Master said. "You will repay when you can. All the White Circle is with me on this. We are rebuilding Veth after the fires; we will rebuild Innman Tor."

"But what of the Tor itself?" Sarah asked. "Can you do anything to restore it?"

"Sarah, he is not a magician," the count said.

"No, but he is the Master, and the Master is said to have strange powers."

"I am sorry, Lord Anderson," Aegis said. "She was but a child when your father ruled, and the legends of his deeds have grown."

"But if the anarchists took the Tor away, could you not bring it back?" Sarah asked. "It is a symbol to our people, and the pit where it stood is a mockery to us."

"How the anarchists removed the true Tor, whether through sorcery or by secret excavations, I cannot say," the Master replied. "But the false Tor, the skull-faced illusion I dispelled, was meant to cover their work. I know of no way to return it to its place, except one shovelful of dirt at a time. It has been much on my mind, of late, why they removed it at all."

"For the treasure," Lizbeth said. "Everyone knows about the treasure."

"Yes, there is the legend," Hope said. "But what was the treasure? Surely more than material wealth, considering the resources necessary to remove an entire hill."

"And that is why you prowled the crater by night?" Sarah asked. "Surely, if you had sent word, we could have done that for you."

Lord Anderson smiled and looked down at his plate. "Yes. I must apologize for my breach of etiquette, but I was summoned by a calling in the night, a thing that has not happened to me before, though other Masters have written of it. I could not disobey. You must have suspected something as well, or you would not have placed a watch around the crater."

"Indeed," Aegis said, "but we erred by half measures. The man you found dead was Strawfast. The sentry on the other side, Harestone, was slain as well."

"Do not blame yourself," Lord Anderson said. "A battalion would not have stopped the creature I faced in the pit."

"We've heard nothing of this," Sarah said. "What kind of creature?"

Lord Anderson glanced down at the table, as if regretting his words. "I didn't mention it in my message because I didn't want to alarm your people. Undoubtedly it will not appear here again. I call the manifestation Lady Order, a Force given physical form by the anarchists. They have done this before."

"A woman?" Sarah asked.

"In appearance, but in reality no more human than a river or lightning bolt. The Balance between Order and Chaos must be disrupted for either force to materialize. Perhaps that is what I sensed in the night. At any rate, enormous energy had to be used to summon Lady Order from a distance, and that indicates desperate need. But I should like to examine the crater as soon as possible in the light of day."

"We can go this evening, if you like," the count replied.

Accompanied by Old Arny, the seven of them strolled together across a brown field, where blight had taken the crop, though sprigs of young wheat stood, defiant, in scattered patches. Lord Anderson seized a handful of dirt and let it slide through his hands. Sarah and Lizbeth paused to wait for him, while Duskin, Hope, Enoch, and the count, lost in conversation, continued on.

"What are you doing?" Lizbeth asked.

"The earth is healing," he said softly. "I sense it. When the anarchists brought their poison, it poisoned everything—the soil, the town, the people's hearts. Yet, it is coming back. The earth abides." He gave a grim smile.

"I suppose you own many farms?" Sarah asked.

The Master looked at her in surprise, a taint of bitterness in his laugh. "I? No, though I am trying to learn all I can, since many of the people are farmers. I have been an orphan most of my life, owning little more than a portrait of my mother and a carved sword."

"But your father was the Master before you."

"Yes. He was." Lizbeth looked up at him and saw sorrow again, close to the surface.

Wanting to be kind, she said, "I don't think you're pompous at all."

"Lizbeth!" Sarah cried.

The Master gave a deep chuckle. "And what made you change your mind?"

"Because you haven't said anything bad about the count. You haven't accused him of anything, and—"

"Lizbeth, that will be enough," Sarah said, unmistakable menace in her voice.

They walked in silence, Sarah's face scarlet. "I must apologize," she finally said.

"No need," Lord Anderson replied. "The Master coming down from on high, is that it? I understand. But the Master is the servant of the house, subject to those he rules. Your father is the same; I see it in him."

"Yes, but I thought you would be different, I suppose, way up in the Inner Chambers."

They continued in silence again.

"Sarah is a pretty name," he said abruptly.

"Thank you. My father wanted to name me Middle."

"Middle?"

"Middle Aegis."

"Oh, no," Lord Anderson said, chuckling. "Not really?"

"Truly," she said. "Mother saved me, bless her. The humor is in the blood, I fear. Father passed it down to me."

Lord Anderson laughed again. "I think it's wonderful."

They came to the tattered edge of the crater. Hope whistled under his breath, and Sarah clutched Lizbeth's hand.

"It's larger than I remembered," Duskin said.

"It's monstrous," Hope replied. "How did they do it, and why?"

"I would like to go down," the Master said.

"The way is less steep to the left," said the count.

Once over the edge, the bowl of the crater sloped gently down, and the company had little difficulty making their way toward the bottom. The red sandstone lay serrated where water had run over the rim. Otherwise, there was little to see.

"Up until the last two weeks a lake lay at the bottom from all the rain," Aegis said. "We had not examined it since it dried. Another mistake, I fear, but there is much to do at Innman Tor these days, and every hand is needed."

They came to the place where the water had stood; the earth lay splintered from the drying. Four men kept watch around the excavated area. The anarchists' bodies had been removed, but all else appeared undisturbed from the last time Carter had seen it; shovels and wheelbarrows lay scattered.

At the lowest point of the crater, dirt had been excavated three feet down in a ten-foot circle, and below this, a hole had been dug, two feet wide and nearly as deep. The Master bent to brush away the loose earth, revealing a smooth white-marble edge. "There's something hard here," he said, "like rock."

The earth upon the marble was less than an inch thick, and at Count Aegis's command, the four sentries shoveled away an area revealing four flagstones, each three-foot square, with the emblem of an archangel etched into their centers. Where the stones should have intersected lay the two-foot hole.

"See," Lord Anderson said. "Whatever stood between the flagstones has been removed. This is what they carried away."

"Yes," Hope said. "The hole is too small to have been merely another flagstone. A metal box, perhaps."

"Enoch," the Master said, "you have lived in the house longer than anyone. Was the Tor always here?"

Enoch shrugged. "Who can say? I visited this country before it was called Innman, shortly after the Lord God called me to wind the clocks in His house. Was the Tor here then? Can I remember? It was many centuries ago. The mind does not always recall clearly. But the etchings of the archangels on the stones, those I have seen before, in other places of great importance."

"And yet, the Tor covered these flagstones," Hope said. "Though the anarchists were able to destroy it, I doubt human hands placed it here. Was it then designed to obscure the flagstones? And you said the anarchists were not just excavating; they were attempting to fill the holes, to cover up their handiwork, suggesting they wanted to hide what they had done."

"Hello," Carter said, reaching farther into the niche. "I see a bit of stone." He brushed dirt away and withdrew a shard, five inches long and an inch thick. A strange expression passed over his face as he held it.

"What is it?" Duskin asked.

"I don't know, but there is power within it. I can feel it trembling, as if wanting to draw me to some unknown destination."

"Let me try," Duskin said.

Lord Anderson gave it to his brother. "I feel nothing," he said.

The Master raised his eyebrows. "Indeed? It is quite strong."

Several others of the party took it as well, though Lizbeth was not allowed, but only Lord Anderson could detect the mysterious pull. "I believe it is a portion of the object the anarchists removed."

The Master slipped the shard into his pocket, rose, and rubbed the dirt from his hands, his face grim, almost angry.

"But what *did* they remove?" Lizbeth asked, not liking his look at all.

But his eyes grew kind when he glanced at her. "What, indeed? We do not know. But what do we know for certain, Lizbeth?"

She looked at the flagstones and the missing portion. "That the anarchists took the treasure."

"Precisely."

"But what does it mean?" Aegis asked.

"It means that whatever was buried beneath Innman Tor has been stolen," the Master said. "And your country, perhaps the whole house, will never be the same until it is returned."

When Lizbeth came down to breakfast the next morning, she found only Sarah and Duskin in the kitchen.

"Hello," she said.

"Morning, little one," Duskin replied.

"I'm not little. I turn twelve in March."

"Oh. Sorry." Duskin grinned at her, though she did not understand why.

"Where is Lord Anderson?" she asked.

"He and Father have already eaten," Sarah said. "They went to visit some of the townspeople. Would you like eggs?"

"Yes, please. Why didn't you go with the Master, Duskin?"

Duskin made a face. "And listen to an afternoon of boring discussion? I do it when I have to, but I don't like it."

Sarah turned back to the stove and added a pair of eggs to the skillet. "But as the Master's advisor, you should learn all you can."

"I help him better at some things than others," he said, giving Lizbeth a wink. "And Hope is a fountain of knowledge. I say, don't you have a cook?"

Sarah colored slightly. "We did, but we dismissed him when things grew difficult. Father refuses to hire another, although he is entitled to use the palace treasury to do so."

"He's a good man. Has he always been in government?"

"More out than in," Sarah said. "He was on the Citizens' Council before the anarchists came, but he eventually resigned in protest after the king was exiled and Settlefrost took over. For a period of time, he was extremely unpopular, until everyone began to see he had been right about the anarchists. After the Bobby was defeated and Settlefrost resigned, they chose him as First Factor. Will you be joining your brother after breakfast?"

"No, I don't think so. I may just loll a bit, if you don't mind. Affairs of state truly weary me."

Sarah smiled. "It must be hard. You are what? Eighteen?"

"Almost. I'm seventeen for another six months."

"Politics will interest you more as you age. If you don't mind being left with Arny and Lizbeth, I may join them myself. I find it fascinating."

"No, I'll be fine. Actually, I'm scheduled to go out to the crater with Enoch and some of your people this afternoon to excavate a bit more."

"Would you like to see our garden?" Lizbeth asked. "I helped plant the wisteria."

"Certainly, little miss."

"I'm not little."

"Lizbeth, what happens to those who wart others?" Sarah asked.

"They get warts."

"A scientific fact. Remember it."

The Master stayed two days at Innman Tor, meeting with townsfolk, discussing crops and food distribution and a hundred other things Lizbeth could not comprehend, but she found in Duskin a companion. And though he never said it, she sensed his sympathy, for like her his father had vanished when he was young, and he knew well the ache in her heart. So he played with her as a tolerant cousin, carrying her across the lawns, spinning her around while she laughed merrily, hearing her tell stories from her favorite books, and dancing with her in the living room, she barely tall enough to reach his chest, sometimes standing on his feet as he carried her across the floor. And if she loved him before for his golden hair and blue eyes, she adored him now for his attention.

But Sarah was strange during their stay, fretful one moment, laughing the next, uncharacteristically checking her reflection in every mirror she passed, never happy with the result, wrinkling her nose at her eyes, or her mouth, or the way her hair touched her ivory neck. Though she owned only five dresses, both mornings she changed three times before finding the proper one, and shoes twelve times (Lizbeth counted the second day). She spoke constantly of what the Master said, or did, and how he looked when he was stern, and the way he smiled, and his Lightning Sword, and the sorrow in his eyes, and how all the people seemed to love him.

"But I thought you didn't like him at all," Lizbeth said.

"And I have every right to change my mind. That is a woman's imperative. He is nothing like I thought. He is truly here to help us."

On the evening of the second day, when Duskin and Enoch were still at the crater, and the count was busy negotiating for goose feathers with merchants from Westwing, Lizbeth found herself sitting on the back-porch swing with Sarah, while Lord Anderson strode the porch length, examining the flaking paint on the eaves. He no longer wore his mantle, his sword, and his hat, but neither he nor Sarah looked comfortable. They spoke of how quickly paint fades, and of the weather, and of the count, and of how Mr. Hope had found nothing in his research to suggest what had been stolen from the Tor, while the

Master paced the porch like a general surveying a battle, though the only thing to see was a pair of robins building a nest on one of the budding apple trees.

"Why is everyone so nervous?" Lizbeth asked as she held Roon, her beagle puppy.

"What makes you say that?" Lord Anderson asked, drawing quite still.

"You keep pacing."

"Lizbeth, unminded manners make mannerless minds," Sarah said. "Lord Anderson has been confined all day in council. He needs to exercise his legs."

"Like a horse too long in a stable?" Lizbeth asked.

The Master sat down rather quickly on the stone balustrade surrounding the porch. "An uncomplimentary analogy. Perhaps I'm simply too old to sit still, for fear of petrifying."

"Perhaps you're both," Sarah said. "An equestrian antiquarian. And since you've been studying farming and the marble beneath the Tor, an agrarian equestrian lapidarian antiquarian."

Lord Anderson held out his hands in mock surrender. "Stop! Please stop. I dare not match your wit. All I know is that in the last three weeks I have done enough sitting for a lifetime. So much of the White Circle was damaged by the anarchists, and everyone needs my help. All the years my father was Master, I never suspected the extent of his responsibilities. I do not complain; it is a marvelous adventure, but wearisome as well."

"And is all the house as wretched as Innman Tor?" Sarah asked.

"Parts are untouched. Others, such as Veth, were almost totally destroyed by fire. Fiffing is in anarchy, appointing new leaders, affixing blame, the hearts of many of its inhabitants rotten with the bile of the Bobby; North Lowing, once a beautiful country, full of rivers and green fields, is a vast ruin, its people refugees. I don't know if anyone will ever live there again. Innman Tor will recover sooner than these; your people have stout hearts."

"I thought us fools' fools."

Lord Anderson laughed. "No. Simply misled. We have all made our mistakes, I more than any other."

"But you are a great man," Sarah said.

He laughed again. "My position would indicate so. I will not rise to arrogance by pretending modesty, for I cannot forget the house chose me, but Evenmere humbles its Masters."

"The house itself?"

He shrugged. "Perhaps life. It humbled my father. And it humbled me when I was young. Yet, it is an exhilarating charge; more than I could wish. There is power in being the Master, both humbling and heartening. Sometimes it makes one presumptuous. I hope I have not been so at Innman Tor."

"In what way?" she asked. "I have seen nothing."

His voice grew soft. "That is because you have not seen everything. I would not want you to feel obligated, simply because of my position."

"But we are most grateful for all you have done. You have seen our poverty; you have been kind in our need."

"I do not speak of the condition of your people. Together, we will remedy that. My presumption lies in having asked your father if I might . . . call on you."

Lizbeth looked up from petting Roon, eager to hear. A

joy suffused Sarah's face for the barest instant, but she subdued it before Lord Anderson glanced her way.

"Of course," the Master continued quickly, "it all lies with you. You may have other suitors, though your father made no mention. At your word, I will not inflict myself upon you."

"I would feel . . . neither afflicted nor inflicted upon," Sarah said lightly, though her voice was strangely hoarse. "You are a strange man, Lord Anderson, wearing power as if it were a cloak, thinking no one sees, speaking always of your service to the house, as if it were alive and both your master and consort, escorted by a mad Jew who believes himself old as time, whose only duty is to wind the clocks, and a butler who speaks of precedence of law and the nature of the universe. And both these men you call your servants, yet treat one as father and the other as brother. It is not your power, or your position, which makes me agree to see you, for my father has both, and in the smallness of Innman Tor, as honorable a position as your own. But it is the way you are amid such power that I find intriguing."

"And you, plainspoken as you are, I believe to be a poet," the Master replied. "And that combination I find intriguing as well."

Then they both smiled.

And Lizbeth lowered her head close to Roon's ear, and whispered that they would marry and Lord Anderson and his servants would come live in the Little Palace, Duskin with them, so she and he could dance forever on the maple floors.

Thus, it was an enormous disappointment when Duskin did not return with the Master on his next visit, or any thereafter. Lizbeth asked about him each time, but the answer was always that he was busy, usually hunting in a far-off country named Naleewuath. Lord Anderson, who she came to call Carter, told her wonderful stories of that land, how both the tigers and the furniture could speak, though the great cats were friendly and the furniture was not, so that tigers and men hunted the furniture-beasts through tiny rooms with many doors. And though the stories were exciting, she still did not understand why Duskin spent so much time there, that he could not visit her. Seeing her sorrow, Carter promised to take Lizbeth, Sarah, and Count Aegis to his home in the Inner Chambers, once things were better at Innman Tor, so she might see Duskin once more.

Lizbeth thought it terribly romantic that Lord Anderson should court Sarah, for he was tall and a great lord, and his quiet humor won her over, until she forgot she had once believed him a schoolteacher. The sorrow that hung about him frayed a bit each time he saw Sarah, as they laughed together and walked the lanes of Innman Tor, or played lawn-darts on grounds returning to green from the blight, or simply sat, Carter listening as Sarah read poetry she composed. Lizbeth he called their "little chaperone," for she accompanied them everywhere, on carriage rides and picnics, or searching for lilies near the portions of the house surrounding Innman Tor.

Food and supplies poured into the town from all the

White Circle, so by summer's end there was indeed bread and potatoes, lumber and nails, paint for the houses, and even root beer. The people said having the new Master court the count's daughter was a grand thing, and ascribed to it all their good fortune, even when the fruit trees flowered again and the wheat arose from the newly tilled earth, for all knew the Master commanded great power.

Because their houses and garments had been drab brown during the years the anarchists ruled, the inhabitants painted everything brilliant hues and fashioned their clothes from the brightest fabrics, so for many years thereafter Innman looked like a carnival. If it was gaudy, Sarah said they should be forgiven being color-blind after seeing so little of it for so long.

There came a day when the winds billowed from the northwest, not yet cold, but fraught with the first whispers of autumn. The leaves were turning; the earth stood rich and brown; the air smelled sweet with summer's end, as it always does so mortals do not mourn its passing overmuch. Carter, Sarah, and Lizbeth had taken the carriage to a little grove, close to that portion of the High House surrounding Innman Tor, where water trickled from the hands of a stone angel, overlooking a small fountain in the midst of a copse of tall elms and Corsican pines, a private place, with a granite bench and squirrels taunting one another amid the branches. They ate a picnic of steamed macaroni and grated cheese, layered with forcemeat, truffled roast chicken, and, best of all to Lizbeth, bread pudding.

The air grew still; the glory of the departing summer descended upon them; clouds drifted in heavy herds across the sky, diffusing the sunlight, leaving all in golden haze. Lizbeth laughed to be alive and walked the edge of the fountain, which was narrow enough she had to place one foot directly before the other.

"Watch me!" she cried, but when she had circled the fountain's lip, she turned and saw they had not observed at all, for Carter knelt on one knee before Sarah, who sat upon the granite bench.

Then Lizbeth shouted no more for them to see, but drew near, and heard him say: "Sarah, you are the fairest and brightest of women, good beyond hope, wise beyond scholarship, clever beyond cunning, radiant with heaven's beauty. There can be no higher honor than to have you for my wife, if only you would consent. Though I am not worthy, I dare ask because my heart requires nothing less. Will you marry me?"

Then Sarah sat quite still, put her hands together, folded her arms, unfolded them, touched her fingers to her face, then clasped her hands to her lap and burst out laughing, until Carter's face gradually reddened.

"My lady, I do not understand what is so funny."

But she took his face in her hands. "Forgive me, my lord, but you seem so serious, kneeling there, with the shafts of sunlight falling upon you. And could you not have sat beside me and asked as well? You have called me a poet, but there is poetry in you when I least expect it."

Tears sprang unbidden to the corners of her eyes and her voice caught as she said, "I was angry when I first saw your face, those months ago at the train station, thinking you proud and haughty, yet, most curious of turns, finding myself loving you as well. Angry and smitten, all at once. Most interesting. I will marry you indeed, sir, if you can keep me so through all the years."

"And if you are more smitten than angry, all will be well?" he asked.

"Ah, who plays with words now?"

And Lizbeth danced and giggled across the yard.

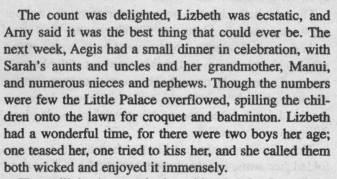

The count was delighted, Lizbeth was ecstatic, and Amy said it was the best thing that could ever be. The next week, Aegis had a small dinner in celebration, with Sarah's aunts and uncles and her grandmother, Manui, and numerous nieces and nephews. Though the numbers were few the Little Palace overflowed, spilling the children onto the lawn for croquet and badminton. Lizbeth had a wonderful time, for there were two boys her age; one teased her, one tried to kiss her, and she called them both wicked and enjoyed it immensely.

The twilight came early, hazed by the clouds, and the young ones drifted in, some coaxed and some carried; the two boys disappeared behind the house in a game of chase, and Lizbeth found herself pursuing the first fireflies alone. She was about to enter the house herself when she heard the soft calling of her name from behind the honeysuckle at the back gate.

"Is someone there?" she cried, thinking the boys had returned to frighten her.

But a man leaned out to beckon from behind the leaves, his face half-shrouded in the twilight.

"Papa?" she cried, drawing near, her heart suddenly pounding.

"Come here, Lizbeth," the man said, his deep voice almost a growl.

"Papa, you've come back!" she cried, rushing into his arms. He knelt to embrace her, and she clung to him. "Oh, Papa, I've missed you so! Where have you been? Why were you away so long?"

"No time for talk," her father said. "Come with me."

"What's the matter? Can't you come in?"

"Not in. Come away."

"But where are we going?"

"I will show you. No time."

"Very well."

He took her hand and led her through the back gate, which stood half-open. It creaked softly as he shut it, and he muttered under his breath, a soft murmuring that continued thereafter, like the whispering of wind across the leaves.

"Papa, your hand is ice cold," she said. "Have you been ill? Is that why you were gone so long?"

"Quiet," he said. "Later."

Ever he refused to answer her questions as they traveled between the houses, down the long alleys, pausing sometimes to hide from stragglers strolling through the streets. Darkness had fallen as they passed the last avenues and angled across the fields, leaving Innman Tor.

"Father, I'm becoming frightened."

But he clutched her hand in a fierce grip and said nothing. She pulled hard and drew away. "I'm frightened, Daddy."

He looked down upon her with expressionless eyes and reached for her hand. She darted away, keeping her distance. "Why are you doing this?"

"Trust me," he said, holding out his hand. "Come."

She wanted to run away more than anything, for at that

moment, her father seemed a stranger, a creature with his face, staring from behind his eyes. She stood uncertain, looking back at the lights of the town, thinking of Count Aegis and Sarah, and Carter, and the warm home she had known for two years. Her lip trembled; she began to weep.

"Don't . . . cry," he said, still holding his hand out like a mannequin. "Come. I am your father."

And gradually, though she wanted to run, she returned to him, drawn by the ache of having lost him before. She put her hand in his, but he snatched her roughly into his arms, and trotted swiftly across the fields.

Then she became truly afraid and began to scream, but he ignored her pleas, and they were too far from Innman for anyone to hear. He fled past the very place where Carter had proposed to Sarah, past the Corsican pines and the angel fountain, and entered a door beneath shadowed eaves.

Corridors and stairways streamed by, and when she could scream no more she wept, and when she could weep no more, she lay silent. As minutes turned to hours, she fell asleep, and dreamed of being rocked in Sarah's arms.

When she awoke she found herself still traveling, but they no longer journeyed alone; a pair of men in gray coats accompanied them, one carrying a lantern through the benighted passages. These she guessed to be anarchists, for they were much like the thin, shrewd men who had once lorded over Innman Tor. They did not speak, but went as those who fear capture. Throughout the night they kept their rigorous pace, not setting her down even a moment. Despite her fear, or perhaps because of it, she slept again.

They woke her long enough to feed her dried meat and crusty bread washed down with lukewarm water, in a bare passageway with wooden floors shining in the lantern light, and white swans floating on the wallpaper. She sat beside her father, chewing mechanically, scarcely hungry.

"Daddy, where are we going?"

Her father looked down, his eyes yellow in the lamp-light. He made no move to touch her. "Not far. Not far now."

"Where have you been, Papa?" she asked, but he did not reply, so she knew she had been a very bad girl to make him so angry. She wept again, in sniffling sobs, ut-terly weary.

After the meal, he carried her once more, and they con-tinued down the passage until they reached French doors, facing east, with the rising sun streaming through win-dows beyond, onto a corridor resplendent with banners of royal purple, purple draperies embossed with gold, and purple carpets bordered with golden fleur-de-lis. A brass plate above the doors read: WELCOME TO BISNEY, UNDER THE KING'S LAW. The sun cheered her, so she believed they had found someplace nice, but there was no one to greet them as they stepped through the French doors.

"You have performed adequately," one of the anar-chists said. "You will be rewarded. Give her to me."

"No, Papa! Don't let him have me! No!"

But he handed her into the arms of the anarchist, who sagged beneath her weight, though her papa had carried her tirelessly for hours. As they took her away, he stood silent at the doors. She kicked and screamed, flailing toward him, begging him to take her back. Over the anarchist's shoulder, she saw him turn away, neither love nor concern upon his face, no expression in his animal eyes.

She fought a long time, until exhaustion took her. After that she did not care what happened, for she knew she was going to be punished, though she did not know why, and she wept for Sarah and the count until she could weep no more.

They traveled many days through the house, along winding ways, some lighted and cheerful, others grim as stone, where the lamp-light wavered like will-o'-the-wisps. After the first hour, they ceased carrying her except when she grew weary, but made her walk, though they tied a rope around her wrist, attaching it to one of their own, so she could not escape. Mostly she was lonesome, for the anarchists did not speak to her; they scarcely spoke at all, and when they did it concerned matters she could not understand. Always they watched her, though where she could have gone, she did not know. She felt the same helplessness she had known when her father had first disappeared, two years before, except this was worse, for then she had anticipated his return; that was lost to her now.

After what seemed many days, they came to a portion of the house all iron and gray brick, solemn and stark. Fierce guards, dressed in chain mail and bearing pikes, defended the corridors, and the anarchists had to present letters of passage to each in turn. Always the sentries asked where they were going; always they said, "Beyond the Borderlands." Then the guards grew silent, their eyes lidded with dread, and asked no more questions, but allowed the anarchists to pass.

They traveled several days through that bleak country, until they descended by a winding stair to a corridor less than two feet wide and six tall, constructed of the same gray bricks. This they followed for hours, until Lizbeth imagined they traveled through the belly of a snake. At last, they came to an iron door, no taller than Lizbeth, that opened by the turning of a steel valve requiring both the men's strength.

They extinguished their lamp and carried Lizbeth into an utter darkness.

"Please," she said to the anarchist who held her, though she could see nothing of him. "Where are we? Why is there no light?"

"There is neither moon nor stars here," the man replied. "This is the country which some call Oblivion."

They waited a time, until she saw it was not as dark as she had supposed, but bright as a sliver-moon night, and her captors appeared as shrouded shadows, though the source of the luminance was hidden from her. Still, if she had considered, there was something uncanny about the light, for she could discern a vast plain before her, sloping slightly upward, and at the horizon, the dim lamps of a witchy house, the only structure in all that great expanse.

They set out across the plain, and as they went she became frightened once more, and fought against her captor. He drew his hand back to strike her, but the other cried, "No! Have pity on her. She is but a child, and will suffer a terrible fate."

"Then *you* carry her!" the other said, handing her to him. And because he had shown a thread of kindness, despite his dreadful words, she struggled no more, but closed her eyes tight, and prayed Count Aegis and Master Anderson would come to her rescue. As is the way of children, she looked hopefully behind, in case they might already be in pursuit, but saw only the great walls and towers of the High House, falling farther and farther behind, all gables and gargoyles, a vast, monstrous heap in the darkness, its yellow lights staring blindly, like goblin lanterns, into the enormous night.

The air was chill on the plain, though no wind blew, and sharp stones of jet littered the ground, glittering as if all the stars had fallen to earth, to lie in ruined mockery of their former glory. The anarchists traveled several hours through the waste, and by the time they approached the lone house, Lizbeth's fingers and ears were stiff from the cold.

They passed down a cobbled lane where a light from a single lamppost spread a vaporous green glow. The house was smaller than the Little Palace, tall and thin, with a wicked red glow radiating from a single rectangular window. The kinder anarchist, puffing from the exertion of carrying her, set Lizbeth down, though he kept a fierce grip on her hand. They approached a tall door, decorated in red and blue stained glass, cut in small, precise squares, with light shining through it. One of the anarchists knocked, and a man appeared bearing a lantern and a revolver.

"We've brought the girl," one of her captors said.

"Come in. *He's* been waiting."

They led her through a drab, ill-lit hall and up a stair,

where they thrust her, alone, into a small room; she heard the turning of a key in the lock behind her.

The chamber was ordinary enough, with wooden floors, a dull painting of gray flowers on one wall, and a single chair beside a rectangular table in the center of the room. On the table, a luminant tube, green and liquid, shaped in an oval, flung flickering light across the floor, rising in spurts to reveal the faces of machines composed of spiraling tubes, cylindrical tanks, lenses, orbs, and mechanical arms, their bulk hidden in the shadowed edges of the room. A bellows blew soft puffs of steam to the ceiling. A heavy stone block, etched with symbols and cherubim, sat on the table as well.

"Welcome," a voice said, from the midst of the darkness, making her squeal in fear. "Welcome, Lizbeth Powell. I am the lord of this house, the Man in the Dark."

She sought to penetrate the shadows, but saw nothing. "Please, sir, let me go home. I haven't done anything."

"You will never go home. You will live the rest of your life in this country, this land of Outer Darkness, for your father has sold you for an exceedingly small price."

Lizbeth burst into tears. As if in answer, one of the shadows disengaged from behind the machinery, and the Man in the Dark approached, garbed all in black, shrouded in a greatcoat and the shadows of the room, like a walking silhouette.

"No tears," he said, and reached out quickly with his ebony hand. She screamed as it passed right through her chest, though she felt no pain, other than a terrible chill. When he withdrew his hand, something pulsed within it. So great was her fear, her tears ceased. He retired back into the darkness, then spoke in barely a whisper: "We have taken your heart, and your soul with it, and you will never, ever know love. Those things are gone from you. You will live in dreariness, in the dull sameness of the house, and you will always be alone. And the years will pass, and no one will remember you, for they will think you long dead. But we will make you our princess, the queen of the anarchists, and we will build a house for you greater than all of Evenmere, and more wondrous; we will conquer the High House, and use its planks and stones for our own construction."

He stepped closer, carrying a necklace, which he placed around her neck as she stood in terror, her back against the table. "When you are grown you will be the greatest woman in all the world, and all will bow before you. This necklace is but the first cold stone to replace your stolen heart."

A single gem gleamed dully on the silver chain, an onyx heart no larger than the end of her thumb, encased in glass, untouchable.

"It's so small," she whimpered. "It's the heart of a baby."

"It is the only one you will ever know."

"You better take me back," she said, becoming angry. "Master Anderson will find me, and he will make you pay."

But the Man in the Dark only laughed a dry, mirthless laugh. "Why, it was Carter Anderson who arranged your abduction."

Thereafter he vanished into the shadows. Other anarchists entered and took her to a tasteless supper, and afterward put her to bed in a gray, remorseless room, where she wept until sleep overwhelmed her.

So it was Lizbeth came to live at the False House. She had free run of it, small as it was, save for the locked room at the top of the stair where the Man in the Dark stayed. The outside doors were likewise bolted, and she could discover no windows, not even the one with the red light she had seen from the outside. The cold, gray anarchists never spoke to her except at need.

When she had been there almost a week, they led her to a walled garden, made of gray bricks, with a brackish fountain at its center, that flowed under the wall in a narrow channel. "You may plant what you wish in this garden," the anarchists told her, and they gave her seeds, but the only things that grew were brambles and thorns.

Another would have despaired, and indeed, for a time she did, but as the weeks passed, she refused to believe the lies of her captors, and vowed that whatever compliance she pretended, she would always seek escape. So she cultivated the thorns and brambles, and shaped them as another would fashion roses, and though only she saw beauty in the garden, it was real enough to her.

And through the years the house gradually grew larger, though she never saw anyone with hammer or saw, nor heard the noise of carpenter's plane.

And one day, overhearing an anarchist say that the stream that ran beneath the garden wall flowed all the way to Evenmere, she formulated a plan. Thereafter, whenever she could steal a bottle, whether wine or any other with a cork, she wrote a letter, sealed it in the glass, and sent it drifting under the wall. She always addressed these to Duskin Anderson, for thinking she had no heart to set on anything, she set her mind on him alone, believing that someday he would hear of her capture, and come to her rescue, with his shining eyes and his glistening blond hair, and he would return her to the count and Sarah in the Little Palace, where she would live forevermore.

The Lampman

Arboreal winds howled outside the High House, moaning down the chimneys, whistling as they tattered the eaves and raked the stone gargoyles, gryphons, angels, and friars scattered across rooftops misshapen and ponderous with snow. The gale bayed its Fenris-howl of winter unchanging, hunting its prey with cold, sharp fangs. The fields of March lay coffined beneath the heavy veil, the ponds frozen, the trees, snow-bearded vagrants, put to sleep standing.

Carter listened to the wind, disturbed by its anger, its strident voices shrieking like the unconsoled dead. But for that, and Chant's absence, he might have been content, tucked beneath the massive fluted arch of the white-marble inglenook, the fire warming the patterned tiles on the walls and Persian rugs of royal purple, adorned with golden sunflowers, lying at his feet. A leather-bound volume of MacDonald's *Lilith* lay discarded beside him, while he pondered an oaken board standing on the mantel, displaying a triple-towered castle with an armored hand wielding a sword rising from the topmost turret, and beneath, the words: "Gainsay Who Dare." From his position beneath the heavy arch he could only see the corner of the carving, but it had been there since his boyhood, and he knew the words well.

"But the storm has gainsaid," he murmured softly, thinking of the endless miles of Evenmere, its towers and gables mantled by the snow, "and who can gainsay *it*?"

"Are you conversing with yourself, or harboring familiar spirits?" a voice asked.

He smiled up at Sarah, who had entered the dining hall and stood before the inglenook, warming her hands against the flames. She was dressed all in green, in a plain skirt, with a richly braided basque, trimmed and faced with Persian lamb, her raven hair pulled back in a bun, so her eyes were everything, and though she smiled, he saw she had been weeping.

"No spirit as mischievous as you," he said. "Come sit beside me."

He moved the book so she could share the cushioned bench. She took his hand and asked, "On what have you been brooding?"

"Charming thoughts—despair, darkness, dread. Especially dread. You mention familiar spirits: can you hear the wind?"

"The storm has been appalling."

"Yes. Cattle dying on the Terraces, lack of food, that is grave enough. But sitting here, I hear a voice in the tempest and a power. It is unnatural, Sarah. I know it suddenly, irrevocably."

"The anarchists?"

Carter shrugged. "Likely enough. My thoughts keep returning to the treasure of Innman Tor. I wonder if the two are related?"

"Perhaps. Or perhaps you remember it because today is Lizbeth's birthday."

Carter cocked his head back. "Is it? Would I have recalled? I wonder."

"It is no fault of yours. I don't always tell you. You never had the chance to celebrate . . . any of her birthdays. She would be eighteen today. If I knew she lived, or even that she had perished, my heart would rest. Do we dare ask the dinosaur once more?"

Carter shook his head. "That old dragon! I think he knows, but he is full of spite. *As one of the departed souls,* he called her. What does it mean? He only uses riddles when he wishes to deceive. I've seen him baffled but once, when I asked him of the treasure of the Tor. But we must accept that Lizbeth is lost to us. Long ago, I told you the house humbles its Masters; it has humbled me in this. That year, when I inherited my father's things, became Master, defeated the Bobby, and courted you, I thought myself invincible. Yet I could not find a lone child. Even today, after all these years, when I wander the manor, I find myself listening, watching for her."

"You did all you could." She patted his hand and sighed. "But she was like both sister and daughter to me. And that we have had no children of our own . . . I know it troubles you. I am sorry—"

"Shhh," Carter said, pulling her head to his shoulder. "We share that grief. Perhaps God will grant our prayers, though the doctor could promise us nothing."

They sat together in silence as a dull pain welled and

subsided in Carter's breast. Finally, he said, "Today, I have another search to make. Chant has been gone too long."

"Chant goes where he wills, and is often absent for days."

"Yes, so I thought, but that was before I heard the voice in the storm. There are things the Master knows. The Balance is changed, Sarah, between Chaos and Order. I've sensed it like an ache in the back of my head ever since I saw Lady Order at Innman Tor, but today—just now—I *know*. It has slipped disastrously. Forces are moving and I fear for Chant."

"Where will you go?"

"That is the question. I should speak with Hope and Enoch."

"I sought you to cheer myself. Why do I feel no better?"

He kissed her quickly on the mouth. "I am the brooding one. I married *you* to add cheer. Why you married me, I couldn't say."

"Perhaps it was as the people of Innman said, so you would bring us shoes and corn. I should have sought higher; I bartered badly."

"You wound me."

"I see no blood. Or corn, for that matter. I will accompany you to find Enoch and Hope."

They stepped from the inglenook, and Carter glanced up at the bas-relief border above it, depicting scores of squirrels bounding between maple branches, with plaster grape clusters alongside. It was a dusky room, the ceiling and walls paneled in dark oak, its centerpiece a massive table with leather border and clawed legs. Etchings of mice scurried around the periphery of the crystal chandelier.

Arm in arm, they left the dining hall and proceeded down the transverse corridor, past mahogany panels glimmering redly in the gloom and flying buttresses carved with kittens swatting balls of yarn. The main staircase stood to their right, all dark oak, with talons for banister knobs, and an ironwood eagle with a six-foot wingspan above the highest landing, surveying its prey below. Beyond it, the corridor turned west beside the garden entrance, ending at two doors, one leading into the gentleman's chamber, the other, the picture gallery.

The door to the gentleman's chamber stood half-open, and a low, tuneless humming issued from within, it being Mr. Hope's habit to spend his hours in the small office he maintained there. Carter rapped on the door, and it swung open, onto a stodgy room, with a tall window framed in a paneled box, a long leather couch beneath dark wainscot, and a pale-rose dolomite fireplace surrounded by an oak mantel with concave panels on either side. The ceiling and border were soft-white, with plaster bells descending. A wrought-iron light fixture in the shape of an "H" supported four lights, draped in ruffled shades, focusing on an oak billiards table. An oriental rug, red, gold, and green, surrounded the billiards table, but had been cut away beneath it, allowing the legs to sit solid on the wood floor. The name *Gavagans* was carefully etched in the wood around one of the pockets.

Hope's desk occupied one end of the chamber, and he had made the area wholly his own, for every table, stand, and bookcase were covered with a wondrous variety of knickknacks: books and pipes, wooden tools, maps and bottles, worthless stones from far countries, drawings six centuries old, ancient humidors, and tiny children's dolls carved in ivory. An enormous magnifying glass sat on his desk beside a small, battered armband with runes upon it, wrapped with an identifying tag, stating, tentatively: *Erreth-Akbe?* A heavily gilded, begrimed mirror sat in one corner, its surface obscured by dried soap.

Hope peeked out from behind an enormous red-leather volume titled in French, a pair of spectacles resting on the bridge of his nose.

"Have you a moment?" Carter asked.

Hope half stood, his version of a bow, then fell back into the chair. "Come in, just reading some fascinating works on ancient treaties. Did you know every three years we are supposed to send two brass apples, fashioned by the artisans of Keedin, to the people of Indrin as a sign of our continued friendship? In return they deliver twelve bottles of their best wine."

"When was the last time this was done?" Carter asked.

Hope thrust his nose back into the book. "Hmmm. We're about four hundred twenty years behind. But since the people of Keedin no longer mine copper, and Indrin has abandoned its grape orchards, it may be just as well."

Sarah laughed. "Do you really spend your time reading that rubbish, or is it all a ploy? I poke my head in occasionally, but have never caught you playing billiards."

"Madame, I am a student of the vagaries of law, not of the assurances of geometry. I cannot proscribe to the ridiculous theory that numbers are consistent, nor that angles remain constant. My acquaintance with this house has assured me that my initial intuition was correct: the precepts of the universe are as changeable as the laws in a courtroom. Why would I wish to participate in a game which supports an insupportable supposition? Chess, now, there is a game, all chaos and confusion."

"But, surely, chess has strict rules," Sarah said. "I have thrashed you soundly using them."

"Quite correct," Hope said, a smile circling his round face. "But if we were to decide to play by different rules, no one would argue its impossibility."

"But, sir—"

"Please don't start," Carter said. "Once the two of you begin, it moves outward in a widening whirlwind. We came because I am concerned about Chant."

Hope's eyes grew grave. "What is it?"

"A stirring. I fear for his safety. He rarely tells me where he goes, but I thought either you or Enoch might know."

"Hmmm. The danger of letting your servants be about their Master's business, I suppose. Enoch is gone to wind the clocks in the Towers; I expect him no earlier than Friday. But Chant's rounds are not the mystery you suppose. I have made it my business to accompany him, as well as Enoch, to know their route, and I keep a record, as did Brittle before me. They report their movements, for their work is too critical to leave to chance. A moment."

Hope withdrew a gray notebook from a desk drawer and thumbed through it. "This is Wednesday. Chant left on Saturday, following the route leading to Lamplighter's Lane. A two-day journey at best, taking into consideration all the lamps he checks along the way. Logically, you should proceed straight to the Lane, since you will likely meet him on his return route, assuming he has simply been delayed. You can arrive in somewhat less than a day by following the most direct course. Should we send a company with you?"

"No. I shall go alone. The servants cannot enter the Lane at any rate—the way is guarded against any save Chant and myself."

"What do you suspect, and what can I do?" Hope asked.

"I do not know the answer to either question. I am simply uneasy."

With his greatcoat upon him and his mantle and his sword, Carter departed the Inner Chambers. Sarah accompanied him down the narrow hall to the doorway beneath the servants' stair. Within lay various remains: a wooden rocking horse, broken and dreaming, a toy sailing ship, sea-green and splendid save for a puncture in its keel, discarded paintings and notebooks, and a green door with a glass knob containing an exact model of the High House as seen from the north. Carter drew the Master Keys from his pocket; the bronze ring shone dully beneath the single gaslight. They sparkled in his hands, each a different color, size, and shape, some with angel's wings or faces upon them. He chose the malachite key, speckled in blue, seemingly made of stone, though strong as iron, then turned to Sarah and held her two hands in his own.

"I will return as soon as I can."

She looked sad, but managed a smile, saying, "I do not play well the waiting wife, pacing the widow's peak, watching the sea. I would accompany you if you let me."

"You would smoke cigars if I let you."

"I would do so whether you would or not, and have done on occasion. You fear I will invade the smoking room where men love to sit and speak of boyish things."

"Not I, my lady, but Hope. I despise the taste. And Enoch prefers his pipe. But when have you seen me sitting and smoking? Or for that matter, wasting time in frivolous conversation?"

"Never," she said, and tears sprang to her eyes, so she hugged him suddenly, with a desperation that startled him. "Take care, Carter. I love you."

"And I you," he said. "Don't cry."

She drew away and brightened. "I do not mean to make too much of it. Heaven knows I've seen you tramp off many times before. Go, now. Find Chant."

He kissed her lips, fit the key into the lock, and opened the Green Door. Beyond lay the Long Corridor, all gray, with a haze hovering at the ceiling. He kept his eyes on Sarah's until the closing door blocked his sight, then locked it behind him with a sigh.

Wonder overtook him, as it always did whenever he entered the Long Corridor, even from the first time when he had stolen the Master Keys from his father as a boy of twelve, on that disastrous day resulting in his fourteen-year exile from Evenmere. The ramifications of that single, thoughtless act haunted him each time he crossed the threshold, and though much of guilt and regret had passed with his ascension to Master, yet the sorrow of so many years' absence from his father due to one childish offense remained ever with him.

He strode down the gray corridor, over the gray carpet, past the gray pictures, waiting for the pain that assaulted any entering the Main Block of the house. It began in his arms, an ache as if the blood had ceased its flow, moved quickly to his chest, then up to head and down to legs, as if he were being shredded and sewn back together. He lowered himself to his haunches, waiting for the aching to pass. He had often speculated on the cause of the distress, and suspected the Main Block of residing in another dimension, with those passing the portal being remade to survive, so explaining how a limitless country could abide within the bounds of finite walls. But at that moment his mind focused only on discomfort, not conjecture.

When the pain ceased, he rose and continued down the passage. The corridor was cold; Carter's breath issued in clouds. He could hear the fierce northern winds moaning over the great house. He champed his gloved hands together and longed for the warm inglenook in his own dining room.

The Long Corridor is constructed in a circle, and most of the countries of the White Circle, those lands allied with the Inner Chambers and granting fealty to the Master, are located along its outer circumference. Inside the circle itself lies Ooz, Veth, Innman Tor, High Gable, and half a dozen others. Near the center, in a place men do not go, is Lamp-lighter's Lane, where stood the most important lamps in Chant's charge.

Three hours Carter strode the Long Corridor; the gray mist gradually lifted; the zinnias on the wallpaper lightened to orange; the carpet warmed to peach. He ate a late lunch beside one of the many hearths scattered along the way, this one well stocked with wood and boasting a great overstuffed chair. Usually on his journeys he ate dried strips of fruit and salted beef, but since his marriage it had become Sarah's custom to prepare one good meal with her own hands. He savored the river trout, cooked plain, with a tomato and garlic sauce, and as he warmed to the fire, his heart warmed to her kindness, so he was briefly content. He wanted to fall asleep afterward, sitting in the chair, but roused himself and went on.

He soon turned to the right, into a gray, unmarked doorway, leading to Ghahanjhin, where he had several times visited the land's mysterious ruler, Baron Koshchei, known as The Deathless because every sovereign in that country, upon entering into his seven-year term of office, was given the same name and required to go perpetually masked. Thus, a Koshchei had ruled in Ghahanjhin through nearly all its recorded history.

Carter passed through a foyer, with a marble bookcase covering one wall, filled with squat, green leather-bound books, each four feet wide and reputed to contain the history of the time before Ghahanjhin, but written in the Histian language, which no living man can read. Two stuffed gnawlings, like finned bears, with six-inch fangs and claws, stood on pedestals between the doorway leading into the country, and a sentry, dressed in silver chain mail with ebony tunic, cloak, and boots, sat at a rosewood desk, reading a copy of an ancient tome by Sir Bela, skald of Eastmarch. At Carter's entrance the man set the volume smartly down and rose, clutching a heavy spear, muscles rippling as he came to a guarded stance.

"Welcome to Ghahanjhin," he said in a low, smooth voice. "Please state the nature of your business in detail neither spurious nor eloquent." He wore a brass helmet with a silver serpent rising from the nose-guard.

"Carter Anderson, Master of Evenmere, here on the business of the house." Carter showed the ring he wore on his left hand, which Mr. Hope had presented to him upon his public ordination as Master. His father had worn a similar band—it was an ancient tradition—but his had disappeared with him in the Rainbow Sea. Seven stones cut in seven concentric circles adorned it—jasper, sapphire, chalcedony, emerald, sardonyx, sardius, and chrysolite—representing the Seven Words of Power. Hidden inside the band were carved the words *L'essential est invisible*.

The sentry gave a brisk bow. "An honor, my lord. Should I send the baron word of your coming?"

"If you wish, but I doubt I will have time to see him. I am passing through to Lamp-lighter's Lane."

"God speed you then, there and back again. You've come about the trouble, I suppose?"

"What trouble?"

The soldier, a square-faced fellow, no more than twenty-five, glanced down. "I assumed you would know, my lord. The guards have reported strange sightings through the windows overlooking the Lane, and stranger noises issuing from it. No one can enter to check, of course, but it has become a place of fear, a watch soldiers no longer enjoy, alone in the quiet hours."

"Then I will investigate. Have you seen Chant?"

"The Lampman himself? No, my lord, but he does not always pass this way."

"If he does, inform him of my coming."

"Most certainly. If you wish, I can gather an escort."

"Time presses or I would. But I can find my way."

"Very well, my lord."

Traveling south, Carter passed into northern Ghahanjhin and soon encountered the Looking Glass Marches, a mile-wide buffer surrounding the country, built three centuries before during the War of Five Countries, taking its name from the mirrors covering every wall, ceiling, floor, and stair. The reflections of reflections, created not for vanity, but as a defense, all along the twisting passages, confuse the senses and make footing treacherous. A company entering the Marches would find itself immediately discomfited, and men describe a vexing task as "hard as a Ghahanjhin charge." Carter went bumping into walls, scarcely able to distinguish the true path; were it not for his maps, he would have been instantly lost.

The passages, the doors, the stairs, became increasingly narrow, until his shoulders brushed the corridor to either side. Ghahanjhin is a country of cozy lofts and petite rooms, a dollhouse kingdom, filled with secret chambers and passages, and a people proficient at striking from concealment. Almost all are adept at the bow and the blowgun.

After an hour, he left the Marches for corridors paneled in dark oak. There were no windows in all that country, and the gas lamps were few, so shadows lay thick upon long tapestries depicting—images within images—the same brooding chambers in which he stood. Ghahanjhin was a populous country, and he spent two hours more navigating the corridors, but saw no one, as if its inhabitants were fairies hiding behind roses and cowslips.

At last, he found seven soldiers warming their hands around a low fire, all tall and pale as ivory, wearing silver and sable, aiming spears and crossbows at Carter's heart. The tallest of them indicated a heavy door and spoke in ceremonial tones: "Behold the door to Lamp-lighter's

Lane, which no man may enter and live, save the Master and his Lampman. Depart if you fear death."

"And if death is certain, what use are the watchmen?" Carter recited, in the required ritual reply.

"The watchmen give warning, least the unwary perish."

"I am the Master of Evenmere, seeking his Lampman," Carter said, displaying his ring.

The young man, seeing the protocol complete, touched his left shoulder with his right hand in salute. "He has not yet passed this way, my lord, for he normally reaches the Lane by an alternate route and exits here. But we are informed he is indeed beyond this door, pursuing some unknown agent of evil. Thus you see these other soldiers with me, to prevent the enemy's escape. Be cautious, if you must enter."

The dread that had pursued Carter all the way from the Inner Chambers clutched at his heart, but he said only, "You make me anxious, indeed. Please let me pass."

The sentry unlocked the door with an ebony key from a ring at his belt, and threw the iron bolt aside. The hinges screeched as he dragged it open. Icy winds shrieked through the portal; snow lay in heavy drifts beyond and turned tree branches to gnarled claws.

"My thanks," Carter said. He stepped onto a huge quadrangle, where quatrefoils and red masonry showed between the drifted snow. The wind, finding its way below the steeples, the spires, the ponderous towers, tore at Carter's face and clothing. The snow swept in, heavy and swift, on a horizontal plane.

The door rattled shut behind him. He stepped farther into the quadrangle. At its center, some distance away, stood a long row of pedestals, twelve feet high, sur-mounted by massive statues and surrounded by a stone maze with walls twice a man's height.

Carter saw no footprints, but knew the snowfall would quickly blot them out. He waded through the drifts, pro-tecting his face with his mantle. Despite his apprehension for Chant, he resolved to survey the quadrangle methodi-cally before daring the maze. Something, perhaps the eerie desolation, the warning of the sentry, or the loneli-ness of the courtyard, prevented him from calling to the Lamp-lighter.

Rounded alcoves lined the outer walls, with scores of angels on the facing and underside of every arch. He searched each in turn, fearing the discovery of the body of his friend. His dread grew as he went, spurred by imagi-nation and hopelessness, for if Chant had been injured, or even slain, his adversaries might have taken him any-where in the house.

Halfway around the quadrangle, his breath froze within him—Chant's hat lay half-buried in snow. He picked it up, to assure himself it was indeed the Lamp-lighter's. His heart began to beat at his temple; a man could not live long in such cold.

He searched the ground for signs, while the wind blew bitter all around. Seeing nothing, he broke into a run, sloshing through the drifts, searching each alcove in turn. On and on, down the length of the quadrangle he sped, his breath blowing in clouds. Still he found no trace.

He was almost to the corner when he spied the tattered sleeve of a coat protruding from the next alcove. A half sob escaped him as he leapt round the corner and found

Chant, lying sprawled against the arch, his head lolled to one side, his garments torn.

Calling his name, Carter cast his own gloves aside and felt for a pulse at his friend's throat. His skin felt cold as a corpse, but at Carter's touch, he gave a faint moan.

Though ignorant as to the degree of Chant's injuries, Lord Anderson could not leave him any longer to the storm. Daring all, he cast Chant over his shoulder and retreated across the quadrangle, passing close by the stone maze. Chant was thin, but tall, and Carter staggered beneath the weight. By the time he stumbled to the door, he was gasping for breath, but the sentries keeping watch through the door-slit threw back the bolt and helped them in at once.

The soldiers carried Chant to a cot beside the low fire, where one fed the flames, while Carter and the tall commander of the guard removed Chant's boots and gloves to massage his limbs. Shortly, the Lampman groaned again, opened his pale pink eyes, and said: *"So hard it seems that one must bleed, Because another needs will bite! All round we find cold Nature slight, The feelings of the totter-knee'd . . ."*

Then he fell unconscious again.

A half hour passed, and as the heat of the room warmed him, Chant gradually stirred. Carter gave him hot tea in a spoon, and he eventually sat up to drink. Afterward, he looked markedly better. Carter had already checked for wounds and frostbite, and found nothing except a bad bruise on his forehead.

"I must conclude this is not heaven," Chant said, his voice weak, "unless all the angels resemble Lord Anderson."

"By God's grace, I should hope not," Carter said, smiling for the first time. "You sound like your old self. It's a miracle I found you when I did. At first, I thought you were surely dead."

"Another few minutes in the storm, and I would have been. You came just in time. *For the Angel of Death spread his wings on the blast.*"

"You could not have been in it for long," Carter said, "else you would have suffered severe frostbite. Where have you been the last few days?"

"Not far from here, but only in the Lane today. There is evil abroad and a force working in the house."

"I have felt it. Are you strong enough to tell the tale?"

"There is no time! The lamps are in danger. We should go at once." Chant tried to rise but Carter pushed him gently back.

"I need information before we plunge headlong into the fray. Be brief, but tell all; omit no details."

"Very well. My head feels stuffed with cotton, but allow me more tea and I will relate what I can."

Carter poured tea into a tin cup. Chant took a few sips, then began. "My troubles originated four days ago. There is a little green lamp at Riffenrose, beside Ionian candles of four disparate lengths, and its oil must be replenished weekly. I set out for it, by way of the Mere of Books, intending to return through Lamp-lighter's Lane, to trim the wicks and inspect the oil there.

"On the second day, at a little after two o'clock, I turned a corner and found myself face-to-face with *myself*. I do not speak metaphorically; the man before me was my exact duplicate. In languid moments, we speak of meeting our own image in the world; it is a charming thought. In reality, it is a horror beyond describing, as terrible as confronting our own annihilation and equally as compelling. *Go from me. Yet I feel that I shall stand henceforward in thy shadow. Nevermore alone upon the threshold of my door.* My breath fled from me; I trembled like a frightened hound. He used the moment to approach; he drew a gun. I fled, foolishly perhaps, for the barrel was nearly level with my heart, yet I do not believe he intended simple capture. Miraculously, though he fired twice before I reached the corner, at a distance little greater than between you and me, he missed, as if he did not perceive the use of the weapon."

"Did he follow?"

"He did. We played a game of cat and mouse thereafter, he in solid pursuit, I using all my wiles to elude him. He chased me up and down flights of stairs, through passages narrow and wide, yet I kept my wits about me, despite the fear, driven by the knowledge that upon my apprehension he would become my replacement. I determined not to confront him unless driven to desperation, for the price of failure was too high. We fired at one another more than once. Ever, I pushed toward the Lane, trusting its Guardians as proof against him. *All by myself I have to go, With none to tell me what to do—All alone beside the streams And up the mountain-side of dreams.*

"I traveled all through the night and heard no word the next day, until I neared the corridors leading to the Lane. From those I encountered I learned one matching his description (or mine, I suppose) had been seen lurking. I was in County-by-the-Lane by then, where I could rally friends about me, and so was escorted to my destination by Marshal Japth and a squadron out of Vroomanlin

Wood. The marshal sent a messenger to you as soon as possible, which probably reached the Inner Chambers this morning, shortly after you left.

"At last, after too much delay—Japth being a careful man—we reached the east door leading to the quadrangle late this afternoon, where we found the guard slain, and the door standing wide. The men, of course, could not accompany me into the Lane, for fear of the Guardians. My one desire was to wait for your arrival, but I could not; the lamps had to be inspected within the allotted time, for the lights of Lamp-lighter's Lane are the lamps of the universe. They, more than all others, cannot be allowed to expire. *All the suns—are these but symbols of innumerable man, Man or Mind that sees a shadow of the planner or the plan?* I gave the soldiers passwords by which they should know me upon my return, and entered.

"The snow had relented for a time, and I soon discovered footprints leading into the stone maze surrounding the Lane. I made a thorough search along the quadrangle walls before penetrating the labyrinth itself. The footprints were still distinct, so I knew he was not far ahead. As I followed, I realized my adversary did not know his way; he wandered the maze at least two long hours, and I with him, before he finally reached the Lamp-lighter's Lane.

"In the Lane, I discovered a shadowy figure, preparing to extinguish the first of the twenty-one lamps. I gave a shout and fired a shot, but missed. He dove behind the trees with an uncanny speed, leaving me no alternative but to pursue. The foliage is heavy there, and the snow gave way at every footfall. No sooner had I plunged into the thicket than he leapt upon me. Apparently, his gun was empty, for he used it as a bludgeon, giving me a bad blow to the head, even as I wounded him at close range. He sped away, whimpering like a hound.

"Dizzy and weak, bleeding from my temple, I returned through the maze, but my injury eventually overcame me. All went dark; I lost my way. The next thing I remember is waking here."

"So he was able to fool the Guardians in your shape," Carter said.

"Yes. And that frightens me. He is still out there. The lamps must not be doused."

Carter drew his Lightning Sword. "I will find him."

"I will go as well."

"You're still dazed."

"But I can watch your back. Despite his celerity, he will not easily surprise two men. Too much is at stake." Chant stood, tottering but resolute, and gave a wan smile. *"Come, then, let us cast off fooling, and put by ease and rest, For the Cause alone is worthy till the good days bring the best."*

At Carter's word, the guards unlocked the door to the quadrangle. The snowfall had thickened, obscuring all; the walls of the maze lay invisible. Together, the companions waded through the drifts to the labyrinth. By his maps, Carter could navigate the maze, but it was unnecessary with Chant as guide. The stone passages were narrow; snow lay heavy atop the walls. Within twenty minutes they stood within the Lane itself.

Two years had passed since Carter first entered Lamplighter's Lane; then he had imagined a park, with a single cobblestone street lined with lamps—it resembled rather a forest, unpaved, heavy with shrubbery and pines. Icicles hung from the branches; the bushes were mountains of snow. The lampposts stood in three groups of seven, all glowing brightly in the gloom, defying the storm. Surrounding these, rising above the foliage, the massive statues glared down, shoulders and heads crested in snow, as if they had donned epaulets and oversized hats, the nival brims on the deep-set brows. These were the Heroes of Evenmere, those who had fought, and often died, for the High House. Some had been Master; most had not. Nearest stood Camped, Governor of Ooz, wise-eyed and thoughtful, a sword and a sundial, one in each hand, who negotiated the treaty that formed the White Circle; beyond him, Œlfwenge, robed as a Greek, three-headed Cerebus straining against a leash held fast in massive fists; Countess T'sychem Tibell, sprung from Logana, First Magistrate of Anwerr, bearing a quill pen and the scales of justice, who slew the Supreme Anarchist at Donnershot; Lord Farnsworth, the great metal-wright, bearing hammer and tongs, deliverer of Aylyrium in the Rooftop Rebellion; Lady Guniel, poet and philosopher, standing before a dragon with Jormungand's eyes; Baron Serscith, surrounded by owls, who gave his life in the aeries of High Gable; D. Latch Relsweizer of Arkalen Demesne, peering out from a little boat, holding a mask in his left hand. There were more besides, and Carter drew a deep breath, for they were marvelously wrought, those protectors of all that was Evenmere.

"The lanterns remain lit," Chant said. "I will take you to where we struggled."

Chant led down the Lane, between the lamps and the statues, but when they pushed their way through the undergrowth to the site of the conflict, the snow had obscured all, including any shed blood.

"If he was wounded, he would seek shelter," Carter said, glancing about.

"There are alcoves in the bases of the statues."

They drove deeper into the pines, sliding on the snow, stumbling on hidden roots, until they approached the nearest statue and discerned a soft, whimpering voice. They slid slowly around the pedestal where the words could be clearly heard.

"Burns. It burns," the voice said, one Carter found vaguely familiar. "Should not have come. No, no. Graycoats lied. Said easy. No easy. Must get away. But it burns."

Carter steadied himself, drew a deep breath, then lurched into the narrow alcove, the tip of his Lightning Sword aimed at the man's brow.

"Stand still," he ordered.

He perceived only a brief glimpse of the face that was and was not Chant's, bearing every physical feature of the man, but combined with an utter beastliness: the rose-pink eyes glaring with a wolf's stare, the thin lips a vicious, soulless snarl, the Greek nose, nostrils flared for the scent, the long face, bereft of intellect. And then the creature abruptly *changed*, with a fluidity too rapid to follow. And as it transformed, it vaulted over the sword point.

Heavy rows of fangs ripped at Carter's collar, massive paws drove the sword from his hand and flung him against the pedestal. He clutched for his pistol, even as the beast careened toward Chant. Carter swung to fire, knowing he would be too late, as the long, scaled body bent all its force toward the Lampman, this gnawling from Naleewuath, this changeling beast. Carter saw the fear in his friend's eyes, saw the slavering jaws, heard the bestial growl.

And suddenly, two massive feet, as fleet as the gnawling itself, landed on the monster's back, crushing its spine, sending it howling and writhing in agony. The Guardian, Cevan the Clever, finally aware, when the gnawling changed shape, of an intruder in the Lane, had descended with all its strength. The titan lifted the dying beast in its heavy hands, and snapped its neck with a quick twist, as a man might slaughter a chicken. The monster's twelve legs ceased their writhing. The colossus tossed its victim into the pines, gave an imperious glance all around, and returned to its pedestal.

"Are you injured?" Carter asked.

Chant looked uncertainly at his body. *"Do I live, am I dead?* Why, I don't believe he even touched me. And you?"

Carter glanced at his arms. His greatcoat had been shredded by the beast's claws, leaving his flesh untouched. "I am well." He glanced up at the Guardian, silent now, still as stone. "They are as fierce and frightening as you said."

Carter saw his own awe mirrored in Chant's eyes. "Yes; *Where he stands, the Arch Fear in a visible form.* Yet for the first time, an intruder successfully entered the Lane. Never before have the gnawlings assumed human form— these are new gnawlings. We will require more guards at the doors and secret phrases for passage."

"We may be able to recognize them by their language,"

Carter said. "This one spoke in the guttural half phrases of its kind. Their minds are no keener, at least."

Together they examined the corpse, which appeared in all ways an ordinary gnawling. After discovering nothing of value, Chant made his usual inspection of the lamps, while Carter, finding himself of no assistance, surveyed the Lane for other signs of foes. Of this he had little concern; the wounded gnawling would have sought its allies if any had been present, yet Lord Anderson drew his Lightning Sword. The Lane ended against Corsican pines, with a narrow path cut between. This trail he followed warily, still shaken by the assault.

He passed between the pines and discovered a narrow stream beyond. Briefly, he was taken by its beauty, for its banks were straight as a channel, the trees surrounding it uniformly spaced as a park, yet a disquiet soon fell upon him, as he realized the trees were *too* evenly spaced, with every third one precisely identical: a half-grown willow, with each branch indistinguishable and every mark on the barks balanced and interchangeable. He drew near the stream; it remained strangely unfrozen, its water as warm to the touch as on a spring day. Minnows darted in and out along the shore, their movements a symmetric dance, thousands up and down the bank, performing the same incessant ballet.

A quiet horror seized him, a fear he could not explain. He felt the skin crawl on the back of his neck.

"Master?" Chant called from behind the pines.

"Over here!" Carter shouted. "Come see."

The Lampman appeared a moment later, and his face went gray, his eyes grim, his mouth slack. *"Ah! my Lord*

Arthur, whither shall I go? Where shall I hide my fore-head and my eyes?" he whispered hoarsely.

"What has happened?" Carter asked. "It was not always so."

Chant shook his head. "It has been changed. This river runs from far to the south, passing through much of the High House. It is a branch of the Fable River, called Plegathanees. But it was an ordinary stream, not this caricature, this artist's sketch. What does it mean?"

Carter glanced along the shoreline. "It means that in the battle between Order and Chaos, Order has achieved a dreadful victory, one boding ill for the world. The anarchists are surely behind it. We should see how far it extends."

Chant led to the left. The symmetry of the shore made for easy walking, and they soon came to the walls of the labyrinth, where the water passed through a conduit. The harmony remained unbroken except at the duct's mouth, where several glass bottles bobbed against a piece of lodged ice, which had broken and fallen from the wall and was quickly melting. Chant removed the floe, and the bottles poured down. Each was corked, with a letter scrolled within.

"Curious," Carter said, plucking the first as it descended. He pulled the cork, withdrew the note, scanned it, and then, with a quavering voice, said, "Chant, we must collect them all."

Several had drifted downstream, but the current was slow, and they recovered them easily, five letters in five bottles.

"What are they?" Chant asked as he uncorked the final

missive, while Carter knelt, unmindful of the snow, inspecting each in turn.

"They are all addressed to Duskin," he said. "From Lizbeth. She is still alive."

Jormungand

Sarah sat at the French console in the drawing room, studying five letters spread across the table, five notes of desperation delivered from the dark past. She had read them a hundred times and wept a thousand tears. Lizbeth had numbered each missive, the last being seventeen, not all having survived the waters. But the very first was there, addressed to Duskin, as were they all, written in a childish scrawl: *Please come rescue me. I am in a house without sunshine. I do not know its name, and no one tells me anything. They leave me in a garden, where I grow brambles and thorns. I am always alone. Please, please, save me. Love, Lizbeth.*

And she had drawn hearts around the word *love*, and a picture of a dog on the back, with the words *I wish I had a puppy* written there.

By the seventeenth letter, the handwriting had become more elaborate, and so dense as to be almost unreadable—the result of experimentation rather than education—but the spelling and vocabulary were surprisingly good:

> *Dearest Duskin: I do not know how long I have been here, for there is neither clock nor sun to guide me. I remain alone in this lightless country, and no one pities me. I have been allowed no books. but have found a torn copy of* Wuthering Heights, *which has been my mentor, my education, and my only guide to all that is human; I have learned no other way. At whiles I steal writing instruments and scraps of paper. I think of you, and Sarah, and Count Aegis. I have forgotten the sunlight, and trees, and grass, and all good things. I am weary to escape into your glorious world, and to always be there: not seeing it dimly through tears, and yearning for it through the walls of an empty heart; but really with it, and in it. But they have taken my soul and my heart, and often I believe I am but a stone carving, given the appearance of a living woman; or the ghost of Catherine Linton, outside Heathcliff's window, whose icy fingers no man may touch. I pray every day for my rescue, that you will come to me, Duskin, and hold these spectral hands in your own warm grasp, that I might be whole once more. Come swiftly, but under no circumstances tell Lord Anderson of your knowledge of my existence, I beg you.*

Sarah turned toward Carter, who sprawled across a floral fainting-couch amid the chairs, occasional tables, bric-a-brac, the throngs of objects saturating the opulent chamber, his left hand drifting aimlessly across the royal-blue carpet as he stared at the intricacies of the Baroque ceiling—the dangling pendants, swarming Atlantides, seraphs, and flowery festoons, the border of somber ancients, gaping out with owl's eyes in judgment over the chamber. Unaware of her regard, he sat quite somber, overmatched by the finery, his face reminding her of the little boy who must once have played war with his wooden soldiers beneath the French console. Seeing him thus, she could not help but recall her love and pride of all that was him.

He glanced up and conferred a sad smile, which she returned, their hearts one in the gesture.

"Despite it all, I keep thinking about the Tor," he said. "But there is no evidence her abduction was related to the treasure."

"And none that it was not. We now know the anarchists were involved. The poor baby! But why should she fear you so much?"

"I wonder. The anarchists have had six years to poison her mind. What might they have told her?"

Just then, the drawing-room door plunged open, and Duskin appeared, dressed as garish as an eastern prince in trousers and shirt of gray and green leather, a white fur cape with ocher trim, and yellow boots, all cut from gnawling skins. Beside him, clad in equal splendor, stood Gregory, four months his senior, tall and red-haired, broad-chested as a stallion, with a hawk's nose, dimpled chin, broad brow above hazel eyes, and the smile of a king. He was Duskin's cousin on his mother's side, the son of her brother, and the two had become fast friends while attending the University at Aylyrium. Both men were grinning like boys and bearing an enormous gnawling skin between them, a floral beast eight feet long.

"The lions' whelps of Bashan have returned!" Gregory cried, looking indeed majestic as a great cat, though one whose hair flamed madly red.

"The conquering lords!" Duskin echoed. The two cousins beamed at one another.

"Behold, Lord and Lady," Gregory said. "A rug with the face of an angel for your fireplace."

He flopped the head of the beast forward, revealing six rows of teeth, a serpentine face, and a forked tongue.

"An angel far-fallen," Sarah said, wrinkling her nose. "I've warned you to bring no more skins. I'm weary of beasts watching at every turn, all teeth and no manners."

"But, Sarah, Duncan says it's the largest he's ever seen," Duskin replied. "Can't we keep it? It could go in the upstairs hall."

"And have its eyes leering at the top of the stair? I'd head for my bed and die of fright."

"If you do we'll have you stuffed and put right beside it," Gregory said.

"We'll turn it toward my room," Duskin said. "You'll just see its back."

Sarah fluttered her hands in surrender. "Do as you will; you were here first."

They set the skin down as Carter rose and embraced his brother, while Gregory gave a low bow and kissed Sarah's hand. "My lady, you look as beautiful as ever."

"And you look like peacocks," she said, grinning back. "Or popinjays." She liked Gregory, but took some pleasure in deflating him, for his beauty had given him the confidence women find attractive, bordering often on arrogance, and he practiced his charm on every lady he met.

"Judging by your garb, the hunt went well," Carter said.

"It was splendid!" Duskin declared, beaming. "Exceptional! I never tire of it. We went unaccompanied this time."

"Without tigers?" Sarah asked.

"Without tigers," Gregory said. "It was exhilarating."

"And rash," Carter said. "The gnawlings are swift."

"We have learned how best to hunt them," Duskin said. "You have to come with us next time!"

"Chant and I had our own gnawling hunt. I pray you do not meet their like."

"Tell me," Duskin said, tossing himself into an overstuffed chair.

Carter related his tale swiftly. When it was done Duskin's eyes had widened. "Gnawlings in the shape of men! This is news."

"There is more," Sarah said. "They found letters from Lizbeth, addressed to you."

"To me?" Duskin asked. "How old are they? Is she still alive?"

"Read for yourself," Sarah said, pointing to the table.

Duskin read them quickly, and when done, all joy had slid from him. "To be alone so long. We must rescue her."

"First we must learn where she is kept," Carter said. "The letter seems to describe the Outer Darkness."

"The Outer Darkness!" Duskin said. "I have never been, but they say it is haunted."

"I nearly agree," Gregory said. "I used to accompany

my father there. He had dealings at its edge. I know it well, but like it little. It's a grim country."

"We may require your help, then," Carter said. "But first I need more information. I want to ask Jormungand."

"I could accompany you," Duskin said.

Carter smiled. "Thank you, no. Hunting gnawlings has made you foolhardy. He nearly devoured you once; we will not tempt him again. At any rate, I will consult Hope first."

"I will go with you and tell what I know," Gregory said. "Will you join us, cousin?"

Duskin shook his head. "It's a warm bath for me and a hot meal." But he sat staring at the letters as the two men departed.

"Sarah," he finally said. "Why did she address them to me?"

"She was taken by you."

"But I only saw her once."

"Yes, but you gave her attention. She used to write your name in a little book she kept. She fancied she loved you then; it has sustained her all these years."

"And I never visited her again."

"You were seventeen years old, ignorant of your impact."

Duskin sighed. "I wonder if I've grown up at all. I spend my time traipsing about the house like a spoiled dandy, stalking gnawlings, fancying myself a great hunter, only to return and discover Carter tracking the true enemies of Evenmere."

"Do you regret his being Master?"

He glanced at her and then away. "I? Of course not!"

She gave him a doubting look.

"Ahh, Sarah, I could never lie to you. I do not regret it and yet I do. I love my brother. He was destined to be Master. He enjoys all the details that drive me mad with boredom—the state dinners, the diplomacy, the endless meetings. I could never do that. But I am no help to him."

"He enjoys it less than you think. But you support him in many ways."

"So you say, but it isn't true. Mostly I frolic, while he handles affairs of state. I'm not made to be a king's counselor. I have no place of my own."

"You may be partially right," Sarah said. "You were born with a restless spirit, which gives you strength. But you must never lose that restlessness; it keeps you true to yourself."

He came and kissed her cheek. "You know me better than I know myself. Why can't I find a woman like you?"

Sarah laughed. "You have found more than enough women; you simply don't keep them long enough to learn their ways. But you don't need one like me; you need one suited for you."

"Yes, but they say a man looks for someone like his mother. Better I should live alone. When I see the faintest trace of her in the women I meet, I flee; I readily admit it. My mother was not . . . good."

"Lady Murmur allowed ambition to rule her. It was a failing."

"Excuses can be made, but when does a failing grow to corruption? My mother became evil; perhaps she was always so. And what does that make me? She caused Carter to be banished from the house; she made my father miserable and may even have provoked his death. And he was a honorable man."

"But a man, nonetheless. I did not know him, but I think his tragedy began when Carter's mother perished, long before he met Lady Murmur. You are the son of your father *and* your mother, neither, and part of both. We must recognize the good and ill in our parents to avoid their path. Doing so makes us strong. You will manage enough mistakes of your own without wearing theirs like a cloak."

He patted her hand. "Wise Sarah. Were you always so wise?"

"All women are wise. It's a scientific fact. Like osmosis and steam engines."

Carter and Gregory passed down the transverse corridor to the morning room, where they found Hope sitting at the claw-footed table with the gulls carved along its borders, staring through the picture window at the white nothing of the blowing snow, sipping tea from a china cup, a heavy volume propped upon his lap.

"What, not polishing the silver?" Carter asked.

Hope grinned back. "I did not leave Dyson, Phillips, and Hope for the purpose of burnishing spoons, though I assure you I see the work is done. I've been reading on Lamp-lighter's Lane and the gnawlings, but have discovered nothing germane."

"Perhaps you can tell us about the Outer Darkness, instead."

Hope grimaced. "There is little good to tell, but it is a fascinating subject. I glanced through a relevant volume not long ago; if we could journey to the library I could find it at once."

He rose and led the men back down the transverse corridor, past the entrance hall, the dining room, and the main stair, to the massive library doors where throngs of carved seraphs and hippogriffs guarded the architraves. The jade knobs turned easily; the doors swung silently; the library stood misty gray, as if the anteroom of some primordial swamp, the watery edges of its walls wavering in the dim light from the windows. A small sitting area stood to the left of the entrance, furnished in long, floral couches bearing carved hunting hawks down mahogany armrests, and beyond these waited the narrow door leading into the chamber of the Book of Forgotten Things.

They crossed the heavy carpet, russet cattails on olive fronds, where gray dolomite pillars supported a low ceiling also gray with tendrils of yellow and brown, and entered the gloomy maze of the stacks, where they sank into the potent odor of ancient wisdom and dark leather. The ceiling rose higher here, revealing a curved staircase leading to a gallery filled with bookcases bordering all four walls of the upper story. Carter sighed; of all the house, he loved this room best.

They passed down the long aisles into the *Geography* section, where Hope fumbled a moment before withdrawing a tall, silver volume. "Just the one."

Carter eyed the shelves. "Someday I shall hire a librarian to put these books in proper order. Legal works under *Fiction*, novels of the fantastic under *History*—how do you find anything?"

A cunning smile rounded Hope's already round face. "At first I was baffled, but the truth eventually surfaced.

The legal works, which are nothing but the fantasies of men's minds, by which we erroneously pretend to control the world about us, have been placed quite logically under *Fiction*. History, our half perception of the order of the past, wholly tainted by our own prejudices, lies in the *Political* category, while the heroic adventures of men and women who never existed, such as *The Volsunga Saga* and *The Wise Woman*, which attempt to explain our experiences and our existence, lie in the *History* section. The latter, I would have placed in *Metaphysics*, but that is mere quibbling."

As he spoke, Hope thumbed through the silver volume. "Ahh, my recollection is restored. This is a fascinating text from three centuries ago, involving the abolition of treaties between the White Circle and the countries to the far south bordering the Outer Darkness. There is murder and mystery between these lines; my blood was chilled at the reading. Chilled. The Master at that time, old Montague Faull, had just hired Brittle; the writing is in my predecessor's very hand. Imagine living so long! But this was a perilous time; Brittle's predecessor had advised Faull poorly. Petty insults incited minor skirmishes evolving into bitter campaigns. Faull himself was assassinated soon after. The people of Wethermel and Starkwall withdrew from the White Circle, and relations have remained cold ever since. The two countries were later split into four in a bloody revolution: Ephiny Edge, Shyntawgwin, Darking, and Broodheim."

"Even in my father's day there were difficulties," Carter said. "One of the few times I saw him angry was over the mistreatment of our emissary to Shyntawgwin."

"Still, we should attempt a reconciliation someday," Hope said.

"It won't be soon," Gregory said. "Not if our troubles stem from there."

"Yes," Hope said. "The girl's letters, if truly written by her, claim she is being held in a benighted country. That would indeed describe the Outer Darkness, a barren plain without sun, moon, or stars."

"Like the edge of the earth," Gregory said, "as when the ancients believed it flat."

"Yes," Hope said, studying the book. "The name itself is from the New Testament, you know: *But the children of the kingdom shall be cast out into outer darkness: there shall be weeping and gnashing of teeth*, but that title is relatively recent. In ancient times it was named, among others, Gunnungagap, Gimokodan, the Hollow Land, the Onyx Plain, and Oblivion. When the first peoples settled the countries surrounding it, they called it Kur-nu-gi-a, the 'land of no return.' But though it lies within Evenmere, surrounded by the four countries, it is said to be paradoxically infinite. No one knows what it is, really. Some claim it is the resting place of Entropy, others the darkness from which the worlds were formed. We know it occasionally grows; the borders of the four countries have fluctuated through the centuries."

"But what, in your own opinion, do you believe it to be?" Carter asked.

Hope hesitated. "Do you recall how Brittle called the High House a Parable?"

"Yes," Carter said. "He said it was the only explanation we could comprehend. I've contemplated it many times."

"As have I," Hope replied. "And I believe the Outer

Darkness to be the same, a representation of the void left by the making of the worlds, the end of Creation."

"How can that be?" Gregory asked.

"It is beyond the understanding of science or reason," Hope replied, "more a matter of feeling than physical substance."

The men fell silent, trying to imagine what Hope meant. Finally, Carter nodded. "Yes. It is at least as much an explanation as Evenmere itself."

"It makes a kind of sense," Gregory said, "especially after having walked its edge. It is like being somewhere not of this world, a land lonely beyond words, where all that is human does not belong."

Carter glanced at Gregory, surprised by his wistfulness, as if he were a child, seeing the darkness again for the first time.

Mr. Hope shrugged. "At any rate, because of the sheer expanse of the Outer Darkness, the house where Lizbeth is being held will be difficult to locate. It could be adjacent to any of the four countries."

"In that, we may have some aid," Carter said, drawing from his pocket the shard taken from Innman Tor. "More than once I have tried to follow the stone's mysterious pull; it seems to lure me vaguely south, though its power ebbs and flows in various parts of Evenmere, making it unreliable. I suspect the Outer Darkness harbors both Lizbeth and the treasure of the Tor. Still, if we could narrow the search . . ."

"Certain of the kingdoms are more sympathetic to us than others," Hope said, "and Shyntawgwin is the most likely to support our enemies."

"But why would the anarchists build a house there, and

what do they want with Lizbeth?" Carter asked. "According to the letters, she is given no tasks and undergoes no training. If she serves as a hostage, what is the purpose?"

"Exactly!" Hope said. "Why have they not contacted us with demands? No one holds a captive six years for no reason."

"I intend to consult Jormungand this afternoon," the Master replied. "Perhaps he can provide answers."

"Odd you should mention that," Hope said. "Twice last night I woke, thinking I heard him roaring, great thunders of rage that shook the rafters of my room."

"Why, I thought the same," Carter said, "but I dismissed it as the howling of the storm. Roars like nothing I have ever heard, and the house jittering as if in an earthquake. I awoke this morning thinking it a dream."

"You and I have shared dreams before," Hope said. "But this was unlike that. Could it truly have been the reptile?"

"I shall go at once," Carter said, though dread descended upon him at the thought of the dinosaur. "Thank you, William. Gregory. Perhaps the two of you could consult maps to find the most circumspect route to Shyntawgwin."

"Yes," Gregory said. "I can help with that."

"Very good," Hope said. "Godspeed. We will anxiously await your return."

Carter left the library, crossing the transverse corridor to the main stair, the eyes of the ironwood eagle glaring down upon him from the highest landing, the dark railing cold to his touch. He ascended to the second floor, turned left at the top of the stair, and proceeded down a long corridor paneled in oak, carpeted in vermilion, the shadows heavy along its length. He entered the familiar door to the room that had been his as a boy. As Master, he had been loath to take his parents' chambers, so he and Sarah still made this one their own, though she had added a wall portrait of her father and mother to match Carter's own, a low bed-table with carved seraphs to match the angel on the mahogany fireplace mantel, and satin quilts to match the scarlet azaleas upon the wallpaper. A saber hung in a silver sheath above the mantel, and a notched wooden sword and four wooden soldiers with red and blue paint faded from countless hands—the toys Carter had carried from Evenmere during his exile—stood upon a heavy dresser with an oblong looking glass. Sarah sat upon the bed, reading Tennyson, three quilts about her for warmth—the room was freezing, for the fire had failed.

"Hello," he said. "Were you waiting for me?"

"If I pretended I were not, would it make it easier?" she asked. "Must you go at once?"

"Better to be done with it. Are you afraid? I have faced him before."

"Yes, and you returned pale as a mime. No, I do not fear your being eaten, though there is always that chance. I do not know what I fear. A waste of time, of course. Still, if you do not mind, I will sit and wring my hands while you are gone; it's the fashion among ladies today. I would not do so if you would allow me to accompany you. I used to hunt with Father, and I handle a shotgun well."

"No weapon can harm Jormungand; there is no defense if he chooses to strike. But the danger is more to my companions than myself. I learned that with Duskin, though why Jormungand spared him that day, years ago, I don't know. Probably, for his own strange amusement."

Carter went to the hearth and pushed against a brick, which slid in at his touch. The entire fireplace swung slowly outward; beyond lay an empty, dust-laden chamber, with wooden floors and a narrow stair leading upward. He lit a lamp and turned back to Sarah. "It never takes long."

They embraced, and her body felt warm, comforting, a protection against both evil and winter. They said no more. He turned and entered the chamber.

His shoes left tracks in the dust; the stair creaked; the paneled walls ran smooth on either side, unbroken by ornamentation. His heart pounded against his chest in anticipation. As he ascended, he felt the temperature plummet, as if the cold air had risen to the heights of the house in defiance of natural law. By the time he reached the top of the stair, his breath came in smoke. His raised lantern revealed the bare floorboards and the central strut of the sloping roof, the attic walls remaining outside the circle of light. Forgotten trunks, hatboxes, ceramic dolls, and broken broomsticks lay strewn across the floor, and silence rested all around, the noise of the storm failing to penetrate the attic hush.

He stood in the silence, intending to call, but a sudden intuition restrained him, a premonition so compelling he immediately extinguished his lantern and drew his Lightning Sword, its pale light scarcely illuminating the path at his feet. He stood still, astonished by his own response, and quickly realized it was the emptiness that had startled him, for he knew, as the Master sometimes knows such things, that Jormungand, who always met him at the top of the stair, was far away, deep within the attic.

He made his way to one of the sloping walls and followed it: bare studs, with nails protruding through, the smell of dust heavy in his nostrils, the darkness before him absolute. The floorboards creaked beneath his weight. A fear fell upon him, that his premonition was wrong, that the dinosaur awaited him, that Jormungand would not respect him as Master. At every moment, he expected red jaws to close upon him.

He halted, fighting an urge to flee back down the stair, drew a breath to gather courage, and continued. The air had become almost supernaturally cold; it bit his face, stiffened his hands, wounded his lungs till they ached. He wondered how long he could bear it.

Far ahead came a brief flash of light and the report of a revolver. He increased his pace, though he dared not run, lest he stumble. After several moments, he reached what he thought a wall, until he recognized it as a rectangular structure, half again his own height and fifteen feet long. He searched and found several others scattered about, none displaying any means of entrance, as if they were the discarded boxes of giants. These did not particularly surprise him, as he had never been so far into the attic and knew it to be filled with every sort of abandoned thing.

The crack of another pistol interrupted his investigation. He sheathed his sword, drew his pistol, and stood listening in a darkness so complete he fancied he had gone blind. A low rumbling rose, seemingly from no direction at all, as if the entire attic growled. The floorboards rattled beneath his feet. This quickly subsided, and as he recovered his courage, he became aware of a pinpoint of light. He approached it, its glow too distant to guide his path, compelling him to grope his way. He forced himself to go cautiously, both to drive back panic and to avoid tumbling over the scattered debris.

As he drew near the glow, he spied eight figures in greatcoats surrounding a shrouded lantern, scarves bundled around their heads, swathing all but their eyes, giving them the appearance of well-dressed mummies. He slipped behind one of the boxes and slid down its length to draw closer.

In his excitement he had forgotten the cold, which had grown continually more intense the deeper he went into the attic. It was unnaturally painful now, stabbing through his garments, clutching at his limbs, tearing at his ears and nose, a frost more frigid than the howling winds outside the house.

The anarchists milled in agitation. Carter could hear them, though they kept their voices low.

"I will not put away my weapon," one said.

"Then fire no more until you have a definite target," another commanded. "It's dangerous, discharging your gun at shadows, seeing a dinosaur at every turn."

"I will continue to do so until we know what happened to Hibbert and Burks. I say the dinosaur consumed them."

"And *I* assert they are lost," the other man said. "Have you no scientific training, man? Dinosaurs are reptiles; reptiles cannot function in the cold. He is poikilothermic, a cold-blooded lizard, crouched in a corner somewhere, somnolent as a serpent in winter. The noises are nothing more than the rumbling of the wind against the eaves. Now, disperse again, and constrain yourself."

"Very well," the other said grudgingly.

The men separated into four parties of two, each bearing a shrouded lamp. A pair approached the crate where Carter stood concealed.

He slipped around the corner as the men reached the point where he had been standing. Using their light for a beacon, he crept to the other side of the box as they passed, then set out to follow.

His mind raced. Anarchists in the attic—if not the authors of the preternatural cold, then using it for Jormungand's destruction. But why? The dinosaur was an enigma, his purpose unknown, an oracle too dangerous for any save the Master. What threat did he pose the anarchists?

Carter kept well behind his quarry; the men were wary to the point of terror, too frightened to speak, turning every direction to glare at the shadows, practically walking back-to-back between the crates. And still, he heard, far distant, the low rumbling. Carter could have slain them easily enough, but he never killed except by necessity. He crept closer, intending to capture these unharmed.

The anarchists passed between an intersection of four crates, pistols in hand, peering in every direction. Suddenly there arose a rush of air, like an eagle descending on its prey. The men gave an odd piping noise, cut short by a cracking, crushing din. The lantern crashed to the floor on its side, flickering but still aflame.

Carter gasped and drew his Lightning Sword, not for protection, but because it marked him as the Master. He bolted to the spot where the anarchists had been and lifted the lamp. A crimson streak stained the floorboards, the only mark of the men's passing. Carter peered into the darkness, and for the barest instant thought he saw a huge, red eye, reptilian and cruel, gone before clearly seen.

He climbed to the top of one of the crates and extinguished the lamp. After a moment's vigil, he detected the lights of the three remaining parties, bobbing back and forth across the attic, fragile in the darkness. One had moved far beyond the others, and was making its way in a half circle around the crates when it was suddenly, silently, swallowed up. Carter watched closely, but it did not return.

He continued his vigil, his sword lying on his lap, faintly shining. When another lantern vanished, he climbed down from the structure and made his way toward the fourth party, hoping to capture at least one for questioning. Since he no longer feared meeting the anarchists, he kept his sword high, guided by its illumination, trusting it to identify him.

Loud exclamations drew him through the darkness; from behind the safety of a box, he spied both anarchists holding their lanterns, staring at Jormungand, who sat utterly still. Carter sheathed his sword and slipped closer.

"You see," one of the men said. "It is as I stated: the cold has immobilized the brute. Intelligent or no, it is still cold-blooded."

As Carter rushed forward he noticed the dinosaur was thinner, and a third smaller, yet still massive, his head six times that of a horse, his skin glistening in the lamp-light like sheets of ice, as if he were frozen in place.

Carter drew his pistol, a warning shout upon his lips, when the great lizard struck, more swiftly than the eye could see. One moment the men stood gaping, the next, their hats dropped fluttering to the floor, their pistols unfired, not even an exclamation from their lips. Bones, devoured in a single bite, broke like sticks. Jormungand swallowed and gave a predatory grin, his rows of teeth glistening pickets. Carter turned his head, feeling ill.

"Cold-blooded indeed," Jormungand boomed. "A good description, and a good epitaph. The Last Dinosaur thanks you, little Master. You should send snacks more often, tiny tidbits, little sandwiches in packages of ten, but next time put salt in their pockets; they needed something."

The dinosaur roared with a violence that shook the attic and sent Carter ducking to the floor.

"Scientific jargon, facts and fractions, data and dogma, hypotheses and hypotenuses," Jormungand rumbled. "Posthumous speculations by pretentious magicians, born of the Modern Age, stripped of their sorcery, made menial by their metals and their locomotive engines, pointing to their brains like monkeys with a newfound toy, certain they have discovered the Oracle of Delphi and the Apples of the Gods, all laid out in one minuscule walnut shell, two of which I have just cracked. A scientific fact for them to digest, had I not digested them first. I liked them better when they made gods of the rain and the wind, fled from my one eye on the Isles of Crete, slew me with a saint's sword and sound tactics in dark Bavarian forests, died beneath my grendel-talons in wooden halls, knowing even as they perished that they faced the uncalibrated, unmeasured, undefined *Unknown*. Now, as I gobble them, I catch their passing thoughts, the screams of scientific men: 'how odd,' 'most interesting,' 'why, this is impossible'; logical minds too analytical to fear the Supernatural, since the Natural has become their deity. Someday I will forsake this attic and once more show them the meaning of naked terror."

Jormungand roared again, the deafening noise making Carter squint and clamp his hands over his ears. When he looked again, the dinosaur had fixed a red orb upon him. His voice grew serpent smooth. "And were you wanting to chat, exchange homilies, talk of weather and spoonerisms? Things like 'How is your stepmother Murmur? Is she still dead?' Have you a point, or have you finally realized that surrendering yourself to be consumed, which would offer me the barest millisecond of pleasure, might be the largest contribution a human could contribute to the cold universe?"

"If I had no value as Master, you would already have eaten me," Carter said, as bravely as he could. "You have shrunk considerably since last we met. And I heard you roaring in rage, last night in my dreams."

Jormungand blew flames from his nostrils, briefly singeing the frigid air. "You would rage too, if your cozy home had become an icehouse. The anarchists do this, seeking to destroy me. Look closely, can you see I am fading?"

Carter dared to draw nearer, though the monster's tongue flickered in the sword-light. To his shock, he saw the dinosaur was partially transparent, the slats of the attic visible behind his sleek snake hide.

Jormungand hissed; Carter flinched. "Yessss, they target *me*! There must be vengeance on these fleas. Do you think I care if they try to annihilate me, to impale me with rifles and spears, to crush me with juggernauts and tons of steel, let them come! I long for the combat! But this, this bleaching of the Last Dinosaur, forcing me to shrivel, to wither into nothing, like an old shirt torn to rags, dissipated and diluted until only threads remain, for this they must pay! And worse, they have made me . . . uncomfortable. You are the Master; it is your responsibility to avenge this insult, for if Jormungand perishes, All will be changed."

"Why do they want to destroy you?"

"The first question, and an excellent one, striking to the heart of the matter, since it concerns myself. Part of the answer is simple: I provide information to the Master, and they wish you blind to their machinations. But the second reason I cannot explain to a mortal mind; I am a Force and a Power; binding me will do them good, or so they believe. And there is a third thing, something even I cannot know: they are contriving a plan in the Outer Darkness beyond Shyntawgwin, where my vision cannot penetrate."

"Our suspicions are confirmed," Carter said. "I have recently learned that Lizbeth, the girl kidnapped years ago, is being held there."

"Yes, there is a connection between the two, though all is unclear."

"Why would they want her?"

"The second question, also of interest, because it concerns the frost in my attic. They are using her, directing power through her, a New Power I do not know, though it smells somehow familiar. But it is causing the Fimbulwinter outside, the unending winter of the Vikings, and it will not cease so long as she remains their prisoner."

"So to save the house, I must rescue her and frustrate the anarchists' schemes beyond Shyntawgwin. How can this be done?"

"The third question, also of value since it would end my torment. Only recently have I perceived that the thing taken from Innman Tor is the key, though it, too, is hidden from me, for it was made with the foundations of Evenmere, in the time before the attic was constructed, before my banishment, when I was free to roam the earth. But the little Israelite who winds the clocks was there. If he no longer remembers, send him to the Book of Forgotten Things. Once you discover what the anarchists have taken, you will know your path. But surely, you must enter the Outer Darkness before all is done."

Carter sighed. "Thank you, Jormungand. I will go, then. I'm sorry if you are in pain."

"In pain? I revel in pain! I *am* Pain! And your pathetic sympathy, sent out with such good intentions, clapping yourself on the back as you do so, applauding your brief moments when you glance up with your mosquito eyes and consider the welfare of anything but yourself, is laughable. You want to do something charitable? Ask me a fourth question so I can devour you. Give until it hurts."

"I will say no more," Carter said, "you are too subtle a serpent; eventually you would dupe me into asking that question. Good day."

"In this you are correct, little Master. But I have not duped you yet; perhaps that makes me merciful. Such nobility! They should grant me an honorary membership in the Benevolence Club. We could hold the meetings here. Bring more of your friends for our next gathering."

Carter hurried from the dinosaur and lit the lantern as soon as he was some distance away. He clutched the lamp close, unable to resist glancing back over his shoulder, expecting to see red eyes and long teeth. He was half-frozen with the cold and weary with a terror only dark jaws and deep darkness could bring.

He forced himself not to run, and it seemed an age before he reached the stair. Just as his hand touched the banister a low voice rumbled, right beside his ear, *"And remember, I am always everywhere."*

And though it shamed him later, he bolted down the steps like a child, while deep laughter rumbled at his back.

Forgotten Things

Enoch was away attending his duties when Carter descended the attic stair, and a day was loot awaiting his return. He arrived just as Carter, Sarah, Chant, and Hope were sitting down for supper according to their custom in the eventide, the Master having dispensed with formalities except for the comfort of guests, when Hope would adopt the guise of butler, beaming like a small boy playing make-believe, and the other two would eat in the servants' hall. As Enoch entered, he did not whistle, as was his wont, nor smile, but threw himself onto a chair and sighed.

"Am I so old to become forgetful?" he asked. "Do I lose my way in the house where the Lord God brought me before Babylon was an empire? Perhaps it is my new boots; perhaps they said, 'Enoch, you've been walking this way too long; we will take you another direction.' I should never have thrown away the old ones. Two hours

I wandered the house tonight, two hours when I could not find my course."

"You were *lost*?" Sarah asked.

Enoch put his hand to his cheek and stared at the plate of braised goose the butler's assistant set before him, his brown eyes enormous, thin as glass in the glow of the gas jets. "I woke this morning and I knew who I was. I said, 'Enoch, it's you again. You're awake. You're not like other old men who can't remember.' Every day it's the same. What will I say tomorrow? 'Enoch who?' "

"You returned from the Towers today," Hope said. "How were you lost?"

"I was walking from Four Dials Tower toward the Long Stair. There are seven small rooms with seven turns through which I must pass. Right, left, left, right, right, left, right. When I came to the third left, the turn was gone. I thought I had missed the path while daydreaming. I stood in a straight corridor I had never seen before. It had lamps every ten paces, and a table beneath each lamp. Every table was the same as the last, to the very grain of the wood, and upon each table sat a rose in a vase. The roses, too, were identical to the petals; I plucked one and compared it. But there are strange things in Evenmere; too many for one man to see, though he live twice my age, so I did not think much of it. After passing twelve tables with twelve roses beneath twelve lamps, I had adventured enough, and returned the way I had come. But though I traced my path to rooms I knew, and set out a dozen times through the seven small chambers, I could not find the proper turning. At last I took another route, and finally made my way to the Long Stair, though it was more from fortune than skill. Should I get more sleep? Was I drunk with wine? What excuse do I have?" He raised his hands in a shrug.

The table fell silent, until Chant murmured, *"The old order changeth, yielding place to new."*

"That would be my guess," Hope said. "You say the turnings were different. You might be mistaken once, but not repeatedly. I have noticed no diminishment of your mental capacities. You defeated me soundly at chess two nights ago."

Enoch, still staring at his uneaten dinner, raised his brow. "It is a better game since they added the bishops."

"Neither have I noted any change," Sarah said, "and I do not believe love blinds us. You are as wise as ever."

"The river at Lamp-lighter's Lane," Chant said.

"Exactly my thoughts," Carter replied, "though it chills me to consider it. The stream had become wholly symmetrical, as if artificially constructed. And you say each part of the corridor was identical?"

"Even to the marks on the floor."

"Then here is no sign of senility," Hope said. "The house is changing, becoming more ordered."

"So the anarchists, the champions of Chaos, seek to overthrow Evenmere by imposing uniformity? Rather like rodents importing mouse traps, isn't it?" Sarah asked. "But we can't be deceived by their name, I suppose."

"No," Carter said. "They intend to enforce their own doctrines on the house, and thus, on the worlds. If they can use either Order or Chaos as their means, they will do so. We must uncover their plot."

"But how?" Enoch asked.

"Through you, old friend. I have been to the dinosaur,

and he says you must look in the Book of Forgotten Things."

"I? But the book is for the Master."

"Yes, but my father showed it to me when I was but a child, before *I* was the Master. It will be safe for you."

"So," Enoch said, frowning. "Maybe tomorrow I will still remember who I am."

"Of that," Carter said. "I have no doubt."

The next morning found an unusually pensive Enoch accompanying Carter down the transverse corridor, through the tall doors of the library. They passed beyond the couches and the gray dolomite pillars, through the four-paneled door into the small, windowless study, with its tall ceiling, blue carpet with gold fleurs-de-lis, and seven buttercup lights in the brass candelabra, which Chant kept always burning. The stained-glass skylight, red, blue, and gold, depicted a man receiving a book from an angel who was both beautiful and terrible, with long, golden hair flowing to his shoulders and a golden belt encircling the waist of his white robe, which had a marvelous sword strapped upon it. Since childhood Carter had viewed the angel with an awe undiminished by time.

The study was furnished with a kidney-shaped desk, having a leather top fastened with brass hobnails and a matching dark-leather chair. Mahogany panels decorated the walls, a fireplace stood beside the door, and a bookcase with blue leaded glass rested behind the desk. Unlocking the bookcase with a small skeleton key taken from the top drawer, Carter withdrew a heavy leather book lined with gold leaf. He set it, unopened, upon the desk, and bade Enoch take a seat in the chair.

Staring at the volume, the Windkeep's face went pale. "Master," he said. "Forgive an old man. Should I fear this book? It terrifies me. It is most holy."

"There is nothing to fear. You will not die if you look within it."

"I have lived for many lifetimes of men. I do not fear death. Life, sometimes, I fear. Men were not meant to remember so many ages, and things slip away. The acts I do today, the paths to the clocks, the winding of their mechanisms, that I remember well, but what if I look into the past, and nothing is as I recall?"

Carter deliberated before speaking. "Jormungand calls our days insignificant, our passing inconsequential. I look at this house and the long life you have led, and I do not believe him. Yet, it strikes me I will never truly understand you, who have seen so many ages. You are a mystery I can never unravel. I do not know how to advise you, my friend."

Enoch shrugged. "The old dragon, what does he know? Much about this life, little of the next. And one of his names is Scorn. Is it necessary I read the book? It is. And Jormungand does not lie, though the truth he holds back can be perilous. I will open the volume and describe what I see."

"You will turn only to the fourth page and no further. The memories beyond are sometimes . . . unpleasant."

Enoch opened the volume as instructed and stared. To Carter, the white pages remained blank, but the Windkeep's eyes soon widened. "An image arises, real as my own hands. I see a flagstone plain, with a village surrounding it. It is Innman Tor, before the hill was raised. I recall it now, in the first days of my employment. I visited here, and a man, who seemed more than mortal, led me across the flagstones, showing me the single stone at the center, and telling of its purpose. It is the Cornerstone, the First Stone of the house, upon which all rests. There are signs and symbols and seals upon it, that no man can read, and it is the Foundation of the whole house. And after he showed it to me, he said a Tor would be raised to cover and protect it from the eyes of men. And when next I came to Innman, it was so, though I never saw my guide again."

Enoch stared a moment longer, sighed, and drew his eyes from the book, horror on his face. "The anarchists have stolen the Cornerstone, to build a new house, to change all that was and is and is to come! We must stop them."

Carter's thoughts darted a hundred directions at once, but he said, "Enoch, if this is God's house, as you say, and as I believe, might He not stop them Himself?"

"We are His agents on earth. It is the task of the Master to protect the house, as it is my duty to wind the clocks."

Carter bowed his head, suddenly overcome. "And what if the Master fails?"

"Can we see the whole plan? It is too large."

The men sat in silence, thinking their own thoughts, until at last, Enoch said, "Master, it is much to ask, but now that I have seen the book, I am not so afraid. And I . . ." His voice caught suddenly in a way Carter had never heard before. "I would like to see Aram once more, the country of my birth, as it was when I was young."

"It may be painful, as I warned you. The book shows what it wishes, not always what we desire."

"Still, could I?"

Carter nodded. "Simply turn the page."

Enoch did so. He stared at the pages once more. A peace suffused his countenance—his eyes grew bright as gold coins, so the wrinkles and the worn planes of his face, his large nose and his heavy brow, were transformed, the weariness of the ages both fallen from him and fallen upon him like a holy shroud. He looked immortal, more than human, nobel as a bronze sculpture. Carter thought, *He is beautiful, ancient as he is,* and his love for the old man brought sudden tears to the corners of his eyes.

Then a troubled expression overtook Enoch's face, so that he was changed again, once more only a weary, elderly gentleman with black Assyrian curls. He turned from the book and tried to smile, but his expression crumbled; he broke into loud sobbing and cast his face into his hands, while Carter stood in confusion and embarrassment.

"Forgive me, Master," Enoch said, after regaining his poise. "I know it is not the way of your people to show such emotion, but I am from a different land, where our hearts sometimes spill into our eyes. I saw Aram, even as I remembered it, and I felt the cool breezes, and heard the wind through the vineyards beside the banks of the wide Euphrates. And I saw my precious wife, as she was when we were young, after the birth of our first son, Methuselah, who I held in my arms once more. Her face was drenched with sweat from her exertions, yet she told me how she loved me, while I stood bursting with pride and wonder, rocking my little boy. And all these have been dead many thousands of years, and I have not been permitted to join them. I do not mind the work, and I do not mind the aches, and I love the life I live, but I miss them with all my heart, and sometimes I wish the Lord God would call me home."

Enoch was silent a time, then said, "Thank you for showing me the book."

"I'm sorry it caused you pain."

The Hebrew shook his head. "There is a sweetness in sorrow. Should I regret it? I have seen their faces once more, and I will not forget."

"So the anarchists are seeking to rearrange reality," Hope said as he thumbed his way through a large, velvet volume. They were all in his office—Carter, Duskin, and Sarah seated across from his desk, which was layered in books, Enoch warming his hands by the hearth, Chant standing, staring out the window, and Gregory practicing positions at the billiards table. "And this Cornerstone, of which I can find no record, is the key?"

"It is the Foundation of the entire house," Enoch said. "Whatever is built upon it will stand."

"And they are constructing a False House beyond Shyntawgwin, a structure of their own design," Carter said. "Out there, in the darkness. As it rises, our own reality changes. We must prevent it."

"*Four courts I made, East, West and South and North. In each a squared lawn, wherefrom the golden gorge of dragons spouted forth a flood of fountain-foam,*" Chant muttered, still staring at the blowing snow.

"Precisely," Sarah said. "And we, the object of that dragon's attack."

Hope fumbled for another book, which he handed to Carter. "This is a map of Shyntawgwin, as cartographed over two hundred years ago."

"But in what strength should we go?" Carter asked.

"With an army," Gregory declared, popping the nine ball into the corner pocket. "Clear them out in one swoop."

"Then we will battle the armies of Shyntawgwin, Ephiny Edge, and Darking before we ever reach the False House," Hope said. "Even Broodheim might respond if it thought itself threatened."

"They will forbid our passage?" Sarah asked.

Hope sighed, drummed his fingers, and stared thoughtfully at the ceiling. "We could have diplomats there in two weeks. But do we dare ask their permission? Perhaps they are in league with the anarchists, in which case we will be showing our hand. Better to surprise them."

"Can we send an army through the house, unseen?" Enoch asked. "Word would spread; everyone would know."

"Perhaps," Hope said, "but I have been reading. During the Yellow Room Wars small parties of troops were sent down diverse routes, to rendezvous later."

"Do the books tell everything?" Enoch asked. "I was there. It was not so simple. Twelve men, walking together, whether in armor or not—everyone knew they were soldiers! Whole companies were sent as diversions. Plots and counterplots, every misdirection was used. It would not be so easy, in a time of peace, to conceal such legions."

"Then do not conceal them," Gregory said. "Mass a force large enough to overcome Ephiny Edge, Shyntawgwin, and the others. Meet them in full strength."

"It would be a long campaign," Chant said. "Thousands would die and a year would pass, while the anarchists continued to transform Evenmere. By the time we broke through, the Cornerstone could be spirited away, the work continued elsewhere. *And while the world runs round and round . . . reign thou apart, a quiet king.*"

"Time *is* on their side," Duskin said.

"I could lead a company small enough to slip through Shyntawgwin," Carter said. "The question is, could we do anything once we arrived?"

"Up to this point, the anarchists have not shown strength of numbers," Hope said. "But it is risky, walking into the unknown, even for the Master."

"We must act soon, but not in haste," Carter said. "Send diplomats to Ephiny Edge and Shyntawgwin. See if we can discover what they know of the border, but be subtle. You had mentioned opening relations with them again. Tell them we wish it now. We will at least discover if they are pliable."

"But that means we must wait, while Lizbeth languishes," Sarah said. "I tremble to think how they use her, to bring this hideous winter."

"Tennyson answers again," Chant said. "They won't do her any further harm than they have already, for *Thereon I built it firm. Of ledge or shelf the rock rose clear, or winding stair. My soul would live alone unto herself in her high place there.* They have made her the queen of all loneliness. They have gifted her a copy of *Wuthering Heights*, a book of unrequited love and dark despair. It is not just to control the winter that they are tapping her emptiness, but to focus it through the Cornerstone, to build the False House itself, a sterile, loveless manor. Lizbeth is the catalyst."

"Oh, but it is hard!" Sarah said. "My blood boils. I would strangle them myself, if I could!"

Carter squeezed his wife's hand. "We will do what we must."

"One thing more," Hope said. "A pair of famous architects, who have done extensive research on Evenmere, are working in Keedin. I have read their splendid work, *Exploring the East Wing*, and have used their services many times on matters of geography—or as they call it within Evenmere—archtography. They are eccentric, but might be of service concerning both the Cornerstone and the navigation of Shyntawgwin."

"Contact them," Carter said. "And send a message to Captain Glis as well, informing him of the situation."

"At once," Hope said. "And other members of the White Circle may also need to know. As Evenmere changes, it will produce first concern, then panic. Some rooms may vanish altogether, and one can only speculate on what will happen to the people within. I will, of course, dispense information only at the highest levels."

At that moment, a noise erupted in the hall outside the office, and a page boy appeared, looking annoyed. "My pardon, Lord Anderson, a house-runner has come and demands to see you at once. I told him you were in conference, but he will brook no delay."

Carter raised his eyebrows. "Send him in, then."

As the page left, Carter said, "I have postponed the construction of a house-wide telegraph system long enough. Regardless of the speed of our relay runners, it still takes three days to cross the White Circle. Next summer we begin the work."

"Did your father trust the telegraph?" Enoch replied. "He said it would send stuttering ghosts down the wires and all over the house."

"It is also recorded he despised vegetables," Sarah said. "Should we declare the house wholly carnivorous? We live in a progressive age; we must move with the times, lest the times move over us."

"They have said the same in every era since Asshur built Nineveh," Enoch replied with a shrug. "But all this running? It's good exercise but too much excitement. Thinking of it makes my feet hurt. You want wires, we should have wires, and men in hats to tap the words."

The page boy ushered a young, obviously exhausted man into the chamber, dressed in the blue and gold livery of the House-Runners of Evenmere. He dropped to his knees before them and bowed his head. "My lords, I bear a message from Duncan of Naleewuath to the Master."

"I am Lord Anderson," Carter said.

The runner quickly produced a document signed by Duncan, affixed with the seal of Naleewuath.

Carter read the letter and gasped. His face turned pale. "What is it?" Sarah asked.

"The gnawlings have massed; they've attacked everywhere, broken the whole country into pieces. There is slaughter in the Puzzle Chambers and fire in Sidebend."

"When did this occur?" Duskin cried, leaping to his feet.

"Yesterday afternoon. The message begs us come; there are tigers dying in Naleewuath."

The Gnawlings

No more than a dozen men accompanied Carter, Duskin, and Gregory to Naleewuath. The cold of the Long Corridor made the journey miserable, the howling of the winter winds above the travelers' heads an incessant reminder of their discomfort. They spent a short night at Halfway Hall, and by midmorning of the next day passed the little country of Indrin, where they saw the first signs of the invasion, as straggling refugees, faces haunted, passed through the Long Corridor. Many stopped to implore the Master for aid, and though it slowed his progress, Carter gave comfort where he could, assuring them that Chant was close behind, leading a party of physicians.

"Why do you think the gnawlings are attacking?" Gregory asked Carter, tramping by his side. "Are the anarchists responsible?"

"Either directly or indirectly," Carter replied. "But there is more: forces have been released. A dread has fallen upon me in the last three hours—the closer we get, the more I sense a shift in the Balance between Order and Chaos. Something has been *done* to Naleewuath."

"Done? What do you mean?" Duskin asked.

"I don't know, and I am afraid to guess, but with the wind howling last night as I slept, I dreamed of wounded tigers wandering a desolate Naleewuath, freezing in the bitter cold."

The men fell silent, lost in their own anxious thoughts, until Gregory said, "Perhaps you should ferret the anarchists out and have them executed. Put an end to this nonsense."

"Not until they've committed a crime. It would be nearly impossible, at any rate. Anarchy is a philosophical movement. You can't use force to prevent people from thinking."

"You can, if they're dead," Gregory replied.

"But that's their way, not ours," Duskin said.

"We've used violence ourselves," Gregory said, "to maintain the status quo."

Duskin laughed. "Always the devil's advocate, cousin! The anarchists are mad, that's all. Killing is a convenience for them."

"No," Carter said. "I wish they *were* simple madmen. I've studied their doctrine extensively. It's frightfully coherent. But they are Utopians, who by their nature seek simpler times; in this case the anarchists desire a simpler universe, one without pain and suffering. Who can argue with that? But the consequences of creating such a cosmos are complex indeed."

"That's unknown, isn't it," Gregory asked, "since it's never been done?"

"You've changed sides, again, Gregory," Duskin said. "He vacillates in every argument. It's intentional. I sometimes wonder if he has a true opinion at all."

"But it is a reasonable question," Gregory insisted, giving Duskin a grin.

"Perhaps," Carter replied. "But I intend for it never *to* be done. The implications are too monstrous."

By late evening, they met a company of the White Circle Guard, proceeding from Ooz, pearl hauberks reflecting the lantern light, metal strips rising from the sides of their conical helms, giving them the look of totem faces. A tall, lean warrior, saluting smartly, presented himself to Lord Anderson, helmet doffed, a young man with a nose like a Greek sword, his eyes almonds in the gloom. "Sergeant Sedger, from the fourteenth regiment, third brigade, my lord. Captain Glis said we might meet you on the road."

Somewhat to the man's discomfort, Carter shook hands. "A pleasure, Sergeant. Where is Glis? Has he reached Naleewuath?"

"He has, sir. He sent word that the Naleewuath militia was driven back, but is holding a line north and east of Middlecourt. Reinforcements have already arrived from Veth, Kitinthim, Ril, and Keedin. There are reports of scattered fires, and the Firemen of Ooz have had a bad time reaching the flames."

"They will torch the country as they once did Veth!" Duskin cried.

"Captain Glis does not believe so, sir," the sergeant said. "It has been the gnawlings' home for hundreds of years; he attributes the fires to accidents. But the beasts are driving east. Their real objective remains uncertain."

"I see," Carter said. "Let us proceed then, if there is nothing more."

The sergeant saluted again and turned briskly back to his troops.

As they passed down the Long Corridor to the Naleewuath passage, the way gradually widened, the zinnias on the wallpaper giving over to deep green foliage, the carpet darkening from peach to dusk gold, with patterns of autumn leaves scattered throughout. Carter watched carefully, hoping to perceive the moment when the forest twilight descended and the leaf patterns became genuine greenery, as was the way in that country.

But he did not hear the crackling of leaves beneath his boots, and the branches descending from the ceiling were not of wood, but stone sculptures of trees. No water dripped from the mist-shrouded ceiling; even the light fell in glaring squares, blinding in a land accustomed to dusk. Duskin touched the unyielding rock of the branches.

"What have they done?" he whispered. "What have they done to the trees? The enchantment of the tigers is leaving Naleewuath."

"No," Carter said. "Not leaving. Being driven out. The anarchists continue to transform the house."

They reached a fork in the corridor and passed to the right between a pair of tall arches adorned with life-size statues of tigers on either side. This at least was a familiar sight, but beyond the arch was a rectangular room, with two doors on each of its three walls, and at its center, where a large willow had once grown, stood only a gray post.

"They will make a ruin of the house!" Duskin cried, his eyes glistening damp. "I loved these lush halls, the hunting of the gnawlings, the roaring of the tigers, the shrouded morning air. They've desecrated the most sacred jewel of Evenmere!"

"I cannot rest until I speak with Glis," Carter said, too horrified for anger. "Sergeant, the men are weary. Set up camp here, if you deem it a proper location. Duskin, Gregory, with me."

They made their way down a sprawling corridor where once the walls and forest had mingled indistinguishably, the leaves now only fading paint on brown plaster. The end of the passage opened to the ruins of the marketplace of Naleewuath, its booths splintered and broken, partially burned by fire. The finery of the craftsmen: clothes, jewelry, furs, carved gnawling tusks, and dozens of other useful and beautiful things, lay spoiled by water and smoke, scattered amidst rotting produce. A sentry halted them at the market's edge, his rifle aimed at Carter's head.

"Identify yourselves," the man commanded.

"This is Master Anderson," Gregory said.

"Stand where you are, sirs, as you value your lives," the sentry said. He gave a low whistle, and another soldier appeared.

"Corporal Cooper," Duskin said, recognizing the man and stepping forward.

"Stand back!" Cooper cried, drawing his own pistol and aiming without hesitation. "Tell me your place of origin and your purpose."

"But, you know me! It's Duskin, and this is Lord Anderson."

"Obey my orders at once," the man insisted, looking plainly frightened.

"We have come from the Inner Chambers." Carter said,

"by way of Halfway Hall, to speak with Captain Glis. Sergeant Sedger, our escort, is encamped behind us."

The corporal turned to the sentry. "What do you think, Private?"

"They sound right, sir. The others couldn't speak that way."

Cooper lowered his gun, though he did not reholster it. "My apologies, Lord Anderson, to all your party. But you are the second Master to appear this evening."

"What?" Carter said. "An imposter?"

"A gnawling, sir. He was slain. There have been others, twins of our own men, and we learned to recognize them only after four from my squadron were killed. Fortunately, they are inarticulate beyond a few words. Private Green, here, killed two of them today, at this very post."

"Our adversaries grow more devious," Gregory said.

Cooper led them through the market; soldiers huddled around the brick fire-pits scattered within the hall, warming their hands—men in the pearl armor of the White Circle Guard, the blue uniforms of Kitinthim, and the gray mail of Veth—most in disarray, having apparently just arrived, with officers caterwauling orders everywhere.

Cooper brought them to a door beyond the booths, which opened on a narrow chamber with five figures and a tiger surrounding a worn table, studying a map of Naleewuath. All rose at their entrance, save the tiger, who sat on a low couch, bandaged and obviously injured. Carter grinned, comforted by the sight of old comrades: Captain Glis, who gave a grim smile and rushed to clasp

Carter's hand, the scar down his right cheek burning red in the firelight; Duchess Mélusine from Veth, the Porcelain Duchess, a diminutive woman, blue-robed, blue-eyed, her face bearing the sweet compassion of a saint; Baron Spridel from Kitinthim, short, barrel-chested, dressed in the dark blue trousers, jacket, and cap of the Burnishers, still holding himself with military stiffness despite his age; Captain Nunth, of the Firemen of Ooz, dressed in black boots and heavy gray jacket, his red helmet beside him on the table, his face as pitted and worn as ever, both aged and ageless as he bowed low to the Master; Duncan, head of the Farmers' Association of Naleewuath, the closest the country had to a leader.

The great cat was Mewodin himself, the Tiger-Lord, but a Mewodin drawn and weak. Dried blood stained the bandages on his left shoulder; where his right eye had been gaped unrelenting darkness. Lord Anderson approached, and the tiger rose unsteadily on his hindquarters to place heavy paws on Carter's outstretched arms. "Mewodin, old friend. I had not heard you were injured."

"Kitten scratches," the tiger said, but his cat's voice sounded labored, and he dropped back on all fours with a grunt of pain. "They have dared too much this time."

"We will punish them for it," Carter said. "I grieve for the deaths of your people."

Jade eyes gleamed, the emotions behind them unfathomable. "The Tigers of Naleewuath do not fear death, which is a cunning hunter. Worse is this death of the land; the forests have gone; the enchantment has withdrawn, the charm of the tigers."

"Why is it so?" Carter asked.

"We are the cause of the magic, not the magic itself.

Where there are tigers, there have always been jungles. How it can be otherwise, I do not know. But I smell the anarchists in it."

Just then, the Marshal of Ril, tall and bookish Charles Inkling, half brother to Prince Clive of Nianar, was ushered into the room. He looked out with honest eyes from behind thin spectacles, his face slender and firm with intelligence. Glis seemed particularly pleased to see him.

"A pleasure," Carter said upon being introduced. "I regret we haven't met before. I have read your book *A History of Warfare in Evenmere*. It is brilliantly done."

"You're too kind. Mostly, it was far too long, I fear," Inkling replied. "But this is a bad business. My militia is small, less than fifty, but we came when we heard. We want to do what we can."

Carter turned to Captain Glis, who indicated the map sprawled across the table and said, "Our forces are confused at the moment. These gnawling spies have all of us gnawing our fingernails. Their forces burst from the Puzzle Chambers two days ago, en masse, without warning. Their first target was the Tiger Lairs—"

"They came in human shape, in large numbers," Mewodin growled. "Otherwise, we would never have allowed them so close. They even had rifles. Three of my people were slain, and two wounded, including myself. We were driven from our Lairs onto the Terraces!" Mewodin gave an angry growl.

"Till today, the gnawlings held sway from the Puzzle Chambers to the Lairs," Glis said. "Duchess Mélusine and Baron Spridel brought their forces in late yesterday evening."

"When we arrived, we pressed toward the Puzzle

Chambers," Mélusine said, eyes flashing. "We rapidly forced them out, though we took heavy casualties—fighting in close quarters against wild beasts is new to us. The baron came in from the west, and we pinned a portion of their forces and drove the rest back toward the Catacombs."

"But not all," Spridel said. "I tell you, Master Anderson, when you appointed me Baron of Kitinthim I didn't know we would be fighting gnawlings in Naleewuath. My people are better at burnishing floors than stalking big game."

"Yet, you acquitted yourselves well," Mewodin said.

Spridel waved his hands vigorously. "Still, still, and meaning no disrespect. We have little training. I'm not a military man. My people are not a military people. I saw more than one of my lads torn beneath gnawling claws today. We cannot stay long; they will not abide it." Spridel's voice was ragged with agony. "We polish *floors*, my lord. That is all we have ever done . . ."

"You are correct, Baron," Carter replied. "We have asked much, and you have answered well. It is true Kitinthim has no military tradition, and little weaponry, and that demonstrates the mark of your courage. But we have brought more of the White Circle Guard."

"Yes," Glis said. "So long as we can contain the gnawlings, the Baron's forces can be placed in support positions."

"But contain them from what?" Inkling asked, studying the map. "Gnawlings, by nature, do not attack in organized units, but slay their prey from hiding, disguised in their furniture-shapes. These have attempted to push east. What is their motivation and purpose?"

"That is the question," Glis said. "On their own, they lack reasoning capacity. They are dumb beasts, for all their ability to speak. There are no clear objectives, but they have massed east of the Catacombs, and are driving toward the Long Corridor."

Carter stared at the map. "As if they were leaving Naleewuath . . ."

Duchess Mélusine gave a quick smile, only a slight upturn in her small mouth. "My very thoughts. But why?"

"And in what numbers?" Gregory asked.

"Many," Mewodin said. "I have never seen so many, nor heard of such throngs, not in my father's father's father's time. And multitudes in the shape of men!"

"Fires have been set," Fireman Nunth said. "A thing never before done by gnawlings. But the conflagrations were designed as distractions, pulling valuable men from the east."

"Currently, they are being held *here*." Glis tapped the map. "If they are truly migrating they will probably strike at Middlecourt before the night is over. We've concentrated our forces at the Puzzle Chambers to protect the citizens behind us, but the Naleewuath militia has re-formed from their first defeat and could relieve our positions. We would have to march tonight."

"Our men are weary," Duchess Mélusine said. "They've fought through most of the day. We're three hours from Middlecourt."

"But it's necessary," Marshal Inkling said in his quiet, firm voice. "If the gnawlings clear a path through Middlecourt, there is nothing between them and the Long Corridor."

"Sir, forgive my ignorance," Duncan said. "You are all

great men, and I am but a farmer in Naleewuath, but if the gnawlings want to leave, why not let them? Send them and be done, I say."

"You might well want to be rid of their kind," Carter said. "That I understand. But I must consider all of Evenmere. In Naleewuath the gnawlings are contained; beyond your borders no one has experience fighting them. If a portion escapes, they pose a threat to the whole house, including Naleewuath again, for you will have enemies both inside and outside your borders. And worse, their new ability to assume the shape of men makes them deadly dangerous. There are many questions. Do all of them have this power? Why have they acquired it now, unless by the design of the anarchists? No, Duncan, we must stop the gnawlings in Naleewuath."

"Then I will send word to Sergeant Sedger," Glis said.

"He won't be happy," Gregory said. "They've probably just encamped."

"Ah, Sedger will be thrilled," Glis said. "He's young, and still thinks battle all honor and glory. He may soon change his mind. Duchess, if you and the marshal can prepare your men? And, Baron Spridel, if your soldiers can follow, we'll keep them behind the lines as reinforcements."

"Aye, they'll come," Spridel said. "For all their inexperience they aren't cowards, once they know where they stand." He gave a fierce grin. "Perhaps we can polish the floors after the fight."

"My kin are scattered," Mewodin said. "But I will rally them to the east, to drive a spear into the heart of the Catacombs."

So long as the gas jets burn, night and day mean nothing in the High House. Thus, there is never reason for a foe or a fight to tarry till morning. Carter stood on a balcony overlooking Middlecourt, contemplating how Naleewuath had changed—where once light had poured from above, and verdant forests rose into the obscurity of the misty ceiling, bare walls stood, dim lamps braziered upon them, making a new sort of forest of shadow and light in a hall bejungled in darkness. He wondered if he would be able to recognize friends from foes in the gloom.

The troops had camped at a main passage leading outward to the Long Corridor, and had even managed to sleep between one and three o'clock in the morning, until roused by reports of gnawling movement.

Carter caressed his pearl-handled pistol, a single-action weapon more powerful than any designed by Mr. Colt, able to slice a six-inch hole in gnawling or man, its recoil so powerful it had to be held in both hands. He also bore a four-foot pike with wide, ornate guards meant to halt a gnawling charge. Glis, with a handful of men, stood beside him, and Baron Spridel sat in a chair, rocking and softly humming.

A soldier appeared, dressed in the blue garb of the Burnishers augmented by bits of armor—a hauberk, a chain-mail legging on one leg, and a battered helmet. His only weapon was a heavy staff. "The gnawlings come," he reported to Glis, pointing to the corridor leading into the hall. Beyond the lantern light, eyes glistened, vanished,

THE FALSE HOUSE   129

glistened again, accompanied by soft scramblings, low growls, the padding of gnawling feet, shadows deeper than the night shadows beyond, the silhouettes of the beasts.

Glis glanced at Carter, who gave a grim nod. "Prepare to fire on my command," the captain said to his lieutenant.

"I want to do something to confound them first," Carter said. He drew himself erect, and raised one of the Seven Words of Power to his thoughts, letting it slowly ascend as if from a pool of fire, its letters glowing with heat. When the Word appeared solid as brass to his mind's eye, he expelled it with effort from his throat. *Rahmurrim.*

The room shook; the surprised shouts of the men in the hall were echoed by animal cries in the corridor.

The soldier beside Glis yelled a warning even as a low hiss erupted at Carter's elbow. He turned in time to see the man who had brought word of the approaching gnawlings transform into an elongated monster, with multiple, taloned centipede legs, a wolf's head, and foaming jaws. It leapt, and Carter dodged backward, half falling, dropping his pike to catch himself on the balcony rail, nearly flipping over it as he did. Somehow he found time to right himself and raise his pistol, though the creature would surely be upon him before he could bring it into line.

Talons and jaws swept down, but were met by a blur of white, as Glis's lieutenant threw himself between the Master and the beast. The man screamed; pistols rang out, and the gnawling shrieked and fell flopping to the floor, its blood streaming over the carpet, its talons raking the lieutenant further in its contortions.

When the gnawling grew still, Carter scrambled to the

fallen soldier. He was badly mauled, the razor talons having pierced his nearly impenetrable pearl armor. Several soldiers tried to stanch the bleeding, but Carter watched in horror as the man's eyes passed into emptiness, his hand clutching the Master's wrist.

"He saved my life," Carter gasped.

"His name was Rupert," Glis said. "From my country, Aylyrium. I know his parents. Are you injured?"

Carter inspected his own frame. "No. Just bruised."

"What word did you speak?"

"The Word of Hope, which ends despair and confusion. Illusion cannot hold against it. I wanted to see if it would strip the gnawlings of their human forms. I never thought one might be nearby."

"The Word saved your life," Glis said. "No doubt the brute intended your assassination. A moment later might have been too late."

"Captain, the beasts have massed!" Spridel called.

Glis and Carter sprang to the balcony's edge, where they saw gnawlings thundering up the corridor into Middlecourt, their eyes reflecting yellow, green, and red in the lamp-light, charging in long, desperate ranks, their roars filling the hall. Even from where Carter stood, the noise was terrifying, but the men, lined up in a half circle before the corridor with the tigers behind them, first row kneeling, second standing, held their ground, and upon command, aimed their pistols.

"Fire!" Glis ordered.

Had they attacked in formation, they could have sundered the men's thin ranks, but they poured from the corridor as the beasts they were, howling, jaws snapping, claws slashing. Pistols flashed across the line; animals screamed. The weapons discharged point-blank into the mass, and the first row of beasts fell, but those behind bounded over the bodies and into the hall. The men managed a second round before proximity forced the use of pikes. The beasts rushed straight onto the glistening points, slaughtering themselves against the iron. The hum of battle, the deadly droning howls and death cries, shrieks and moanings, melted into a single clamor. Carter aimed his Colt, but his own men blocked a clear shot. Immediately he wished he were below with his fellows, though his duty clearly lay above.

He caught a glimpse of Duskin and Gregory, fighting side by side along with a young, sleek tiger, and a prick of envy stung him. In the last year, during their many gnawling hunts, the two had become close friends; they were in their element now, working as one, using their pistols and pikes to shield one another, their precise teamwork hauntingly beautiful. If not for his fear for their safety, he would have found the sight exhilarating.

But even in the midst of his admiration, he saw a gnawling, more massive than all the rest, bound through the ranks and leap toward Duskin. Carter's breath caught in his throat as wicked jaws sprang for his brother's jugular, only to be blocked by Gregory's pike, wedged between the gaping maw. The monster shook its heavy head, raising Gregory from the ground, then slamming him down with terrible force, but by then two tigers had leapt upon the beast, rending it from neck to foreleg. The gnawling's knees gave way; it dropped straight to the ground, covering Gregory from sight.

For an awful moment, Carter thought the man crushed, until a triumphant mop of red hair popped from beneath the massive corpse. The cousins clapped one another on the shoulders and returned to the fray. Lord Anderson soon lost track of both in the rising smoke of the guns.

The forces compacted at the corridor entrance, then spilled into the hall as the men were driven back by the charge. Tigers rolled across the ground, wrestling the gnawlings. Between the shadows and the light, Carter glimpsed the varied forms of the creatures, some squat with heavy hands, others clawed or taloned, sleek as serpents, or massive as bulls, jaws gaping, tongues lolling, foaming and shrieking, barking like dogs and screeching like hawks. The largest fell easy prey to the pistols; the others, disarrayed, were forced to retreat.

"The Word of Power did it!" Glis cried. "They entered the corridor as men, and the transformation took them by surprise. Without human hands, their rifles were useless."

"They're coming again!" Gregory shouted, where he crouched beside Duskin in the chamber below.

"Prepare to fire!" Glis called, and the men drew back into half-circle formation.

The gnawlings burst through, and again gunfire devastated their front lines. Then they were upon the men, striving against their pikes. Bodies piled up along the border between the forces; screams and growls, the horror of the sanitarium, filled the court. Carter held his pistol ready, looking for an opening.

The gnawlings plunged deep into the defenders' line, stretching it thin, but the soldiers held, and the beasts were repelled once more. Again they retreated into the corridor.

"Stand fast!" Glis called. "Prepare to fire!"

They stood in the dim hall, panting and bloody, awaiting the next charge. But before it came, a messenger bounded up the balcony stair. "Captain, they've found a secret passage and are bypassing our forces!"

"Where?" Glis cried.

"Sixty strides south. They were moving to take us from behind, but the Burnishers stopped them."

Spridel, who had remained seated throughout the battle, arms clutching the sides of his chair, leapt to his feet. "My boys are fighting? They're barely armed!"

"They drove the gnawlings back, sir. The beasts are retreating east toward the Long Corridor."

A glint of pride lit the baron's face. "Lord Anderson, by your leave! I must join them."

"Go," Carter said, and Spridel hurried away.

"Can you send Mélusine to the Long Corridor?" Glis asked one of his lieutenants.

"No, sir, the duchess is engaged in the passages to the north, but Marshal Inkling is moving that direction."

"Not enough," Glis said. "Lord Anderson, I have twenty men in reserve in the chamber below. Can you lead them?"

"I can," Carter said, wondering if he spoke the truth. He was no captain, though at Hope's insistence he had studied military tactics.

He sped down the spiral stair into a room behind Middlecourt, where Sergeant Sedger waited with a score of the White Circle Guard.

"Sergeant, you and your men, with me at once," Carter ordered. "We have gnawlings to catch." As they went, he opened the maps within his mind and plotted an interception course. They trotted through gloomy, winding ways, guns cocked, pikes held high.

They turned a corner and their lanterns revealed a line of gnawlings passing east down the next intersecting corridor. One roared and pointed a falconed hand, answered by a chorus of growls and hisses; animal eyes gleamed sanguine in the lamps. Several beasts turned to face the men, but Carter shifted his pike to his left hand and drew his Lightning Sword. It shone golden starlight, pure and blinding; he squeezed its hilt, taking strength from its radiance.

"Maaaster comes!" a gnawling cried, and a shudder went through the beasts.

"Fire!" the sergeant commanded, and the men in front released a dreadful volley. Smoke filled the air; the reverberations magnified the blasts to cannon fire. Gnawlings screamed and fled both directions down the intersecting corridor. Carter led quickly after, but hesitated at the turning, wary of being caught between his foes, should any choose to return. Wounded and dying beasts lay all around, but the rest had fled. He stood in indecision, torn between pursuing those escaping toward the Long Corridor to the left, and those still contained within Naleewuath.

"Hold this position, Sergeant," he ordered. "I will return." He darted down the left passage.

"Sir, take some men with you!" Sedger implored.

"Three, then, no more, in case you need them. And watch for Marshal Inkling. He should be nearby."

As the four raced after the fleeing horde, Carter cursed his misfortune at failing to intercept the entire company. Still, all was guesswork in the windings and the gloom. Gnawlings could travel at tremendous speeds, and the soldiers strained to overtake them, their breath coming in gasps. Finally, they spied the end of the procession. The four men sped up, and were nearly upon the beasts when one turned and shrieked in fear, a sound akin to a horse scream—the gnawlings were never brave; bereft of their human guises and their rifles, fleeing through unfamiliar corridors to unfamiliar lands, they were growing panicked.

During their pursuit, Carter had brought the Word Which Manifests to the forefront of his mind. *Fulan.* He spoke it with effort, and the force swept before him in a golden, blistering wave. The gnawlings screamed and fled faster, mindless in their terror, but the wave overtook them, bowling several off their feet.

The soldiers fired, and three gnawlings dropped, writhing and howling in pain. The men advanced, fired again, and more fell. Then they were treading cautiously past the frenzies of the dying and wounded, avoiding the raking talons, bobbing horns, and heaving bodies. By the time they were safely free, the gnawlings had vanished around a corner.

The soldiers plunged blindly after, but as Carter rounded the bend, a massive tail raked his chest, clipped his chin, and sent him sprawling. Gunshots and gnawling roars rang all around as he lay dazed and blind.

He recovered his senses to find two of his men down, the one farthest away screaming in pain as a rolling beast with heavy jaws mauled him, the other inches from death from an enormous bird, with thin stalks for legs, a razor bill, and rows of tiny, serrated teeth. Carter leapt to his fallen sword, swept it up, and with a twisting motion that sent him tumbling to the ground, slashed at the bird-creature's legs, severing one in a shower of golden sparks.

As it fell, the gnawling pecked at him, driving its long, thin beak an inch deep into the wood floor beside his head. Then its weight crashed upon him, smashing the air from his lungs—he was caught amid the writhings; beak and claw flailed the air. He kicked free with his legs and scrambled away.

Down the passage, the rolling beast had finished its victim, and along with two others, was closing with the soldier who still remained standing. Carter drew his pistol and shot an apeish brute in the chest. Before he could fire again, the second gnawling charged the standing soldier, who brought his pike into line. The creature impaled itself up to the hilts before it died, leaving the man pinned against the wall. The final gnawling, seeing its companions slain, fled down the corridor.

"Stay here!" Carter ordered, though none of his men appeared able to follow. He sprinted down the hall to the low gate leading from Naleewuath, which the gnawlings had easily surmounted, vaulted over it and bounded into the Long Corridor. The beasts were fleeing in both directions, and though he fired until his chambers were empty, they soon disappeared beyond the gentle curve of the passage.

Carter sighed and returned to his followers. The man who had been mauled was dead, the soldier who had halted the gnawling's charge was injured, and the remaining soldier was dressing his comrade's wounds. Once the man was sufficiently bandaged, they supported him as they made their way back to Sergeant Sedger.

"Thank the Lord, sir!" the sergeant cried when he saw them. "We couldn't afford to lose you."

"What's the situation?"

"The gnawlings have not returned. We've heard from the marshal, who occupies the corridor to our west. We've halted their retreat."

"But some escaped," Carter said.

"No more than a handful, sir."

"Yes," the Master said. "A handful. And I may not regret it tonight, this week, or even this year, but someday I think I will regret that handful very much."

Carter soon learned of victory at Middlecourt. The army had pressed all the way back to the Puzzle Chambers, soundly defeating the beasts. Because of their superior weaponry, and because the gnawlings had been forced into an unaccustomed form of fighting, the men had suffered minor losses. But by the time all was done, little of night remained for rest, and the morning, which once shone down gloriously from the soft skylights of Naleewuath, brought no day to a country windowless and changed.

Shortly after breakfast, Carter met with the duchess, the baron, Duncan, Glis, Nunth, Marshal Inkling, and Mewodin, and swearing them to secrecy insofar as their positions would allow, told of the theft of the Cornerstone, and the abduction of Lizbeth, so they might plan for the protection of the White Circle.

"This, then, is why the jungle has failed," Mewodin said.

"Yes, and there will be other, stranger things," Carter said. "Portions of the house have changed, corridors have shifted, and it will probably grow worse. I must journey to Shyntawgwin to seek the source of the evil. We have agreed we cannot go in force, and I need all of you to be wary, particularly with gnawling spies about."

"It chills the bones," Spridel said.

"It chills the soul," Inkling replied.

"But one question remains unanswered," Duchess Mélusine said. "Why did the gnawlings decide to leave Naleewuath, their ancestral home?"

"I don't know," Carter said. "But I am certain of one thing: they were terrified. At first I thought it was fear of the soldiers, but it was more than that. I have never seen them so desperate."

"M' lord," Duncan called, from the door to the chamber, where he conferred with one of his people, "I may have the answer. We had our suspicions, but no certainty till now. If you wouldn't mind stepping outside."

Beyond the chamber, four men guarded a heavy armoire, worn and faded with age.

"This is a gnawling," Duncan said.

Carter stepped back and placed a hand on his sword; Duskin and Gregory reached for their pistols.

" 'Tis nought to fear," Duncan said. "It's dead."

"Impossible!" Duskin said. "Gnawlings revert to animal form when they die."

"Are you certain it's a gnawling?" Spridel asked.

"Yes," Duncan said. "In its furniture-shape, a gnawling's skin shows signs of segmentation. See the legs?"

Carter drew closer. The extremities displayed minute sections, like the joints of an insect.

"This explains the gnawling's fear," Inkling said.

"I don't follow," Nunth said.

"I do," Carter said. "The anarchists have betrayed their

servants. The Cornerstone is creating a more orderly house, where furniture remains furniture. No wonder the beasts were so frightened; they are facing annihilation. This was not an attack planned by the anarchists, though certainly at one time they gave the gnawlings their new abilities and supplied them with rifles."

"Which explains both their lack of tactics and their clumsy attempts to infiltrate our ranks," the duchess said.

"I doubt we will have any more trouble from the beasts for a time, then," Carter said. "The rebellion is quelled, and few will be willing to serve the anarchists now. But we must remain wary, since they possess this new power."

After further discussion, Carter, Duskin, and Gregory departed, escorted by a dozen of Sergeant Sedger's men. Duskin was especially pensive on the return trip.

"Are you well?" Carter finally asked him as they passed along the Long Corridor.

"Well enough, I suppose, though furious at the anarchists, at their intellectual foolishness, their plots and schemes. They are all supposedly educated men."

"Most of them," Carter said. "The one I captured at Inman Tor, who later died, claimed to be a professor of history."

"Then he learned nothing from his studies. How can they think the destruction of the house desirable?"

"It is idealism mingled with evil," Carter said. "It leads to fascism—or anarchy."

"Gregory saved my life at Middlecourt," Duskin said.

"I know. I saw. I owe him a great debt."

"I've never seen death's hand so close. I wonder if it will affect me?"

Carter laughed. "If you fear becoming a coward, don't bother. You won't succumb to terror."

"No, not that. But in all our adventures together, you and I, and in all the hunts since, I never thought I would die, not really. I saw it for the first time yesterday—someday the jaws will close, the bullet strike, the sword hit home. It sobers one."

"It does indeed," Carter said.

Journeys

Once back at the Inner Chambers, Carter spent a day in speculation with Mr. Hope, discussing their journey, and two days awaiting the appearance of the famous architects. When a hall boy announced their arrival, the Master and his butler were sitting in the drawing room devising plans, drinking hot tea, and watching the snow blow beyond the golden damask curtains.

They entered shivering, bundled in hats and coats and gloves, hugging themselves against the cold of the Long Corridor, elderly men, one tall and thin, the other short and stocky.

"Phillip Crane," the shorter man said. "And this is Howard McMurtry, my senior partner. Architects at your service, sir. Isn't that right, Mr. McMurtry?"

"So we might be described," the other said. "Architects retired, as it were, seeking to map the architecture of all the High House. A task we will probably never complete."

"But I think we will," Crane said. "It's for a book, shouldn't you say, Mr. McMurtry?"

"A scholarly book, chronicling the wonders of Evenmere. We're retired, you know."

"You said that, Mr. McMurtry. But we're happy to be . . . retired that is. Worked together—"

"For forty-two years," McMurtry said. "Same firm, owned by our fathers. The fine old establishment—"

"Of McMurtry and Crane," Crane said. "We kept the name. Forty-two wonderful years."

"Some weren't so precious," McMurtry said.

"Forty-two wonderful years," Crane said. "It's the enthusiasm for a matter that counts."

"That's one way to look at it," McMurtry said.

"The only way to look at it. You're a pessimist, Mr. McMurtry."

"And you an idealist, Mr. Crane. But we are, Lord Anderson, as we said, at your service."

McMurtry possessed a few sprigs of silver hair, most of which had migrated to his eyebrows, wondrously delicate hands, and earnest blue eyes. Crane bore a lion's mane of long white hair, a bulbous nose, and brown, impish eyes framed in laugh lines.

Carter and Hope shook the men's hands and gave them seats near the fire and hot tea. Once their shivering subsided, Hope inquired concerning the Cornerstone.

"Ahh," Crane said. "The Cornerstone. Yes, we know much about it. Practically experts."

"We know a little," McMurtry corrected. "Mostly legends."

"More than anyone, I should say," Crane said. "It has been of interest to us. A cuneiform tablet, once hidden in an alcove at the apex of a vertical slab of rock in southern Loft, now stored at the university in Aylyrium, describes it as a block, roughly seven stones weight, twenty-eight by twenty-eight inches, with numerous inscriptions; I would have to consult my notes for more information."

"And it is said to have powers," McMurtry said. "Of that the legends are specific."

"Have you any familiarity with the country surrounding the Outer Darkness?" Carter asked.

"Assuredly," Crane said.

"Somewhat," McMurtry replied. "We spent three miserable weeks in Shyntawgwin."

"Had a splendid time," Crane said. "Except for the soldiers."

"They accused us of spying," McMurtry said. "Nearly didn't return alive."

"Required a bit of diplomacy," Crane said. "A bit of chat."

"I despise diplomacy," McMurtry said.

"Which is why he travels with me," Crane said. "To save his life occasionally. The architecture surrounding Shyntawgwin and Ephiny Edge is quaint—"

"Oppressive," McMurtry said.

"Like a rustic farmhouse."

"A nightmare of architecture."

"We plan to go there," Lord Anderson said, drawing the shard from his pocket. "Quite soon. I tell you this in confidence, gentlemen. We seek the Cornerstone stolen from Innman Tor. This is a small portion from it." As Carter gave the shard to Mr. McMurtry he felt its power pulsing in his hands. "Would you be interested in accompanying us? Your expertise may be needed. You would receive compensation and the gratitude of the Inner Chambers."

"Seems like ordinary rock to me," McMurtry said.

"It isn't," Carter replied. "It contains enormous energies unperceived by any save myself."

"Sounds rather dangerous, don't you think, Mr. Crane?" McMurtry said, returning the shard.

"Sounds rather exciting, don't you think, Mr. McMurtry?"

The two men exchanged identical grins.

"We'll go, of course," Crane said.

"Couldn't miss the opportunity, even if it kills us," McMurtry said.

"As long as one gets out alive, we can still finish the book, wouldn't you say, Mr. McMurtry?"

"Not as a 'we,' Mr. Crane. Not as a 'we.' But I would dedicate it to you."

"And I to you. When will we depart?"

"I have diplomats testing the waters of Shyntawgwin," Carter said. "They should return in two weeks."

"Excellent," said Crane.

"Acceptable," replied McMurtry.

The ambassadors returned with ill news, for the leaders of Shyntawgwin had detained them at the border, and after three days delay, forbidden them either audience or entrance into the country. Even more disturbing, the envoy had learned that Moomuth Kethorvian, a member of the White Circle bordering Shyntawgwin, had closed its gates amid rumors of revolution or disease, allowing no one to enter or leave the country. That Carter's contacts within the White Circle could glean no information implied a secrecy ominous enough to keep the Master and Mr. Hope awake and fretting several nights. The anxiety was useless; by the end of a week they knew nothing more.

Late on a Thursday evening, when the lamps were low, and the storm howled overhead, Sarah helped Carter don his Tawny Mantle, his Lightning Sword, his traveling boots, and his warmest coat and gloves. When all was done, she tied a red and black checkered muffler about his neck.

"I made it for you," she said. "Warm neck, warm heart. It also doubles as a checkerboard."

"All purpose, eh? But I haven't any checkers. Can it be used for semaphore?"

"And semaphive." She eyed him appraisingly and smiled. "Wrapped like that you could pass for the ghost of checkered past."

"I am what you made me."

"No, you are wearing what I made you."

Carter bent forward and kissed her on the cheek. "I haven't a chance."

"Not a ghost of one, checkered or plaid."

They went downstairs holding hands, into the library where Hope and Chant waited, all the lamps lit. Duskin and Gregory arrived shortly thereafter, then McMurtry and Crane, followed by a short, bandy-legged lieutenant leading fourteen of the White Circle Guard.

"Lieutenant Nooncastle reporting," the man said. He had a plain, honest face, marred by pockmarks on the left side, the protruding eyes of a frog, and a handlebar moustache curled in tight circles. A squadron of medals covered his chest, including the prestigious White Cross of Inglenook.

Carter gestured toward the decorations. "As Glis told me, you are obviously well qualified, Lieutenant. I've seen fewer ribbons on majors."

"Didn't want to be a major, sir. Didn't really even want the medals. A man is what he is, regardless of how much jewelry they pin on him, but Glis makes me wear 'em. When we're in the field, I'll put them in my pack."

"You're from Innman Tor?"

"Yes, sir, born and bred."

"That was one of the reasons Captain Glis recommended you. He thought it might be useful."

"More than likely he wants to get me out from under his feet, sir." Nooncastle gave a lopsided grin.

"That I doubt. Is the squadron ready?"

"At your word. Would you like to address the men, sir?"

"I would."

Carter spoke with everyone gathered around him, including Duskin, Gregory, and the two architects. "Captain Glis has already told you our journey leads through Shyntawgwin to the Outer Darkness, where we hope to recover both the Cornerstone of Evenmere and a young woman kidnapped by the anarchists. The urgency of our mission is acute. Unless we succeed, Evenmere will fall and Creation will be forever changed. Never has so much been placed in the hands of so few. Therefore, you have been carefully chosen by Captain Glis and myself for your bravery, intelligence, strength of arms, and ability to keep a secret. The latter is most important; the enemy must not learn of our mission.

"Further, the Master must often travel alone, using secret ways critical to the security of the house, and known only to himself. But the danger is too great; risks must be taken, and I intend to take you through those passages. You have each sworn to remain silent. I can do no better, though one of you might betray Evenmere in the end."

"Not willingly, sir," one man said.

"Not under pain of death," said another.

"My lads are trustworthy as they come," Nooncantlo said. "But I admit it hasn't been done since the Yellow Room Wars. It's a great responsibility."

Carter smiled. "I have complete confidence in all of you. You are the best soldiers in Evenmere. We will be passing through Bleak Passage for the first leg of our journey. You know what that means. For those of you who have never been, nothing can prepare you, but stay together, work as a unit, and we will soon be through it."

Lord Anderson turned to Sarah, who took both his hands and smiled, though her eyes were sad. "Find her, Carter. Find Lizbeth and bring her back."

"I will," he said, and kissed her fiercely, treasuring the taste of her mouth, while his men turned their heads in respect.

"Good hunting, Master," Chant said. "Go cautiously *Into that ominous tract, which, all agree, Hides the Dark Tower.*"

"Thank you, Chant, for your gloominess," Carter said, smiling ruefully, recognizing it as the Lamp-lighter's show of affection.

Enoch was gone on his rounds, but Hope was present

and looking morose. Carter shook his hand warmly. "Keep the house together, William. I'll send messages if I can. Try not to worry."

"I'll do my best. I'll bury myself in research, instead. Perhaps some of it will prove useful. We've made certain all your men carry the garb of Shyntawgwin in their packs, in case you need to go disguised. I can think of nothing else to do. Be careful, Carter."

The Master led the party, twenty in all, toward the stacks.

It is not unusual for diplomats and dignitaries to step from among the shelves of the library of Evenmere, as if slipping from between the covers of a book into the real world. As a child, Carter had thought that the way of it; later he learned its aisles served as a doorway unique in all the house. He had walked its path twice before, but it was always an unpleasant journey, for within those passages his maps were useless.

He glanced up at the rows of volumes stretching higher than his head as the party marched with measured steps, seeking the way, imperceptible unless looked for, and easily missed.

At last, from the corner of one eye, he glimpsed a trembling, as if a heat wave quivered between the shelves. As he approached it, the whole room shimmered, growing indistinct. Before him rose an ebony gash, an unsupported rent looming amid the *Geography* section. It expanded as he drew near; he slipped between its lips into milk-warm darkness.

For those watching, Carter and his followers grew insubstantial and indistinct before vanishing into the quivering air.

"For the one face I looked for was not there, the one low voice was mute; Only an unseen presence filled the air, And baffled my pursuit," Chant's voice drifted ghostly after the company.

Carter assembled his troop in a wide corridor, with walls bare of either baseboards or borders, ordinary enough to the touch, but colorless and indistinct in the lamp-light. The air was warm, and dry as twigs, as if the men had entered passages untouched by the vagaries of weather.

"Hello," Crane said, turning his lamp the direction they had come. "Look at this, Mr. McMurtry!"

Where the library should have been stood a tall portal, composed of green malachite, etched with the symbols of the twelve apostles poised on twelve thrones, surrounded by a sea of the risen dead, overlooked by cherubim and seraphim, their archangel wings forming the portal arch, the throne of God hidden in smoke upon a Sea of Glass. No part of the adit remained uncarved; the four horsemen of the Apocalypse rode the upper air; Lucifer careened like a star from heaven; men and horses fought by the thousands across the panoply, and in the bottom corner stood a single lamb beneath a star. The portal itself was hazy as a fogged mirror.

"It's terrifying, Mr. Crane," McMurtry said. "It chills the blood. A man could not enter that door unbidden, I say."

"In that you are correct," Carter said. "Only the members of the Inner Chambers, or those invited, may pass."

"If only we had time to make plaster casts," Crane said. "The world should see it. We could make a fortune displaying it."

"Or lose your lives in the doing," Nooncastle said. "Not for nothing is it called 'Bleak Passage.' You don't want to remain long. There's legends of men lost in its windings, grown insubstantial as shades, haunting the corridor forever, unseen, unfelt, undying till the end of time."

"Superstition," McMurtry said.

"Walk Bleak a mile before you so judge it," Nooncastle replied.

"There are only five charted exits," Carter said, "each cutting through the middle of the Long Corridor, leading to a different portion of the house; to use any others can result in tragedy—those lost seldom see the Inner Chambers again. But we have nothing to fear if we stay on the main corridor, and are assured of traveling unobserved; no man dares keep watch within Bleak."

Despite his show of confidence, Carter dreaded the journey. He felt blind without his maps, and staring down the length of the blank corridor filled him with apprehension. Nonetheless, he gave the order, and they set out, Nooncastle leading. The whole company, seized by disquietude, tramped in silence, listening. Occasionally, a man lifted a snatch of song, or a joke, or tale, but his voice quickly faded, his spirit quelled. The heat, at first a relief, quickly grew oppressive, forcing them to remove coats and hats, armor and gloves, as sweat beaded their temples. Shadowy forms writhed in the intersecting corridors, suggesting wonders and terrors too dreadful to be borne, as if the men walked paths scored by angels, in whose immortal faces they might soon find their own frail eyes reflected.

Day, night, time—none had meaning in that drear tunnel. As its sanctity seeped into their minds, they went as sleepwalkers, overawed, their eyes vacant with despair. They camped in silence, ate in silence, slept in silence, clutching their souls about them like children in the dark.

On the third day, they passed a doorway of four-paneled oak with a brass knob, incongruous amid the nebulous halls, the first of the five exits, this one leading to the Mere of Books. As one, the men turned their heads, watching it pass, craning their necks to see it retreat, as crewmen on a ghost ship, cursed to sail forever, stare in longing at the lights of a passing freighter.

They marched two days more, past another door, this one leading into Ooz, where stands the headquarters of the White Circle Guard. Again they gazed with yearning; one man gave a half cry, as if his wife or sweetheart waited beyond the threshold. A despair overtook the company; the younger men silently wept, though they knew not why.

Soul-sick, they continued, until at last they reached the third door, their destination. A murmur passed among them; step by step their pace increased, until they raced wildly down the corridor, boots thumping in the stillness, like shipwrecked sailors beckoning distant sails.

They pressed against the locked door; they beat upon it madly. Nooncastle scattered them with a shouted command, while Carter took a silver key from his brass ring and slipped it hastily into the lock. He flung the door wide and everyone rushed through, gulping the chill air of Evenmere as if rising from beneath the sea. Nooncastle slumped to the floor and his men followed suit.

Carter shut the door behind him and locked it carefully, then stood shaking his head, as if to clear it.

"Hideous," Duskin said. "Ghastly."

"I've never felt anything like it," Crane replied.

"Each time I enter, I swear it will be the last," Carter said.

"I shouldn't wonder," Duskin replied. "I won't go there again."

They were in a long room, windowless, but cheerful, with white carpet, white walls, and white Atlantides descending from the ceiling. An amber fresco depicted a scene from the *Kalevala*, of Wainamoinen, sword in hand, approaching the giant Wipunen. A birch tree grew upon the titan's shoulder, an alder on his chin, an oak from his forehead.

"There is a great awe in Bleak Passage," one man said, "like the holiness of God."

"There is a terrible despair there," another replied.

"No, it is the edge of insanity," a third said. "It is the cold halls of old age and the failing of the mind."

And none could agree what lay in Bleak, but all swore they would not willingly return.

"But you may have to," Nooncastle said, rising to his feet. "I have been through it six times, and it grows no better. But beyond this room is a larger chamber, made for guests. It can be bolted from the inside for protection, since none have the spirit to keep watch now. Come along, come along!"

The men sluggishly obeyed their commander. The chamber was indeed pleasant, painted with swordfish and whales, with white pillars, a tall ceiling, and golden sunflowers on Morris tile. A gallery stood above, all in dark oak, containing a small library. Wood lay in the large, circular fire-pit in the center of the room, and the whole company was soon eating roasted potatoes and dried meat from their packs.

Little was said, and they soon drifted into slumber, to dream of pacing Bleak Passage once more, and by so doing, dispel its emptiness from their souls. Despite his weariness, only Carter could not sleep, but lay restless among the piles of slumbering men, his mind on Lizbeth, Sarah, and most of all, on the terrible imbalance he sensed throughout the house, waiting like a gaping maw. He fell into a troubled sleep while holding the shard, feeling its pulsing drawing him toward a darkness deeper than night.

It was midmorning before anyone awoke. The fire lay in ashes; the room lay chilled. The men rubbed their eyes like little children and stumbled about for kindling, which they found in a rack by one wall. They ate a large breakfast and set out in silence.

The door had brought them three days' journey past Naleewuath into a country with the enigmatic name of The Bridle of Sooth. Because Carter wished to pass unseen, he led his men a winding way, through narrow secret ways with walls and floors of bare boards and low ceilings, their heavy boots clattering in the stillness. Lord Anderson wondered how many such drab passages he had walked since becoming Master.

Eight hours brought them to a low room with flaking paint on yellow boards. Beside a stone hearth they found a wooden box, and within it, carved toy soldiers, maps drawn with the hand of a child, and a piece of faded paper wrapped in a scroll and tied with a golden ribbon, declaring itself a charter in a misspelled scrawl of "The Secret Society of Simrana," whose bylaws demanded its members "protect the land from lawbreakers, brigands, and pirates."

"How did children find their way here?" Gregory asked.

Carter smiled, recalling his own boyish explorations. "Sheer resourcefulness. This must have been a great adventure, a hidden world all their own. I envy their discovery. But see how the paper crumbles! The author of this page is older than any of us now."

"They must have prevailed against the pirates," Gregory said. "I daresay none have been sighted for decades."

Carter smiled again. "Then let us make supper within these sacred halls and rest a time. We have to cross the Long Corridor soon, and I want to do so in the hours before dawn, when few travelers are abroad."

Ancient wood still lay on the hearth, and a cheery fire soon blazed. They cooked no food, but ate bread and cured meat from their packs. Despite their weariness, a general camaraderie arose; the soldiers had trained together; they loved Nooncastle well, who bantered lightly with them, and they were beginning to grow accustomed to the Master, who seemed only a man, after all.

"A wonderful place, this," Crane said, glancing all around, brown eyes blazing impishly. He glanced at his comrade, who even seated was much taller. "Wouldn't you say so, Mr. McMurtry?"

"It could use a window," McMurtry replied, drawing out his pocket watch, "though it's after six—"

"—and already dark outside, anyway," Crane said, brushing his silver hair back. "We couldn't see a thing.

But these secret passages are ingenious. I understand there are many within the house."

"Hundreds," Carter replied. "Perhaps thousands. Actually, it's a wonder more aren't found."

"They were, back in the Yellow Room Wars, long before you were born," Nooncastle said. "I was only a private then, young as some of these wide-eyed chicks." He waved a hand broadly at his men, who grinned all around. "The Master himself, your father, was in his twenties, and newly come to his inheritance. He knew of the passages as the Masters do, but the enemy discovered them occasionally, and both sides built walls to block their course, until few were trustworthy. That was a bloody war, as we drove the anarchists back to the south. We took a terrible toll on them, especially in the Fiffing Campaign, where the struggle gets its name, when we caught them in the Yellow Rooms between Fiffing Downs and Mommur. Their numbers have been thin ever since."

"I'll bet you were a hero, weren't you, Lieutenant?" one of Nooncastle's men asked, and it was obvious all his company had heard the story before, but liked listening to it again.

"We were all heroes. I remember coming home afterward; the Golden Boys of the Yellow Rooms they called us, and Constance, she was waiting for me, eyes shining as if I were a knight of old. Threw her arms right around my neck as I marched into Innman Tor, which wasn't considered proper, of course, but everyone acted the same. Women were weeping, and some of the men, because we had seen a lot of death. It was glorious, coming home."

"Not for all of us," McMurtry said.

"You were there?" Nooncastle asked.

"I was."

"And what was your company?"

McMurtry stretched his long legs to their full length and stared into the fire. "It doesn't matter. They all died. Only I survived."

"Well," Nooncastle said after a moment's pause, "there was that, too. Not all our battles were victories, and many paid the price. I lost several good friends in that war."

"And though I didn't serve, many of my school chums did," Crane said. "A number of those did not return. Yet we can be thankful that some, like Sergeant Nooncastle and Howard McMurtry, did."

"Yes," Carter said, but he was thinking of Sarah, and of returning to meet her, like Nooncastle to his Constance, after this journey was done.

❦

Driven westward by the need for secrecy, the company roused at three o'clock in the morning and marched dead-headed until they reached the Long Corridor. They hurried through it and entered a hidden way opening into the country of Westwing. The air smelled ocean-sweet, for the waters of the Sidereal Sea flow there through the Fable River to Runaway Bay, where are the greatest ship-yards of Evenmere, and the country was much warmer than the Long Corridor, owing to a refined heating system. But the men had little time to enjoy it, and were soon traipsing back through secret corridors bitterly cold by comparison. Their breath rose in clouds; the storm howled its monotony overhead; Carter wished he could fall asleep behind a tall chair before a blazing hearth, as he used to do as a child on long winter days. The memory warmed him, and he nurtured it many miles.

They spent a wearisome morning in that passage, which wound through the house, bypassing intersections by detouring either above or below, so the men traipsed up and down stairs until their calves and knee joints ached.

"This reminds me of the way to the Room of Horrors," Duskin said.

"Very astute," Carter replied. "This passage is part of the Curvings, which indeed lead there. Although they sometimes fragment, they connect much of the White Circle. This portion is one of the longest unbroken sections."

Even as he spoke, pain stabbed through the center of his head, so that he clutched his skull, gave an involuntary cry, and fell to one knee. The soldiers massed protectively around him, weapons ready.

"What is it?" Duskin cried.

For a moment he could not see. As his vision cleared, he said, "The maps . . . have changed. The anarchists are rearranging the house again. The passage before us is transformed."

The agony subsided and he stood, knees trembling. "I was concentrating on this section of Evenmere when it occurred. It was like having my brain wrenched at a right angle. No, I'm fine. It was just a shock. But the way before us is altered. I'm uncertain just how."

Through another hour's journey Carter was prodded by a conviction he chose to disregard, hoping it might prove false, but his fears were realized as they reached the end of the corridor and found no lever allowing egress. "The exit at this end of the passage is gone," he said softly.

"Then the anarchists know we are here," Duskin said.

"No. I thought so at first, but there has been a general alteration of the house just beyond this wall, affecting many chambers. We happen to be here by coincidence."

"Do we turn back?" Sergeant Haggard asked, Nooncastle's second in command, a freckle-faced, red-haired man with a boy's grin, though he was not smiling now.

"There is no time," Carter said. "Gentlemen, some of you have axes. I need a hole in this wall large enough for us to pass, but no larger."

Two of the soldiers drew broad-axes and hacked their way through the plaster. When they were done, both were covered with white dust, but a two-foot hole gaped in the wall. The company crawled through into a corridor.

"Find lumber," Carter said. "Take it from wherever it can be spared. I want this wall boarded up, to hide the passage beyond. We will send repair crews when we can."

Carter examined the corridor, then abruptly sat down. "Gentlemen, if one of you would be so good as to locate an empty room, we might as well have lunch."

"What's wrong?" Duskin asked.

"Can't you feel it?" Carter grimaced as soon as he spoke. "No, of course not. Sorry. Sometimes the maps are so strong, I forget it is not so for others. I intended to cross this corridor and open a secret passage on that far wall, but more than just its doorway has vanished; the passage no longer exists. I'll have to plot an entirely new course. It will take time."

Haggard returned a moment later and led the company into what proved to be a small church, with glazed tiles, brass candelabra, stenciled chancel, and stained-glass windows representing the signs of the twelve apostles.

Several of the guardsmen genuflected and crossed themselves before filing into the pews and unpacking their rations. Carter wandered to the front, sat on the floor beside the altar, and leaning against it, eyes closed, let the detailed, colorful maps drift into his mind. The images granted him a dual vision—the first as if he looked at ordinary charts, the second as if he wandered the halls shown therein—while he saw and comprehended both simultaneously.

He traced a course, seeking hidden passages and unpopulated ways, but though he could envision the corridors, the maps did not reveal if any were occupied. After thirty minutes, he sighed, withdrew from his reverie, and found Gregory, Duskin, and Nooncastle seated around him, his brother taking great bites from an apple.

"Were you praying?" Gregory asked.

"No, studying the maps."

Gregory nodded and glanced around the church. "A waste of beauty," he said, indicating the altar with his chin. "These superstitious relics won't survive the next century."

"Have you no room for faith?" Carter asked.

Gregory eyed Lord Anderson with steady confidence, his gray-green eyes bright with fervor. "You mean in God?" He dismissed the altar with a wave of his hand. "I have faith in the destiny of man. God, Christianity, all claptrap for the ignorant."

"Enoch would certainly disagree," Carter said. "But you believe the whole world insane, then?"

"Not that I know of," Gregory said. "How so?"

"Man has required certain basics for thousands of years: food, shelter, the desires of the body, and the need to seek God. When we are hungry we eat, when weary we rest. Is our longing for deity the only need we have which cannot be met? And if so, if we carry an eternally unrequited desire throughout our lives, are we not then, as a race, insane? No, Gregory, the destiny of man, grandiose as it sounds, will not fill the gap."

"I think it will," Gregory said, undaunted. "I need nothing larger than myself and scientific reason to build a better world. Who knows what inventions we will create in the coming decades?"

"I'd have none of such talk, myself, sir," Nooncastle said. "It's unnatural. Wholly unnatural. Men running about, trying to replace the things God made. What will they do next? Flying machines? Icarus's wings! Give me the old ways any day."

"But surely, good Lieutenant, if there is improvement . . ." Gregory said. "The world is changing; the old order is moving aside. The mechanical age will lift men from common toil. Certainly, I admit there are problems, yet how glorious it all is; mechanisms doing the labor while men stand watching! The age to come will be one of poetry and philosophical speculation. Imagine the music that will be written, the dramas, the books, when all humanity has time to pursue higher callings."

"You have a greater expectation of man than I," Nooncastle said. "No, sir. Give him enough leisure and a man will take to the bottle, I say. And I guarantee it won't be the poor with all the free time; they will be stoking the machinery. The rich will stay rich, meaning no disrespect to you noble gentlemen. But at least there will always be a need for good soldiers."

"But, Nooncastle, surely you understand that man must evolve?" Gregory said.

"From the cradle to the grave, yes, sir, and plenty will happen between."

"But there must be more. The golden age—"

"He goes on like this at times," Duskin said. "But unless I miss my guess, there will be no meeting of these two minds, the dreamer and the pragmatist."

"The world is built by dreamers," Gregory said.

"Yes, sir," Nooncastle replied. "But it is run by pragmatists."

"As for faith, Gregory, you may change your mind as you age," Carter said. "Was it Plato who said that no old man dies an atheist? I cannot recall."

"You sound like my professors from university," Gregory said, grinning, clearly enjoying the debate.

"Ah, I do not think of these things much. I accept my faith as best I can, though I will admit this mission tests it sorely. Sarah is my philosopher. If you want a real debate, you should spar with her. She could argue your professors to the ground."

Howard McMurtry and Phillip Crane wandered up, the latter carrying a set of maps of his own. "I was just pondering our path, Lord Anderson."

"As was I," Carter said. "May I see your chart, Mr. Crane?"

"Certainly," Crane said. "Mr. McMurtry and I drew these ourselves—"

"—ten years ago," McMurtry concluded. "One of our first publications."

Carter placed the map on the floor before him, won-

dering how long it would be useful as the house continued to change.

"Several of you have traveled this territory," Carter
said. "I need your counsel. We have two choices: we can
go here and here"—he pointed—"through these corridors. This is my choice, for it will lead soonest to
Moomuth Kethorvian, though it requires taking the Long
Corridor some distance before striking another hidden
passage. The alternative would be to turn here, into the attics leading to High Gable. We would not find another secret way for some time, but the path is less inhabited.
What are your thoughts?"

"I have never been either direction," Duskin said.

"I have only passed through the Long Corridor," Gregory said. "That portion is particularly busy, or was at that
time."

"Too busy," McMurtry said. "There is extensive trade
between Himnerhin and Westwing. I would not recom-
mend it—"

"—for our travels," Crane said. "For the very reason.
The attics surrounding High Gable, on the other hand, are
quiet, and I think I can show a way through these passages here"—he tapped the map—"which will lead to no
chance meetings."

"The gentlemen are correct," Nooncastle said. "You
could never reach Moomuth Kethorvian undetected. Half
the White Circle would know before we ever entered the
hidden corridor."

Carter frowned. "Very well. You have already paid for
your passage, for I would have gone the wrong direction."

"Traveling the attics is always an exciting experience,"

Crane said. "Full of marvelous things. It's like wandering past buried treasure."

"Very dusty treasure," McMurtry replied.

As they finished lunch and departed the church, Carter gave one backward glance at the worn pews, the stained-glass windows, the unadorned cross upon the altar, quite beautiful in its simplicity, and perhaps because of his mentioning her to Gregory, he felt a sudden longing to see Sarah, to sit with her among common things, and listen to her speak of books, and colors, and familiar concerns, revealing in every word only a fraction of the mystery that was both simply herself, and the embodiment of every woman. He said a prayer under his breath for the success of their journey, and departed.

They turned left into a corridor paneled in oak, with pristine Prussian blue carpet. Though Carter feared they must soon be detected, they passed down its length without incident, taking an intersection to the right, then back to the left. Windows stretched along one wall, opening onto a quadrangle, revealing snow still falling in deep drifts, though the wind no longer howled. The sun remained wholly shrouded, the day gray and bitter. The men shivered.

Thereafter, they reached a narrow servants' stair, its carpet worn and lamps unlit, dim but not wholly dark. They followed it past four floors into a high attic, stretching far into the distance, faintly illuminated from octagonal windows of beveled glass overlooking the rooftops of Evenmere. Dust lay thick upon the bare floorboards; boxes and crates lay stacked in the center, forming an aisle on either side.

"What a wealth of lore undoubtedly lurks in these cartons," Phillip Crane said.

"A barrage of debris," McMurtry said. "The old adage is true; no one in the High House ever throws away anything."

"And an interesting phenomenon it is," Crane said, "resulting, I believe, from the limitless spaces in the structure. People do, indeed, grow into whatever room they have. I have been on several 'digs' as they call them, where parties enter attics such as this, seeking forgotten treasure. On my mantel are Roman coins and a bust of Ozymandias dating to his era."

"If the house had any order, such things would never be lost, Mr. Crane," McMurtry said.

"But," Crane said, "in Evenmere, nothing is ever lost forever, wouldn't you say, Mr. McMurtry?"

"Only for centuries, Mr. Crane. Only for centuries."

The attic was low-ceilinged, and the walls, like the windows, were eight-sided. The men marched in ranks of two down the left aisle, through a gloaming of diffused light, and the silence fell upon them as they stirred dust first fallen when Tharmaldrun was king. Walking kept them warm, living in such an enormous, drafty house having enured them to the cold, and it occurred to Carter that his former melancholy had fallen from him, leaving him suddenly happy, with a joy that comes in the midst of adventure, even one barbed with danger and hardship. The endless complexities of Evenmere held a constant fascination for him, this house where there would always be another secluded nook, a hidden closet, a virgin attic, to explore. His eyes ran happily over the assorted crates; occasionally he reached into one, beckoned by the shape or color of some abandoned gaud. Most were useless—meaningless ledgers computing wealth long dispersed, trinkets and beads valuable to one deceased, springs and parts for machinery with purpose unknown—but occasionally he found something of beauty, a pair of ruby slippers, a crystal globe with figures depicting the battle of Hrolf Kraki against King Adhils, a copy of *Historia Regum Britanniae* signed by the author, a child's marble of the lightest blue. He carried each as he walked, examining it, before depositing it into another box. He kept the marble, with a twinge of guilt that some boy grown to adulthood might come seeking it—a notion he dismissed with a smile, for the toddler who once held that gem was likely dust. And, as Mr. Hope would have reminded him, the Attic Law of 1367, which stipulates that no attic may be salvaged except with the express permission of the underlying country, also allows for attic gleaning, so long as no more than a specified poundage is removed. He laughed aloud, recalling it, and wondered how much of his mind was filled with the rules and regulations of the High House. Yet, he also knew these laws were not trivial, but the basis for a grandly diverse civilization.

The attic continued, hour by hour: a window every twelve paces, the bare boards, the dull boxes, the only variety an occasional bend to the right or left. Twilight fell, obscuring the blowing snow against the glass, before Nooncastle finally called a halt. There were no hearths in the attic, but the soldiers assembled a portable, iron fire-pit, called a *fetchfire*, and with scraps of wood collected during their trek in the halls below, created a passable flame, the smoke drifting to the high ceiling and roiling down the attic length.

Nooncastle stretched his hands to the blaze and sighed. "We'll have few such comforts if we stay up here where there's no wood. But at least there's enough for tonight."

"I won't risk wood details in the house below," Carter said. "Not yet. There's too much danger of being seen. Perhaps later. But this attic extends for days, and I intend to follow it as long as possible. We'll have to bear the monotony as best we can."

"A soldier's life is monotony, interspersed with brief moments of terrible excitement," Nooncastle said. "The monotony is the best part."

They made a meal of their rations, set a watch, and turned in. Carter wrapped himself in his blankets, and listened to the wind, risen with nightfall, shuddering the attic walls, moaning over the eaves. The sentries' mantled lamps burned on either side, like stars across the ether. Carter closed his eyes and dreamed he lay in an enormous tunnel, with the wind howling forever and ever down the way.

High Gable

Twelve days the men traveled the attic, passing above Himnerhin and Ooz, and though those countries are well settled, they saw no one, though they often heard voices and songs drifting up the attic stairs. In Himnerhin, where the windows overlook the Terraces, Mr. Crane tried to show the orchards for which the country is famous, but the snowfall covered them, leaving white mounds for trees, and Carter wondered if there would be a spring with peaches at all.

Despite his misgivings, he found this portion of the journey pleasant, because he enjoyed a hike. Since Duskin and Gregory wore no uniforms, he sometimes sent them slipping downstairs for firewood. At night, the men sat around the *fetchfire* blaze, telling stories and jokes, Nooncastle smoking a briar pipe, and as is the way of such things, everyone becoming better companions. Carter found the lieutenant to be solid as old boards, both in strength and character. Crane and McMurtry, despite their oddities, were likable enough, Phillip Crane for his enthusiasm, Howard McMurtry, his steady reasoning. Although Gregory had hunted often with Duskin and occasionally eaten with the family, Carter did not know him well, and found him impertinent as young men sometimes are, but steadfast enough in his way.

Crane loved to tell stories of the countries he had visited: the Palladian towers of the villages of Keedin, the Evythian vastness of the halls of Aylyrium, the Rococo carvings on the cupboards and wardrobes of Nianar, the Baroque steeples and minarets of Ooz. He and Mr. McMurtry had journeyed as far as Capaz, and seen the Sidereal Sea by way of North Lowing. He could describe the beauty of the veins of a stone statue in minute detail, and though it might have been dull in another, he made it interesting, for he told of those who had carved it, and what loves they had, and how they had died, often in murder and blood. The two men had crossed the mountains to Far Wing in the west, and even beyond, to lands with exotic names and wondrous customs, where the languages were distorted and changed. Mr. Crane even claimed dragons dwelled beyond the tiny kingdom of Thimble, sunning themselves on the stone steps of the dark eidolons dedicated to heathen gods. And though Carter did not believe dragons still existed, save for the dinosaur in the attic, he enjoyed the stories well.

After several days' journey, they came in late afternoon to the edge of High Gable, which lies only in the upper stories, with Himnerhin below. Carter sent Duskin to make discreet arrangements for their passage, there being no secret corridors leading into that country, and no way through without passing the border guard. Instead of having Duskin enter from the attic, he sent him through the Long Corridor, as an ordinary traveler would go.

His brother was absent nearly half a day, and the last two hours Carter did nothing but pace, despite knowing a hundred reasons he might be delayed. At last, when daylight had sunk to the gloaming of winter, Duskin appeared, accompanied by a short, plump gentleman in ludicrous garb. The forced smile on his brother's face brought an amused grin to Carter's own, for he had dealt with the Grandfalcons of High Gable before, and recognized the approaching dignitary.

"Lord Anderson, a surprise beyond surprises," the man said, his own smile a polite nothing, his voice betraying nervousness.

"Grandfalcon Thintillian," Carter said, shaking the man's hand with equal fervor. "How long has it been? Two years, I think, since that problem with the Eekee?"

"Ah, the Eekee. I want to forget them." The grandfalcon had a bulbous nose, weak eyes, a red moustache, and loose jowls. In the custom of his people, he wore a long cloak, fastening in the front over a wool tunic, with an elaborate headdress, two feet tall, adorned with bird feathers of every color, all collected from creatures having died from natural causes. The cloak was heavily embroidered with arcane geometric shapes, and a badge hung on his right breast with a semblance of a cloth falcon rising in flight. "The Eekee, small men with small minds," he said to Duskin. "I'm sure your brother told you. The Eekee thought it wrong for us to use the gliders. Said it discomfited the birds. But, of course, the birds are where we learned it. The Eekee!" His voice warbled on the last word.

"I hope all is well in High Gable," Carter said.

"You've heard rumors?" Thintillian asked, a trace of fear in his eyes. "Is that why you've come?"

"No, we are simply journeying through. Is there concern?"

Thintillian hesitated. "It is . . . not well. Mysterious happenings; disastrous events. It's . . . oh, it's the birds!" The man seemed suddenly close to tears. "You're here and you must see. I said nothing to your brother, young *Dutton* here, because I promised to give Dr. Vandermast, our Master Ornithologist, a chance to study it before spreading the alarm. I told him we should contact the Inner Chambers, but you know how difficult the ornithologists can be! But I'm glad you've come, regardless of what Dr. Vandermast says."

"I want to see this, of course," Carter said. "But I'm certain Duskin has told you we are traveling in haste and wish to remain unseen."

"I will guarantee your anonymity. The border guards will be sent away, and we will pass into Eggshell Mission, straight up to the Aeries."

"So far!" Carter said. "I hoped to journey through Hedging Lane, then down to Dovecote Passage and into Moomuth Kethorvian. Our need for secrecy is great."

"Our need is equally immense, Master Anderson," Thintillian said stiffly. "High Gable resolves its own difficulties, as you know. But we have an enigma and you must see the Aeries. I will conceal your escort in the Middle Haunts and we will ascend the heights alone. Your face is not well known in High Gable, as it might be in Naleewuath or Veth, and if you conceal your mantle and sword, you will not be recognized. At any rate, few will walk the Upper Air tonight."

Carter sighed to himself. Thintillian was eccentric, and stubborn within it, a mark of his people; their country had been founded by philosophers and scientists and sometimes their erudite leanings surpassed rational thought.

After seeing to the removal of the border guards, Thintillian led the company from the attic into grand chambers walled in dolomite the color of ocher, with tiled floors etched in gold. They soon reached a massive chamber built of blue marble, surmounted by a dome of staggering height, painted sky-blue, with blue birds and butterflies and twinkling stars sketched between royal-blue ribs descending downward like falling rain from a central wheel embellished with a portrait of an owl in flight. Farther down, the bird illustrations flitted in the thousands between painted greenery. An elegant spiral stair, also of blue marble, ascended with stones cut to fit, so that as it wound upward, the steps meshed with one another, folded hands soon lost in the heights. The men stood gaping.

"It's beautiful," Duskin said, and all agreed.

"With few exceptions, the rock on this stair uses no mortar, but is freestanding," the grandfalcon said. "It was made by the artisan, Ieegin, at the behest of King Feg, over a thousand years ago."

"And do we watch our step then?" Nooncastle asked.

Thintillian gave a scathing look. "It's as solid as the day it was built."

"That's what I mean," Nooncastle said, under his breath to the Master.

By the time they paused, halfway to the top, their legs ached. Thintillian led them into an elegant side chamber, also in blue, with enormous pictures of bird heads on the walls.

"The soldiers will remain here for the night. I will return for the Master momentarily," the grandfalcon said.

As the gold-trimmed door closed behind Thintillian, Gregory said to Duskin, "An exceptional country, wouldn't you say, young Dutton?"

Duskin reddened and shook his head. "Two hours I spent, lurking around his office, seeking an interview, while his secretary made certain I understood how important and busy the man was. I represented myself as a messenger, so of course they wouldn't stoop so low as to be civil to a mere courier. Once inside, even after he knew I was your brother, I had the devil's time convincing him you were really at the doors of High Gable. I don't think he wanted to believe it. Whatever the trouble, he's terrified. We talked an hour about nearly nothing; I still don't know what he said."

"He thinks well of himself," Carter said, grinning. "By the time I finished negotiating with the Eekee, I was sick of High Gable. Their group thought the aerial gliders, which the people have used for over two hundred years, were having a deleterious effect on the nests. Both factions acted mad as hatters."

"They think much of their birds," Nooncastle said.

"It's practically a religion," Carter replied. "Or, at least, a state obsession. Ornithology is the most respected study in High Gable, and the owl their national symbol. But don't think them totally deranged; it's impressive to see their gliders drifting off the high towers on summer's days, hundreds of feet above the ground, men sailing like birds on the wind. And they are masters of hot-air balloons as well. They have many scholars and have designed hundreds of useful inventions. They also keep an extensive library."

Thintillian returned at that moment, "Are you ready, Lord Anderson?"

Carter handed Nooncastle his sword and mantle. "You may want to come, Duskin."

"Could Mr. McMurtry and I go as well?" Crane asked. "I have never been to the towers."

"It is a long climb," Thintillian said.

"Ah, never mind these gray hairs," Crane replied.

"The years have made us tough as leather," McMurtry added.

They proceeded up the stair until they reached a door near the very top. Carter had no particular fear of heights, but standing on the high balcony, looking down to the blue circle at the bottom, he kept his hands on the rail.

"An architectural miracle," Crane said, beaming.

"A work of genius," McMurtry agreed, an identical smile on his face. "How could they think it would stand—"

"—for a thousand years?" Crane asked.

"If it stood at all, a thousand years would be as a day," McMurtry said.

"Quite right," Crane replied. "As a day. I can hardly wait to see the Aeries. I have heard so much about them. Wanted to see them before—"

"—but we were pressed for time when last we came," McMurtry said. "Depressed for a week."

"You will see little glory in the Aeries today," Thintillian said, leading them onto a landing that opened into an enormous rectangular chamber, its windows overlooking an immense quadrangle. Snow blew against the glass; the sky beyond was hidden by storm clouds. Laboratory tables covered with beakers, alembics, and test tubes were neatly laid out in one corner; telescopes of various sizes and shapes jutted through ceiling slits. Enormous birdhouses crowded against the windows, their doors to the outside made fast against the winter wind. The room was surprisingly warm and filled with rasping sounds, like metal against file, quite different from the cooing, chirping, and squawking Carter remembered from his last visit.

"They use an innovative steam system to pump hot air through the chambers," Carter told Duskin. "It purifies the atmosphere as well; notice the lack of odor despite the birds. I haven't had time to study it, but I intend to one day."

As they stepped closer, Carter paused. "Wait! The windows are changed. They were circular before, weren't they? And gabled? Not these square frames lined up in rows."

"I had read they were Catherine wheels," McMurtry said.

"They were!" Thintillian cried. "Round and beautiful! Look at them now. Ugly, squat things. And that is the least of it. Look at the birds!"

Carter felt a chill not caused by the cold. Through the windows of a birdhouse stood a thin caricature, the head rectangular as a box, the beak a forty-five-degree angle, the pinions jagged as those of a thunderbird, the body two squares for the upper and lower torso, and the legs, thin sticks with lines for claws. Had it been dead and mutilated, it would have been less horrid, but it lived and functioned in meticulous, mechanical patterns, seeking scattered seeds not in the rapid movements customary to the avian, but in precise swings of its head. It made no extraneous movements when not eating, but remained motionless as a sculpture save for the rhythmic pounding of its heart against its chest.

"This was an emerald cuckoo," Thintillian said.

"It's all gray now," Duskin said.

"Every bird is gray, even the peacocks," Thintillian said.

The bird gave a metallic cry, echoed by thousands of others, throughout the Aeries, a cacophony that made the men shudder.

"They all emit that ghastly noise," the grandfalcon said, "every twenty-two seconds, without fail. Can you help us, Lord Anderson?"

Carter pursed his lips, his face flushed with shock and outrage. "This is the anarchists' work."

"But can you do anything for us?" Thintillian asked. "You are the Master. The Words of Power, perhaps?"

"I must try. If you will give me a moment."

Thintillian led the companions apart, and Carter focused on the Words, uncertain if any might be useful. Gradually, the Word of Hope rose before him, the heat of its burning letters nearly palpable to him, so the flame warmed his face. He brought it gradually to his throat and released it with a low gasp. *Rahmurrim*.

The room shook. For a moment nothing occurred, but then, gradually, the bird before Carter expanded, unfolding like paper, its colors blossoming into green and yellow, angles and lines giving way to rounded, downy softness. It hopped twice, gave a happy chirp, and began to sing. Birdsongs and fluttering wings filled the Aeries with a jubilant passion.

Thintillian, forgetting his dignity, bounced up and down in excitement, beaming. "You did it! The birds are returned! The luck of High Gable! How did you do it?"

Carter smiled. "The Word of Hope, which heartens and ends confusion. I used it to unveil illusion, as on Innman Tor, years ago, and in Naleewuath most recently. But though the nature of the transformation was similar to the false Tor, this was not completely insubstantial—see how the gables did not revert."

"What does it mean?" Crane asked. "Is the transformation of the house somehow more real?"

"So I would guess," Carter said. "Which mutated first, the gables or the birds?"

"The gables, certainly," the grandfalcon said. "By a week."

"Then I think Mr. Crane is right. The core of the alteration is the transformation of the house. Other objects will follow. Next time I may not be able to right it."

"Thank you, my lord," Thintillian said.

"I don't believe it will last," Carter said. "Unless we stop the process, the birds will eventually return to their previous form. And worse, my pity for the creatures has exceeded my judgment. I could not bear their suffering, but by employing the Word of Power I have announced to all the High House that the Master is at High Gable."

"Perhaps," the grandfalcon said. "But we have kept the transmutation of the birds secret, though rumors abound. Everyone knows something is going on, but we've quarantined the Aeries to prevent the people from panicking. We couldn't have done it much longer, of course."

"Panic over birds?" Duskin asked.

Thintillian gave a piercing look. "The birds are the symbol of all that is High Gable. Our government rests on their feathered shoulders. I wouldn't expect you to understand."

"At any rate, I have done all I can," Carter said. "If you could return us to our room tonight, then provide escort through the borders tomorrow, it would be appreciated."

"It shall be done," Thintillian said. "We can guide you around Wattlepole early tomorrow morning, before anyone is astir. But it will take two days to reach our borders."

The use of the Word had wearied Carter, and he returned to the room dispirited, terrified by the transformation of the birds, wondering what would become of Evenmere.

They reached the borders of High Gable by a thin passage spiraling downward, alternating between sloping halls and sets of short two- and three-step stairs. Thintillian led them himself, his pomposity lessened by gratitude. They parted at Dovecote Passage, a corridor with both walls covered by a vast William Morris forest tapestry, done in brown and olive with orange tulips, depicting every variety of bird disporting on an acanthus-leaf ground. Likewise, avian statues, covered in gold, roosted on brass poles depending from the ceiling. The corridor served as a buffer zone between High Gable and Moomuth Kethorvian; ages before they had warred, and each had finally donated rooms to set the peace between them. Because the lowest portions of High Gable inter-sected the highest of Moomuth Kethorvian, Dovecote was one of only two corridors connecting the countries.

In order to remain unseen, they soon departed Dove-cote, journeying through doors painted red, blue, ocher, and saffron, into rooms deserted save for one containing a sleeping tramp, who fled at sight of them, his boots echoing down the passages. Soon after, in a wide corridor, Carter moved a single lever, cleverly hidden at the base of a tall statue of a cherub with broken nose and marred face, and a wall panel slid away, revealing a secret passage de-signed to take them deep into Moomuth. It began as wood paneling, but quickly changed to black marble. The men's boots rang upon the dolomite floor; by the lamp-light they saw fanged, eleven faces carved in the architraves, staring down upon them with hungry eyes. Ancient pictographs chiseled into the marble depicted gods and demons garbed in a blend of Minasian and Old Eastwing splen-dor; gryphon and ibis heads jutted from the walls like tro-phies in a tomb. The air lay thick; the black stone sucked the light from the lanterns; the soldiers' shadows wan-dered lost in the jet.

"Anywhere else, building a hidden passage of such ma-terials would be sheer extravagance, wouldn't you say, Mr. McMurtry?" Crane said, running his hands over the cold stone in admiration.

McMurtry's eyes sparkled. "It would indeed, Mr. Crane."

"Have you been to Moomuth before?" Duskin asked.

"Four times," Crane said.

"Five, actually," McMurtry corrected. "We pass through Moomuth when we can, to study its vast edifices.

Its architecture is unlike anything else in the house. Quite gaudy."

"Gaudy, but fascinating," Crane said. "They have retained the ancient splendor of the court of Nothopolassar, and the Singing Gardens of Moomuth Kethorvian rival their ravaged counterpart in antediluvian Ankhnan. It is believed to be one of the oldest inhabited portions of the house, where the first Master is said to have been born."

"If it's all this dismal, I don't much care for it," Nooncastle said. "Keep alert, lads."

Beneath such gloom the men's spirits sank. They journeyed all that day through the fundamental darkness, until they felt like shadows' shadows themselves, but toward evening entered a corridor with four narrow windows cut through the foot-thick marble.

"Odd," Gregory said. "A window in a secret corridor. Mightn't that give it away?"

"Apparently not," Carter said, peering out one of the panes. "Even though we descended from High Gable, we're still two stories up, practically invisible from below."

Frost had gathered upon the glass, and a light snow fell, but Carter could distinguish a courtyard, piled high with drifts, its statuary transformed into grim ghosts, their eyes and mouths vacant circles.

Duskin, who had manned one of the other windows, suddenly gave a sharp intake of breath. "Carter, look at this," he said softly.

Lord Anderson stepped to the casement, but saw nothing. "What is it?"

"The snowflakes. Each is identical. In nature no two should be alike."

Carter shuddered as he studied the wisps upon the glass. Not only was each flake indistinguishable, but the elegance of the crystals had been replaced by three overlapping triangles, as if designed by an unimaginative mathematician.

"Let's move on," Carter said roughly. "We've no time for gawking." He led the men quickly away.

They camped that night before a hearth with winged zebras on either side and a gaping totem face for a mantel. Though it did little to disperse the gloom, the fire brought comfort to all save Carter, who lay upon his bedroll, unable to forget the snowflakes. The anarchists were changing not just Evenmere, but the whole world. He wondered if the transformations were more prevalent near the Outer Darkness, or if the Inner Chambers were being drastically altered as well.

He slept fitfully that night, amid dreams of terror and the abyss. More than once he woke, thinking he heard the screams of a young girl alone in the darkness.

The days ran together like water as the passage gradually curved to the east. The companions followed the dusty, cobwebbed ways past brass urns and clay jars large as men, until they reached a landing, where they gaped at a series of intricate stairs carved to the tiniest detail with scenes of ships and sailors and armies marching to war, the soldiers spilling over the balustrades, filing in long lines down the handrails, both armies descending and ascending the banisters toward one another, as if they marched from the hills, all meeting at a central staircase, the heart of the battle. With the lamps of the travelers the only illumination, the carved warriors appeared to tramp out of the night.

"What exquisite craftsmanship!" Phillip Crane said.

"But why build it in a hidden passage?" McMurtry asked.

"Perhaps it was not always hidden," Carter said. "There must be thousands of individual figures. If one man carved it, it must have taken years."

"I've seen many curious things in my wanderings," Nooncastle said. "Quirks and peculiarities. Some artist, no doubt, working here for reasons unknown. It must be quite a story."

"The tale of a madman," Gregory said. "And one we will probably never know."

"Lord Anderson, if I could but make a hasty sketch," Howard McMurtry said. "A rough drawing."

Carter shook his head. "No, Mr. McMurtry. These passages must remain secret as you vowed. There is no point in raising curiosity."

"But it's an architectural marvel!" McMurtry said. "Do you see the way the stair is underpinned? It should be in the Great Museum at Aylyrium—"

"If it were possible to move it, of course," Crane said.

"At the least a photograph," McMurtry said. "But a simple sketch . . ."

Carter sighed. "A sketch, so long as you never reveal its location. A few moments rest will do no harm."

While the remainder of the company relaxed on the steps, McMurtry strode back and forth, pad in hand, making thumbnail drawings, while Mr. Crane gave suggestions. Carter and Duskin found a seat against a paneled wall apart from the others.

"You're annoyed," Duskin said.

"I am," Carter replied. "We are on a grave mission; I feel the entire house swaying around me, as if it were tottering. I cannot explain the feeling. And McMurtry wishes to make illustrations."

"You could have stopped him."

Carter sighed again. "Yes, I suppose so. But we do need a rest, and there's little point in aggravating the man. He's dour enough as it is. It was gracious of them both to come. I just wish they were more serious about our objective."

"The only thing they are serious about," Duskin said, "is architecture. That's why you brought them."

"True enough," Carter said. "They can't remove their eccentricity like an old coat. I wish we were home, and this whole affair ended." He spoke softly, so the others would not hear.

"We should make camp early tonight," Duskin said. "You've been ghost-pale all day. Are you catching cold?"

"I wish that were it. Duskin, we are walking into a great darkness. I feel its pull. I sense the whole house being sucked into it, as if it were an enormous chasm. The Balance is threatened and the center is rotten. All the maps have altered. The nearer the Outer Darkness, the more changes I perceive. It frightens me. Everyone and everything I love is in danger."

"What can we do?"

"Nothing," Carter said. "Not until we find the source."

"That's a great weight to carry."

"Yes," Carter said, nodding. "Before we left, Sarah and I talked of our lack of children. Our efforts have been in vain; our prayers have not been answered. I can't drive it from my mind. Will my supplications go unheeded here as well? Might the whole world slide into the abyss, regardless of what I, or anyone else, desires?"

"I don't claim to know God's will," Duskin said, "or how the universe works, but you're asking two different questions, a prayer for a child, and one for all Creation. They seem to be in dissimilar categories."

Carter laughed. "How pompous I must sound! Yet, if the universe should end, and I never to have known my child's touch . . . I know it sounds foolish."

"No, it doesn't. Any grief looms large as the whole world to the griever. But have faith, brother. You are the Master of the house; there is no one like you in all of Evenmere. Don't let the obstacles discourage you."

Mr. Crane appeared suddenly beside Carter's left elbow, grinning like a boy, startling both men by having come from behind. "Marvelous! Incredible! Can't thank you enough, Lord Anderson. Mr. McMurtry drew only vague sketches, of course. We couldn't begin to capture the beauty of the stair, but it gives the idea. Someday I shall ask to come back and make tracings."

"Perhaps when all is done," Carter said. "But we should go."

They continued another day down the corridor, which began a gradual transformation: the black Doric columns changed into square posts; the arches lost their curves; the sculptures of eagles, warriors, and gods evolved into angular, abstract depictions, geometric monsters hulking in the darkness.

"I've never seen anything like this in Moomuth

Kethorvian before," McMurtry said. "The statuary is almost . . . disturbing, though I can't explain in what way."

"We are nearing the territories of the anarchists," Carter said. "The transformation is their doing."

After several hours of suffering through the endless dark, they came to the remnant of a sculpture, a rectangular block with six squared hands protruding from it. Carter searched its base until he located a mechanism along its edge, which caused the statue to swivel aside, revealing a descending ramp.

"I expected a stair," Carter said. "More of the anarchists' doing, no doubt. Very well, we are done with secret ways for a time. This leads to the Great Wheel of Moomuth, and is the only way through. We will camp here until midnight, and enter the inhabited portions thereafter."

"The Room of the Great Wheel is the center of commerce," Crane said. "I've seen thousands pass there in a day. How can we go undetected?"

"I have a slim plan," Carter said. "If we are noticed, I will simply present myself to the authorities, though it will announce our arrival."

"Wouldn't it be better to work through official channels, as we did at High Gable?" Gregory asked.

"Mr. Hope and I discussed it at length. What works in High Gable will not do so in Moomuth Kethorvian. The Usherites rule here. Their allegiance to the White Circle has always been tenuous, and they border Shyntawgwin, to which they have sometimes been allied. I do not trust them. And the recent closing of their borders does nothing to reassure me."

At the stroke of midnight, the company followed the ramp, which proved to be narrow, but immaculate, bereft of spiderwebs or dirt, its boards polished to a slippery sheen.

"If this is the anarchists' idea of a perfect world, they can keep it," Nooncastle growled, bracing himself against the walls to avoid a tumble. "Can't even design a usable stair."

They finally exited from behind a duplicate of the six-handed statue and followed a gradually ascending corridor leading to ladder rungs extending from one wall. These ended, in turn, at a square tunnel, which could only be traversed on hands and knees.

"Look!" Duskin cried, pointing at a hairless, rectangular creature resembling a child's toy, which skittered from them, emitting a noise like a spring. "Is that a mouse?"

"It was, once," Carter said, feeling the blood drain from his face.

Twenty minutes of crawling brought them to the end of the shaft, where a narrow ledge, four feet wide, extended over a marble chasm two thousand feet deep.

"The Great Wheel!" McMurtry exclaimed. "What has been done to it?"

Once it must have been a vast sphere, with marble braces extending from a stone core to form spokes. Now, two square frames set ninety degrees apart fashioned a cross, connected by marble beams, giving the structure the look of a gigantic, black fence, still imposing due to its size, but stripped of its complex beauty. Chambers were carved inside the beams. The surrounding room was vast as a canyon; monolithic standing stones reared from the floor, hulking even from the company's position, so the men knew them to be enormous.

"This was the ancient wheel and monuments of Moomuth Kethorvian," Crane said sadly. "One of the seven wonders of the High House, built in the ageless past."

"It's ghastly!" McMurtry cried.

"It is certainly *changed*," Mr. Crane said. "Yet, though it is no longer a wheel, it possesses a bit of charm, wouldn't you say, Mr. McMurtry?"

"I would not, Mr. Crane. It's an indecency! Even you should see that. The marble was of many colors, an exquisite blend. Now, look at it, all black and looming, like a mausoleum."

"Indecency or no, we must cross the expanse," Carter said. "The way is narrow and unnerving, but not particularly dangerous. This late, those few about will not likely glance upward. But we should move quickly to minimize the risk. Single file."

"I'll lead, sir," Nooncastle said. "I rather fancy heights myself."

"Very good, Lieutenant."

Although not particularly bothered by altitude, Carter did not share Nooncastle's enthusiasm. The soldiers went first, onto the narrow ledge that passed through a opening in one side of the immense squares and continued toward the center. The Master stepped out across the dizzying gulf, and immediately pledged to keep his eyes to the ground. Four feet wide an inch from the earth is a broad expanse on which to walk; seven hundred yards high it becomes a narrow ribbon quivering from the breath of the air currents, a beckoning gulf, daring the hardiest soul to defy death by casting himself over the edge. Carter shot a quick glance downward and recoiled from the impulse; the great hall far below lay dim, most of its lamps extinguished.

They soon reached the center column, where the jets of a furnace blazed within its hollow heart, blowing hot upon their faces, making their shadows dance until they feared their shades would stumble beyond the edge and drag them screaming down. They passed close to the fire, walking the path encircling the column, then hurried away from its revealing light toward the far side. Now, their shadows bobbed before them, grotesque puppets with long hands and faces.

The end of the ledge came without an alarm being raised, though a pair of men stood beneath a lamp on one of the beams not far below. A mild tremor ran through Carter as he looked upon them, for in the lamp-light they appeared strangely contorted, stick figures scarcely human. He hurried on.

They crawled through a tunnel identical to the first, and descended a ladder onto a corridor. Carter led down a flight of stair and through another passage leading into a gallery, where a peculiar buzzing noise rose from the room beneath. The men listened in silence, until Nooncastle, satisfied they could pass undetected, guided them single file along the gallery wall, protected from sight by the balustrade. The gallery was long, lined with works signed by Opperpebb, the great painter from Ooz, though changed beyond recognition to colorless geometric shapes. The buzzing rose in singsong fashion, and the company was nearly through the gallery before Carter recognized it as a simulation of human speech.

He paused, seized by dread. At his signal his followers departed the gallery, while he crept to the balustrade and peered over.

Half a dozen men stood in the room below. At least, Carter knew they had once been men. Like the birds of High Gable, they had been changed, their heads made angular as a rectangular box, with all their features drawn to a forty-five-degree angle at the nose. Their chests were thin boxes, their legs and arms connected rectangles. Their hands were the claws of sparrows, the fingers bending at repulsive angles. They moved with a rapidity, a blasphemous lunging, like a cuckoo clock mechanism gone astray. Because of the droning buzz of their voices, it was difficult to interpret their speech, though he finally deciphered what the two nearest said.

"I will be going to Shyntawgwin," one spoke, the words in steady rhythm, without emphasis.

"I will remain here a time," the other said.

They stood in silence, eyeing one another like ducks.

"I will be going to Shyntawgwin," the first said again.

"I will remain here a time," the other replied.

They waited motionless once more.

"I will be going to Shyntawgwin."

Carter slipped out the door, his gorge rising, scarcely able to breathe from his horror, understanding at last why the borders had been closed. He reached his men and led them quickly away, telling them nothing, certain they must not be captured in Moomuth Kethorvian.

At the next corridor, Carter slid a painting of triangles and circles aside, and ushered the men into a secret way.

After it closed behind them, he heard a rustling beyond the wall. Peering through a spy-hole, he saw one of the Moomuth soldiers marching down the corridor, wooden, helmeted, striding stiffly, staring straight ahead, wholly inhuman. Carter turned away, face pale, and led his men down the passage, away from the central halls.

Three days they traveled that country, up and down stairs, through winding ways, slipping across passages in the hours before dawn, seldom finding wood for a fire, and always cold. Those few inhabitants they saw through spy-holes had been transformed, while the passages were but a twisted remnant of their previous plan, forcing Carter to consider the maps often, and even then the route he chose at morning might be blocked by noon. So it was they approached a passageway so narrow a man would have to turn sideways to advance.

"Is this the way?" Duskin asked.

"It was not like this an hour ago," Carter said. "Nor even fifteen minutes." His search of the maps showed that it remained narrow for a half hour's walk. He mentally threaded his way through a number of options, saw none requiring less than two days' retreat, and said, "It is the only course. Lieutenant, you might want to send a scout forward."

"Merritt at the point," Nooncastle ordered. "I will follow after."

Duskin stepped up to Carter and said softly, "Are you certain you want to do this?"

Carter tried to smile. "No, I'm not certain at all. But if we made it through the tunnels of Kitinthim, I can make it through these."

One by one the men entered the narrow passage. When

Carter's turn came, he gave a grimace and stepped into the shadowed way, Lightning Sword drawn, head down. After his battle with the Bobby in the well, when he first became Master, his fear of darkness and drowning had lessened, but not his dread of closed places. He would have given much to bypass this route, might have even done so if he had not seen the transformed soldiers. But he dared waste no time on his own concerns; the needs of the house drove him.

As he passed into the gloomy passage, a wave of fear threatened to unman him. He fought it, not with any courage, but rather with another terror: that of being seen a coward. His pulse quickened; he could not breathe; his heart beat against his chest, pounding to get out. He glanced up. The corridor was high, an endless plain stretching into darkness; the other wall constantly touched his back. Even in the cold, he broke into a sweat.

He shuffled behind Duskin, and McMurtry followed in his tracks. As the minutes passed, his fear lessened and his breathing slowed. Save for the footsteps, it was quiet as falling snow: a score of men sliding through the narrow way, the marble walls very white, no one daring to speak.

Twenty-five minutes into the passage he felt a trembling, as if the walls had shifted. His terror returned.

He could see the marble quivering, as if it, too, were afraid. He could feel Order and Chaos bending, struggling against one another.

"Hurry!" he cried. "We have to get out!"

At his urging, the men scurried as quickly as their shuffling steps allowed. He sensed the power increasing, the house tensing as if to spring. The vibrations increased.

"I'm through!" the point man called.

One by one they slipped from the narrow way. The wall was a quivering blur.

Duskin escaped, then Carter, McMurtry, and Crane. But just as the ancient architect exited, the passage vanished, leaving a half scream hanging in the air and two of the soldiers forever lost. Carter roared in pain, clutched his head, and was driven to his knees from the pressure of the rearranging maps.

Nooncastle rushed to the wall where the corridor had been. "Arnold! Burroughs!" He pressed his hands against the hard marble, then turned desperately back to Carter.

"Is there nothing we can do? A Word of Power? We have to get them out."

With Duskin and Gregory supporting him, Carter staggered to the wall, sickened, grief-stricken, but helpless before it. He shook his head. "No Word of Power can bring back the dead. The passage is solid stone now."

Several of the men sat down; others turned their backs to the wall. Nooncastle bowed his head.

"We shouldn't have come this way," Carter said, running his hand over his brow. "I shouldn't have brought us."

"Place the blame in its place," Duskin said, his voice shaking in anger. "With the anarchists."

Carter nodded and said no more.

"Arnold was from Keedin," Nooncastle said. "A farmer's son. And I will miss Burroughs's mouth-harp."

Several of the men nodded, for Burroughs had entertained them in the evenings with his playing.

After a time, Nooncastle raised his head. "This is their tomb, then. We should say words before it."

The men rose, and said such phrases as were proper to

their comrades' burial. Carter led a prayer, consigning their souls to eternity. They departed in silence.

That evening, still traveling the secret way, they crossed into Shyntawgwin. At the border, Carter found a spy-hole, and observed the station guards, burly men dressed much in the manner of the people of North Lowing, whose clothes are wrapped over their bodies, though in Shyntawgwin this was done in sections, using small, clasping hooks affixed to an undertunic called a *heeki*. Customarily, different hues were used for each section, but the guards went all in crimson, with chain-mail jerkins over all, and swords and pistols fastened to their sides. Their sleeves were long and loose in the Loftian manner, and they wore neatly trimmed beards and round caps. But no one guarded the Moomuth Kethorvian side at all, and after Carter watched a moment, a pair of transformed men approached the Shyntawgwin guards. Up close, they were even more hideous, all symmetry and precision, their eyes clear lenses, their sharp teeth standing in perfect rows. Carter bade Duskin look. His brother's face turned pale.

"Is this their plan for all of us?" he asked.

"Apparently. They have enslaved Moomuth Kethorvian by transforming its population."

As the mutated men tramped down the hall, the sentries exchanged frightened glances. Carter turned away, wondering how the people of Shyntawgwin felt about their alliance with the Outer Darkness. He had never met their lord, but his nickname from the Yellow Room Wars was "Bloody" Jegged.

"Gentlemen, we are in enemy territory," he said softly. "Act accordingly. There is one advantage: I doubt we will see any more transformations of the house while in Shyntawgwin, since it is under the anarchists' protection."

Beyond the border, the stone of Moomuth Kethorvian gave way to dark wood, ebony-stained floorboards, plaster, and the clammy odor of decay, an aroma generally unknown in Evenmere, despite its vast antiquity. The secret corridor narrowed to a cramped, miserly passageway, but after the weight of Moomuth, it seemed almost cheerful.

They camped that night without a fire, lest the smell of smoke betray them, for a vigilance pervaded Shyntawgwin, as if the very walls were watchful. Through a spyhole Carter observed a wide corridor, with chandeliers, long mirrors, and floral carpets, an elegance of earlier days. The people who passed appeared in haste, their eyes set, their faces cold and stricken. The Transformed went among them, traveling deeper into Shyntawgwin, making men flinch and women draw their children close. Whatever Lord Jegged had told his people, the sight of the changed brought terror to the land.

That evening, Carter conferred with Gregory, who had spent time in Shyntawgwin as a young boy, and knew its corridors well. Together they laid out a course.

The following morning, the men changed into the patchwork Shyntawgwin garments brought from the Inner Chambers, and slipped from the concealed corridor, for all appearance farmers and merchants. Their disguises were not tested immediately, for they made their way into the upper stories, journeying through vacant portions of the house. Apparently, under Lord Jegged's tyranny, many of the Shyntawgwin people had fled the country, for whole portions of the house had been abandoned. It was a desolation similar to what Carter had seen at Innman Tor, under the anarchists' rule, fashioned in despair, as if the whole system was disintegrating. The portion of the house where they traveled was dreadfully cold. The stairs were worn and often unstable, doors had fallen from their hinges, and glass lay shattered, the pieces uncollected.

They kept to the upper stories most of the afternoon, and descended at early evening. Though this portion of Shyntawgwin was inhabited, there were countless signs of disrepair: wallpaper peeling back, carpets tattered and threadbare, the gaslights dim, casting a yellow-green gloom. The clothes of the people were frayed, their shoes thin, their faces pinched.

To remain inconspicuous, Carter divided the company into two groups. They had gone scarcely a dozen paces before Gregory turned to Nooncastle, who was in Carter's party, and murmured anxiously: "It is not the habit of farmers to march in military formation." The chagrined lieutenant dispersed the company along the corridor with orders to look casual, and matters went well thereafter.

They soon came to rows of ornate, paneled windows overlooking an absolute, starless night, though an hour remained before sunset. Gregory leaned to Carter's ear and whispered: "The Docks opening into the Outer Darkness." He felt a shuddering at the base of his spine.

Crowds massed along a corridor that gradually widened into a great room with finish worn to the boards from countless feet, dim lamps, and boys pushing heavy carts laden with bags of grain, boxes of gears, lengths of lumber, and hosts of other goods. Heavy oak doors, once undoubtedly built as bastions against the darkness, were flung wide; ramps led downward to the black earth, where wagons, driven by gray-cloaked men, were loaded. Several anarchists strolled within a few feet of the companions.

They traveled a mile down the Docks, passing several of the Transformed. Carter watched as a pair of the mechanical nightmares passed down the ramps and vanished into the night. The air from the open doors was chill, but not frigid, as if the darkness existed beyond the reach of the storm assailing all of Evenmere.

"It should be a simple matter to leave the Docks," Gregory said, "so long as we go a few at a time." He gestured toward a uniformed soldier, dressed all in red, with a crimson helmet. "They are scarcely wary, for who would wish to enter the darkness?"

Word was passed among the men, who broke into groups along the length of the Docks. Carter drifted toward a side door, past the disinterested sentry. The dingy brass knob turned with difficulty; the door scraped as it opened, a noise thunderous to Carter's ears. He did not turn to see if anyone noticed, but marched down the shaky wooden steps, past a pair of men reclining against the dock-poles. He heard their murmured conversation as he passed, and feared they would call to him. His boots crunched chalk-dry earth scattered with stones; the lamps surrounding the dock cast his shadow long before him, soon fading into the surrounding ebony.

Once lost in the gloom he moved toward the left and crouched to await the others. He could see the full length of the Docks, which from a distance truly resembled piers on a dead sea. One by one, he watched his companions drift down the ramps and vanish into the night. He drew his Lightning Sword a fraction, letting its soft light peep out, a guide to his followers, not easily seen by a chance observer. Like moths, his men fluttered to that flame, Nooncastle last of all, smiling grimly.

"That was a light piece of work," he said.

"Yes," Gregory replied, "but why should they bother to guard the Docks, with this vast expanse as sentinel?"

As one, the men stared into the stony plain stretching strangely visible before them, though their own faces were lost in shadow. No wind whispered; no night birds sang; no stars shone in the sky. They stood transfixed.

"What is it?" one of the soldiers finally whispered. "What makes the dark?"

It was Gregory who answered. "It is the End of Creation, the nothingness between the stars. It is Emptiness."

"But it isn't empty," Carter said. "Look."

Far away bobbed a string of dim lamps beneath the foreboding eaves of a mansion sprawling, mile upon mile, across an onyx plain, casting shadows on shadows down the hills and valleys of its steeps and gables, its courtyards and spiraled towers. Only a handful of lights, crimson and spectral, whispered from its enormity, witches' lights, foreboding, forbidden, like quavering lanterns in a city of the dead. Carter felt its evil beating down upon him, this horror, this house that should not exist, which could not exist in the ordinary world.

"I never dreamed it would be so vast," Duskin said hoarsely.

"They have wrought more deeply than we suspected," Carter replied, shaken. "It truly rivals Evenmere itself."

"Form lines," Nooncastle ordered. "We won't get there by gawking."

The illumination of the plain, little brighter than moonlight at the waning crescent, rose from no visible source, and lit distant objects more than those near at hand, leaving the men in a world of half shadows. Whatever its properties, it made torches unnecessary, allowing the company to go undetected. Glistening obsidian, scattered across the bare rock, made the plain sparkle. Carter picked up a rough stone the size of his thumb, undoubtedly of little value, but nonetheless lovely, and wondered what had created it—magma from antediluvian mountains, scattered debris from the forming of the worlds, the castoffs from the making of the High House? Whatever its source, he knew beyond doubt, it had nothing to do with his world. He looked upon it and saw it was not of Evenmere, just as he recognized that everything he had ever seen before, even when living outside the manor, *was* of the High House, for Evenmere encompassed all Creation save this darkling plain. It was indeed, as Gregory had said, an Emptiness. He thought of the years he had spent as Master, armed with Words of Power and Master Keys, able to accomplish whatever he willed. And now he felt all his strength ripped from him, here where the laws and regulations of Evenmere held no sway. Struck by an awful absence, he let the stone slide from his hands. It rattled on the bare earth.

Duskin, a shadow among all the other shadows, walked beside him. Gasping, Carter clasped his shoulder to steady himself.

"All right?" Duskin asked.

"No," Carter spoke softly, lest the others hear, though he felt rising panic in his own voice. "The Words and the maps are gone. *Gone*. I felt them depart just now."

"How can that be?"

"Once we moved beyond Evenmere, they deserted me. We are *Outside*, beyond Creation. The Words do not apply. I have not felt so lost since I was a child," he spoke rapidly, battling his own terror. "Losing them—it is like being stripped naked to run through this wilderness. Oh, how confident we are with our possessions, our power, all the wealth of Evenmere behind us. And then to have them taken! I believe I have been led by God to be the Master; I have walked in the path He chose for me. Brittle himself, back from the dead, told me as much. And now I am forsaken."

Duskin clasped his hand harder. Both men were whispering. "But you were given a great gift—the knowledge of an afterlife, a heaven," Duskin said. "It strengthens me to know of it, but you saw Brittle with your own eyes."

Carter nodded desperately. "Yes. I should be grateful. Yet the promise of heaven does not sustain me amid the troubles of earth. Would God allow the anarchists to destroy all reality? And if so, does that make their way His choice? I know it does not, but evil has been allowed to exist. Will it overcome us; will all the earth become mindless, mechanical slaves? I feel small, my brother, as I have not felt since I became Master. Help me!"

The last was a desperate, whispered cry. Carter's hands trembled; he could not breathe; he thought his soul ripped from his body, leaving a puncture wide as eternity.

Duskin pulled his brother close. "What of your mantle, and your blade?"

Carter clutched at his sword hilt, ran his fingers through the Tawny Mantle. Gradually, the fear lessened. "They are still with me. I sense their power. But, Duskin, don't you understand?" His voice nearly broke in his agony, and he could not help it. "I am responsible for Everything! *Everything!* All Creation rests on my shoulders. You, Sarah, the house, Enoch, all of them. I don't know if I can do it. Not without the Words."

"No, brother. It rests on *our* shoulders. Heaven will aid us."

"Brave Duskin. Beloved brother! You are idealistic, and I love you for it, but there are horrors in the world, dire circumstances, people in pain. Death everywhere. I lose faith sometimes."

"So do we all," Duskin said. "It is easy to believe in God when we are strong, but easier to rest on Him when we are weak. The anarchists will not overcome us. I believe it with my whole heart."

Carter's breathing slowed; he steadied himself and managed a wan smile. "Then I will take my strength from you."

Looking about, he realized they had halted their march. The entire company stood milling, staring into the darkness, as if not to hear.

Carter took another deep breath and mastered himself. "I apologize. I'm all right now. It . . . is difficult to explain."

"Of that I'm certain, Lord Anderson," Nooncastle said. "But enlisted men need have no ears for the Master's high concerns. It's the left foot and the right for soldiers. Move along now, lads."

"Yes, sir," the men replied.

When the company had journeyed three hours, they entered a series of canyons, and so lost sight of the False House. Scouts were sent ahead, and soon reported an army upon the plain. Going to see for themselves, Carter and Nooncastle raised their heads above the ridgeline and saw row upon row of the Transformed, standing in the darkness, bearing neither lantern nor torch, rigid as scarecrows, silent as the dead.

"This is where they come when they leave Moomuth Kethorvian," Carter said, "after they are changed."

"They fill the plain," Nooncastle replied. "Eerie, is what it is. The whole population of Moomuth must be out there. I'd estimate at least thirty-five thousand. We can't pass through their ranks."

They returned to the company and reported the situation.

"But why do they just stand there?" Howard McMurtry asked. "It's inhuman."

"But wouldn't you say they were the perfect army?" Crane asked. "Willing to wait at attention for days on end. Do they even eat?"

"I would not call them perfect, Mr. Crane," McMurtry said.

"Nor I," Nooncastle said. "At least, not until I see them fight. As for why they remain there, they're probably a barrier only by chance; far easier to leave them encamped on the plain than in the house."

After some discussion it was decided to circumvent the army by following the canyons. Not only would the company remain hidden, but the ravines appeared to circle behind the False House. Nooncastle sent scouts before them.

They went in silence, disheartened by the news. The air was not so cold as the snowbound corridors of Evenmere, but filled the travelers with a chill that seeped into the soul, making all seem hollow and insignificant. The men and the hours trudged on.

They camped in the midst of a ring of mounds, lighting no fires, eating their meal in silence, and throwing themselves into their bedrolls to cover their heads against the infinite, terrifying Night above them. In all his life, Carter had never known such quiet; no animals, no wind, no stir ring of insects. When he closed his eyes it seemed he was falling forever into darkness, the Words of Power lost to his grasp.

He woke two hours later and stumbled up, filled with anxiety, determined to check the sentries. He made a slow circle around the camp, speaking to each guard in turn, and came at last to Corporal Howard, who sat on a boulder but rose at Carter's approach.

"Keep your seat," Carter said. "I'm just taking a stroll. I want to take a look above those rocks." He gestured toward a knoll near the canyon wall.

"I'll have someone accompany you, sir."

"Unnecessary. I have my Lightning Sword. I'll only be a moment. It will ease my restlessness."

He made his way along the cold stones. He had not

wished to alarm the sentry, but an intuition of dread had grown as he circled the camp. He moved as quietly as possible around the curve of the knoll, then climbed partially up the canyon wall to a narrow shelf. From there, he could look down upon the whole encampment. The peculiar properties of the country, which illuminated distant objects better than those near at hand, allowed him to discern the slumbering forms of his comrades, a viewpoint superior for keeping watch. He determined to move the sentries farther out, and was about to return to his bedroll when he saw a shadowy form creeping between two of the guardposts.

At first, he thought it but a trick of the gloom, but gradually realized the figure was slipping from the camp rather than toward it. Inch by inch, it skulked past the watch and drifted toward the canyon wall.

Wary of crying a warning to the sentries, Carter groped his way along the canyon wall, but as he neared the phantom, he lost the advantage of the light upon his quarry. By the time he reached the spot where the figure had been, it was gone. The camp lay clear below him, but he could see almost nothing near at hand. As he strained his eyes, a brief flash of light occurred beyond the canyon lip, passing so quickly he fancied it imagination. But he climbed higher and saw it again.

He was nearly to the rim when a handful of stones dislodged and rattled to the rocks below. His hope for stealth gone, he raised himself above the edge in time to see a shadowed form shrouding a signal lantern and slipping behind a rock formation.

Carter drew his pistol and followed, but soon lost sight of his quarry among the stones. He searched for precious moments before suddenly drawing up short. "Curse me for a fool! I'm giving him time to return to his bed."

He hurried down the slope more quickly than safety allowed. Seeing Corporal Howard, he barked, "Did anyone pass you?"

"I saw no one, sir. Should I alert the rest of the watch?"

"No. Keep your position."

Once in camp, he inspected each bedroll in turn. Finding none vacant, he woke Nooncastle and related his tale.

"We'll interrogate the guards," the lieutenant said. "A bad business, if a man can enter and leave our camp without us knowing."

"Could it have been other than a member of our party?" Carter asked. "An anarchist scout, who stumbled upon us and was signaling his forces?"

"Stranger things have happened in war. But I doubt it. You said he slipped *from* the camp. The simplest explanation is often the best."

Inquiries to the sentries proved vain; no one had been seen entering or leaving. Since the anarchists now knew their position, Carter and Nooncastle roused the company and ordered a march.

As they wound their way down the canyon, groggy with lack of sleep, Carter's thoughts made slow circles. By treachery he had been exiled from Evenmere as a boy; now a new traitor had arisen. As he considered the possibilities, the cold uncertainties of the night seeped into him, until it seemed any could be the betrayer; he saw Nooncastle's openness as the ruse of a clever mind, Gregory's friendship as patient deceit, even Crane's, and McMurtry's quaint mannerisms as cover for dark machinations. Each of the soldiers in turn became devious conspirators.

He drifted deeper into gloom, until the whole world seemed secretly allied against him. It was only when he imagined Chant, Enoch, even Sarah and Duskin, as his enemies that the absurdity overtook him like a wave—the lieutenant had served the White Circle over thirty years; Gregory had saved Duskin's life in the basement of the gnawlings; McMurtry and Crane were undoubtedly the eccentric gentlemen they appeared. That left the soldiers, all decorated men, proven and carefully chosen for the White Circle Guard. Unlikely as it seemed, one of their number must have succumbed to the promise of wealth and position.

Carter spent the next three hours pondering the identity of his foe, but knew no more when Nooncastle called a halt to men stumbling on their feet. They threw themselves down beneath a shelf along the canyon walls and posted sentries at its rim to watch the plain. Carter and Nooncastle climbed up to take a look themselves.

The plateau before them glistened in dull onyx, barren save for the altered soldiers, whose lines ended less than a hundred yards away. The False House stood nearer, lights glowing green and gold, like fairy lamps hung in the distance. It was not the sparse, symmetric structure Carter had expected but surprisingly diverse, its towers scratching the sky like claws. A dread filled him as he looked upon it; it seemed to beckon, fey and aberrant, a thing outside Creation, wholly supernatural.

A howl arose from the direction of the manor, a mixture of a wounded wolf and a shrieking woman.

"What foul cry was that?" Nooncastle asked.

"I don't know," Carter said. "A beast of the anarchists, perhaps. Or some wild thing. Lieutenant, do you see a shape against the house?"

"I don't, Lord."

"There to the left! See how the lights are obscured."

Because of the distance and the dark, it was difficult to be certain, but it appeared a monstrous shadow loomed against the gables, a creature a third the height of the building itself, pacing before the house like a hound.

"Is it the anarchists' watchdog?" Nooncastle asked.

"If so, I wouldn't want to enter its yard," Carter replied. "It must be ten feet tall. Another obstacle for us, Lieutenant."

"Yes, sir. I'll have the men keep an eye on it, to make certain it doesn't come near. If it advances we'll see how it reacts to lead."

"Only if necessary. I don't wish to give away our position."

"Nor I," Nooncastle said.

Carter descended to the camp, and flung himself exhausted into his bedroll to dream in the darkness of darkness, and of great dogs that tore at his flesh.

The Onyx Plain

Carter's pocket watch read six o'clock when Nooncastle roused the camp in that country where dawn would never break. The Master sat up on his bedroll, dragged his hands through his hair, sighed, and wished for hot tea. Unlike Sarah, he did not like morning, could not understand her love for the peace of the new day and the glory of sunrise; he often told her he thought sunset much better, just for the sake of her reply that sunrise was merely sunset backward. He certainly did not like waking to the dark, where the world seemed pointless and vain and dim, and human enterprise but a worthless show. A pang of longing to hear her voice pulsed through him.

He shook his head to clear it and stood. The men milled for a time, stamping their feet against the chill, and eating a breakfast of dried rations. Then they were winding their way through the canyon, always hidden from any watchful eyes within the house, ever farther from the army on the plain.

After two hours a scout reported an unknown number of men pursuing along the canyon floor, and Nooncastle brought the alarmed company to a dull trot, an uneasy pace in the vague light.

They had traveled less than an hour when one of the scouts forward and to the left gave a shout and discharged his pistol. A chorus of shots rang back, and with a dying cry, the man tumbled from his position halfway up the canyon wall.

"Take cover!" Nooncastle bellowed, dragging Carter to the shelter of nearby boulders. Gunfire pelted the company's position; cries went up from the wounded. To Carter's left, young Jakes went down, clutching his head. By the time the Master reached him, he was dead, blank eyes staring into the dark. Carter moaned and returned to the lieutenant's side.

The scout's warning had saved the company from walking headlong into the trap, so they were yet several hundred yards from their assailants. When the anarchists charged from the gradual slope of the right canyon wall, the White Circle Guard cut them down, sending the survivors shrieking for cover. Still, they were penned, with an enemy firing from much higher ground.

"We can't stay here," Nooncastle said. "The anarchists behind us will arrive soon."

"If we press forward we'll be slaughtered," Carter said. "If only I had the Words of Power! But I do have my Tawny Mantle. Lieutenant, I will slip behind our opponents and create a distraction. Use the time to escape. If I can, I will rendezvous with you."

"My lord, you are the purpose of our mission. Better you should seek the False House than risk your life."

"Could I leave you behind, and my brother with you? No. I will turn their guns away from our men. Be ready."

Carter drew his mantle close; it cascaded down, lengthening to his feet, shrouding his form in its chameleon dusk, making him one with the darkness and the stones. Nooncastle raised his eyebrows in surprise as Lord Anderson merged with the shadows.

"Hold your position, Lieutenant. In this darkness, I could slay an army."

"Aye, sir, I believe you could."

Despite his bravado, Carter slipped away in trepidation, for the odds were firmly against him. At Innman Tor, using the Words of Power, he had successfully faced eight men, not the score or more before him. Keeping low, he slipped up the slope, picking his way between the boulders, circling the enemy forces to come from behind. Chance bullets danced round his feet; he danced away in return.

The first anarchist he met was a lone rear guard stationed above his comrades on the slope. Carter struck him from behind with a heavy stone; the man's skull cracked; he fell, gurgling. Carter felt dreadfully sick.

He banished his revulsion and slipped along the canyon edge, keeping low, being now in danger from his comrades' fire. The anarchists were grouped behind a granite ridge lying beneath a rock shelf, their white faces jutting from their gray coats and hats, solemn as penguins. Carter stood bewildered—if he fired upon them he would face the onslaught of a dozen pistols; his diversion would last only a moment before his death, leaving his companions unaided. Neither would slipping into their midst avail him, for he would quickly be discovered.

He glanced about in desperation. The ledge suspended above the anarchists was held to the canyon wall by a slender stone bridge, four inches thick and a foot wide. He crawled to the link and studied it closer, hesitant, weighing the power of his Lightning Sword against the stamina of solid stone, knowing he would have time for but one or two blows before the enemy was upon him, drawn by the light of the blade.

His decision made, he rose to his feet, while bullets ricocheted around his head. In one smooth motion, he drew the sword and struck downward, grunting at the force of the impact. A golden blast lit the canyon wall; shards exploded all around his face. The ledge gave way and slid down. For an instant he swayed upon the lip, overbalanced by his efforts, then toppled with it.

He fell four feet, struck the edge of the careening ledge, and dropped behind it, where he rolled to a jarring stop. Without pausing to inspect his wounds, he spun around and saw the ledge sweeping down the canyon, mowing through the anarchists, their shrieks and the rumbling stone masking all other noise.

By the time the mass roared to a stop, Carter had sheathed his sword and slipped behind concealment. Across the canyon his men pressed forward, firing heavily into the stunned anarchists. When he began shooting as well, the enemy, thinking themselves surrounded, panicked and charged straight into the sights of the White Circle Guard.

The fighting grew thick as the forces closed. The destruction caused by the ledge left the opponents nearly equal in number, giving Nooncastle's men a clear advantage, for their armor was resistant to pistol fire. Carter added to the bedlam by shouting at the top of his lungs and waving his sword.

All might have gone well if not for the arrival of the second party of anarchists, who charged the rear of the company. With foes before and behind, the soldiers faltered, then formed a circle to meet the new threat. The anarchists close to the canyon wall rallied, crying for vengeance.

Bullets tore all around Carter. He leapt behind tumbled boulders, sheathed his sword, and weathered the barrage. When the direction of fire shifted, he crawled among the stones some distance, then lifted his head, keeping his mantle close about him. His companions were pinned worse than before. His plan had failed; there was time for little more. He cast about for a new stratagem, found none, and determined to pick his foes off, one careful shot at a time. If he could clear the enemies on this side, Nooncastle could bring the men forward. He laid his pistol across a boulder to steady it, and trained the sight on an anarchist leader. In the dimness it was difficult to get a clear view, but he aimed at the man's chest, held his breath, and gently squeezed the trigger. The anarchist dropped from the line of vision. Carter hid himself behind the boulders, then raised again and sought a new target. He would have given much for the accuracy of a rifle, but they were seldom used in Evenmere, being too cumbersome in small chambers.

As he aimed again, a hideous roar at his back sent him diving facedown behind the boulders. He rolled onto his side to see a monstrous figure leap over his head, clearing the stones as if they were pebbles, howling like all the world's wolves crying at once.

He scrambled to his feet. The beast landed on all fours among the anarchists and struck with teeth and claws; it took the first man by the collar and shook him like a dog with a rabbit; even from a distance Carter heard the neck snap. It cast its victim aside, and with a half-animal voice, cried to the heavens: "The Dogs of Doom! The Red Rose in the Blue-stained Glass! The Hordes of Heaven on a Hellish Shore! Away! Away! And none will stop us!" It finished with a descending howl.

Carter stood mesmerized. Though the body was that of a mangled hound, the face was that of Old Man Chaos—the antithesis of Order itself, given physical form: the gray, half-melted features, the glowing yellow eyes, one far larger than the other, the misshapen shoulders—but with the long jaws of a wolf, the rows of rending teeth snarled into a death's-grin. It pawed the man it had slain, sat back on its haunches and howled again

"The First and the Last! The End of All! The Doors of his Face, the Lamps of his Mouth! Pull down the house, the Order-Beast, Daughter of Hades!"

It tore at the anarchists, and though several scored direct hits to its mottled hide, their weapons proved ineffectual. It slew twenty in a minute's time, then leapt away toward the White Circle Guard. It landed in their midst, scattering them like lead soldiers in the hands of a child. Screams echoed down the canyon. In his wild rush to help, Carter tumbled over a low stone shelf, banging his shoulder and knee. He rose again, Lightning Sword held aloft, running with all his strength.

The hound looked up from its bloody work, one baleful eye gleaming yellow from the sword-light. "The Hymns of Ecstasy! The Dead Thing in the Hidden Room!

The Master himself, the Words of Power now gone from him!" It forgot its other victims and turned, all blood and bone, toward him, crossing the distance in a few bounds, halting not ten yards from where he stood.

Carter drew up short. With the Words at his beckoning, he could control Chaos; without them he could not. "Why have you come?" he demanded warily.

"The house on the borderlands draws me and gives me form. The anarchists within seek to exchange new worlds for old, to establish all Order, never changing, stolid, implacable. A universe of dry dust and utter mechanism, without beauty, without desire, without the brilliant spark of imagination. I arrive, Incarnate, to bite at the heels, to break the walls of the house, if I can. But Order is too strong, too strong! She burns me down, little by little, like sun through slow glass. I die, melting, dissipating, and if I perish all beauty dies with me; the summer breeze on the trembling leaf, the sudden rain in a cloudless sky, the musty scent from the opened book. You are the Master, the holder of the keys! Why have you deserted me for Lady Order?"

"I have not. I, too, seek to destroy the house."

"Then help me enter. I cannot penetrate this structure. Her power holds me at bay. Help me."

"I shall," Carter said. "And you must help me in turn."

"I will," the hound said.

And then it sprang.

Carter clutched his sword with both hands, point up before him; the blade flashed golden light as it met the dog's head. Lord Anderson was slammed against the rocks by the impact; the world went black, then returned. He lay on his back, with Chaos beside him, divided from head to tail into two equal parts. The hound neither bled nor writhed in death, though dark shapes thrashed within the halves. The eyes, still gleaming yellow, stared up at him. And then the head abruptly lost all form as the two parts melted and ran together, only to reappear, seamlessly whole.

"The Barking Dog on the Moon-Swept Moor," the mouth said, while the body continued to regenerate. "The Crying Eyes!"

Carter leapt to his feet and dashed between the boulders, filled with a terror only the loss of the Words of Power could bring, that he who had been master of both Order and Chaos now fled helpless before their avatars. Even as he ran, his mind raced; Chaos was not a living being, but Primeval Force—it had struck at Carter not because of reasoning or logic, but because its nature caused it to destroy even those who might aid its cause. No doubt it was drawn to the Outer Darkness, given form in response to the growing power of Order, reaction to action, like water rushing into a newly made fissure. But having found Carter, the one person capable of containing it, it would surely stalk him. Though in the past, it had sought to seduce him to its cause, his destruction was clearly preferable.

A wild baying rose at his back. He had ascended to the lip of the canyon, and glanced behind to see the hound loping along the rock floor, scenting the air, having apparently lost sight of its prey. Carter drew his Tawny Mantle close and looked across the dim plain, where the False House stood beckoning. He measured the distance with his eyes; he was far behind the ranks of the transformed soldiers; the house was close, little more than a brief sprint across the tableland. He looked back and could no longer see the great shape; the dog was lost amid the shadows. If it caught him on the plain . . .

There was no time for thought. Though he might expose himself for all the house to see, he had no other choice. But at least this flight would draw the dog from Duskin and the others. He caught his breath for the space of a dozen heartbeats, adjusted his mantle once more, though he doubted even it could hide him on the bare plateau, and vaulted over the rim, where he broke into a dead run, leaving nothing to spare.

He had always prided himself on his athletic abilities. At Bracton College, he had excelled at fencing, boxing, and track, but had been a distance-man and no sprinter. He kept in condition, and upon beginning his dash, feeling the power of his muscles, it seemed he could run forever. But he was ten years past his college days, the house was farther away than he had thought, and a dreadful stitch soon throbbed at his side. He wondered if he could go the distance at all. His mantle and greatcoat scarecrow-flapped around him, the rocks jarred his legs even through his boots. He was breathless with fear, desperate for survival.

He heard the howling at the lip of the canyon and pushed harder.

He was almost to the house when footfalls, loping breath, and low growls arose behind him. He dared a glance backward; the hound was almost at his back, its grotesque, melted face, tinged with blue, hideous on the canine form. There was no escape.

There is no terror like that of a charging beast; the teeth, the jaws; it freezes the blood, yet Carter cast his fate on a faint plan, and dropped to his knees. The hound could not arrest its onslaught so swiftly; foul breath blew in Carter's nostrils, grinding teeth scarce missed his head, but the brute passed over, carried by its own momentum, its legs straddling his body; and Carter thrust upward with his sword, ripping its stomach wide. Twenty feet it traveled before dropping to the earth.

Carter raced to it and severed its head with a single blow, then drove again toward the house. But he covered only a dozen paces before a voice rasped, "The Mouth at the Door! The Head of Bran the Blessed! The End and the Beginning. The Worm Ouroboros Biting Its Tail! So I! Come back! You cannot escape!"

But Carter was already in the bare yard of the house. Even through his fear the eerie shape of the manor filled him with dread, its black boards and onyx bricks, the twisted gables, the hideous sculptures upon the rooftops, the slanted, rickety eaves. So close, it loomed enormous, a meandering hulk, of no architectural style at all, as if a child had designed its facade and drawn its portals. An unidentifiable foliage grew from the upper windows. All this he saw in a glance, in his desperate search for a door.

He sped down the length of what he imagined to be the front of the house, always listening for the coming of the hound, ears dulled by the rattling of the stone beneath his feet, but though there were alcoves and embrasures, no doors could be seen.

He turned under an arch leading into a bare courtyard, but though he searched on every side, again found no entrance. Panic nearly took him as he realized he had reached a dead end. He sought to retrace his steps and came face-to-face with the Chaos-hound. The dog lunged;

Carter swiped at it with his sword; neither blow struck home. He fled along the side of the house, stumbled, fell among the stones, rose, and fled again.

A trellis, covered in black, vicious thorns, wound its way up the side of the manor. Carter leapt and frantically climbed ten feet before the weight of the hound slammed against the structure, nearly jarring him from his perch. He glanced back and saw the beast in the courtyard below, preparing to spring again.

As Carter drew even with a low eave, Chaos lunged onto the trellis and scrambled up using its massive paws. Jaws snapped inches from Carter's feet. As the hound lurched closer, the trellis, unable to bear the weight, gave way at the top. As the whole arrangement toppled, Carter instinctively stepped on the dog's head, using it to spring toward the eave. He fell short, but caught a supporting strut, and hung momentarily suspended.

Jaws snapped close to his neck; the wicked teeth closed on Carter's pack, nearly jerking him from the eave. He hung on with all his might and the straps broke, freeing him. He scrambled onto the rooftop and glanced down to see Chaos worrying the contents of his pack.

"The Threshold of Madness!" the hound howled, vainly leaping at him once more. "The Fires of Doom! Fly, fly, but I will rend you. I will rend the whole house! What will you do? Give me answer!"

But Carter did not answer, any more than he would answer the wind when it murmurs the words of men, for it is dangerous to speak to Chaos.

An unlit window hung three feet above his head and the artless ornamentation gave ample toeholds. As he started to climb, a pain shot through his left arm where the thorns had cut through greatcoat and flesh, leaving a stain of bright blood. He grimaced but went on. The first two feet were difficult, but after that he steadied himself on a statue with the head of a grinning gnome and a body of numbers and symbols, math and art poorly mixed. With the sculpture beneath his feet, he reached the casement easily.

The window was ordinary enough, but fastened. He broke the glass with the hilt of his sword, unlocked it, and forced it open after prying with the tip of his blade. He slid into the darkness.

When the Chaos-hound first struck the White Circle Guard, Gregory pulled Duskin into a clump of boulders, probably saving both their lives, for the beast tore through armor and bone, slaying on every side. Duskin saw both Leiber and Brackett go down beneath those savage jaws. The other soldiers scattered, while the hound stood baying and mouthing its gibberish ten feet from where Gregory and Duskin knelt in concealment. They crawled among the rocks to escape, while it roared and snuffled the earth all around.

Then, with more rantings and a rush, the hound, having sighted Carter, vanished. Duskin, unaware of the reason for the beast's departure, stayed low; he had seen the monster's power and knew no man could stand against it. In the distance, he heard voices and battle, but the cries of the wounded anarchists drowned out the words, so he did not know of his brother's struggle with Chaos. Afterward, a long silence fell, and the two men peered from beneath their concealment, to find Nooncastle and the others gone, and the second group of anarchists nearly upon them.

"We've lost the others," Gregory said.

"Yes, and Carter!" Duskin asked. "We should find him."

"There is no time to search. He is the Master. He can look after himself, and perhaps we will see him on the way to the house. Hurry, they are almost upon us."

They slipped between the boulders and spent a long hour avoiding their foes. Duskin kept a careful, but vain, watch for their comrades, all the while wondering how many had survived.

They wound several hours through the canyon before casting themselves among the stones for a meager supper of dried beef, the only consolation to constant hunger being that one was too tired to care. As he lay down to sleep, Duskin thought of nothing save his brother. He had tremendous confidence in Carter, but his sibling's reaction to the loss of the Words of Power had shaken Duskin more than he dared admit. He considered himself the one given to moods and Carter the immovable mountain, steady and uncompromising. If he was dead . . .

He turned on his other side, turning the thought from him. Believing with stubborn idealism in the strength of good, he could not truly accept the power of evil. Carter was Master; the heavens would split asunder before he should perish. Yet, their father had been honorable, too, and had died. His own mother had been swallowed up by evil, much of it her own design. Duskin turned on his back, choosing to look at neither side of the issue. As Sarah often reminded him, they were all in the hands of

God. That thought sent him drifting into a troubled sleep, full of Carter being rocked in great, alabaster palms, the face of the rocker unseen.

Several hours later he awoke, wishing he carried a pocket watch, glad no danger had found them in their unprotected sleep. He rose with a sigh; the noise roused Gregory, and they were soon sharing a cold breakfast of dried beef and bread. While Gregory rolled up his bedroll, Duskin climbed to the canyon rim and peered over. They were much closer to the house; he could see its back side, and estimated they could be there in another two hours by following the winding canyon. He spied the hound circling the manor, nose to the ground. If not for it, they could cross the plain, a ten-minute stroll. He grimaced and scrambled back down the slope, and they set off.

"I would give much for an apple," Gregory murmured.

"I would give much for the sun," Duskin replied. "Then we could go find an apple."

"There will be no sun here. There never has been. It's a part of the universe left empty."

"That house certainly gives me the shivers," Duskin replied. "Few lights, nothing but that great hound guarding it; it seems almost deserted."

"Why do you suppose the anarchists do it? What drives them to build in the darkness?"

"They're mad, that's all. Hungry for power, like my mother."

"But surely not all of them," Gregory said. "Many have given their lives for their cause. And those we have captured have been quite educated."

"Yes," Duskin admitted. "They are intelligent men. But

they're deluded, thinking they can change the entire universe. What egotism!"

"I suppose. But with the power of the Cornerstone, they might be able to do as they claim."

Duskin shook his head. "I pray not. Oh, we've had this discussion a hundred times before, and as always I see your point. The universe is a dreadful place sometimes. Death and savagery, injustice, poverty. Yet, their course can't be right."

"Because the world was made this way? But shouldn't we attempt to improve our lot? Is the wheel an evil thing? Are fire and heat wicked? Certainly the anarchists are extremists, but we live in an extreme world. Should we let one child go hungry a day if we can do something about it? I look into this darkness and I wish all were light."

"You sound like a convert."

Duskin sensed Gregory shrug in the darkness. "Oh, you know I like to play with ideas, to try them on and see if they fit."

"How well I know," Duskin answered. "It's well and good to speak of one starving child, but there is your error. They have captured one innocent child, Lizbeth, and made her dwell alone, in sorrow, for the sake of their plans."

"For the good of the many. They have sacrificed much to follow the anarchist philosophy. Is one person too great an offering for all humanity?"

"I think it is, somehow," Duskin said.

"For hundreds of thousands of children?" Gregory asked. "You would give your own life in such a cause."

"I like to think I would, but still I disagree. Perhaps it makes no sense, but Lizbeth didn't ask to be sacrificed.

She was given no choice. It is fine for the anarchists to offer themselves, but to ask it of a child . . . Would we trust the universe to such men?"

"Perhaps not, but we trust our world to governments, our lives to our leaders. The entire house is entrusted to your brother."

"Yes, but the house itself chose him. I daresay God Himself chose him. Brittle said so, when he appeared to Carter and Hope."

"Do you really believe that?"

"Why, yes I do. Why shouldn't I?"

"Certainly your brother and Mr. Hope are men of veracity—"

"They are indeed. My brother does not lie."

"But he might be mistaken. The guilt of losing the Master Keys as a child, of causing your father's destruction, must have weighed heavily upon him. And when he learned your sire was truly dead—what man wouldn't need to be justified, and what greater justification than the hand of heaven?"

"You think him deluded? What of Hope? Did he fantasize as well?"

"No, not Mr. Hope. And he is an honest enough man, in his way. Yet, he went from a common lawyer to custodian of a vast empire. He would not be the first to overlook some quirk in his Master for position and power. And do so with the best of intentions, wanting to help your brother in his grief at first, later sticking to the story out of loyalty. Or perhaps only your brother saw the miracle; perhaps he spoke to a blank wall which he thought Brittle. Mightn't Hope, ever one to admit the possibility of the fantastic, truly believe Carter had seen the dead butler, though he himself saw no one?"

"I suppose anything is possible," Duskin conceded, "at least while we are speaking hypothetically. But I don't think so in this case. Simply because it is miraculous, should we say it is impossible? A primitive man would consider the iron horse a tremendous magic. Can't we assume that because two people have claimed the occurrence of an event, it truly has occurred? If you and Sarah tell me it is raining, must I go to the window and look, or should I assume it isn't, because you said it is? And if two people I trust say they have seen the dead walk, should I call them liars?"

"A smooth point," Gregory said. "But it is much more likely to be raining, than that the dead should rise." Gregory slapped Duskin on the shoulder. "How often have we had such talks, cousin? How many angels can dance on the head of a pin? If the present is but the passing of time, and the past and the future do not exist, because one is over and the other is yet to be, how can we say 'a long time in the past,' or 'a long time from now'? What is the nature of the universe, and the age of man? What have we not debated?"

Duskin chuckled, his irritation draining from him. "We were worse when we were twenty. Those nights in Aylyrium, at Arkovor College, you and I, and Devine and Weston, certain we had all the answers. We were pompous boors."

"We were trained to be so," Gregory said. "Remember Professor Bellgrove?"

"That old lion? We ridiculed him. Everyone at university did."

"But we adored him as well."

"You did. If he wasn't an anarchist himself, he knew their philosophy better than they. But he did know how to argue. He was the spark that led us to debate through the long hours of the night."

"You know he's dead?" Gregory asked.

"What? No. When did it happen?"

"I thought you'd heard. He was one of the anarchists your brother killed in a midnight skirmish at Keedin."

Duskin stopped and put his hand on his friend's arm. "You must be joking!"

"No, Bellgrove didn't just spout anarchist philosophy. He was one of them."

Duskin felt as if the earth had shifted beneath him. "He was really an anarchist? Of course, he always favored their creed, but I was only jesting before. I had no idea."

"Few did. I was one of them. He told me as much in an unguarded moment."

"You never said."

"He pledged me to secrecy."

"And you kept your vow? An anarchist teaching at Arkovor! You had a moral obligation to inform the authorities."

"But I had given my word."

Duskin turned and they trudged again. "The whole world is topsy-turvy. Old sedate Bellgrove, dying at Keedin, in the dead of night, slain by my brother! What a sad end for such a wise man."

They walked in silence a long time thereafter, as a hundred thoughts rattled through Duskin's mind. He felt vaguely naive. True, he hadn't known Bellgrove that well, only in the way students recognize their favorite instructors, the flash and dash of the outer man, but he had admired his booming voice, his leonine head, the look he had, all wisdom and surety. For Carter to have had to kill him—

They came without incident to that part of the canyon directly behind the house, and climbed to the rim. The mansion stood before them, stark and strange, stretching on and on across the plain. Duskin gave a shiver.

"Do you see any sentries?" he whispered.

"None," Gregory replied. "Odd, isn't it?"

"Not if the whole house itself is a guard. The architecture is so eccentric, it's hard to see the doors."

The hound bounded around the corner, sniffing the air, pawing the bricks, howling and whining. It darted back and forth, weaving toward the men, but turned again, and vanished behind the mansion. Duskin could almost follow its course by its baying.

Crossing the distance to the house took a lifetime; Duskin could feel his heart pulsing against his chest in rhythm with his pounding feet. Guns drawn, they slipped beneath the eaves. Like Carter, they discovered no doors, and Duskin found himself holding his breath in fear as the baying of the hound drew near. But when they had searched only a short distance, Gregory abruptly paused before one of the bricks, saying, "What's this?"

There came a soft click, and a part of the masonry rolled outward, revealing a secret entrance.

"Good job," Duskin whispered, clapping his cousin on the back.

Together they stepped into a wide hall, and as the cries of the Chaos-hound drew closer, frantically searched for a means to close the entrance. Duskin found a lever nearly frozen with rust, and the bricks slid closed, leaving the men in absolute darkness. Despite some panic, Duskin fumbled in his pack for matches and a lamp, and a flame soon cast a narrow circle of light.

The pair squinted down the midnight hall, and Duskin gave a gasp. Twisting tendrils, some a foot thick, with four-inch spikes, snaked along the corridor, twining through the doorways, sending spiny hands to test the ceiling strength.

"What are they?" Duskin whispered.

"Thornbushes," Gregory replied. "They are thornbushes."

When the Chaos-hound struck, Phillip Crane thought it lucky he and Mr. McMurtry had been near the front of the company, for several soldiers behind them were immediately slain. Not being fighting men, the two architects fled at once, and so were ahead and to the right of their companions. The noise of the rampaging beast, the screams of men, the rending of flesh, were dreadful, but in an instant a silence fell.

Mr. Crane dared a peek over his shoulder. "The monster is gone, Mr. McMurtry, but our soldiers are moving at right angles from us. We best hurry, if we want to rejoin them."

They shifted direction, but were unable to catch up before a ring of anarchists, apparently lying in wait, rose from among the boulders and surrounded the White Circle Guard at close range.

"Surrender!" a voice commanded. "You haven't a prayer."

Nooncastle must have agreed; the company, outnumbered three to one, was taken wholly by surprise after the monster's devastation. "Do as they say, lads. We've lost enough men for one night."

Crane pulled McMurtry back behind the boulders.

"Worse and worse," McMurtry said. "What shall we do, Mr. Crane?"

"We can do nothing to help, at least not yet, Mr. McMurtry. Neither can we stay out here with that creature roaming loose. I suggest we follow. Perhaps we can slip into the house behind them."

"And do what, Mr. Crane? We are not warriors."

"Why, find the Cornerstone, of course. That is our mission."

"I thought we were advisors."

"Not at all. Not at all. You were in the war, after all."

"Forty years ago."

"But the courage hasn't drained out, has it, as if you were a bottle with a bad crack? Come, Mr. McMurtry. It's all quite exciting."

"Only because you were *not* in the war, Mr. Crane. We should return to Evenmere and let them know what has occurred." Yet, already McMurtry had begun following the captives. "If I don't survive this, I should like my picture on the inside of our book, as part of the dedication."

"And so you shall get it," Crane replied. "Unless you live, of course. It would appear pompous if you live."

"Presumptuous."

"In poor taste."

The anarchists drove their captives hard, undoubtedly

hurrying to avoid another meeting with the Chaos-hound. They soon came to the opening of a cave, hidden among the dark stones, and entered without the comfort of light.

The architects hesitated at the entrance. For a time they heard the anarchists scrambling over the rocks, then the clatter of a closing gate.

"I shall enter first, Mr. McMurtry."

"Perhaps we should go together."

"It may be dangerous. Best to risk only one."

McMurtry drew his lean frame up to his full height and produced a pistol from his pocket. "I *was* in the war, Mr. Crane."

The two men grinned the same grin at one another. "After you, then, sir," Crane said. "But I have a firearm as well." He patted the pocket of his greatcoat.

"Then produce it, Mr. Crane. Produce it, It does no good in your pocket. But try not to shoot me in the back."

They entered the cave, and felt their way awkwardly around a corner, where a dim light became evident. A gas lamp had been installed into the rocks, and by its shabby light they saw an iron gate, locked by a skeleton key. Beyond the bars stretched a corridor paneled in oak.

"Odd," the taller man said. "No guards."

"But there is the lock," Crane said. "Should I go at it, or should you?"

"You're the lucky one. Give it a try, Mr. Crane. Besides, it's close to the ground, as are you. I would have to stoop."

From his greatcoat, Phillip Crane drew forth a massive key ring. "This has served us well in our explorations of the house, wouldn't you say, Mr. McMurtry?"

"More than well, Mr. Crane. Except for the time at Fiffing."

"Oh, yes. Fiffing. An extraordinary experience, Fiffing."

"A dreadful experience, Mr. Crane. Of course, that was your fault. If you hadn't wanted to see the Pool of the Blue Flamingo—"

"Then we never would have finished chapter eight. And the excerpt from chapter eight won the Bethmoora Award for Realism in Architectural Literature. You never complained when we accepted the award, Mr. McMurtry."

"Of course I didn't. I had already lived through the deadly peril. I deserved an award for that alone."

"It's true, though they don't give out awards for deadly peril."

"Except in Adventurers' Clubs."

"Perhaps we should join one, Mr. McMurtry. Might be pleasant."

"Might be ghastly, Mr. Crane. A bunch of boors boasting of their accomplishments. Let the work speak for itself, I say."

"Even if the work involves deadly peril?"

"Even so."

While the architects spoke, Crane had been trying the various keys in the lock. The bolt turned with a loud groan.

"No problem at all," Crane said.

"Then we are fortunate. If you call entering a house full of men willing to kill us a lucky stroke."

Crane locked the gate behind them and slipped the key into his pocket.

"Do you think that wise, Mr. Crane? We may need a rapid escape."

"Perhaps, but I have no desire for that wolf-creature to enter the house. But we must be cautious. There should be guards. I can't think why there wasn't one here."

They made their way up the corridor, McMurtry in the lead, the crimson sputter of gas lamps lighting their way. They traveled several hundred yards before the passage ended at a gray portal with the inscription LET HIM WIIO HAS NO FEAR, FEAR HERE above the lintel. Phillip Crane opened the door, while Mr. McMurtry thrust the muzzle of his pistol into the crack, followed by his head and shoulders. Crane could see nothing from his vantage point behind the door. McMurtry leaned back out. "Empty, Mr. Crane. Shall we proceed?"

The door opened into what appeared to be the house proper. They were in a large, dimly lit hall. Hulking statues stood in the corners, formless abstractions with the heads of men.

"Is it my imagination," McMurtry half whispered, "or is the entire chamber tilted?"

"I believe you are correct. It's not an illusion. Look at those pillars in comparison to the wall behind. It's all lurching to the right."

"But there's so much more," McMurtry said. "Look at the pillars themselves! Tuscan with Eastwing fluting. And they, too, bend slightly to the right, like wavering light across a heat mirage. And the telemons and caryatids, geometric but suggestive. Ugly things! And there aren't any windows."

"What point windows in a lightless country, Mr. McMurtry?"

"True. But look at the molding. It's all pieced together with various patterns. The whole room has the feel of the first drawings I did in school. Worse! It's almost childish in its lack of continuity. Whatever the anarchists are, they aren't architects. How did they build it at all? And there, covering that entire wall; it's difficult to see in the dim light. Are those thorns?"

Crane crossed the hall, his footsteps ominous in the silence. He approached the tendrils, examined one closely, and gave it a tentative poke. "They are, and living ones at that."

"They're everywhere," McMurtry said. "I've never seen such an abomination! Whole thing should be burned to the ground."

"And perhaps it shall, Mr. McMurtry, if we can only locate the Cornerstone."

"And what shall we do once we find it?"

"We shall cross that span when we get there, wouldn't you say?"

"I suppose. But the stone could be anywhere in the house, and the manor is vast. It might take weeks, Mr. Crane."

"Then best we begin, Mr. McMurtry. Best we begin."

Deep Passage

The natural acumen of the courtroom rose within Mr. Hope as he stared at the slender messenger before him, as if he might, with his eyes, peel away, onion-wise, the thin layers of the young man's soul, and in so doing, reveal the truth of the dubious message lying beside its crumpled envelope on the oak desk. They were in Hope's office in the gentleman's chamber, and though the hour approached noon, the room remained gray, a casualty to the overcast heavens and the collected snow along the ledge obscuring the panes of the tall, single window. No matter how briskly the logs burned in the fireplace, the snow fell faster, and Hope was always cold—and at that moment, chilled to the bone.

"Tell me again how you received this message," he said, keeping his voice calm.

"It was brought by courier to High Gable from beyond Moomuth Kethorvian. I know no more."

"And you are from High Gable?"

"No, sir. I am the third to carry the message. I received it at Ghahanjhin. It was sent with all speed."

Hope noted the weariness in the man's eyes, his dark hair daubed to his head with perspiration, his clothes damp from his efforts; he had arrived panting for breath. Though Hope questioned him for twenty minutes, he perceived no guile.

"You have done a great service to the Master of Evenmere," the lawyer finally said. "Go into the kitchen and have the cook find you something to eat. You are to remain within the Inner Chambers until I give leave, for the good of the house. Understood?"

"Yes, sir."

When the messenger departed, Hope studied the letter meticulously before rising from his desk. Clutching the missive, he made his way past the garden entrance, turned left down the transverse corridor, past the main staircase, the dining room, and the morning room, and approached the drawing chamber. The door stood open and the sight within momentarily eclipsed the urgency of his mission. Enoch, Chant, and Sarah were there, embedded among the massed chairs, couches, ottomans, and tables upon the carpet field of blue, beneath the ceiling of plaster seraphs, pendants, the copious Atlantides, surrounded by the border of gaping, peeping ancients. The old Hebrew sat on the floral couch, grinning appreciatively, while Chant, standing before the golden damask curtains, recited a poem by Yeats. No sooner had he begun than Sarah sprang to her feet from a low couch, and with a mischievous grin, joined in:

"I will arise and go now, and go to Innisfree,
And a small cabin build there, of clay and wattles made:

Nine bean-rows will I have there, a hive for the
*   honey-bee,*
And live alone in-the bee-loud glade."

She began to walk a slow circle around Chant, who turned slightly to keep her in view, both reciting together:

"And I shall have some peace there, for peace comes
*   dropping slow,*
Dropping from the veils of the morning to where the
*   cricket sings;*
There midnight's all a glimmer, and noon a purple
*   glow,*
And evening full of the linnet's wings."

Their voices flowed together, tenor and soprano, and echoed sweetly through the chamber:

"I will arise and go now, for always night and day
I hear lake water lapping with low sounds by the
*   shore;*
While I stand on the roadway, or on the pavements
*   grey,*
I hear it in the deep heart's core."

They ended together; Sarah grinned and clapped her hands before her chin, and even Chant managed a wry smile, while Enoch applauded heartily.

"Amazing," Hope said. "And I, scarcely able to recite the alphabet."

"Oh, you quote your books of law well enough," Sarah said. "And never miss dot nor tittle. Come join us. There is little else to do in this endless winter, and poetry makes me forget my apprehensions."

"I fear this message may change that," Hope said, tapping the letter. "It professes to be from the Master, but the instructions are disturbing."

"From Carter!" Sarah's eyes flew wide. "Do read it!"

"Very well. It is addressed to myself, and states: *I am in urgent need. I cannot explain for fear this message might be intercepted and all come to ruin, but I require Sarah, Chant, and Enoch to come to me at once. There is a way I have discovered, named Deep Passage, which you must use. If any doubts the letter, remind Sarah we spoke of our lack of children on the night beside the fireplace. Remember I would not put you in danger except at great need.*

"Thereafter, it gives directions for the finding of the passage," Hope said, "and ends with what appears to be Carter's legitimate signature."

He handed Sarah the letter; she examined it hungrily, and cried, "It *is* his signature. I do not doubt. We must go."

"But wait, my lady," Hope said. "Signatures can be forged. The anarchists surely have the skill."

"But the message he gave, of our talk by the fire. Who could it be but Carter?"

"We must ask ourselves that question," Hope replied. "Could any other have the information?"

"None. We were alone."

"Could he have told someone?"

"No stranger, certainly," Sarah said. "It is not a matter for casual conversation. He might have mentioned it to

Duskin, perhaps, but no other. It is unlikely an enemy could have been close enough to overhear."

"Could they have discovered it any other way?" Hope asked.

"You need not be delicate," Sarah replied. "No, Carter would not reveal such knowledge under torture; if anything he would give false clues."

Hope pondered a moment. "If Carter knew of this passage, why didn't he use it himself to go to the Outer Darkness?"

"But he did not know," Enoch said. "The maps of the Master must be studied. He could not simply say, 'I wish the shortest route to the Outer Darkness,' and have Deep Passage appear before his mind's eye. Unless he stumbled upon it through long contemplation, he would not have known. It seems we must accept the message as true."

"Must we?" Hope asked. "When it required endangering the lives of the most important members of the house?"

"My quest, meseems, is here," Chant said. *"Or devil or man, Guard thou thine head."*

"Exactly right," Sarah said. "But Enoch and Chant, yes, they are of great value to Evenmere; I am not."

"You underestimate yourself," Chant said.

"A hostage perhaps?" asked Hope.

"If it were only myself, yes," Sarah said. "But not all three."

"The others mentioned as a ruse?" the lawyer suggested.

"A poor one, then," Sarah replied. "If they wanted only me, they would ask I be sent with a dozen troops, to avoid suspicion."

Hope struck the table lightly. "You should have studied law, madam! I tell you I don't like this!"

"The laws of the universe do not alter so easily as legal customs," Sarah said. "Whether we like or not does not belie the facts: Carter asks us to come. The request seems believable. Oh, I know I speak from the heart; if he is in need I would run to him without regard to fact! But there is logic here as well—we have his signature, along with a statement only he would know. Still, if passion does not rule, we should well ask the question: why does he need us?"

The room fell silent.

"Can we say?" Enoch asked with a sigh. "No. Who knows what witcheries Lord Anderson has found that only we can prevent?"

That evening Enoch and Chant brought two men into Hope's office, where he studied them with an appraising eye. The first was tall and dark, with gray beard and bee-tled brow. The other was short, bald, and wore spectacles. Both men appeared spry but ancient.

"Ebeneezor Prim," the first said. "I am Enoch's apprentice."

"Clarence Shandon," the second said. "And I am Chant's."

Hope stood with ceremonial elegance. "Gentlemen, it has been two hundred twelve years since either the Wind-keep's or the Lamp-lighter's Apprentice has been called to his duties. Never in the history of Evenmere have both been activated at once. Generations of apprentices have lived and died, having never performed their function, for though the High House by God's will makes the Wind-keep and the Lamp-lighter long-lived, the same longevity is not given to their assistants. Beginning day after to-morrow, you will undertake the tasks for which you have been trained and continue until your supervisors return, or you yourselves perish."

Hope stepped from behind his desk and shook hands with the two, who, displaying nubbed teeth in primeval grins, bowed and departed.

The lawyer sank into his chair.

"You look pale," Enoch said. "What troubles you?"

"We are delegating the most important of tasks to two octogenarians I do not even know."

Chant shrugged. "You can trust them well. We have trained them since they were fourteen years of age. They are equal to the task."

"They are," Enoch said. "But the last time I surrendered my duties, save for my journeys to wind the Hundred Years Clock, was seven centuries ago, when my leg was broken by a falling beam. I, too, am uneasy."

"And I am being left alone," Hope said. "Bereft of all companionship."

"Brittle administered the house when Carter's father disappeared," Chant said.

"Brittle had both of you." Hope put his hands to his chin. "I hope I do not become the last butler of Evenmere."

"If it comes to that, you needn't concern yourself about a long career," Chant said. "For it will mean the anarchists have won."

Hope grimaced. "Thank you for your pessimism."

Mr. Spaulding sat in his overstuffed chair lined with the stained fur of a white gnawling, drinking morning tea boiled over the dainty hearth built into the wall beside him. He was a small man, very old, and a little deaf; he liked reading and thinking; he hated conversation and large gatherings. Sixty years before, he had been appointed Door Warden to the Towers, and every morning since, without fail (save the day of his mother's funeral), had arrived at ten minutes to six, wearing a large bow-tied cravat and a long frock coat with velvet cuffs, to take his place at the end of the long corridor, beside the single white, six-paneled door, with sprigs of holly carved about its borders, and the emblem *Per ardua ad astra*, meaning "through struggle to the stars," carved upon the lintel. A heavy iron bar, painted white, protected the door. It had another lock as well, but since that one could be opened only by the Master Keys, it was left unlocked except in times of crisis. Mr. Spaulding kept the key to the bar. Pouting stone lions crouched upon either side of the entrance; the corridor was paneled in oak; the carpet, all orchids and nosegays, had a hole worn down to bare wood, beneath the place where the warden kept his feet. Since Enoch was the only one to use the doors, insuring the warden solitude for days at a time, he spent the hours dozing before the fire, reading, and watching the maids drift like paper ships along the corridor. Through the decades, he had devoured more books than most librarians, the weight of the words adding to the thickness of his spectacles, until his eyes gave the appearance of brown apples.

During the night his place was taken by his counterpart, the owner of the other chair beside the hearth, the equally reticent and ancient Mr. Bradbury. In short, Mr. Spaulding had reached the full extent of his capabilities.

He was just browsing through the first pages of a translation of a promising ancient work, *The Red Book of Westmarch*, when he glanced up to see four figures striding down the corridor. At first he assumed they would dissipate into one of the rooms, as had occurred innumerable times before, leaving him to ponder their mission with all the acumen of a cow regarding the skyline. At their continued advance, a vague unease fell upon him, which gradually grew as door after door was bypassed. The set of their jaws and resolution of their gait seemed a revolver aimed at his head. Worse, he sluggishly recognized them as the Lady of Evenmere, the chief butler, the Windkeep, and the Lamp-lighter, the most prestigious members of the household, save for the Master himself. Mr. Hope was in his usual attire, but the other three were garbed for travel. Lady Anderson wore a full-length winter coat and bore a shotgun nearly as tall as herself.

As they passed the last doors, utter horror gripped him. He fumbled his teacup onto the side table, spilling half its contents, and rose hastily, hiding his book beneath the cushion and brushing at his moth-eaten suit.

"Good morning, friend Douglas," Enoch said. "How fares the watch?"

Spaulding gulped, unable to speak for a moment. "It is ... It is well, Master Windkeep."

He stood paralyzed. All words escaped him, but he soon realized Mr. Hope was speaking.

"Sarah, I have given it great consideration. This Deep

Passage, if it truly leads into the enemy camp, is a tremendous opportunity for our armies. I will wait ten days, no longer, then I will have Captain Glis send a company, perhaps more, through its portals."

Sarah considered. "Very well, William. It seems prudent. But Glis must be cautious. If this is indeed Carter's plan, he must do nothing to ruin it."

Hope nodded miserably, shook hands with Chant and Enoch, and took Sarah's hand between his two. Tears sprang to the corners of his eyes, so that she said, "Ah, my friend, do not look so. All will be well."

He nodded, like a round-faced boy trying not to weep, released her hand, and pulled his collar close about his cheeks. "Yes, madam. Good-bye. I will take care of the house. I just wish we could send you the swifter way through the Green Door rather than by the Towers, but without the Master Keys this must serve. Even so, Deep Passage is only a day's journey. Godspeed."

With that he hurried away, head sunk between his shoulders.

Mr. Spaulding, seldom brought so close to human drama, stood entranced. At last, Lady Anderson turned to him expectantly. He looked at her with dull eyes.

"Have you your key, good man?" Chant finally asked.

Mr. Spaulding looked at him like a frog. "My key." He turned around, stared at the chair, then back at Sarah. "Lady Anderson, I did not know of your coming."

"As we intended. Neither shall you mention where we have gone."

"I? Who would I . . . ? I mean, of course not. Of course not. I never speak to anyone. My key."

He did another circle before digging into his pocket, retrieving the key, dropping it on the way to the door and once more while unfastening the bar. He pulled the bar back, stepped away, then realizing he had not opened the door, nearly ran into Enoch in rushing back to fling it wide with a crash. His face went crimson. "This way, your lor—your ladyship."

"Thank you," Sarah said.

The three stepped through the door. He closed it, and looked through the peephole in time to witness Sarah burst into laughter behind her hands.

He lowered the bar and locked it, trembling. There had never been a day like this in all his sixty years. He crept back to his chair, amazed with embarrassment and excitement that Lady Anderson herself should use his door. Contemplation of the episode would occupy several weeks thereafter.

Sarah's laughter vanished as she gazed upon the great stair leading up to the Towers. The room, which contained only the door they had entered, one other, and the stair itself, was paneled in dark oak. The moaning of the storm seemed to radiate from the shivering shadows of the high ceiling; the stair, fifteen feet wide, stretched straight into a night broken by regularly spaced lamps leading like stars to the first landing high above, with utter darkness beyond. A green, golden-flowered carpet covered the floor and the stair except where gray marble peeked from the edge of the steps. Monks, carved upon the balusters, turned their faces toward the top of the stair, mouths open as if in Gregorian song, gaping and toothless in the gloom.

Sarah scanned the long slope of the stairway, overawed as always by its sight, but she said, "Enoch, does it make your feet hurt?"

Enoch followed her gaze and gave a grin. "How could it not? But it does not trouble me. As a boy I liked to climb. Still, that is not our path today."

He approached the other door and withdrew an iron key from his belt. The lock turned with a click. "I will lead, Lady Anderson."

Beyond the opening, all lay in darkness. Chant lit his lantern expertly and gave it to Enoch, who led them through, then locked the door behind them. Following the instructions given them by the letter, they made their way in the direction of the Long Corridor. Their course immediately descended, then turned back south, so that Sarah knew they must be passing below the room they had just occupied. The corridor was narrow, covered with a thin, saffron carpet, with paint peeling off the yellow walls, and bitterly cold. They walked in silence, in single file, Chant bringing up the rear, all subdued by the emptiness of the passage and the wind roaring outside the house. They went quickly, but with little fear of encountering anarchists, who seldom came so close to the Inner Chambers. *Unless,* Sarah thought, *it is indeed a trap, in which case they might perceive our direction of travel.* But knowing the futility of fretting over the future, she soon put her fears behind her, and found herself enjoying the walk. She was usually denied the chance to accompany Carter on his missions as Master, and despite her apprehension for her husband, it thrilled her to partake in a mysterious journey. Even more, it gave her a task, which was always better than waiting.

They were traveling through the Empty Reach between the Terraces of Naleewuath and the Gray Edge, and would turn east long before they came to tiny Indrin.

A half a day they journeyed, soon leaving the yellow corridor behind, to wander amid other passages and stairs, but few chambers—the Empty Reach was a path, not a destination. Mostly the carpets were bare, the banisters dull from wear, the wallpaper sagging wearily. Sarah wondered if anyone ever traveled this way; certainly they saw no one else. Yet it was a shame for it to be forsaken. *I should like to build skylights, and cover them in flowers,* she thought. *And perhaps plant trees as in Naleewuath, their branches reaching up toward the sun. But no greenery would grow in these windowless halls.*

They ate lunch in an alcove with a low table and faded Powdered wallpaper, its flowers green, gold, and orange. The floor was bare save for a Kidderminster carpet in lily pattern, with holes where mice had chewed it. Sarah produced enough food for a banquet: slices of beef, green vegetables, even tea, though it was ice cold.

"Is this a picnic?" Enoch asked. "I should eat so well on my rounds."

"A few decent meals we will have, before we are reduced to salted meat," Sarah said. "If not for the chill, this might even be pleasant. I would have brought a tablecloth if you had not laughed."

"A perfect woman, nobly planned, To warn, to comfort, and command;" Chant recited. *"A creature not too bright or good For human nature's daily food."*

"Fiddle faddle on quaint verse," Sarah replied. "Men are too lazy to consider details. You are all great hulks, wonders at master plans, vast battles, tremendous constructions, build the pyramids and send in a thousand workers! But ask how to feed or clothe your armies, and you haven't considered it. If not for women, men would live in hovels, thinking deep thoughts while eating with their hands. You haven't a practical idea in your heads."

Chant and Enoch exchanged wry glances.

"Is she right?" Enoch asked. "She might be."

"I suppose so," said Chant. "But I have been with you on journeys, and we have never eaten poorly. Do not be deceived, Lady Anderson, Enoch is a master chef."

"Because he has lived the lives of a hundred men," Sarah replied. "Learning comes even to the male of the species, eventually. But what are you wearing beneath your greatcoat, Enoch?"

In answer, the Hebrew stood and unbuttoned his garment, revealing a glistening coat of chain mail and a two-handed sword with a long, silver scabbard, heavy with runes, inlaid with topaz and lapis lazuli, with ivory and pearls adorning the guards of the gleaming hilt. "The sword, called Aroundight, I carry always with me outside the Inner Chambers. The mail I have owned from old; it is honed from the same metal as the armor of the White Circle Guard and will stop even a bullet." His brown eyes shone brilliant as he grasped the hilt of the blade, and with his Assyrian curls and fierce, ancient face, he looked indeed a great warrior.

"I shall keep my shotgun," Sarah said. "It is better for distance."

"Yes," Enoch agreed, "but is it good at close range? Experience has taught me a knife or a sword, obsolete in the outside world, is still of use in the house, with its endless corners. And I carry a pistol as well." He patted his greatcoat pocket.

"So with your pistol in one hand and your sword in the other you are four-armed, and by inverse definition, fore-warned," Sarah said.

"On that military observation, perhaps we should go," Chant said. *"Let us, then, be up and doing, With a heart for any fate; Still achieving, still pursuing, Learn to labor and to wait."*

They put away their supplies and were soon pacing the corridors, climbing and descending stairs until Sarah's ankles ached. By midafternoon, she began to whistle softly; Enoch caught the tune and they whiled away a happy half hour. After that, the old Hebrew told tales until evening, of his early days in the house, and of the times before, when the world was young, and the Medes but scattered tribesmen.

"But who was the first Master of Evenmere?" Sarah asked.

"The very first I did not know," Enoch replied. "It has been said that Evenmere has always been, since the beginning of the world. But the man who was Master when I first came was Mardos, a lordly man, broad of shoulder, stout as a lion, deep of mind. He handled a spear like no one I have seen before or since. The house was much different then, for it has changed over the ages, and I have seen it when the halls were of bronze, and its gardens, standing where the morning room is now, rivaled those of Babylon. But in the days of Mardos, all of Evenmere was made of stone—the walls were dolomite, onyx, chryso-lite, the tableware of copper, the shields and doors of brass. Was it more beautiful than now? Who am I to judge? And in that day, there were dragons in Eastwing; not the great worm who dwells in the attic—he was more than all of them and called Behemoth then—but lesser dragons, still three times the size of a man."

"Did they breathe fire?" Sarah asked.

"Of course, though how the house was kept from burning I do not know. But these could not, or would not, fly; legends say they were descended from even older serpents, immense enough to cover the sky. Mardos it was who rid the house of them, not because he wished it, for they were beautiful; their scales glistened purple, gold, and green by torchlight, and their heads were long and smooth, velvet as horses, for their skin was soft where there was no armor. But they were always snatching sheep from the Terraces and men from the halls, and at last Mardos had to confront them. For three years he and his men hunted the dragons through the chambers of Evenmere, with his great hounds, large as Fenris wolves. The lesser ones they slew, until only old Tiamat remained, the greatest of all the dragons, and the most wily. Mardos chased her across Eastwing, until, at last, he thought her cornered in the lowest regions of the house, and with his hounds before him, entered a low dungeon far ahead of his men, yet unafraid, because of his good sword and his dogs.

"No sooner had he entered, then the door dropped closed and Tiamat sprang her trap, leaving only the hounds and Mardos to face her. So mighty was Tiamat, she slew the beasts as if they were pups, and those the apples of Mardos's eye. Enraged, the Master drew sword, in that time before the Lightning Blade was forged, and smote the dragon, but the edge did not bite deep and she broke the weapon in twain with a powerful swing of her tail. Mardos was struck by the dragon's breath; half his body was scorched, though he was not slain. His weapons were gone, save for his spear, but in that he was master. This he hurled and it flew true, entering the left eye and then to the brain, slaying Tiamat in one stroke.

"No one saw that battle, and the Master, who was grievously wounded, had no time to recount his exploits before he perished, so a full telling cannot be told. When the men broke through the door, I with them, we found our Master and the broken sword, and the spear embedded in the worm. He was a brave lord, and that was the last seen of dragons in Evenmere. The story is told in many lands, but that is the truth of it."

By early evening they came to the Long Corridor and traveled its gentle curve a half hour before exiting to the right, down a short stair leading into a squat, paneled passage. Following the instructions from Carter's message, they counted six inserts from the wall and depressed the ornamental knob at the center of the seventh, which caused the entire panel to open with a click. Sarah exchanged satisfied and somewhat anxious glances with her companions—the panel revealed a bare passage, less than four feet tall, smelling of dust and dry rot, filled with cobwebs and silverfish fleeing from the light.

Enoch led, stooping low to enter, bearing the lamp. Chant followed and then Sarah. The floor was bare oak. Even on her haunches, Sarah's head brushed the ceiling. Chant gave a start as a lizard scampered down the wooden steps of a stair, which curved away to invisibility.

"Can this be it?" Enoch asked, then shrugged.

Sarah found a lever near the floor and shut the panel; it closed with a dull thud. "Surely it is. But it must have been built for dwarves."

Indeed, the ceiling above the stair remained low, and the companions were forced to walk doubled over, waddling their way down the wooden steps like ducks. Within thirty seconds Sarah's back ached. She was nearly eye-to-eye with the spiders and slugs strolling along the ceiling, and the walls felt like soft pulp to the touch. The passage seemed to close in around her as they descended, deeper and deeper into the earth, as if into ancient tombs.

"Are you well, Lady Anderson?" Chant asked, in a mole-soft voice.

"Quite comfortable, sir," she replied, just as quietly, knowing she spoke to still her own fears. "I cannot help but thank my father, who never barred me from recreations normally reserved for boys. I can still hear him saying: 'Sarah, you must not depend on others for strength, but be strong for them instead.' As a girl, I wrestled my boy cousins, sometimes winning, hunted, skinned rabbits, built forts, crawled through tunnels, a hundred other things. Only I do not recall it being so difficult then."

"Nor I," Chant said.

"It is the knee joints that cause the problem," Sarah said. "The knees of the young are well lubricated with butter and oil, you know. All children are ninety percent butter."

"They neglected to impart that fact before awarding me my medical degree," Chant said.

"You attended Lang College, didn't you?"

"Yes," Chant said, with a touch of pride.

"Ah, I see the problem. You should have gone to the College of Butter and Oil. Then you would have your facts straight."

"I stand corrected."

"No, sir, you do not stand at all. Nor do I. That is the whole dilemma."

Chant gave a soft moan in reply.

In this manner they descended forty minutes, accompanied by the noise of their popping joints and their shadows on the moldy walls, often forced to rest their aching limbs. Sarah yearned to flee screaming back up the stair; the air was stifling; she felt suffocated, but at last they came to a landing before an iron door, wholly encrusted in rust, its locking mechanism a large valve.

"This was made to keep whatever is behind it out," Enoch said, climbing to his feet and stretching his limbs. "Dare we open it?"

"We have no choice," Sarah said. "Most likely the door was constructed to keep the countries bordering the Outer Darkness from close access to the Inner Chambers."

Chant drew his revolver. "Nonetheless, we will take precautions. If you would open the valve, Enoch."

Sarah raised her own shotgun to her shoulder, wondering if she had chosen the proper weapon; the way was narrow, and the Windkeep might be caught in the spray. She determined to aim as far right as possible to avoid hitting him.

Enoch set himself to the valve, but could not budge it alone, and Chant had to put his lamp down to help, leaving only Sarah to protect the way. Inch by arduous inch, they turned the mechanism, the groaning of the metal reverberating through the passage beyond. She kept her shotgun poised, her pulse beating at her temple, as they strained against centuries of rust. At last, with a final shriek, the door roared open on its hinges.

With a rush, black shapes swarmed through the portal, chittering as they came. Sarah almost involuntarily squeezed the trigger, but Chant was too close, and as she hesitated she recognized the creatures as bats. She dropped to her knees, protecting her face with her hands as the horde passed cheeping up the stair, their shadows obscuring the ceiling.

"How could they live so deep?" Chant asked after the bats had fled.

Sarah stood. "I'm glad I recognized them in time to avoid shooting. But I'm trembling all over."

"You have nerves of bronze," Enoch said. "I would have fired. There must be a shaft in the passage to allow them entrance."

Chant raised the lantern higher, and two more bats twittered through the doorway, causing all to duck again. The Lamp-lighter stayed low, and pushed the door wide, revealing a square, eight-by-eight red-brick passage, extending in a rolling line into the darkness. The white spoor of the bats covered the floor for several feet, but beyond was clear.

"Deep Passage," Chant said. He stepped over the threshold, clutching his pistol, and said softly, *"But now farewell. I am going a long way With these thou seest—if indeed I go—For all my mind is clouded with doubt."* And his voice came echoing back like a murmuring sea.

Sarah followed and Enoch brought up the rear. The door had no locking mechanism on this side, but the Hebrew pulled it shut to the accompaniment of a tremendous, wrenching noise. "If anyone lives down here, how could they not hear us?"

"Hopefully, none do," Sarah said. "Is the air warmer? That is some comfort, at least."

They walked abreast, Chant carrying the lamp, their shadows lurching across the floor, walls, and ceiling, distorted by the channels of grout on the brick. The passage sloped like rolling hills; the bricks were cracked and split at intervals, some loose and lying on the floor, as if the corridor was subject to earth tremors. Their boots clicked, and the clicks returned as reverberated drumrolls; even speaking softly, their words ricocheted into myriad whispers muttered at their backs. Sarah abruptly paused, and the others followed suit.

"Listen," she said, and the walls sang back *listen, listen.* When the echoes died, she suddenly knew for what she harkened. All her life, she had been surrounded by the sounds of Evenmere, either in the lanes of Innman Tor, or the corridors of the Inner Chambers. No house is ever silent; the gas jets hiss, the stairs creak, doors open and close, but in Deep Passage the hush was complete. Not even the winter storm could penetrate so deep within the earth, beneath tons of dirt and stone. They were alone.

"Nor wintry leaves nor vernal, Nor days nor things diurnal," Chant said. *"Only the sleep eternal, In an eternal night."*

Enoch nodded and patted Sarah's shoulder, and they went on. By the time they stopped for the night, her feet were numb from walking the uneven bricks; she removed her boots, massaged her toes, and sighed. They stretched out upon their bedrolls and shared a meal of bread, cheese, and preserved apricots, all sitting in a circle around the lamp, only their shadows, the bricks, and their own stark faces for company. Yet, there was about the tiny flame and the sharing of food a comfort Sarah had not known all day, so she was briefly happy.

"When I was a young man," Chant said softly, "shortly after receiving my degree at Lang College, war broke out between Westwing and Moomuth Kethorvian, the Three Years War we call it now. I served during that time as a medical officer for Westwing. Much of the fighting was in the lowest levels of Moomuth; it has basements under basements, a torturous labyrinth, passages much like this. *We, quivering upward, each hour Know battle in air and in ground.* The hospital had to be near the fighting; we were in darkness for days at a time. Once, the enemy forces overran the medical unit. They didn't even know what they had found; they fired straight into the hospital; the screaming was ghastly. It took precious moments to convince them of our identities. Even then, their officers could scarcely halt the slaughter; the men were crazed from too much darkness, too much blood. *I hear even now the infinite fierce chorus, The cries of agony, the endless groan.*"

"Is that why you no longer practice medicine?" Sarah asked.

"Partly. But the Master himself, old Lord Chesterton, was wounded and in the hospital during the attack. I managed to conceal him from the Moomuth forces—not an easy task. We became friends thereafter, and when the last Lamp-lighter died he offered me the position."

"You are long-lived, I know," Sarah said. "Though not nearly so old as Enoch. The Three Years War is a dozen decades past."

Chant nodded. "Yes. I will be a hundred and sixty in March. Of all the servants of Evenmere, only the Wind-keep is given immortality, but the Lamp-lighters and the master butlers usually live several generations."

"And did you never take a wife?"

"When I was young there was a lady from Ghahanjhin who was very dear to me, but our marriage was forbidden, for I lacked sufficient position to gain her father's approval. I pressed the issue; I was a medical student, arrogant, selfish, swearing she meant more than life itself, but willing to tear her from her family in the name of love. She was not a strong woman. Her father would not relent. Neither would I. He swore to banish her from the family if we wed; I swore I would die without her. She hung herself from a beam in Totman Abbey."

Chant dropped his head so the shadows fell across his face. "I completed my degree. In the war I learned further the meaning of the sacredness of life, which can be concluded in an instant. I had gone from misery to misery, and had often thought of ending my own contemptible existence."

"But you did not," Sarah said.

"No. There are times, my lady, when one must either find the forgiveness of God, or perish altogether, either in flesh or spirit. I left Evenmere a time, until the Master summoned me back to serve him. I think he suspected my circumstance; I never understood why such a wretch as I was made Lamp-lighter of Evenmere. But shortly, thereafter, I found heaven's mercy, on my knees, beneath that very same beam in Totman Abbey. That night I dedicated myself to the service of God, the house, and my fellow man. I have lived that life ever since."

"Have you not been lonely?" she asked.

"We are all lonely, Lady Anderson. I am a solitary man, but I have many friends in the house, many more lonely than myself, that I visit as I go about my rounds. And God's grace sustains me. I could ask for little more."

"You work is very important," she said.

"It is, but that is not the lesson. *Bright star! Would I were steadfast as thou art*— I would live my life as if every action is important, as if all, no matter how large or small, lead, metaphorically speaking, to Totman Abbey. For, indeed, they might."

They finished their meal in silence, then Sarah said, "We should keep a watch, tonight. Should I take the first turn?"

"Chant and I will watch," Enoch said.

"You will not. With only three present I must shoulder my share. I will brook no dispute."

"Very well," Chant said. "We know better than to argue with *that* look. We will need to extinguish the lamp, I fear. We dare not run out of oil before journey's end."

Sarah glanced at the surrounding shadows. "It will be pitch-dark, but we need not fear. Nothing could creep upon us in these whispery halls. I'm not yet ready to sleep, so I will watch first." She drew her shotgun to her shoulder and showed a stout chin.

"You will wake us if you hear anything?" Enoch asked.

"You will be awakened. Any noise other than your breathing must be that of an enemy, and I will fire this." She patted the shotgun. "It will be your alarm."

The lamp was extinguished; darkness wrapped them like a gloved fist. Sarah sat, staring, reminding herself it would grow no brighter. She put her hand before her

eyes—it seemed the proper practice in such situations—
and discovered, certainly enough, she could not see it. She
grew somber. *I am like a hound in the yard at night,* she
thought, *whose only defense is his nose and ears.* She gave
a deep sniff with her delicate nostrils. *It smells like brick.
The ears will have to do. Best I perk them.* In such silence
the breathing of her comrades sounded turbulent as factory
engines; her own breathing threatened to overwhelm her;
she could picture her lungs filling and emptying, an image
she found disagreeable. She soon felt herself drifting; staying awake was difficult in the dark. Nothing felt real. She
sat up and tried to recite poetry to herself, but her thoughts
sailed to a hundred different things, to Carter, the Inner
Chambers, the Azalea Room that she meant to redecorate,
her father and Innman Tor. She remembered the last night
she had seen Lizbeth, and the day the girl had played with
her puppy on the front porch while she and Carter talked.
She wondered if Carter had indeed found her; he surely
would have said as much in his message, whether for good
or ill, if it were so. And she passed through the fears and
hopes all people feel for those they love when the only
substance comes from imagination.

Down and down a long tunnel Sarah's thoughts descended, until she jerked awake, sat up straight, pinched
herself on the leg, and began the journey over again. She
wondered how she would know when her turn at watch
was over; perhaps when she could bear no more. She felt
her lids closing again.

Suddenly she was wide awake, uncertain what had
roused her. Her heart fluttered frantically; she strained to
listen.

Down the corridor, a faint snuffling noise approached.

She drew her gun closer. She had spoken bravely of firing at the first sound; her actual dilemma was less certain. It was impossible to tell the distance of the noise, the echoes ran everywhere; the creature, man or beast, could be ten feet away, or fifty. And if it could see in the darkness, as a bat, and she missed her target, it might charge. She dared make no noise to wake her companions.

The snuffling grew louder; she envisioned a great bear. There was no more time for thought. She strained to pinpoint the noise, then in one motion brought the shotgun to her shoulder and fired.

The light was blinding after such darkness, but too brief to illuminate her target. She was thrown backward by the recoil, for she had been sitting cross-legged when she fired, and she struggled to right herself, even as she heard the beast screaming into the night, padding away while Chant and Enoch fumbled awake.

The Lamp-lighter quickly lit the lantern. The passage stood empty as far as the circle of light. Chant was on one knee, lamp in one hand, a pistol in the other, and Enoch had risen, long sword glistening, face as stern as an Assyrian god. Sarah found herself violently trembling.

"Are you injured?" Chant asked.

"No, it didn't touch me," she said.

He rose, holding the lantern high, and went to a spot less than six feet away, where blood lay glistening on the red bricks. His eyebrows rose in respect. *"And hast thou slain the jabberwock? Come to my arms my beamish . . . girl.* He strode a few paces down the corridor, lantern high, stared into the darkness, and returned. "Could it have been a man?"

"No," Sarah said. "Those were animal screams as it fled."

Chant nodded. "We can assume it will not return, then."

"But we should move back up the corridor," Enoch said, "lest the scent of its blood attract something else."

"There's a cheerful thought," Sarah said, rising and lifting her bedroll. "A beast large enough to eat that one. Does anyone have the hour?"

Enoch removed his pocket watch. "It is shortly after midnight. I will take the next shift. Would it be best to leave the lantern burning?"

They made their new camp two hundred yards back from the old. Sarah lay down and pulled the blankets over her. Though she closed her eyes facing the tiny flame of the lantern, she did not sleep well, but kept starting awake from dreams of the beast plodding toward her through the darkness.

The remainder of the night passed quietly, and they ate a cold breakfast and set out again. With less than five troubled hours of sleep, Sarah felt unimaginably weary. But since neither of her companions, who were seasoned travelers, looked better, she assumed she wasn't supposed to feel well, which cheered her in turn, so she was soon well enough, though longing for a cup of hot tea.

They followed the bloodstains down the passage until the trail vanished into a drain pipe, four feet in circumference, the first of a number of such conduits that they passed in silence lest they rouse a pack of the creatures. Sarah wondered if the corridor was susceptible to flooding.

The rest of the day proved uneventful, save for encountering three intersections stretching into darkness, which they ignored. By evening Sarah was unimaginably bored by the endless monotony and had to constantly restrain herself from counting the bricks. Chant, too, became pensive; only Enoch retained his good humor, and told stories he had heard in his long life: of the splendor of Carcassonne, golden and glorious in the morning sun; of the small country Dorimare, with its rich plain, watered by two rivers; and the forests of the Vale of Erl, home of ancient kings; of the peaked gables and green cottages of Ulthar, where no man, by law, may kill a cat; and the great city Celephais, in the valley of Ooth-Nargai beyond the Tanarian hills, whose pavements are made of onyx and whose spires lift themselves into the very clouds. He spoke of ancient Hyperborea, where the old magicians practiced their craft; of antediluvian Poseidonis that sank beneath the ocean waves; and of fair Vandarei, where the Khentorei ride their great stallions across the vast plains. There could not have been a better companion than Enoch, who had learned to tell tales beneath the full moon of ancient Aram; his eyes flashed when he spoke, and his deep voice rumbled until Chant had to remind him to speak softly.

The days that followed were without incident or meaning, a dreary nightmare of traipsing through the unchanging passage. They neither saw nor heard any more beasts. All day they traveled the red bricks; all night Sarah dreamed she walked them, so day and night became one continuous journey. By the fourth morning Enoch wearied of telling tales, Chant of reciting poetry, Sarah of games with words, and nothing remained but silence broken by shuffling feet. A crawling beetle, of which there were few, became as wondrous as a whirlwind, to be fastened with eyes hungry for variety. A break or crack in the bricks brought an hour's speculation.

By the sixth night, as they shared a bland supper, Sarah said, "We shall all be crazed before we reach the end."

"Times such as this remind us of what life is about," Enoch replied. "How often do we waste a day waiting for the next? But who knows? Tomorrow's pain may make us wish for this silent hall. This is what adventure is, after all, discomfort enough to make a memory."

Sarah smiled. "Live for the day? You must be correct; you certainly have more experience at it than I. But I would be done with this adventure, nonetheless. I would rather know how the story ends."

"I agree," Chant said. "I would rather return to the quiet lighting of the lamps, and to journeys with comfortable beds at their end. *And the night shall be filled with music, And the cares, that infest the day, Shall fold their tents, like the Arabs, And as silently steal away.* Hot food and hot tea, there's an adventure."

"One we will not soon share," Sarah sighed. "Not unless bricks can be burned."

By the eighth day they discovered the end of Deep Passage, marked by a granite stair cut from the wall. The hewn steps, narrow and bereft of a guardrail, ascended into dimness. Air currents whispered around the companions' heads as they climbed, steadying themselves against the beckoning gulf with one hand upon the wall. Enoch kept his sword ready, Chant his pistol. Sarah's shotgun was useless with the Windkeep blocking her line of sight. The stair zigzagged from landing to landing. After a dizzying half hour, they reached an iron door identical to the one used to enter Deep Passage. To their vast relief, the valve was un-locked, though it took both men's strength to pull the door wide enough to enter. They stepped into a lightless room, barren save for a cracked onyx table, with the beginnings of a gallery visible in the circle of their lamp-light, and bizarre machinery peering from the gloom.

As they stepped toward the center of the room, the door slammed shut with a heavy clang and a voice commanded from above: "You will cast down your weapons and sur-render. You are completely surrounded. There is no hope of escape. The door is sealed behind you; a ton of dyna-mite could not blow it open. I declare you prisoners in the name of the Society of Anarchists."

Hope sat reading in his study, huddled before the fire, wrapped in a red muffler. He was restless and found him-self scanning the same paragraph over and over. Sarah, Enoch, and Chant had been gone slightly over a week; the snow had ceased, and the world outside the window, sheathed in frost, was still as any portrait. The house con-tinued to run relatively well, though there were scattered reports of passages being transformed. He had received a message that the main corridor to Eastwing was impassi-ble, and had dispatched soldiers to investigate. He was lonely more than anxious, and had spent the evening din-ing with Rector Williams and his wife, moderate acquain-tances who helped to pass the time.

Currently he perused a red leather volume: *The Unabridged Records of Evenmere*, a companion to the slender *History of the High House*, looking for information concerning the anarchists. As an organization, the Society had existed for little more than two hundred years, and was actually a remnant from the old Zeitgeistheim Party, which had held significant power for more than three centuries. Hope, who always endeavored to work methodically, had made his way up to the time of the Yellow Room Wars. After reading a general history, he turned a page to discover both a dead moth trapped between the pages and a lengthy list of the officers known to have served on the anarchists' side. He brushed the corpse from the page, intending to turn to less tedious reading, when a name, formerly hidden by the insect, caught his eye.

His heart fluttered; a wave of heat passed across his head. For an instant, he could not breathe. Then, impassioned, he clutched the volume, sprang to his feet, and rushed to the library as quickly as his bandy legs would allow.

He left the great doors of the library banging against the wall, scurried past the dolomite pillars and hawk-armed couches, and plunged into the stacks. Within five minutes, he had discovered two cross-references confirming his fears.

A hall boy, having observed Hope's hasty charge, appeared before him. "May I be of assistance, sir?"

"Assistance?" Hope said. "I'm not certain if anyone can help us now! I need to speak to Captain Glis at once. The fastest runner, the greatest urgency. I will prepare the message. Men must be dispatched, an invading army to follow Sarah. We are undone."

He looked again at the list of anarchist officers. Half way down the page, leading the fourth regiment of the second brigade, was Lieutenant Howard McMurtry.

The False House

Lizbeth walked the gray halls of the gray house. A low mist swirled about her feet, and the thorns glistened star points from the yellow glow of the lamps. She wore a midnight-blue velvet dress, with a jacket of bronze velvet and a bouffant and skirt of pale blue cashmere, and her shoes shone black as marble; her hair lay all in curls and bounced against her cheeks. She was happy, because she knew she looked pretty, though she did not recall how she had come to be so. She wondered about the mist, for it was unnatural to the house, but she did not allow it to trouble her much. She skipped as she went while the shadows snapped soundlessly at her heels, and she chanted the words of Hindley from *Wuthering Heights*: *"Wait till I get hold of those elegant locks—see if I won't pull them loooooonger,"* holding the vowels out in the last word, a child's repetition to a tune Sarah had crooned to her often.

She came to white French doors nailed shut by heavy

iron spikes driven into the casement and immediately fell to work prying at the spikes. At first, she could not move them, but then her gaze fell upon a pry bar, and with its help, she soon withdrew the pegs, one by one, though they cut her as she did so, and blood dripped down her wrists.

With the last spike withdrawn, she flung the doors wide, and a clear, sweet wind blew upon her brow, wafting her hair. She raised her arms in triumph and prepared to step over the threshold into a starry darkness.

At that moment, a shrouded figure appeared out in the night, his face just beyond the circle of light cast from the hall lamps. She found herself trembling, though she did not know why.

"Who's there?" she called, her voice unnaturally heavy in the mist. The figure did not reply, but drew nearer.

It occurred to her it must be her father, come to fetch her from the house. She reached small hands toward the threshold, but it was Carter Anderson who lurched into the room, the left half of his face covered in darkness, his eyes and grin those of a jackal. He towered above her. Lizbeth shrieked and fled down the corridor, while he stamped after, all blundering rage. She could surely outdistance him, for she knew the house better than anyone, yet she found she could scarcely run at all. It was as if she fled through water, straining with every stride against some unseen force.

He caught her effortlessly, snatching her wrist in a rough grasp. "You'll come with me," he rasped. "To a place even more terrible."

She screamed and screamed and screamed, all the world's terror ascending to the top of her head.

And then she woke.

She lay still, too frightened to move, reassuring herself it was but the old dream, the same dream as always. Her heart, which she believed was not her heart at all, but the heart-pendant given her by the Man in the Dark, shredded itself against her chest; she still trembled. *"I had the misfortune to scream in my sleep, owing to a frightful nightmare,"* she whispered to herself. *"I'm sorry I disturbed you."*

She sat up. The fine dress of her dream was gone, replaced by her gray rags. Her hair was uncurled; she knew it would never be curled again; it hung in a heavy mass past her waist, an animal tangle. The anarchists allowed her neither brush nor scissors, though she combed it each day with her fingers. Her one consolation was that it was clean; she bathed fastidiously in the fountain in the garden. It was her defiance against them.

She glanced about the room that had been hers for six years: the dingy lamp, a tilted dresser with a broken leg, containing nothing but a few simple things that she called her treasures, a mattress lying on the floor, chewed by mice on its left side—she had made one of the creatures her pet until the Man in the Dark learned of it and took it away. She owned no shoes save the pair she was wearing when she arrived—though now too small by half, she kept them wrapped in soiled cloth among her hoard.

Anytime she woke from the dream she never knew which was more terrible, the fear or the reminder of who she had once been, before the Man in the Dark snatched her heart from her breast. She hugged her knees, remembering the feel of fine clothes. She did not cry, not even in these moments of horror; crying was for those with souls, and hers had been taken from her. Yet she always ached, deep inside, and wondered what it was if not her heart.

She went to her treasures, withdrew the battered copy of *Wuthering Heights*, and clutched it to her breast. She owned no other book; why the anarchists had given it to her she did not know, but she always kept it well hidden, in case they should decide to take it back. She fled whenever she saw her captors, anyway, partially because she feared them and partially because she had grown shy in the long years, for months passed without her seeing anyone at all, though she occasionally heard voices in the distance. Four times a year, as Lizbeth reckoned time, the Man in the Dark summoned her. Him she feared even more, but when he spoke she listened, though he always said the same words: that if she ever left the house she would blow away, insubstantial as smoke, because she had no soul, and that all her feelings had been taken from her, because she had no heart. Then he would strap her to the dreadful machines he kept, and send bolts like colored lightning passing through her body and into the strange stone kept on the onyx table. As he did so, he would speak of ice, frost, and endless winter, until the hollow where her heart had been would freeze numb with cold; and of order, harmony, and the beauty of constancy, until she imagined a whole world of squares, lines, and perfect peace. The lightning rays never hurt, but the hum of the machines and the passion of the Man in the Dark terrified her, and she often wished the stone would go away, and the ritual end.

The last time the Man in the Dark summoned her, the stone had indeed been gone, and he asked many questions concerning it, as if she knew where it might be. He said awful things would happen if it was not returned, but she was glad it was gone, though she knew his words were true; the Man in the Dark never lied. He had told her where her food could be found, and what her punishments would be if she sinned. He had explained how the house, little more than a cottage when she arrived, would grow to a vast manor. She always believed him, and because of the hunger within her, looked forward to their talks, despite her terror. The other anarchists would never speak to her; she thought they were not allowed. Besides, he sometimes gave her twelve short candles that she could use any way she wished and a replacement for her gray dress.

She rose, her long hair rustling. It was golden still, as it had been the day Duskin leaned down beside her at Innman Tor and held her locks against his. She did not look at it without remembering, and she always thought of him after one of her nightmares, when she would rise and flee down the long, ill-lit corridors, a shadow among shadows, past the dark doors and dim embrasures to her garden, where she raised the thorns that covered every portion of the house. Within the garden ran a little stream, and while the dream was still fresh, if she had a bottle and paper, she would send another letter bobbing away to Duskin.

She turned to the door, intending to follow that very course, having recently found a fat flask with a cork stopper tucked into a cabinet in the newest portion of the house, but she gave a shriek to find a vulture-nosed anarchist standing at the threshold, eyes obscured by the brim of his hat.

"What does he want?" Lizbeth muttered under her breath, not knowing she spoke aloud.

"I've come to fetch you," he replied. "To see the Man in the Dark."

Her heart quailed, yet she replied bravely enough, "Very well. I shall come. Lead the way." She always spoke to the Man in the Dark's minions as if she obeyed them by choice, for he had told her she was to be a princess, and if she seldom felt like one, still she would play the part.

They wandered down the halls into that part of the house Lizbeth called her own, all hulking statues and red lamp-light, and then through a door normally kept locked into the Inner Chambers. They paced down the transverse corridor, a gloomy hall without ornamentation, and by-passing several rooms, ascended an angular stair to the second floor, where they followed the corridor to the left until reaching a pair of large, double doors, which the anarchist opened with a key. The room beyond marked the beginning to the inner sanctum of the Man in the Dark, a series of compartments that had grown, along with the rest of the house, since Lizbeth's capture.

She was guided through a sequence of passages ending in the room where he had first taken her heart. Her pulse quickened as she stepped to the onyx table at the center of the chamber, where a single, flickering gas lamp cast only a small circle of light. With relief, she saw the stone had not returned.

"Be seated," the anarchist ordered. She chose a carved chair from among the nine surrounding the table and began tracing her fingers along the cold armrests in anticipation. Finally, a deep voice rumbled from the shadows.

"How is my little princess?" The heavy form of the Man in the Dark loomed above her.

"I am well, thank you, sir," she replied.

"The thorns grow thicker every year, though I have told you to raise them no more."

"They are my sole amusement," she replied.

"You will cease this activity. This is to be an ordered house. The chaos of the thorns interrupts our progress."

Ever since her kidnapping, Lizbeth had to repress an urge to giggle when lectured. She did not know the cause for the impulse, but this time an involuntary laugh slipped from her tongue.

The Man in the Dark's fist struck her in the head, sending her sprawling across the floor. She cried out, but did not weep.

"There—that will do for the present," her tormentor said calmly, without passion. "I thought I had cured you of laughing, yet still you stare back with your belligerent eyes. When will you surrender to your fate? There will be order in this house, and in the world to come. You will be princess of that order. Remember that."

But Lizbeth's face had become a mask. She rose to her feet.

"Ahh, that's better. Your countenance is closer to being suitable. Yet still, you hold out hope; I see it in the house around me, in the thorns. Why is it so? Your life has been nothing but misery. Those you once loved have betrayed and forgotten you. Ah, I saw a glint of disbelief in your eyes concerning the latter. It, at least, I can prove. Perhaps then you will abandon your childish hopes, and realize the world must be changed. Behold!"

Lanterns were lit, revealing other anarchists standing close to the Man in the Dark. She tried to perceive his face, but it remained in shadow. From a dark door behind him, three horrid figures were led, their bodies all angles, their footsteps mechanical, only the barest hint of curvature on their cheeks, shoulders, and eyes. Their noses were sharp as the beaks of birds.

The first carried a long, black, stylized key, all squares and rectangles. A square clock was embedded in his chest, though the only number shown was zero, set at the 12 position. His dark hair fell upon his shoulders in angles resembling ringlets.

The second carried an ovoid lantern; the light issued from it in rectangular beams, like sunlight passing through dust. He wore a tall, square hat. His garments were black, with bits of poetry embroidered in jagged fashion upon them.

The third was clearly a woman, though her roundness had become all angles. She wore a pyramidal crown; her hands were fingerless, tapering points.

"What are these?" Lizbeth asked, her voice trembling.

"The new house requires a Lamp-lighter, a Windkeep, and a Lady of the House. This is Enoch, Chant, and Sarah, brought from the Inner Chambers."

A speechless terror fell upon Lizbeth. She stood trembling, and nearly toppled to her knees.

"Yes, we have changed them," the Man in the Dark said. "But they are unharmed. These are actually less geometric than those who stand upon the plain, proof the process is improving. Other transformations will follow, until they are more human than you or I have ever been. Indeed, they will be as gods. You may speak to them if you wish."

Lizbeth did not understand all of the Man in the Dark's

words, but she drew close to the woman and whispered, "Sarah? Is it you?"

"It . . . is," the creature replied, her mouth moving at inhuman angles.

"Are you . . . in pain?"

"I am . . . content," the voice sounded as Sarah's might if intermixed with the creaking of a rusted hinge. Lizbeth fought the tears welling in her eyes.

"I am . . . content," she said again. "I remember . . . a summer's day . . . when you and I and Carter picnicked beneath the trees, both your faces shining."

In all the years of suffering, this was more than Lizbeth could bear, that the anarchists should destroy the one person she loved most in all the world. Yet, she did not weep, but shaking violently, fell at Sarah's feet. "I hate you!" she screeched to the Man in the Dark.

"Perhaps, but surely you see you cannot return to the life you left. We are changing all the world; nothing will be the same when we are done. Never mind it will be a better place; for you there will be only despair. Yet, I will offer you a bargain. Last time we met, I asked you to imagine where the Cornerstone might have gone. Have you thought on this?"

"I don't know where it is," Lizbeth replied, wondering why he continued asking her about it.

"I want you to try harder to envision its location. And if you do, and we find it, I will return Sarah to her natural form. The others must remain changed."

Confused, Lizbeth sought to comply, but nothing came to her mind. Finally, in desperation, she said, "Perhaps in the attic?"

"Are you certain?"

"No, it's just a guess."

"Very well. You will return to your chambers now. If you think of anywhere else, you will report to us at once." The Man in the Dark turned to his followers, "Search the attics, and send the Windkeep and Lamp-lighter about their duties."

The anarchists left her outside the locked double doors leading to the Inner Chambers, where she fled to the walled garden at the back of the house. The thorns she had raised all emanated from this place, the roots massive, twisted, forming a maze only she could traverse. She went hurriedly, never stopping until she fell trembling beneath the roots at the very center of the thorn patch. The branches, thick as posts, fountained upward, forming a canopy over the garden walls before entwining through the rest of the house.

Though she did not weep, she shook and whimpered like a wounded pup, great gasping moans and groans and half-articulate cries. She burrowed as far beneath the predatory branches as she could, the cool earth her comfort. "Oh, Sarah," she murmured. "It's because of me! They've taken you because of me! It's dreadful. It's just too dreadful!" So chanting, she gradually drifted into a black slumber, with Sarah, Chant, and Enoch marching around the halls like strutting monsters.

A twinge of despair swept through Carter as he stood beside the crooked window and watched the beast rend his bedroll and devour his supplies, while a detached part of him considered the human capacity to cling to familiar things, be they only old blankets and a weather-stained pack. But the loss of his lantern was a real blow; he would have given much to regain it, though he saw it lying shattered, its glass glistening against the onyx.

He turned regretfully away and searched his pocket until he found a match. By its transient light he found himself in a tiny room, with unpainted walls and unfinished boards. He crossed quickly to a lopsided door and eased it open to discover a narrow stair with two-inch thorns trailing along one wall.

The light failed, leaving him once more in ebony. At least he had but one choice: to descend the stair. He drew his Lightning Sword, but it shone so dim as to illuminate nothing, as if its power had been quenched upon entrance to the house. He sheathed it once more, and felt his way along, staying to the left to avoid the brambles.

Once, his terror of the night would have overcome him; it did so no longer, but every man naturally fears, with primeval terror, the invisible jaws and claws of the dark. And this night was complete, redeemed by no flickering, no starlight, no reflections. The stair spiraled down; his boots sent hollow echoes; he kept his hand on the rail, eyes blindly gaping, breathless from the image of miles of nothing.

A thorn tore his hand; he recoiled from its bite. The tendrils must have crossed overhead from the right side to the left. He sucked blood from his palm, felt for the right railing, and was stung again, the brambles on both sides now. Feeling momentarily helpless, he reached back to the left, but lower, and located a part of the railing beneath the thorns, which he used to guide himself down. He traveled only six paces before the barbs thickened, forcing him to revert back to the right-hand rail. In this manner, he made his way, growing more angry each time the thorns cut him. The stair might well extend forever; he wished he had remembered to count his steps.

Then the railing gave way to empty space. He crouched on the bottom step and listened, but heard nothing, saw nothing, sensed nothing, save the creaking of the house. He knew he must either find a lamp or return back up the stair and through the window, in the slim hope of locating another, lighted entrance.

With a flourish of courage summoned because he knew he *was* afraid, he rose and drew his Lightning Sword, determined to explore before yielding to flight. He stepped forward and discovered a wall to his left, its plaster cool to the touch. He proceeded along it, ears straining, every footfall measured lest he stumble and fall. He numbered his steps, and at twelve reached another wall and received a nasty jab; every place he set his hand was thick with thorns. He turned to the right, keeping track of the wall by trailing his sword against it, and after another five paces, struck his ankle against more brambles. Grimacing in pain, he sprang back, and sat on the floor to nurse the wound. The thorns had penetrated his trousers; his shin was wet with blood. For a moment, his courage deserted him.

He sat still, rallying his strength. Sheer persistence kept him from returning to the stair, and he began rapping at the thorns with his sword to discover their boundaries. The brambles had grown from the wall and formed a solid mass extending outward four feet. Like a blind man tapping with his cane, Carter used his sword to steer around the tangle, but when he turned back toward the wall, it seemed to have vanished. At first he was uncertain, thinking to reach it any moment, but soon knew he had passed the position where it should have been. Apparently it had opened to another room or corridor. He shuffled back to the left, expecting to find where the wall turned, but again found nothing, and was now ten to fifteen paces off his course.

In desperation, he struck another match, leaving but two remaining. Its brief light revealed he had indeed wandered wholly from the previous room, having passed through one of two doors that now gaped before him from either side of a corner. He entered the one to the right, since at first glance it appeared the correct choice, its corridor running to right and left, but his flame expired before he could see more. Unwilling to use his remaining matches, he made his way to the right side of the corridor, which he anticipated would end shortly, bringing him back to the room where the brambles had cut his shin. When the corridor continued for twenty steps, he turned back, certain he had taken the wrong path. He found the doorway easily enough, entered the room, and took the left door. To his frustration, a wall stood to his right, and he chided himself for not realizing it would be so, since otherwise it would open into the corridor he had just departed.

He stood wholly baffled, uncertain where he had made the wrong turn. He took a few tentative steps to the left, but found it wholly illogical; only by going right could he regain the original room leading to the stair. He examined the right wall for doors, but discovered only thorns. Thirty paces he walked, but found no doorway. He decided to retrace his steps back to the room of the two doors; surely the right door was correct after all. He followed the wall back to the room, groped his way back down the right wall, and followed the corridor to the right. He reluctantly used another match, and discovered only a straight passage, the gray stones covered in brambles and gray mold. He hurried down the passage as long as his tiny torch would last, discarding it only when unable to bear its heat. The light had not illuminated the end of the corridor, so he did not know how long it was, yet felt certain it was the way he had come before, and must end soon.

He had walked thirty-two paces when his foot slipped into nothingness. He tottered precariously at the unknown brink, arms flailing, then tumbled, hands before him. Time froze as he fell; centuries passed before he struck the hard ground, jarring his shoulders and arms, and banging his knees. He lay moaning, all fear of discovery expelled by the agony in his shoulders. He gradually sat up and inspected his members, fearing broken bones. His left bicep hurt when he moved, and his left wrist was mildly sprained, but he was otherwise intact. Reviewing the plunge, he believed it had been only a few feet, but when he rose and tried to reach the ceiling, with the hope of climbing back out, he found nothing.

He reluctantly struck his last match, which snapped in two rather than igniting, the head vanishing into the darkness. He fumbled along the stone floor until he found it, but when he struck it again, it hissed and expired without flame.

Carter cursed and flung the match away. He sat back down, despair nearly driving him to tears, like a little boy left comfortless in the dark.

But he soon reminded himself such thoughts did no

good. *Things have been too easy the last few years. As the Master I had the Words of Power, and a thousand resources at my bidding. I could summon whole armies. Where are my armies now?* He forced himself to sit quietly, to calm his mind and consider his course, and after a moment, became aware of a dim, distant light. Using the left-hand wall as guide, he followed the corridor around a corner, where he discovered a flickering red gas jet, mounted at eye level. The crimson flame, the crumbling stones, and the thorns tendriled over the brazier gave the whole passage a hellish look, an image reinforced by a barred window in the ceiling. The brambles, which he saw clearly for the first time, sprouted barbs two inches long, extending from white, leprous branches soft as mushrooms, surely the only vegetation capable of living in such darkness. He gave an involuntary shiver.

Though he had light, it did no good; he was still trapped in the lower regions of the house, but at least the gas jet provided a reference while he searched for an exit, and eventually he might find material to use as a torch. He sighed. There was nothing to do but explore.

He found a scrap of paper and a dull pencil in his pocket and leaving the light behind, began mapping the area by feeling his way along the labyrinth of chambers and corridors. It seemed a bitter irony—he who had borne all the maps of Evenmere, reduced to scrawling lines on foolscap. He found less than a dozen doors, more than half of which were locked. The search wore on his nerves since he always expected to encounter an occupant sleeping on a bed, but the rooms were empty of either furniture or inhabitants, though not of the wicked thorns that cut him. He journeyed as far as he could remember before returning to the lamp to scrawl his map.

Hunger crept upon him; by his watch it was long past noon and he had eaten nothing since breakfast. Neither had he any water; he sat studying his simple map beneath the solitary hiss of the gas jet, trying to disregard his rising thirst. A dread was growing on him each time he plunged into the darkness, a fear of finding something, of something finding him, a beast with teeth of iron and claws of brass.

"Imagination," he spoke aloud, though the sound of his own voice startled him. "Childish fantasies."

He wanted to sleep, to forget this nightmare of hunger and darkness, but he pushed himself to his feet. He was not yet finished with the corridor to his right. He determined to follow it as far as he could, so long as he could remember his way. He drew a deep breath and stepped out of the circle of light, down the turning of the passage.

Hours later, he stumbled back, weary beyond hope, having followed the main corridor to the blank wall of stone at its very end. He had found no stair, though there had been scores of intersecting passages, any one of which might lead him to freedom, could he but choose correctly. More than once he had nearly lost his way; it was so easy to inadvertently pass through a doorway and leave the main corridor. And it was hard to concentrate in the darkness; prayers and snatches of song drifted through his mind.

He cast himself upon the stone floor. For the first time it occurred to him he might be hopelessly lost, that he might die of thirst here, alone. He had known failure before—his inability to find Lizbeth had haunted him for years—yet from the day the spirit of Brittle proclaimed him ordained to be Master, he had thought himself protected by the hand of God. Still, he always knew, in the depths of his soul, he was but a servant to the High House. No man given such a charge could be immune to vanity, but the Masters before him had not always met pleasant fates, though they, too, must have been chosen. And every man was ordained once to die.

He gave a grim chuckle, wondering if that included Enoch. Or would the old Windkeep live till the end of time itself?

It would be so unfair to die here, he thought. *In the dark, after surviving my battle with the Bobby in the well. Especially with the threat of the False House hanging over all. Yet, isn't the cry of "unfair" that of a child? I've spent my whole life calling things unfair—my exile, my father's death. Unfair compared to what? What standard of perfection does the smallest child use to cry "unfair"?*

"I'm rambling," he muttered. "And I'm thirsty."

He glided into an uncomfortable sleep, and dreamed of wandering endless black corridors without a lamp.

Since reading her book, raising her thorns, and visiting the latest additions to the house were her sole occupations, Lizbeth had become an explorer. She never saw any workers building the new wings, never heard the scrape of plane or saw, but often discovered a new door opening into a fresh addition, made as if by magic. Each section in turn she learned by heart, and could traverse most of the house wholly in the dark, save only those portions in which she was forbidden.

She left her dingy bedroom and proceeded down a narrow, high-ceilinged corridor, a landscape of red gas jets, havens of light between heavy darkness. Statues dotted the gloom, angular monsters, eyes all asymmetric, leering abstractions, given life by the twilight. She did not fear them; she had given each its name.

Floor grates provided a view of the basement below, where, too, burned the red-flamed lamps. She had journeyed there as well, though it had taken two years to find her way down through a winding maze of passages. She had even been lost a time, and had wandered many hours through the darkness, finally forced to use two of her precious candles to return to the main halls. Thereafter she became as expert in that part of the house as any other.

She passed through the Master Hall, a vast chamber with a high ceiling, geometric carvings within rectangular naves, and massive, triangular chandeliers that were never lit. From the center of the room, an ebony staircase swept like a bat to the upper stories. Against a wall stood the only furniture, a table of heavy, black onyx, with a headboard down one side. It could have seated twenty, but there were only five chairs, their backs shaped like scallop shells, rounded forward like black waves crashing toward the table. There, she took her meals, which were lowered from a dumbwaiter in the corner.

She passed through the chamber, her bare feet slapping the swirled marble floor, sending angel-wing echoes flapping to every corner, absentmindedly reciting: *"He imagines me in a pet—in play, perhaps. Cannot you inform him that it is in frightful earnest? Nelly, if it be not too late, as soon as I learn how he feels, I'll choose between these two; either to starve at once—that would be no punishment unless he had a heart—or to recover and leave the country."* Another passage lapped her up; the echoes died to cherub flutters. For reasons no longer remembered, she called this corridor the Stone Lanes.

As she crossed another of the grates, she abruptly pressed herself against the wall, having glimpsed a form in the corridor below. She leaned her head forward, peering cautiously down, and saw a man propped against one wall, sitting beneath the red fire of the gas jet. His face remained hidden; he appeared asleep. At first she thought him an anarchist, but his garments were not their customary gray.

Here was a wonder beyond belief! A stranger in the house. She stood breathless, heart trembling. Had someone dared the black plain? Was it a wanderer, a vagabond, an outcast, or perhaps, even, a deliverer? She dared another look; the hair was neither gold as Duskin's, nor gray as her father's, but jet-black. The leopard-spotted mantle awoke a memory, both happy and frightening at once, but too dim to recall.

She crept around the grate, keeping her eyes upon him, longing to see his face. She lowered herself, cross-legged to the floor, determined to keep vigil until he should rouse. Five minutes passed, then ten, before her natural impatience overtook her; she was quite used to doing exactly as she wished within the miserly limits of her captivity. She searched the floor until she found a pebble, held it over the grate, and released. It bounced off his shoulder, but he did not respond. She sought another stone, slightly larger, though still no greater than her little finger. Chance favored her this time, for the missile struck his head. He stiffened, glanced from side to side, and looked up.

Lizbeth shrieked; she could not help it. Here was the face of her hated enemy, the monster from her dreams, her betrayer, Carter Anderson. She leapt to her feet and fled, blind from fear, expecting at any moment to be seized from behind. She bounded through the halls, past cracked walls and half-formed sculptures, her bare feet slapping wood and stone, reaching, at last, her garden sanctuary. Beneath the tender mercies of the cruel thorns she lay still; all thoughts left her; her terror was too great.

She roused, yet another hour passed before she could think clearly. Then she wondered whether he could find his way up the stair—she attributed to him many awful powers—but began to believe he might not be able to reach her. Never once did she question why he had come; just as easily ask why the storm breaks, or the maelstrom wails. To her he was such a force, like summer clouds turned to hurricane heights, a friend who had forsaken her.

She slipped from beneath the brambles. The gas jets on the garden walls cast half-light for her way as she retraced her path through the thorns. She gave no thought to the bloodstains on her arms and legs from her earlier head-long rush; the thorns had cut her many times before.

Because she kept expecting to confront Carter at any moment, as she had so often in her dreams, it took much skulking to return to the grate. When she finally peered back over its edge she saw him standing, consulting a hand-scrawled map.

He's lost, she thought in wonder. *He can't get out*. A

flood of exultation filled her. She wanted to shout! The monster was trapped! She knelt by the grate to observe.

With disappointment, she saw he did not appear frightened, but calmly consulted his map, then vanished into the darkness.

Terror overtook her as she realized he had gone down the corridor that might lead to the stair. Her mind whirled. It was difficult to find, yet if he did . . .

She scurried out the corridor through a series of rooms, down a passage into a narrow chamber, where lay a solitary flight of steps. She flew down the stair that ended at a thin, sliding door and searched frantically for a piece of wood to wedge behind it, to prevent its opening, but the flickering lamp revealed nothing useful. Heart fluttering, she bolted back up the stair and after a frenzied search, located several boards in the back of a narrow chamber. They clattered against one another as she crept cautiously down, her fear of encountering him almost unbearable. The stairwell remained empty; the door shut.

She struggled to wedge the boards into place, then stepped back to judge her work. It would not prevent Carter from breaking through the door if he learned of its existence, but in the dark, with it barred, he would think it only a panel. She quietly ascended, casting many glances behind her.

She scampered to the grate and sat down to wait. More than an hour passed, and she soon returned to the top of the stair and listened for any sign of Carter trying the panel. Hearing nothing, she returned to the grate. This action she repeated innumerable times before Carter finally stepped into the gaslight. Sweat beaded his brow. He slumped against the wall and slid down, looking weary and lost.

A wisp of sympathy moved her; he looked much smaller than she remembered, almost fragile. Time had not blocked her early memories of him, his kindness, his gentle laugh, the way he had looked at Sarah, but these she considered villainous ploys, meant to entrap her. She had often lain awake wondering what evil he had done to Sarah. Still, he did not seem so wicked, sitting there exhausted.

She clenched her fists, pushing such thoughts away. She was older now and could see through the deception. "He's like Heathcliff," she said, "promising love, giving only ruin in the end."

"Who's there?" Carter asked, peering up toward the grate.

She backed against the corner, hand to mouth, wild with terror. It was hard to keep the inside and outside thoughts separate.

"Someone is there," Carter said. "Won't you speak? I've become lost in the house."

She crept closer to the grate, fascination overcoming her terror. *"He is really here, madame."* she quoted softly. *"Not as phantom, or illusion, but in the flesh."*

"What's that?" Carter said, his own voice hushed. "I couldn't hear."

Lizbeth bit her lip. *Inside thoughts and outside thoughts.* Yet she could not resist addressing her adversary. She lowered her voice. "I am the ghost of Catherine Linton. Have you come seeking proof the place was haunted? Well, it is—swarming with ghosts and goblins. *Last night I was in the Grange garden six hours, and I'll*

return there tonight; and every night I'll haunt the place.
Why have you invaded my house?"

Lizbeth could see Carter squinting to catch a glimpse
of her. She knelt with her face close to the grate, but at its
edge. "I don't believe in ghosts," he said. "Can you help
me find my way to you?"

"You will never find a way," she said. "Begone! I'll
never let you in, not if you beg for twenty years."

"Will you give me no aid?"

"Perhaps I could help you, if you would tell me why
you have come. *Have you nothing to show your cousin
anywhere about, not even a rabbit or a weasel's nest?*"

Carter cocked his head in a knowing way. "I am seeking a young woman named Lizbeth Powell. She has been
here many years. I want to take her home, if she will
come. Do you know her?"

Lizbeth mused aloud, not knowing she did so, *"It was
not because I disliked Mr. Heathcliff, but because Mr.
Heathcliff dislikes me and is a most diabolical man, de-
lighting to wrong and ruin those he hates, if they give him
the slightest opportunity."*

"I do not understand," he said. "What cause have you
to disbelieve me?"

"I have seen your works and know your ways," she
replied.

"I ask again, do you know her?"

"Perhaps I do. Perhaps I am her friend. Why would you
bother to help her?"

"I have sought her all the years since her disappearance. She was kidnapped from Innman Tor. I want to free
her from this house."

"Lies!" Lizbeth cried, forgetting her role. This was not

going as she expected. "You're lying again!" She gave a high-pitched squeal of rage.

"Lizbeth, is that you?"

It was all too much. Even trapped, he was gaining the upper hand. Already, he knew her. Eventually he might deceive her into freeing him. He was too persuasive, too powerful, a dark god of evil. She backed away, shrieking the words: *"It is twenty years—twenty years. I've been a waif for twenty years!"* and tore down the halls, back toward her garden. Once more she fled through the maze of thorns and threw herself beneath the great root. There she remained several hours, reciting over and over, *"You should not have spoken to him! He was in a bad temper, and now you've spoilt your visit; and he'll be flogged—I hate him to be flogged! I can't eat my dinner. Why did you speak to him, Edgar?"*

At last she quieted herself and said triumphantly, "I will say no more until he is weak with thirst."

The Inner Chambers

Duskin and Gregory sat resting beneath the cyclopean eye created by crimson gas jets encircling the center of a vast ocher dome. The dim lamps illuminated nothing of the chamber below, which lay void of all design, as if the storage room for every architectural flaw. Other lamps hung suspended thirty feet in the air, lighting nothing. A stair climbed halfway up the center of the room, landing by landing, only to end in empty space. Beams and pillars crossed, supporting no structures; parts of the floor opened into an empty abyss. The galleries hung vertically rather than horizonal. One-dimensional frescoes, blue, green, and gold, circled the chamber, their content non-sense, heads and hands mingled with random objects, without form or balance, hieroglyphs gone mad. Geometric gargoyles squinted from the moldings and upon the baseboards and lintels were carved random sequences of numbers and numerals, nonsense words. Angular bats, harsh-winged, with faces sharp as quill pens, performed symmetrical dances between the rafters, emitting shrieks like nails on glass. Tiny spiders skittered up the walls like eight-legged levers.

Duskin had extinguished his own lamp while they rested. He was covered in sweat, half-blind in the dim light, and certain they were hopelessly lost. They had been wandering through the muddle of the house for three days without sighting a soul. Duskin glanced at his cousin; he was sound asleep, his mouth working as if he dreamed. He gave a startled cry and sat up abruptly, eyes flung wide.

"You all right?" Duskin asked.

Gregory glanced around, realized where he was, sighed, and rubbed his eyes. "Just a bad dream."

"Who wouldn't have nightmares here? No furniture, no inhabitants, little light, as if it were a giant mausoleum."

"It isn't ready for dwelling yet," Gregory said. "It's unfinished. But I expected to find more anarchists as well."

"It's a madhouse. Odd-shaped rooms, corridors going nowhere, ceilings too low to walk under. I thought it would be more scientific. If the anarchists are tapping Order, why is it so chaotic?"

"Perhaps they're learning how to proceed," Gregory said. "Imagine a group of intellectuals banded together for the common purpose of altering the universe, men daring to transform the physical laws of nature. Foolhardy, perhaps, but brave. The Cornerstone gives them a means; they must discover the method. It requires experimentation. The transformation of the people of Moomuth Kethorvian is a preliminary step, obviously much less than what the anarchists want. So, too, this part of the house. Chances must be taken to create a perfect world;

their ability to modify portions of Evenmere shows some success."

"They're certainly successful at concealing themselves." Duskin peered up at the black rafters. "You make them sound like heroes."

Gregory gave a grin. "I like to look at an issue from all sides. How can you know your own opinion unless you know that of your opponent?"

"I don't know, but we better be on our way. As large as this house is, we could be wandering for weeks."

Duskin rose and lit the lamp. They passed beneath the grand dome into a drab corridor, which immediately split into three angling passages. Carved masks hung on every inch of the walls, staring blankly at the lantern glow, and the vicious, ubiquitous thorns twisted through the eye slits, the lamp-light turning their twining shadows into coiled adders, spiked crosses, witch faces, and the maws of sea serpents. The air was chill, but stifling, unnatural as everything else within the house. The wood, the walls, the knobs of the doors, all had an unearthly texture. Duskin could find no words to describe it, except it seemed utterly alien. It wore on the spirit; he was hopelessly weary, unable to concentrate on his mission, worried about his brother. Was Gregory right? Did the anarchists have a valid viewpoint? Were he and Carter simply part of an old order, the intractable leaders of a dying union? Duskin realized he actually knew nothing about anarchist doctrine.

They wandered the architectural waste another eight hours, crossing rickety bridges surmounting limitless drops, opening doors to brick walls, turning corners to contorted carvings leering in the lamp-light, until both men were nervous and cross-eyed from squinting in the gloom. After making a meager supper of their rations, they threw their bedrolls on the bare floor, where Duskin spent the night turning through dreams of carrying dirt from one hole to another with a spoon. When at last Gregory roused him, six hours later, he gratefully dragged himself up, muttering, "I hate the dark."

Five hours into their journey they stepped through a pair of four-panel doors, into a corridor with oak wainscoting, carpeted in malachite green, with a rosewood console near the entrance. Regularly spaced gas jets burned in their braziers, and a coat of arms hung on one wall with the words *Mundus Vult Decipi* emblazoned upon it. A tapestry hung farther down the way, depicting a large body of brooding men in tall hats, peering into the passage with guardian eyes.

"It appears more orderly," Duskin whispered.

Gregory smiled. "Let's go."

Duskin shivered involuntarily as they passed the watchful figures in the tapestry, for they were clearly garbed in anarchist gray.

They passed several doors without encountering opposition, and quickly came to a staircase of most unusual design, its steps supported by metal poles, lacking banister and balustrade, hanging stark and brutal, as if from another, futuristic era. They stood at its top landing, where an abstract, silver depiction of a bird of prey descended from the ceiling, its beak a triangle, its wings severely angled. Duskin glanced at the corridor below, then back to the stair.

"This looks like the anarchists' version of the transverse corridor within the Inner Chambers of Evenmere," he said. "Amazing!"

"Yes," Gregory said. "we have penetrated to the heart of the house."

The slam of a door echoed down the passage.

"Down the stair," Gregory whispered, and quickly led to the second floor, where lay another deserted passage. Footsteps followed on the steps.

Gregory tried the knob of the double doors beside the staircase, which opened into a mercifully empty room. Together they fled through compartments and corridors, until Gregory paused at last in a long, shadowy chamber, lit by a single red lamp, with various mechanisms standing at the lamp-light's edge. An onyx table surrounded by nine chairs stretched into the shadows. Duskin peered into the darkness, uncertain if they were alone. Gregory threw himself into a chair and propped his feet on the table.

"We should be safe here," he said at last, almost nonchalantly. But he had always been a confident man.

"Are you certain? Anyone could enter."

"As dark as it is, I doubt it's much used."

"We need a plan to locate the Cornerstone," Duskin said, taking a chair.

Gregory sat up and drew close to his cousin, so their faces nearly touched. "Duskin, what if the anarchists are correct in their designs?"

"Are you mad? We've no time for philosophy."

"I no longer speak philosophically. The anarchists have harnessed energies capable of changing the face of civilization. Has it never occurred to you they might be as dedicated, and just, as you, Carter, Enoch, or any of us? Certainly, wrongs have been done in the name of anarchy, but wrongs have been done in the name of government, religion, in the name of mercy itself."

"What are you saying?" Duskin asked. His weariness made him angry. "All you've talked about for the last three days is the nobility of the anarchist cause."

"I'm asking you to examine your beliefs. Why did your mother become an anarchist?"

"For the love of power."

Gregory shook his head. "Too simple, cousin. Have you ever wondered why the Bobby cast her into the Room of Horrors? She had many connections in the house; she could have been valuable to his cause."

"He was evil. It was pure spite."

"Nonsense! The Bobby was not given to emotion. Even as a tool, Aunt Murmur would have been useful. No, she was punished because she was no longer trusted. She had been a member of the anarchy party most of her life, even as a little girl in Meszria. She was raised an anarchist."

Duskin sat stunned, uncertain whether to believe. Yet, he *had* wondered why the anarchists cast his mother aside. "If what you say is true, the Bobby should have embraced her."

"And he would have, if she had not betrayed him before. When she met and married your father there was rejoicing in the anarchist camp. The engagement had not been planned by the party; Aunt Murmur met your father by chance, though of course she ran in the necessary circles. Naturally, the anarchists expected to take advantage. Imagine their shock when Murmur turned from them; she did indeed seek power, and was willing to betray her own people to have it. She forgot the cause, forsook the grand revolution, for the splendor of being First Lady of Evenmere. In the end she regretted it; Uncle Ashton never allowed her the power she craved. When she aspired to destroy Carter, so you might become Master, she contacted the Bobby, thinking to return to his graces. But the Society of Anarchists requires loyalty, sacrifice, heroism if necessary. She was a traitor, and paid the price."

Duskin sat, fists clenched.

Gregory studied his comrade closely. "I know it's a bit of a blow. Are you all right?"

"A bit? You say my mother was a traitor not only to Evenmere, but to the anarchists as well? Was there nothing she wouldn't do? But how do you know all this, unless . . ." Duskin rose to his feet. "Are you an anarchist as well?"

"Most of your family are anarchists," Gregory said, leaning back in his chair. "Your uncle Corinius, for example."

"Corinius? That kindly old man. You must be joking!"

"Grandfather Gorice has served twice as Grand Marshal of the Western District. My father, most of your cousins. Myself. Anarchists all."

Enraged, Duskin hurled himself at his cousin, knocking him from his chair to the floor, then leapt upon him before he could rise.

Light bloomed from one corner of the chamber. Duskin bounded to his feet, while Gregory broke away and made a sweeping gesture around a room containing a high gallery, with dozens of forms watching from the shadows. Duskin reached for his pistol, but Gregory stepped before him.

"Don't be foolish, cousin. You would die instantly. You're surrounded. Put that away."

Duskin gripped the Colt. It was all too much. Despite Gregory's betrayal he could not bring himself to train the weapon on his comrade. He let it fall to the floor. "What will you do with me?"

Gregory gave an encouraging smile. "That depends on you." He turned expectantly toward the area beneath one of the galleries, where a round door opened and a figure stepped out, swathed in black, his face hidden by a slouched hat, like ancient Odin walking the worlds, a powerful man, even discounting his heavy garb. He made his way to the table.

"This is the Man in the Dark," Gregory said. "The Supreme Anarchist. He has led since the passing of the Bobby."

"A butcher," Duskin said.

"No," Gregory replied, eyes on his cousin's face. "A saint. He will save the world."

"Well done, brother," the Man in the Dark said in a muted voice, shaking Gregory's hand. "And greetings to you, Duskin Anderson. No doubt Gregory has given you much to deliberate."

Duskin glanced at his cousin. "Has it been your assignment to spy upon me all these years?"

"You wrong me," Gregory said. "My mission was to return you to the fold, a familial duty. Our friendship has not been counterfeit."

"It has not," the Supreme Anarchist said. "Gregory has twice saved your life, the first time by persuading the Anarchist Council to cancel your assassination, planned to weaken your brother's resolve. I understand he also recently kept you from a gnawling's claws at Middlecourt."

"The last, at least, is true," Duskin said. "You are well informed."

"And you were born to a proud tradition," the Man in

the Dark continued. "Even your mother was once a patriot, though she proved irresolute in the end. It is that kind of moral lapse we wish to eliminate. The anarchy party has existed for decades. Have you never wondered why? The High House is a monarchy, whatever we call it. Oh, there are councils and parliaments within the countries; the dukes and barons do not possess the power they once held, but at the very top, the Balance, which determines the laws of the universe, is controlled by the Master."

"That's certainly a simplification," Duskin said. "The Master serves the house, and is no true monarch. The countries govern themselves, while the Master coordinates efforts involving the stability of Existence. But even if what you say is true, if the Master is just, what of it?"

The anarchist gave a nod beneath his heavy robes. "Yes! If the Master is just. And Carter is a just man, in his way. An honest man. But there is a higher justice. The founders of anarchy saw the potential to create a world of true equality, without pain, illness, poverty, or death. Is this a worthy goal?"

"You have murdered in its name."

Plates of steaming beef and flagons of wine were rushed to the table just then.

The Man in the Dark sat down in a chair and made a broad gesture. "Sit! Eat! I know you are starving for real food rather than cold rations."

Duskin reluctantly resumed his seat, though he did not eat.

"Yes, we have murdered," the Man in the Dark said. "Blood is spilled in any revolution. Did the patriots of Nianar take arms against Kitinthim rule? Were the gallows of Ooz necessary to sweep away the aristocracy? And our calling is even more lofty! We seek a universe containing nothing but good because it *can* contain nothing but good, its men like gods, immortal, wholly moral, minds balanced between art and science. A goal worth slaying millions! But when the killing stops, it will end forever. When the war is won, eternal peace will reign."

"You are persuasive," Duskin said. "But what do you want of me? Why should you care if I follow your cause?"

"First, because you are one of us. Secondly, this house, like Evenmere, requires a Master, a man to shake his fist at God and the saints, to take the reins, whip the steeds into frenzy, and carry mankind screaming into a golden age."

"You blaspheme," Duskin said.

"Perhaps I do. But if there is a God, He has fashioned a world of sorrow; I should expect His blessings on those who would change it. And if He built Evenmere, as it is said, why did He leave the Cornerstone to be found? Could it not have been His intention for men to use it to forge a better world? Could that be part of our own evolution? And if this were true, might you not be defying God's will by opposing us? You can be the commander, guiding all to light, the ultimate rebel in the final insurrection."

"You offer the role of Lucifer. I assumed you would reserve that privilege for yourself."

"You misunderstand. I have other plans, more momentous than the mere acquisition of power, ambitions neither of you can comprehend. I have always been a deep well compared to those surrounding me, beyond the understanding of common men."

"Why do you need me? Any of your followers could serve as Master. Gregory, for example. He's competent enough to make a great show of finding a way into this chamber, presumably to have more time to convert me."

"You're wrong about that," Gregory said. "Except for the secret entrance, the house has changed since last I was here. I did take the opportunity to seek to convince you."

"Gaining control of the power of the Cornerstone has proven most difficult," the anarchist said. "Even as Evenmere chooses its Masters, so too does this house. We have tried . . . other Masters. The results were unsuccessful. We believe the house will accept you, if you volunteer to serve."

"I see," Duskin said, inwardly shuddering at the possibilities in the word *unsuccessful.* "Your creation has a mind of its own. Or are the thorns part of your plan as well?"

The Supreme Anarchist gave a grim chuckle. "We are not wizards, just men seeking a scientifically rational universe. The thorns are a by-product of Lizbeth's psyche. She has free run of the west wing, and we cannot control all her impulses."

"So she is the catalyst?"

The Man in the Dark shrugged beneath his cloak. "Yes. We knew you would suspect. The power of the Cornerstone is directed through her. This house is a combination of her construction and our own. We have kept her isolated in an empty environment that passions might be removed from the New Creation, and given her only *Wuthering Heights* as a guide, that she might see the futility of humanity's cravings."

"And you use her as a weapon to maintain the winter?"

"We do. I make no apologies. We take whatever means

necessary to confound Lord Anderson, to keep him occupied until our work is complete. We regret innocents must
suffer."

"As Master, I would become as the mechanized men
upon the plain?"

"Yes and no, for they will not remain as they are now.
I admit their horror; I grant their repugnance, but they are
but part of the first step, which is to eliminate death. That
must be done earliest, for it will require more than one
lifetime to achieve ultimate perfection, and the changed
men upon the plain, however repulsive, are immortal,
save some accident befall them; eventually, even chance
mishaps will lie outside the realm of probability. When
they are risen to their fullness, they will be glorious. Glorious! I speak of metamorphosis as complete as the but-
terfly breaking from its cocoon."

"You speak of limiting choices."

"Yes!" The Man in the Dark's voice rose in passion.
"Choices toward evil and death. What man would not
choose the good if only he knew how? Everything we
have done has been for the greater benefit."

"As you can see, cousin, we aren't the wretches you
imagined," Gregory said. "The anarchists have always
been intellectual warriors in a noble battle."

"And what does that make my brother?" Duskin asked,
thinking Carter was probably within the house by now.

"An unenlightened man," the Man in the Dark said. "We
will welcome him into our brotherhood, in time. But, for
now, Gregory will show you to quarters, so you may consider all we have said. There you will find a copy of *Cults
de Résistance,* written by the founder of the anarchist
movement, Ludvig Prinn. Perhaps you might peruse it."

"Perhaps," Duskin said.

The Man in the Dark followed Duskin and Gregory to the hallway door, with two armed anarchists behind.

"Before we go, brother," Gregory said to the Man in the Dark, "I need to know our situation. Why is the house so empty? Materials are pouring in from Shyntawgwin. Where are they taken? When I return to Evenmere, I must report to our comrades, who have been concerned by the lack of correspondence."

"The materials are being stockpiled for eventual use. As for the men, I sent most onto the plain," the Supreme Anarchist said gruffly.

Gregory gaped in astonishment. "Onto the plain? You . . . changed them?"

"They are more compliant that way, and nearer to perfection. What has been done for one will eventually be done for all. I saw no need for them to wait."

Gregory's eyes blazed in anger. "What is the meaning? Is this the man to whom I pledged my loyalty? Has the darkness driven you insane?"

"My plans are deeper than you can know. You must trust me, if I am to lead the world into perfection."

Gregory stepped forward, fists doubled, before the shrouded face of the Man in the Dark, as if he would strike him. "I demand an explanation!"

It was the opening Duskin sought, and in that instant, with Gregory between him and the guns of the anarchists, his time spent learning to strike quickly while hunting the gnawlings served him well. Even as Gregory stepped forward, Duskin drew a knife from the inner pocket of his coat, grasped his cousin from behind, and pressed the blade to his throat.

"Back!" Duskin cried as the guards sought to close. "Though I have loved him as a brother I will slay for Evenmere's sake."

"Put that aside!" the Supreme Anarchist demanded, though he waved the guards behind him. "You cannot escape."

Under normal circumstances, Duskin could not have handled Gregory so easily, but the actions of the Supreme Anarchist had clearly bewildered his cousin. Duskin backed down the corridor, Gregory in tow, while the Man in the Dark and the guards stood helpless at the door. At the corner, Duskin cast Gregory to the floor and fled, bounding for the next turn as running feet and rifle bolts clattered in place behind him.

Gregory cried, "No!" at his back, and a shot slammed wild into the ceiling above Duskin. He rounded the corner as more bullets hammered the wall.

The corridor turned several times, presenting various outlets, and Duskin quickly lost himself in the vagaries of the house. Finally, he halted, panting and dripping with sweat.

Thank you, cousin, he thought bitterly. *You have saved my life a third time. But it will not stay my hand when next we meet.*

But his anger burned away, leaving him morose. Arrogant Gregory, spouting anarchist philosophy since their college days as if it were a parlor game, and even then seeking to convert him.

He needed to find Lizbeth, who he now knew was the key to the house. Though he did not know her location, she was surely near, and had written of raising thorns in her garden. If the brambles originated there, he might find her by following those trailing along the wall.

He pursued the tangle swiftly, his mind a blur of thoughts, of Gregory, Bellgrove, his uncles, and his grandfather, all anarchists. It was his cousin who had insisted he take Bellgrove's class at university. How much of his life had Gregory manipulated? They had rampaged like boys since college, hunting gnawlings, seeking sport everywhere, taking nothing seriously. Perhaps Duskin had chosen to feel alienated from Carter's world of politics, but Gregory had been there to offer other, more exciting diversions.

Duskin paused, wounded to the heart by Gregory's betrayal, shattered at knowing they would never hunt gnawlings together again.

As for the anarchist doctrine, certainly society should better itself, but if the Supreme Anarchist imagined creating an unselfish world from the dreams of selfish men, could the sum be greater than the parts? The loss of personal will could not be worth an end to pain and death; the creatures on the plain proved that. And despite the anarchist's confident words, something was wrong both in the house, and with the Man in the Dark himself, else he would never have transformed his own people.

Duskin increased his pace. He had to find Lizbeth and prevent these idealists from destroying the world.

The Clock Tower

Carter grew weaker each hour. He had run out of water two days before; his lips were parched; it was difficult to think, and there was only the darkness and the red flame of the gas lamp. A despair was upon him, a fear God had forsaken him, a fear of failure. More than anything he longed for Sarah. If he died here would she know? Would her gentle heart sense his passing? He was anxious for her as well, as if she were in danger, though he ascribed such concerns to delusions wrought by thirst.

Following his most recent ordeal seeking a passage in the dark, where he had found a barred, impenetrable door, he fell to his knees in prayer and meditation, uncertain if he could go on. His mind wandered; for a time he slept, still kneeling, and dreamed of wandering a desert place, with wind stirring the leaves of the arid vegetation. All alone he went, looking for he knew not what, and at last came to rest beside a great rock, with cherubim and runes etched upon it. And in the dream he knew why he wandered the waste, for as the prophets of old, he had come seeking wisdom.

He awoke, and as he rose stiffly to his feet, his dolor fell from him like a cloak. Though still imprisoned, he felt free for the first time since learning of the Cornerstone. With sudden clarity, he realized he had walked without faith or hope throughout his mission, overwhelmed by the forces against him, overcome by the burden of responsibility, vanquished before having fought. He had deceived himself to his own undoing.

For the first time in many days he laughed, a grim cackle from his parched throat. I've . . . been . . . a . . . fool!" he said, tasting each word, knowing them to be true. And despite his situation, though part of him feared it might be mere fantasies wrought by hunger, he was happy, there in the darkness, to be alive, to strive against hopelessness, to defy the anarchists with all his strength, whether in victory or defeat.

And in that strangely triumphant moment, deep within him, he sensed the barest touch of the Words of Power, as if he might yet be a lesser conduit for their might.

Not daring to question the possibilities, he pulled himself to his feet and paced down the corridor, sighing as the slender beams of the lamp vanished at the corner turning. With the darkness all around to aid his concentration, he sat akimbo and meditated upon the Word of Secret Ways. He dispelled his doubts and concentrated, thinking of how he had first seen the Word in the Book of Forgotten Things, its letters glowing like flaming brass; and of the times he had used it in Evenmere. He searched for it, eyes closed, as if he stared across a black, infinite plain, but saw only darkness as empty as the endless halls of the

False House. His despair came rustling like moth's wings. His concentration wandered, drifting to thoughts of Sarah, the house, his father—a dozen other things. He brought his mind back into focus and began again.

Several moments passed before he saw, deep in the darkness, a single dot of orange light. He waited as it rose toward him, not bursting in his mind as it had always done, but hovering, a firefly flame, in the distance. Still, he could read it and feel its faint power. Had it been the Word Which Gives Strength or the Word Which Seals, it would not have been enough, but the Word of Secret Ways, which requires less potency, might give sufficient light to show *his* way. He called it with his thoughts, felt its warm regard, knew it as Force Incarnate in slight form, not power wielded, but power wielding. He could not stoke the flames; they stoked themselves.

He spoke the Word, a whisper. There was no manifestation, no shaking of the room, no noise at all save a soft murmur pattering down the passage. He did not know if he had succeeded, and peering down the corridor he saw no square of light.

He drew the shard from his pocket. Its pull was strong; it would lead him to the Cornerstone if only he could escape. A distinct impression came to his mind that encouraged him further, a certain knowledge that the Cornerstone itself was *resisting* the anarchists' attempts to change the house, almost as if it were a living entity.

Accepting the paradox as fact, he gave a grim smile, pocketed the shard, and shuffled forward, counting his steps. The first door was twelve paces and opened into an empty room; the one after lay twenty-seven steps from that one. On and on the corridor went, as he made the circuit, finishing at last in a series of rooms where he had spent more than one lost hour. He kept to the right, persevering even when thorns wounded his hands, and quickly discovered another doorway, which he left unexplored until he had made a full exploration of the room. Finding nothing but brambles, he retraced his way back to the other door.

Again, he kept to the right, and his breath caught in his throat as he detected a luminous glow, faint in the distance. Keeping one hand on the wall, he approached the glimmer; almost it seemed a trick of his eyes, so subtle was the shine, yet it was surely present—dull blue and wavering. He ran his hands along the wall and pressed a rectangular button at the edge of the baseboard, causing a panel to pop open with a sweet click. Reaching into the darkness, he discovered a narrow stair.

He took the first step and immediately banged his head against the ceiling, a blow that sent him to his knees, softly moaning, clutching his skull in pain. As the agony subsided, he felt his forehead; a knot was rising but without blood, and he ruefully considered the irony of escaping the basement only to die by clumsiness.

He returned to the opening, felt the low ceiling, then crouched and began a gradual ascent up a spiral stair, its steps so unevenly spaced as to make climbing awkward. The air lay still and stifling; he drew a deep breath to steady his fear as he climbed, one careful step at a time, through the night. The terror of every child fell upon him, of being seized by hidden hands, even as part of him wondered why it should be so for one long without light.

He paused, clutching the rail, mustering his courage. The resolute face of his father came unbidden to his memory, looking as it had the day he smashed the door to free Carter from the Room of Horrors. He envisioned the eyes quite clearly. The recollection strengthened him; he resumed his ascent.

When he had taken a hundred steps—he could not help but count—he became aware of a distant light, high above. As he drew near, its illumination revealed the stair to be not only spiraled but angled, rising upward and out, a clumsy architectural wonder of dark oak, with surrealistic cubes—the anarchists' version of sculpture—carved atop the newel posts.

He stepped onto a landing where the red, flickering gas jet scattered spindly shadows across the wall. Finding no exit, he continued upward, and the light dwindled below. Up and up he went, past seven lighted landings, coming at last to another floor, its polished boards shining beneath the eye of a single, yellow lamp. The light crept hardly far; the ceiling lay shrouded in ebony. The slow echoes of his footfalls hinted a cavernous space. He searched about and to his wonder found a torn glove, a discarded hat, and a toppled lantern a few feet from the stair. He snatched the lamp, inspected it for oil, and being satisfied, lit it from the gas jet. As its soft glow expanded he saw a smear of dried blood beside the glove and hat. A broken sword had been cast several feet away. He drew his pistol and raised the lantern high.

He stood in a long hall extending far beyond his lamplight, its walls glistening wetly, its ceiling lost to darkness. As he followed one of the walls deeper into the chamber he became aware of a ticking so slow and sonorous the floorboards vibrated, a resonance creating the disquieting effect of draining the mind of all thought during its sounding, as if time itself ceased with every stroke. It took Carter several moments to adjust to walking between the paralyzing lapses. As he neared the source he spied a dim light high overhead, which he gradually recognized as the face of a clock tower, its enormity made more incredible by being encapsulated beneath the vast ceiling of the room.

As he approached its base, he drew the lantern far over his head and discerned a plain structure, cast wholly of iron, rising into the darkness. At first, blinded by his own light, he could make nothing of the display, which was square and illuminated by a dull, phosphorescent glow, but finally perceived it as possessing but a single hand, and a single digit, a zero standing at the *12* position. The dial slid like liquid around the face, making an entire circuit with each slow tick. With quiet horror Carter recognized this as a tortured version of the Clock Tower. A portal opened to its interior, and an iron stair within spiraled, landing after landing, up to the mammoth mechanism. As Carter, neck craned, peered along the stairwell to the heights, he discerned a circle of light dancing far above. He extinguished his lantern, stepped back from the stair, and watched a single figure descend. When the staircase began trembling from heavy footfalls, he retreated outside the tower and pressed himself against its cold, iron base.

The stranger soon passed from the portal, and the dim light of his lantern showed him to be another of the Transformed carrying a long, rectangular key, a clock identical to that of the tower embedded in his chest. To Carter's shock, the figure resembled Enoch in a mechanical way— jagged curls spiraled down in imitation of the Hebrew's, and the face was an angular version of the Windkeep's own. Carter shuddered and pressed himself farther against the column, but then, incensed at this tawdry mockery of his gentle friend, considered slaying the abomination. His hand crept toward his Lightning Sword, but as the creature lurched across the chamber, feet shuffling, torso twisting with every step, pity stayed him.

Glancing neither right nor left, the Windkeep followed the chamber wall, deeper and deeper into the darkness, until his light vanished in the distance.

"Dreadful," Carter muttered as he relit his lantern.

"Yesss," a voice hissed at his back. "Dreadful."

He turned and fired instinctively at a heavy bulk looming at the edge of the circle of light. The shots had no effect, and he backed into the tower portal for protection, gripping the hilt of his Lightning Sword.

The beast strode full into the light, a gray, mechanical monstrosity fifteen feet tall, walking upright, its body an isosceles triangle with dials, gauges, springs, and valves in the center of its chest, surrounding a whirring pendulum synchronized to the ticking of the clock. The triangular head held a steep snout with a box for a nose, oblong eyes without iris or pupil, and square teeth with edges jagged as saw blades. Steam, whistling like a teapot, blew from a hole in the top of its head. It had a thick arrow for a tail, short, angular front claws, and rectangular feet. Despite its bizarre appearance, Carter recognized it at once.

"Jormungand?" he half whispered.

"Yeesss," the thing hissed, a bellows voice. "Jormungand faded. *Puff.* Jormungand stolen . . . *puff* . . . from his attic."

The dinosaur abruptly whirled like a mechanical doll,

marched across the floorboards to a large tub of water, bobbed his head into it, then marched back to his original position, where he emitted a pathetic burst of flame, illuminating nothing.

"What can I do?"

Jormungand rumbled like a toy winding itself. Carter could not help thinking of a steam engine.

"The first question. *Puff*. But you are not the Master here. *Puff*. I should devour you, as I did the last fool to enter this attic. *Puff*. Only the Windkeep is forbidden to me."

Carter thought of the dark stain and broken sword and stepped deeper into the Clock Tower. "I am still Master in Evenmere. Besides, you need my help."

"Jormungand needs nothing," the dinosaur snorted.

"Only if you wish to remain a mechanical contraption."

Steam billowed from the spout in the dinosaur's head after every tick of the clock. "*Puff*. Gloating are we? *Puff*. Is that it? All very pleasant, very gracious, very *fearful* when you enter my attic and find me in top form. *Puff*. But let me have a bit of adversity, a small handicap, a touch of bad luck, and you're on me like a jackal. *Puff*. Where's your Christmas spirit? Where's your compassion?"

Jormungand took a clumsy step forward. Carter retreated deeper into the shadows. The monster leaned down and stared, blank-eyed, into the portal.

"Will you advise me?" Carter asked.

"The second question. *Puff*."

"You never answered the first."

Jormungand bobbed his head so long Carter thought he had not heard. Finally, the dinosaur said, "The girl. *Puff*.

Find her. She is the key. *Puff.* Take her to the Cornerstone. Only she can release . . . all of us. But hurry. The anarchists have erred. They have dared too much. *Puff.* To fetter pain and death they must end the passing of time; this clock is their first attempt. But the universe cannot exist in this dimension if time ends. *Puff.* Don't squint in confusion—time, space, and mass are all related. Even a mortal should know that. *Puff.*"

"Then the universe will be destroyed?"

"It will pass into Eternity. *Puff.* I cannot see the result; I am a creature of this plane of existence, but I doubt it will survive. *Puff.* By binding me, they begin the process of ending death, for I am the horror of darkness, the Slough of Despond, the dark road down the Marches of Antan—I am Despair. *Puff.* If they bridle me they win much. Too much for their own sakes."

"Is Duskin in the house?"

"My vision is narrowed. *Puff.* I cannot see. But there are traitors. Beware. Beware especially the girl's magic. Once she is found, you should kill her."

"I have come to save her."

"Heroics! *Puff.* Locust rescuing crickets, while Jormungand, the only being of merit, waddles like a cuckoo. But find the Cornerstone and free me. I will make them pay. *Puff.* Now flee to the door at the far end of the attic. I have resisted devouring you as long as I can. My will is not my own in this form, and you are not the Master of this house."

Jormungand marched to the tub again, bobbed to drink like a mechanized bird, then reared his head and gave the most agonized cry Carter had ever heard, a cross between the rending of metal and a horse scream. Carter threw his hands over his ears, dodged out of the doorway, and fled at a furious pace, certain the dinosaur, true to his word, would kill him if he could.

He had covered almost thirty yards before the first booming footfall resounded at his back; Jormungand was much slower in this new form, though each stride covered seven yards. No stranger race was ever run, for each tick of the clock halted the contestants in midstride. The far wall remained lost to the dark.

Carter wove his way through aisles of square boxes in tidy rows, which the dinosaur would normally have trampled flat, instead of waddling carefully between them. By the time Lord Anderson passed through the stacks, he had gained fifty yards. He broke once more into full stride, breath falling in gasps, the lantern rattling with each footfall, all halting at every clock stroke.

The attic stretched forever; Carter had no hope of reaching its end. Thus, when he spied a door in the wall to his right, he veered toward it, redoubling his efforts. He ran into it with jarring force, not daring to slow, then clutched the knob, which resisted his hand. Jormungand's footfalls drew closer; the walls shook from the pounding; Carter heard the grinding of machine-gear teeth. The dinosaur emitted a burst of flame, which hung a split second in the air, as the clock ticked. Carter tugged at the door, rammed it twice with his shoulder, and twisted the knob again. It came off in his hand.

He glanced behind him; Jormungand approached, all gears and dials and groaning jaws, leaving him with the absurd thought that he was about to receive his death from a mechanical goose.

He drew his sword, slipped the slender blade between

the jamb and lock, and pried. Though the weapon scarcely glowed, it still retained a portion of its power, for the door splintered and burst open, and Carter leapt through, even as Jormungand struck at the place where he had been, jaws snapping empty air.

"Good! *Puff,*" the dinosaur said. "This once I rejoice to be thwarted."

Carter slipped down the corridor without replying, knowing in the attic in Evenmere, with Jormungand in his true form, he would now be a dead man.

Lord Anderson did not travel far through the midnight halls before finding water in a hip bath within one of the rooms. He drank his fill, and though it was brackish and tasted of metal, he thought nothing had ever done him more good.

It took nearly a day to make his winding way down from the attic, through torturous turnings, endless inter sections, and dead ends finally leading to a long stair curving gradually to left and right, as if the builders had been intoxicated. For the first hour, before the power of the Word of Secret Ways dissipated, he saw many blue squares, faintly shining in the darkness, but without his maps he did not know where they led. The walls and ceiling varied in size, a twisted, chaotic ruin, unlike the symmetrical environment he had expected in the house, often forcing him to turn sideways or bend low to pass. And everywhere grew the puzzling, threatening thorns.

The stair seemed eternal. Though weak from hunger, and wanting only to sit and sleep, he pressed on, coming at last to a strangely familiar chamber, which he soon recognized as a duplicate of the hidden room in Evenmere leading from the attic stair to his bedroom. Dismayed, he searched the wall and found, at the precise location as in the High House, the lever to open the secret door. The wall shifted with a slow, scraping groan; his lamp-light spilled into a room not dissimilar to his own chambers, the windows arranged identically, the bed and dresser in the same positions. As the fireplace closed behind him, he saw above it an abstract representation of the sword kept above his own mantel, the blade too narrow at the hilt, too wide at the tip.

As his lamp played across the room, he saw a reflection of its beams cast from the eye of a figure sitting in a rocking chair beside the bed. Carter shouted in surprise and drew his Lightning Sword.

The figure rose, a scarecrow man, one arm and one leg shorter than the other, so it lurched like a misproportioned mannequin. It wore a patched hat; its hair hung ragged before its eyes, and its skin was white as bone. Breath hissed from its lungs in flutters. Yet the mangled face staring at Carter was a twisted version of his own.

A splotched cloak, a careless imitation of the Tawny Mantle, lay upon its shoulders. It drew a jagged sword shining with crimson light.

"Master of the House," it said, its voice graveled as a grave, and Carter did not know if it identified him or itself. It staggered toward him; their swords met and exploded in blinding light and choking smoke, as if an encounter of opposite charges, sending both Masters reeling back.

Carter drew his pistol, horrified at facing this travesty,

at once both repellent and fascinating. He needed to end the battle swiftly, before others arrived. The smoke obscured his vision; his lamp lay smoldering sideways upon the rug.

An arm shot out from the haze and seized Carter's gunhand. Instinctively, he reached for the creature's left wrist, pushing it up in time to divert a stray bullet to the ceiling. They struggled, seeking to overthrow one another, the distorted white face, patched as a mummy's, pressed inches from Carter's own.

"Mmmmmnnnnnaahahh" the creature bellowed like an animal, then said in a slurred voice, "Words of Power."

A terror passed through Carter, of this beast controlling some version of the Words. He struggled harder.

"Naalaaaf!" it spat through lips quivering with spittle.

A solid wave of power sent Carter flying into the wall. Everything went dark; he recovered to find his pistol gone and the shambling horror almost upon him. He grasped a small wooden box by his side, splintered by the force of the Word, and hurled it with enough accuracy to down his twin with a blow to the forehead.

By the time Carter staggered to his feet, the false Master, bereft of its weapons, had risen as well. Fearing another Word of Power, Carter charged and struck several jabs to his opponent's midriff. A man would have doubled over; the creature did not. It clipped the side of Carter's brow; he shook off the blow and rammed his fists into the creature's kidneys, again without apparent effect.

Carter reeled beneath another stroke to the head. Finding himself clearly overmatched, he looked for a weapon, and sighted the two Lightning Swords, lying side by side across the room. He ducked beneath his enemy's next buffet, rolled across the rug, and clutched the blade of his own sword. As he rose and turned, the creature kicked the weapon from his hand. Without pausing, Carter spun round and seized the crimson blade as the false Master struck at the small of his back, sending him tumbling.

He rolled against the bed, gasping in pain, still grasping the sword. The doppelgänger, seeing Carter armed, reached toward its pistol, which lay three feet away.

Carter thrust, striking near the heart, all his weight thrown into the blow. The beast went down, grasping at the blade, while Carter lurched for the gun, uncertain if even steel would stop his foe. But by the time he retrieved the weapon, his twin had grown still. Yet, as he drew near, it opened its eyes, just before it died, and whispered: "Thank . . . you."

Upon its death, it shed all vestige of the strange transmutation wrought by the anarchists, its form quivering as it became a pale, young man. Carter wondered whether he had been victim or volunteer.

The double's use of the Word of Power disturbed Lord Anderson, for the force released had been that of the Word Which Manifests. Thinking back through the heat of battle, he realized it was indeed *Falan* the false Master had spoken, but *backward*.

He took up his pistol and his Lightning Sword, and after some debate, the crimson blade of his opponent—if his own sword would not wholly function in the house, the facsimile might. He entered a hallway surprisingly unguarded, identical to Evenmere even to the vermilion carpet, and passed down a bizarre representation of the main stair to a dimly lit version of the transverse corridor.

Seeing no one, he stole to the dining room, hoping to

find food. The door stood open; the room lay empty. Though the table was bare of sustenance, a search of the servery soon produced enough for a feast: preserved meat, dry bread, and a pitcher of water.

With his hunger and thirst satisfied, he became more aware of his surroundings. The chamber was both like and unlike the dining room in Evenmere. The massive fireplace with inglenook below dominated all, though carved of black marble instead of white. Sculpted roses, shaped in squares, replaced the plaster grape clusters upon the arch; above it, the bas-relief border depicted not squirrels but cubed baboons bouncing between angular maple branches. The patterned tiles were chaotic, forming no particular design, their imitation of Morris stained glass depicting crude stick figures rather than pre-Raphaelite ladies. Stone chairs, made sinister by the shadow of the ebony mantel, replaced the comfortable cushioned benches on either side of the fireplace. Dull gray carpets supplanted the Persian rugs of royal purple with golden sunflowers. The ceiling and walls were of gray stone; the metal table contorted itself into a senseless figure-eight, its edges sharp as knives. Smoking gas lamps hung in place of the crystal chandelier.

What kind of world will they create, who contort all beauty? Carter thought. He drew the Cornerstone shard from his pack and felt its gentle pull, leading him from the dining room into the transverse corridor.

Lizbeth passed easily through the thorns tangling her garden. She had dreamed the dream again, the dreadful nightmare, and fled back to her sanctuary once more. But after an hour, a new terror confronted her, a fear Carter had escaped his prison. With trepidation, she deserted her haven and made her way through the halls, murmuring, *"Oh, it will be something worse. And what shall I do when Papa and you leave me, and I am by myself?"*

She came to the grate, dropped silently to her knees, and searched the passage below. Carter was gone, leaving only the flickering gaslight. She felt her pulse throbbing at her temple.

"We were left at peace on our beds as long as the summer moon shone, but the moment a blast of winter returns, you must run for shelter!" she whispered. "Surely, he will return." But she was not reassured. She imagined him catching her unawares, creeping upon her from the shadows. For the first time in many years the dim halls frightened her.

She determined to wait for him, yet sat still only a moment before rising and padding down the stair to the door she had barred. She gazed at it a time, expecting it to move, expecting she knew not what.

"Mrs. Heathcliff, I'll ask you to do nothing, but sit still and be dumb. Tell me now, can you? I'm sure you would have as much pleasure as I in witnessing the conclusion of the fiend's existence; he'll be your death unless you overreach him, and he'll be my ruin," she said. She made her way back to the grate, drifted to the floor, and waited for what she thought a long time. She rose and stood, first on one foot, then the other; she wanted to jump up and down in anxiety, but dared not because of the noise.

"He has extinguished my love effectually, and so I'm at my ease," she whispered. *"I can recollect yet how I loved*

him, and can dimly imagine that I could still be loving him, if—no, no! Even if he had doted on me, the devilish nature would have revealed its existence somehow. Monster! would that he could be blotted out of creation, and out of my memory!

"Hush, hush! He's a human being," she changed voices to the imagined tones of Nelly Dean, the housekeeper. *"Be more charitable; there are worse men than he is yet!"*

Again she reverted. *"He's not a human being, and he has no claim on my charity. I gave him my heart, and he took and pinched it to death, and flung it back to me. People feel with their hearts, Nelly, and since he has destroyed mine, I have not power to feel for him, and would not, though he groaned from this to his dying day."*

In such wise she continued, until a distant noise froze her in fear. She leaned over the grate to look down, but saw nothing, then glanced around and spied a figure striding up the hallway, visible only between the dim lamps. The intruder paused and called softly, "Lizbeth? Is it you?"

She bounded down the corridor in panic, thinking only of escape; he stood between her and her sanctuary amid the thorns, so she fled the opposite way while footfalls rose at her back. In her dreams she had been unable to run; now she tore through the house, frantic for a hiding place, periodically looking over her shoulder to find him still in pursuit. She passed down the hall into a series of rooms, unused like most parts of the house, resembling pantries, chambers she called the Slanties for the way the walls leaned inward.

She fled through random doors, not even noting her way, going left, then left, then left again. With every step, the words: *I have run the whole way from Wuthering Heights, except where I have flown* danced through her thoughts.

Suddenly a figure loomed before her, his face hidden in shadow. He stretched out his hands. "Lizbeth, is that you? I won't hurt you."

She was trapped in a corner. At first she thought he had used enchantment, then realized she had fled in a square. She backed against the shelves along one wall, where hung an assortment of unidentifiable instruments.

She grasped the handle of one and flung it at him, catching him unawares. As he protected his face, she darted from the room, this time dashing in a straight line through the Slanties, down a corridor filled with geometric sculptures. She turned a corner and rushed up a short flight of stair where tottered, slightly unbalanced, on either side of the landing, two statues, vague representations of Heathcliff, wicked chin outthrust, a staff in one hand. On impulse, she hid herself behind one of them, holding her breath, waiting for her foe.

Long moments passed before she heard heavy boots pause at the intersection, then approach the stair. She peered from behind the base of the statue and saw the intruder place his foot on the first step. He ascended uncertainly; she hid herself again, counting the steps as he rose, knowing his position because she knew their number. While he was yet ten paces from the landing, she shoved the statue with all her strength; it withstood her an instant, then gave way with such haste she nearly toppled with it.

The statue struck headfirst, then rolled end over end. Lizbeth's pursuer threw up his hands to deflect the blow, but the base slammed against his arms, driving him down the steps, both falling together. At the bottom, they separated and clamored to a halt, the man prone, the shattered sculpture lying across his legs.

Lizbeth was torn between fleeing and staying to watch—in her dreams, she had never turned upon her assailant; it seemed too miraculous to be true.

"Ah! He was in such a fury! If he had caught me!" she whispered, hands to her lips, as she crept down the stair. The figure lay so still she wondered if he was dead. A trembling excitement overtook her—destroying her enemy had been easy, and after six years of boredom, this game of life and death seemed suddenly great fun.

She drew one of her sacred candles from a ragged pocket, lit it from the single gas jet upon the wall, and approached her tormentor.

The light fell softly upon him, but to her dismay, she saw not the black hair of Carter Anderson, but gleaming, golden locks. Though fearful, she drew closer, then gave a pitiable shriek as the flame revealed Duskin's battered features. Whimpering, she dropped the candle; its light went out.

She trembled like a fawn; her hands waved spastically up and down. She turned to flee to her comforting thorns, stopped, then turned again, all animal instinct. She scurried to the corridor intersection, then froze, uncertain, only her hands moving, still flaying the air. Her head darted bird-wise as she tried to choose between the corridor and Duskin's fallen form.

The words of the book rose unbidden within her: *Oh, well! I'm no coward. Save yourself; I'm not afraid.* Slow, silent sobs, bereft of any tears, shook her as she turned back to where he lay.

"It was not to be like this," she mourned. "He was to come and save me."

She relit her candle and drew close to his side. When she sought to push the statue from his lower body, it resisted her strength, but finally, bracing her hands against the floor and thrusting with her legs, she shoved it from him.

Knowing nothing of doctors or medicine, she knew not how to help, but reached out and stroked his face, tentatively at first, for the touch of another human was both strange and exhilarating. Her anxiety melted away as she remembered their first meeting at the train station, how he had leaned over her and held their golden hair together. She clutched her tangled locks against his own—they were still almost the same color—but to her wonder, he was smaller than she remembered. And he was probably dead.

She began to tremble again, until it occurred to her to see if he was breathing. When he was, she laughed in relief and considered what next to do. The left side of his face was red and beginning to swell; a bump was rising on his forehead. After a moment's thought she leapt to her feet and scurried back to her garden, where she filled a bowl with water from the fountain, returned to find him unchanged, and bathed his brow with a ragged cloth. Even struck down, she found him handsome.

"But it cannot end well," she murmured. "Just like in *Wuthering Heights*, it must all go astray."

The Woman in the Dark

Gregory waited three hours in a room the Man in the Dark had claimed as his own, a cramped, ill-lit chamber barren of all save two wooden chairs. Apparently, comfort was irrelevant to the Supreme Anarchist, but Gregory was troubled by more than the lack of luxury: two of the Transformed guarded his door, and he was uncertain whether he was guest or prisoner. He wondered if he, too, might soon become one of the changed. For the first time, he faced the awful reality of testing the dogma he espoused. It was one matter to speak of turning men into gods; the annihilation of his own will filled him with dread.

Still, he had been trained to the possibility of sacrifice—yet if the anarchists were transformed, who would direct the process? No individual, not even someone as great as the Man in the Dark, should have such responsibility; tyranny was one of the failings the False House was to eliminate. Events were happening without the approval of the Anarchist Council.

By the time the Supreme Anarchist returned to the chamber, Gregory was pacing and prepared to demand explanation.

"Have you occupied your time well?" the Man in the Dark asked.

"I have been with my own broodings," Gregory replied. "There is little here for entertainment."

"I contemplate the nature and beauty of order in this room. It is endless pastime and eternal joy: the symmetry of the corners, the angles and lines of the chairs—they bring peace after the chaos of the house beyond."

"Why have you altered our anarchist brothers? What is your plan? I require an accounting. I am well respected within the Society."

"There is no time for questions—"

"Time must be made!" Gregory declared, slapping the wall with his palm. "Have we sold our souls to the ambitions of a despot?"

"No," the Man in the Dark rasped softly, though there was power in that voice. "I assure you, when all is accomplished, we will have order, and with it, peace. The machinery is complex; balances must be kept. The anarchists were changed to maintain equilibrium. Two days of mathematic formulas would be needed to convince you. And then, how would you understand? Do you fear you will be transformed as well? It is not required, at this time."

Gregory's fury dimmed. He had followed this man for almost a decade and knew him to be a genius worthy of trust. He sighed, and ran his hands over his eyes. "What will we do now?"

"I have received an important message that prompts us to action. Our hopes of persuading Duskin have failed."

"Do not dismiss him too soon."

The Man in the Dark raised his hand for silence. "Events move quickly. Carter Anderson is within the house and must be found. Duskin, too, must be captured, lest he encounter the girl; I want no random variables, for these I hate. I have sent soldiers to Lizbeth's room. I have summoned the forty thousand Transformed from the Onyx Plain. The house is vast, but they will be enough for a thorough search."

"What can I do?"

"Take some men and apprehend Duskin. Reason with him if you can, but once Carter Anderson is captured, his brother will no longer be required for our plans. Then, we will transform Duskin as well, and he will no longer oppose us. There will be order."

Duskin dreamed of being dragged through a stubble field, bouncing over the rows, the stalks jamming into his back. The sky was dark; he could not see who conveyed him and wanted to ask them to stop but could not speak. After a time, his wrists were released, and he was left lying on a low hill amid the shattered stalks. Falcons wheeled overhead, sending oddly metallic cries echoing through a clear sky.

Darkness covered him a long time, but he woke to candlelight haloed through layers of gold. At first he thought it the straw of the stubble fields, but it pressed against his eyes and face, wonderfully soft, smelling pungent and tiger-sweet. He must have made a noise, for it withdrew, and he saw it was the jumbled hair of a young woman. Her face was thin and somber, despite high cheekbones and a pert nose, her eyes the palest blue, made huge by her slender countenance. She was the most haunted and haunting person he had ever seen.

"Lizbeth?" he said hoarsely.

"I didn't mean to," she said. "I didn't know it was you."

"Quite . . . all right," he replied, touching the aching bump on his forehead. "But you're not a little girl. I thought you would be a little girl." He laughed weakly. "Stupid of me. And you're so pretty."

So saying, he drifted back into gray darkness, where he thought he heard a soft voice crooning a children's song.

When next he awoke he was alone, the only illumination the distant red glow of a lamp. He turned his head and discovered himself surrounded by a forest of thorns. It took time to recall all that had occurred—his escape from the anarchists, his pursuit of the girl through the shadowy halls, his encounter with the falling statue. He remembered Lizbeth's face, angelic, bending over him.

His face and jaw hurt; his shoulder and left calf ached. He tested his limbs and was amazed that nothing was broken, though rotating his wrist brought pain. He sat up awkwardly and saw, nearby, a three-tiered fountain with carvings of men's heads upon each level, their open mouths covered in moss, as if suffocating. Water overflowed the font into a stone channel passing beneath thorns grown nearly as tall as the gray, granite walls beyond, a seemingly impenetrable forest on every side of the clearing where he sat. Overhead gaped the empty, starless sky.

He heard a rustling close behind and reached for his gun, but remembered it was gone, taken by the anarchists. He half turned and found Lizbeth making her way through the thorns, threading a path invisible to his eyes. Tall and too thin for good health, she knelt beside him without speaking and shyly presented a plate with dry bread, gray meat, and a mug of water.

"Thank you," he said. "Where am I?"

"This is my garden, where I grow my thorns."

"How did I get here?"

She cleared her throat and did not look into his eyes. "I feared the anarchists would discover us, so I brought you."

Duskin glanced around. "How did you carry me through the thorns?"

"*At any rate, Nelly,*" she said, "*whatever were my wanderings, the clock chimed twelve as I entered the house; and that gave me exactly an hour for every mile of the usual way.*"

"Who is Nelly?" Duskin asked.

"From the book," she said, still not meeting his eyes. "You know. The book."

"*Wuthering Heights*, you mean?"

She nodded.

"A dangerous thing, dragging a wounded man. You might have caused me serious injury."

Instantly her head dropped, and then he saw her body racked with a wholly singular sobbing, in that she neither made a sound, nor shed a tear.

"What is it?" Duskin asked. But she gave no reply.

Realizing his error, mentally cursing himself for a fool, he touched her shoulder, but she withdrew as if struck.

"I'm sorry," he said. "It was a thoughtless comment. I'm grateful for your care. Here, now, cheer up. Can we not be friends?"

But she would have none of it, and Duskin, amazed that anyone could weep so hard yet so silently, finally cried in passion, "Oh, Lizbeth, what have they done to you?"

And at that, her crying slowly ceased, and she looked at him, in a curious fashion. *"I'm not wandering; you're mistaken; and I'm conscious it's night, and there are two candles on the table making the black press shine like jet."*

He did not understand what she meant, but he said, "We found the notes you sent in the bottles, less than a month ago. We came here seeking you. Of course, Carter has been searching all along, but had no idea where you were."

She gave a hiss, like a snake. "He's here! I've seen him. I won't let him take me. I won't!"

"Who? You mean Carter? But he is your friend."

She hugged her legs to her chest. "He's not! He has deceived you. He brought me here. He works with *them*!"

"You say you have seen him. Where?"

"Down below. But I think he escaped. He could be anywhere in the house. Oh, do not speak of him! I fear him above all others!"

Duskin sat silent, uncertain how to address this strange creature. After a time she spoke again. "This isn't going as it should. This isn't the way it's supposed to be."

"How should it be?"

She looked down, suddenly shy again. "Different. It's supposed to be different."

Duskin suddenly felt very tired and slightly dizzy. His

head began to ache. "I'm going to have to lie down again. Thank you for the food."

She nodded, fell silent, and then blurted, "I sang to you before. While you slept."

"I remember, I think. You have a pretty voice."

His words had a remarkable effect; she beamed, her smile all radiance, the unabashed grin of a praised child, and Duskin knew in many ways she had been twelve years old forever. He fell back into an uneasy slumber beneath her soft crooning.

When he woke, she still waited by his side. In his dreams he thought he had felt her hands caress his face, but she sat back shyly as he ate again.

"I feel better," he said, after drinking water from the pewter mug. "My head was in a haze earlier. Thank you."

She did not reply but sat staring, and he saw more clearly her ragged clothes and uncombed hair. Yet her eyes bespoke intelligence.

"Tell me, Lizbeth, how were you brought here?"

She looked down, hunched her shoulders, and squirmed. "Carter did it. It was Carter."

"It could not have been."

"It was! I swear!"

"Then how was it accomplished?"

"Stop! No more running away? Where would you go? I'm come to fetch you home. He wants to know how it was done," she muttered the last, as if to herself, then spoke more loudly, "How was it done? He took me during the celebration. He carried me to the anarchists, and they brought me here, to the Man in the Dark, who removed my heart."

"Carter could not have brought you. There was no time.

You vanished and a search began almost at once. I wasn't there, but Sarah told me the way of it."

Lizbeth's face became a mask, her pupils pinpoints. "It is how I remember it."

"I see." Duskin dared not press her further. "But what did you mean when you said the Man in the Dark removed your heart?"

"He asks senseless questions," she said, though her expression relaxed. *"Foolish, silly boy! And there! He trembles, as if I were really going to touch him.* The Man in the Dark can do anything. He is great and terrible. We must never defy him. He knows what will happen and when. He gives me food every day and I must stay here because he says so. He stole my heart so I would never love anyone. Not anyone at all."

"Yet you want to escape the house?"

Lizbeth scrunched herself together, knees pulled up to her chin, making herself small. "Like Isabella, fleeing from Heathcliff. But it can't end that way. It has to follow the book. I want to leave, but I can't." Her voice turned pitiful.

Duskin would have taken her hand, but she drew back.

"Do you fear me?" he asked. "I have traveled a great distance, through severe danger, to bring you home. I am your friend. You say the Man in the Dark must not be defied, but I have come to defy him. He has not stolen your heart. That is a lie. Come, have you felt no hand of friendship all these years?"

Tentatively, shyly, she drew forward. He sat with palm open, as one would lure a beast. Their fingers touched. She placed her palm in his. As he covered her slender hand in his own, she whimpered.

And suddenly she threw her arms around his neck and cried desperately, "No one has touched me. No one has touched me at all." She wept uncontrollably, tears streaming down her face, and clawed her way close to his chest. Her sharp fingernails bit through his coat into his back; he could do nothing but hold her and ride out the ferocity of her need. He was abashed; at that moment she was a lost child, all little girl, and pity swept through him, yet she was a woman as well. Not knowing what else to do, he comforted her as he would a youngster. She cried; she whimpered, while he rocked her softly and whispered, "It's all right. I have you. It's all right. I'm here now."

"Don't let me go," she repeated, over and over. "Please don't let me go."

Finally, her passion spent, she crept from him, her face drawn once more into a mask.

"You must forgive me," she said. "I don't know what came over me. Is it not strange, that I, who have not wept for years, should weep so?"

"It isn't strange at all."

She sat silent, lost in her own thoughts, while he, in turn, pondered their next action. Lizbeth was pivotal to the anarchists' plans and should be spirited from the house, yet his duty was not just to rescue her, but to restore the Cornerstone. And he had to find Carter.

In the distance, Duskin heard heavy feet on floorboards and a commanding voice. He stood, startled, and saw, through the obscuring thorns, the shadowy forms of men at the threshold of double doors leading into the garden. Lizbeth clutched at him, dragging him back down, her eyes wide.

"Quickly!" she said. "Under here!" She rolled beneath

a mass of the brambles, vanishing instantly. Duskin was slower, but soon found his way under the tendrils.

"It's my sanctuary," she whispered. "They can never find us here."

Duskin thought it certainly true, for he saw nothing but thorns from where he lay, and could scarcely turn on his side without being cut.

For several moments, the anarchists could be heard, marching along the edge of the thorns, until finally, a familiar voice echoed off the garden walls: "These barbs are impenetrable. He couldn't hide here. Let's move on."

Even after the noise of the pursuers had departed, Duskin and Lizbeth lay side by side and face-to-face beneath the threatening thorns, like children hiding in a game. Duskin could just see her eyes through the crimson glow of a distant lamp.

"That was Gregory," Duskin whispered. "My cousin, and until today, my friend."

"You won't go to him?" she whispered. "You won't leave me?"

"I will not," he returned. "Do not be afraid. We will escape together."

She looked stern, as if unable to believe. "I do not think I can return alone to my room; I cannot bear the emptiness now I have found you. I've had no friends in so long."

Duskin smiled, his heart going out to her, and he was suddenly glad, despite the danger of discovery, to be hiding beneath the thorns. For an instant the days of marching, the running, and the jeopardy fell from him, and he was suddenly happy, like the thrill of a gnawling hunt, to face this adventure with his mysterious companion. But waiting seemed useless.

"Lizbeth, we cannot stay," he whispered. "We need to escape the house. Can you get us out of the garden unseen?"

"There are a hundred ways from the thorns—none can catch me within them—and entries into the manor only I know. But all the doors leading out of the house are always locked; I have tried many," she said. "And the few windows are unreachable."

He paused, suddenly realizing she had no concept of how large the house truly was. Undoubtedly, the anarchists kept her imprisoned in a small portion. He glanced at the garden walls, gauging whether they could be scaled, but abandoned the hope; the climbing thorns covered the bricks, creating an impassable barrier, and shards of glass were embedded in triple rows on the top of the wall. They would have to go through the False House.

"We must find a way," he said. "Are you willing to try?"

Lizbeth froze, like a hunted deer, as if the thought were more than she could bear. She glanced at the thorns. "I grew these," she said, opening her hands to encompass the vile foliage. "The Man in the Dark told me not to, but I grew them anyway."

"Yes, you did. They fill the house."

"They are the house." Then, as if speaking to herself, she said, "but Duskin is wrong about my heart. The Man in the Dark has surely taken it."

"Lizbeth, why do you speak of me as if I were absent?"

Lizbeth frowned, a pretty pout. "Do I? I haven't spoken to anyone in so long, I confuse my inside voice with my outside voice."

"Your thoughts from your speech?"

"Yes. I will do better, with someone to talk to. If we are to leave, I will get my things."

"What things?"

Lizbeth looked away. "I will show you. I cannot leave without my treasures."

Thinking the items might be important to their cause, he agreed. She took his hand and led from beneath the thorns. Together, they wound through the brambles, weaving a path where Duskin thought none existed, as if the vegetation parted beneath Lizbeth's feet. They entered a corridor in the main portion of the house by crawling through a round door, hidden beneath the barbs, then passed through several passages and a large hall, but when they peered around the turning leading to her room, an anarchist stood guarding the door.

They ducked back behind the corner. "What does *he* want?" she hissed.

"Undoubtedly, so long as I am free, they wish to take you into custody."

"There is another way into my room that they do not know," she said, eyes impish, as if it were all a game.

"It is too dangerous, Lizbeth."

"I cannot leave without my treasures," she replied. "Come."

She led back the way they had traveled and soon opened a door into a narrow, empty closet. Using the flame from a gas jet, she lit a twisted candle from a pocket of her dress, and they stepped inside, shutting the door behind, leaving them in darkness. Lizbeth knelt and ran her fingers along the rough baseboards until the soft click of a latch sounded, and the back of the closet opened inward.

They wove their way through the secret passage until

they reached a spy-hole, which Lizbeth used to survey the next chamber. "Look," she whispered. He obeyed to find a room containing a single mattress lying on the floor, a broken dresser without a mirror, and a battered chair. Righteous anger flared within Duskin at the cruelty of her captors. And then he felt sick, knowing Gregory as one of them.

"This is my room," she whispered. "The anarchists never come here, except to fetch me, or as they did when they took my pet mouse, Roon. That is the only mattress in the house. It is very comfortable."

"It must be frightening, living alone."

"At first I was afraid, until I named all the rooms. I know the house better than anyone. Nothing frightens me now. Nothing at all. Except the dreams. Sometimes nightmares wake me in the night. But every time I have one, I pray to dream of ballerinas, because they're so nice."

Duskin looked at her in wonder, her honest features framed in the dim glow of the candle. Despite her wild hair and baffling behavior, or perhaps because of it, she fascinated him.

She peered through the spy-hole again, then, satisfied, turned a lever and they stepped into her chambers, where a single lamp burned crimson in its brazier.

Duskin desperately wished the anarchists had not taken his pistol. He glanced around the room, looking for a weapon, but saw nothing. Fortunately, the door was shut; unless they were heard they could complete their mission and be gone.

"Come," she whispered. "I will show you my treasures."

"Please hurry."

She carried her candle, which remained lit, to the decrepit dresser in slow strides. Standing before it, she passed the flame ceremoniously to each of the four cardinal points, while softly intoning: *"I got the sexton, digging Linton's grave, to remove the earth off her coffin lid. And I opened it."*

She turned to him and said, "You must promise not to tell." Then, without awaiting an answer, she silently slid the top drawer open.

"What did you do just now, with the candle?" Duskin whispered.

"It keeps my treasures safe," she said. "One must have ceremonies."

One by one Lizbeth brought her hoard from the drawer: a photograph of Sarah, a leather-bound copy of *Wuthering Heights*, a stained silk handkerchief, seven buttons that she had named, a hair ribbon, a pair of shoes, and three homemade dolls cleverly made of rags tied together. Then she beckoned back to the secret way.

Once safely behind the hidden door, they passed farther down the passage, into other hidden chambers, finally pausing a great distance from Lizbeth's room.

"No one can hear us beyond these walls," Lizbeth said. "We are safe. Now we can put up my treasures.

"These are my dolls. This is Catherine," she said of one mostly pink, hugging it before lifting it to him. "And here is Edgar. And this one is Hareton, who is like you. When I first came to the house, I played with them all the time."

Duskin saw Lizbeth had drawn faces on the cloth dolls with pen and ink. "How is Hareton like me?"

"Though he and Cathy were separated many years, in the end they lived happily together. I haven't a bag to carry my treasures. Some will fit in my pockets. Can we put the dolls and my shoes in your pack?"

"Certainly," Duskin said, smiling to hide both perplexity and irritation at having risked both their lives to rescue the articles. But as she handed him the small shoes, his annoyance faded to pity.

While he opened his pack she placed the buttons, hair ribbon, and handkerchief in her dress. The picture of Sarah she held before her before hiding it away. "She is here, you know," she said, "within the house."

"What do you mean?" Duskin asked. "She cannot be. Sarah is safe in Evenmere."

"I have seen her," Lizbeth said. "And Enoch and the Lamp-lighter as well. They have been . . . changed, made into mechanical creatures. The Man in the Dark told me he lured them here."

"He deceived you," Duskin said. "This can't be true!"

"But it is," Lizbeth insisted. "I spoke to her."

Duskin stood silent, thinking of the transformed men on the plain, uncertain what it meant, not knowing whether to believe, his heart suddenly beating at his throat. "If what you say is correct, we must save them."

Lizbeth nodded. "Her smile was gone, which is what I loved most."

"She's a gracious woman," Duskin said, then added without thinking, "her marriage to Carter has been good for them both."

Lizbeth froze, fawnlike, as if the words were more than she could bear, and began to tremble in a way Duskin had never seen before, a teeth-rattling quaking.

"Are you all right?" he asked, clasping her shoulder.

She tore herself from his grasp, flung herself down to

her knees, her head buried against the wall, and grew so silent he thought she had fainted. "How long has it been?" she finally asked.

"How long?" Duskin repeated, then realized what she meant. "You were captured six years ago in October."

She stood quickly. "So long?" She looked all around the passage. "It's always dark. I didn't know." She paused and stared at him. "I'm taller than I was."

He laughed. "Much taller. When I met you, you were a little girl. You're a woman, now."

"Silly. I thought I had forgotten your height. You carried me in your arms. You probably couldn't, now. I'm nearly as tall as you."

Duskin looked at her slight frame. "I'm certain I could. I doubt you weigh a feather."

"Would you?" she asked, her eyes alight. "Would you swing me around as you did then?"

"Why . . . I suppose. But we have little time."

"You don't want to?" Her face clouded and she turned away. He could not bear the thought of seeing her soundless crying again.

"Yes, yes, of course. Of course I do. But only for a moment."

She turned back, smiled, and approached him, suddenly shy, but he lifted her easily, supporting her back and knees. He guessed her weight at less than ninety pounds. He turned her in a slow circle, and she suddenly began to giggle, utterly innocent, her face all child, in what he thought must be the happiest sound ever to echo through that room. He only hoped the anarchists could not hear.

She reached up, grasped his hair, and held her own

against his, then laid her head upon his shoulder, looked straight into his eyes, and said, "I love you, Duskin."

Embarrassed, he gradually halted his spin. He set her down gingerly. "We must go. The anarchists will be searching for us."

"Have I said something wrong?"

"No, no, not at all. Not at all. We just . . . we are in danger, you because you are with me. We must flee."

She appeared puzzled, and then her face reverted again to a mask, purged of all emotions. "Is Sarah really married to Carter?"

"Yes, happily."

"And he treats her well?"

"Quite well."

"I don't understand."

"Lizbeth, Carter had nothing to do with your kidnapping. You must believe me. And I need to find him. He may be dying. Could he still be where you last saw him?"

"I doubt he has escaped. I used to see him sleeping through the grate, and then he would vanish into the dark, looking for an exit, I suppose, though there is only one way out."

"Will you take me there?"

"Should I?" she said huskily to herself. And though she appeared terrified, she said, "I will. It isn't far."

They left the secret way by another exit and entered a gloomy corridor. "This is Jabes Passage," Lizbeth said, "and the turning before us I call Gnasher Row."

"Unusual titles. Did you remember the way better after naming the rooms?"

"No, but it helped me like them."

They reached the Master Hall. Already Duskin could

not have found his way back to the garden of thorns; there were too many turnings. The hall, all shadows and dim red lamps, reminded him of the bleak portraits of the portals to hell, red glows and bizarre statuary, blackness all around. One of the sculptures caught his eye, an abstraction of a standing scholar, his body geometric shapes, only his face a realistic portrayal. Duskin drew close to the strangely familiar figure.

"Who is this?" he asked softly, for the chamber sent his whispers swirling back at him.

"It is old master Earnshaw, he who first took pity upon Heathcliff, an abandoned waif, and adopted him into his home. It caused terrible trouble, yet he was kind."

"It resembles Count Aegis."

"Yes. All of the characters from *Wuthering Heights* look like people I have known. I don't know why."

"Nor I. Rather incredible, isn't it?"

"Is it? I did not know."

"Why would the anarchists carve sculptures of your acquaintances?"

He hurried to a pair of statues and found Sarah's likeness stamped on one, but the other he could not identify, until he recognized it as an abstraction of himself, though the features were less accurate than on the previous sculptures.

"This is Catherine," Lizbeth said. "She and Heathcliff were in love, though she married Edgar Linton for position and power. And this is Hareton, who loved Catherine's daughter, Cathy, with his whole heart."

"Who carved the sculptures?"

"I don't know. They were here when I found the room."

Duskin nodded thoughtfully, baffled by the images.

"I don't care for this one," she said as they came to the next figure, a brooding statue, cruel-mouthed and scowling, with a hat pulled over its eyes, barely recognizable as Duskin's brother. "This is Heathcliff, who sought to destroy all the inhabitants of both Thrushcross Grange and Wuthering Heights."

Footfalls sounded far down the hall. In the gloom, Duskin saw no one, but Lizbeth said, "An anarchist comes. We must hide."

They crouched down in the midst of a group of the statues, which looked out in every direction. From their vantage place they could see, between the crooks and arms of the grotesque statuary, all across the Master Hall. At first Duskin could discern nothing, Lizbeth's eyes being superior in the dimness, but at last he caught a glimpse of first one of the Transformed, and then many more, streaming down the hall, one after the other, with thirty paces between. He saw others ascending and descending the great ebony staircase and along the shadowed galleries, flowing in wave after wave, their movements mechanical, their hats conical as their snouts, their gray, anarchist garb streaming, bat-winged behind them. A thousand men passed their position, and then a thousand more, close enough they could see the glass lenses of their eyes and hear their bellowed breathing, like the last rattles of the dead. The noise of their footfalls echoed across the chamber, a trudging cacophony. And always they searched, heads jerking, eyes seeking, as flocks of birds, protected by scores of eyes, look for danger.

A quarter hour passed, and still the procession continued. One of the creatures looked directly at Duskin as it passed, and he froze in place, not daring to breathe, as its eyes swept him. It gave no alarm, being deceived by the sculptures, and moved on.

"What are they?" Lizbeth whispered. "Where do they come from?"

"The Man in the Dark has surely emptied the Onyx Plain," Duskin said. "How can we escape them?"

"There must be a way out," Lizbeth said. "But we cannot run; they would see us at once. There are many secret doors in the house. Perhaps there is one among these carvings."

Duskin raised his eyebrows, thinking they could not be so fortunate, but Lizbeth reached up and touched a statue's arm, which twisted slightly. A door slid away at its base, revealing a tunnel leading down.

Dumbfounded, Duskin followed as Lizbeth crawled into the opening, a narrow squeeze, utterly dark, smelling of mortar, dipping for several feet before leveling off. Once they had crept several nerve-wracking feet, Lizbeth lit a candle with a match Duskin gave her; the flame arose, haloing her face. She smiled sweetly. "This will take us to safety." But a shiver ran through Duskin, and he wondered if the tunnel had always been, or if Lizbeth, using the power channeled through her to the Cornerstone, had created it with her desire.

They crawled a long time through that cramped space; unlike his brother, he was not given to claustrophobia, but not even knowing how the passage would end wore on his nerves. Beetles scampered across his hands, bugs dropped on his face, squishy things hidden from the tiny candle pulped beneath his palms. And Lizbeth led as if it were all a grand adventure.

They came up through a hatch opening into another,

nondescript corridor, but Lizbeth knew immediately where they were. They almost immediately reached a narrow, descending stair, apparently ending at a blank wall. Lizbeth halted at the landing.

"Carter is down there," she said. "It is a secret door."

Duskin descended and found a board jammed into the opening mechanism. He removed it and depressed a lever, which caused the wall to spring wide with a sharp click. The way lay dark before him. He drew the lantern from his pack, lit it, and looked up into her fright-framed face.

"Lizbeth, do you know the way?"

She turned from him, arms crossed, apparently agitated. "Yes, but I dare not go. *He* is down there. Do not ask it!"

"Will you trust me?" he asked. "Come, take my hand. We will go together. You cannot stay here; the Transformed are everywhere. Do not believe the anarchists' lies. Think back. Remember the times you and Carter and Sarah spent together. He loves you. They both do. Your loss has been a heavy burden on his heart."

At first she looked as if to bolt, but her face took on the impassive veil acquired whenever she could not confront her own thoughts, leaving her looking devilishly cold.

"I will do it for you," she said, "though it leads me to ruin. *You and Edgar have broken my heart, Heathcliff! And you both came to bewail the deed to me, as if you were the people to be pitied! I shall not pity you, not I. You have killed me—and thriven on it, I think.*"

She took Duskin's hand, while he found no words to answer. He became acutely aware of her delicate fingers easing into his own, the porphyry hands of a doll.

Together, they entered the darkness of a room empty save for the trailing thorns. Like two lost children they made their way from chamber to chamber, down corridors dank and crumbling, not daring to call to Carter for fear of being overheard. In this manner they spent several hours, finally reaching a space with an exit opening onto a stair. Lizbeth halted in puzzlement. "This was not here before. I know all these rooms."

Duskin examined the portal. "It's a secret panel." He drew the lamp closer and peered up the stairway. "Carter must have found it. We should follow."

"No, we mustn't," Lizbeth said. "It leads to the beast in the attic."

"A beast? Like Jormungand? Have they replicated him as well? But how do you know where it goes? You said you had never been."

"I haven't. But sometimes I know where passages lead, as if the thorns tell me. But if he survives, he will be in the Upper Reaches. I can take us there by another route."

"Can you? But what if Carter hasn't found the attic yet?"

"Many hours have passed since I saw him through the grate. Of that I am certain. He is no longer on the stair."

"We should retrace our steps then, and follow the new way."

"Very well," she said, but suddenly stumbled.

"Are you well?"

"Only weary. I have neither eaten nor slept since first I saw you."

"But that was hours ago. When you fed me, did you keep nothing for yourself?"

"The anarchists lower food down a dumbwaiter. I gave you all I had."

"Brave girl, to have said nothing. But I have supplies;

you must eat from my pack. Afterward you will sleep while I keep watch. We will rest here, which is as safe as any."

Duskin unrolled his bedroll upon the stone floor, and they sat together to make a meal. Lizbeth pulled a tough piece of dried meat off with her teeth and grinned. "This is good."

Duskin arched an eyebrow. "Do they feed you so poorly as that?"

"You have sampled the best of it; all quite bland. I have wondered how they make so many foods tasteless. I remember I used to refuse when Sarah asked me to eat my vegetables. I have eaten much worse here. I was a spoiled child."

"Twelve year-olds are supposed to be."

"Perhaps," she said, though she did not look certain.

Afterward, as she lay down to sleep, she looked up at him with the innocent concern of a child. "You won't leave?"

"I'll be right here. Where would I go?"

She smiled, turned sideways, and closed her eyes.

Duskin studied her upturned countenance. When first he had seen her, after being struck by the falling statue, he had thought her an angel, her face haloed by lantern light, her wild hair framing her face. With a bit of nourishment and a decent comb, she might be quite beautiful.

He glanced around the bare chamber. *I should have died here, alone in all this. She has taken thorns and made a garden.* He looked back at her face. *Yet she is so vulnerable as well. Perhaps that is why I am drawn to her. So naive, yet wise in her own world, made ancient by her prison. What strange notions she must have! Does she re-*

*member the sun? Have the clouds of heaven become as
dreams to her?*

Lizbeth gave a soft moan and turned in her sleep; her
fingers moved; she was dreaming. At first the vision
seemed a happy one; she beamed, but gradually the smile
faded and a look of fear fell upon her.

At that same moment an enormous face appeared outside the circle of the lantern light. Duskin leapt to his feet.
The features were those of his brother, though twisted with
hate, four times normal size, and transparent as a ghost.
The shoulders and part of one arm were also visible. The
vision turned and passed through the wall. A dread fell
upon Duskin, that this might be the specter of Carter, a
sign of his death.

Lizbeth made soft whining noises in her sleep. As
Duskin knelt to wake her, the room before him abruptly
shifted. Unlike the former visitation, there was nothing insubstantial about this transformation. The walls opened
up, parting like water; the floor changed from stone to polished wood; ivory statues stood on either side of a long
hallway, carvings of Sarah, Count Aegis, even Duskin
himself. Moonlight poured through two open French
doors at the end of a long hall, and a cool breeze ruffled
Duskin's hair. He saw a young girl, Lizbeth as he remembered her from Innman Tor, approaching the doorway. As
she reached the threshold, a shrouded figure stepped from
the darkness beyond. She shrieked and fled; the man pursued, and Duskin saw his face shifting in the light, so that
sometimes it was Carter's and sometimes another's. The
man grabbed her wrist, and she screamed in terror.

Bewildered, Duskin turned to Lizbeth, who flailed
against the bedroll, echoing those screams precisely with

deep moans. He reached down to touch her; she woke, shrieked, and frantically sought to escape him.

"It's Duskin!" he cried, throwing his arms around her to prevent being scratched by her nails.

She fought a moment more, eyes wide, before recognizing him. "It was Carter, it was Carter," she said.

"It's all right. He's not here now," Duskin said. "It's all right."

"I have to go to the garden!" she cried, seeking to pull away. "Only the garden is safe!"

Ho drew her back as gently as he could. "Lizbeth! No! You're safe here!"

She struggled hard, terrified as a wild animal, saw she could not escape, and stood trembling. He took her by the shoulders, and when she did not withdraw, held her face in his hands, stroking her hair, soothing her.

"You don't have to go back to the garden ever again. I'm going to take you away from here. We're going to escape."

Duskin was never certain thereafter who kissed whom, but suddenly they reached for one another; their lips pressed together in a long embrace. He drew away first, and then she turned her back upon him, arms folded, hugging herself.

"I'm sorry," he said. "I didn't . . . I mean, you're a young woman alone. I wouldn't take advantage. Dreadful of me. Won't happen again."

She turned back, perplexed. "No! How could . . . ? He has taken my heart." She shivered, and her expression became a mask. "It was the dream again, and Carter chasing me. Except sometimes it was Carter and sometimes someone else."

Duskin glanced around; the hallway was gone; the chamber was as before. "And were there French doors?"

"Yes! There are always the doors. I try to go through, but he waits on the other side. How did you know? He pursues me, catches me, and then I awake. I go to the garden to hide. Duskin, I don't have the strength to help you find Carter; I fear him too much! Oh, you say he is good, but how can I know?"

"The vision has changed my mind, at any rate," Duskin said. "Carter has freed himself from his prison, and I can best help him by spiriting you from the house, to prevent the anarchists from channeling power through you. I see that now. Once we are out, I will return for my brother."

She looked at him sharply. "The Man in the Dark told me if I left the house I would die, since I no longer have a soul. One cannot live in the real world without a soul."

"He lied. I don't believe him."

She turned around, agitated. "If I go with you, and if we come to the door where Carter waits, will you protect me from him?"

"I will. Can you find it?"

"Yes. I think I have always sensed it, though I never went because I knew *he* would be waiting. And if you lead, I will accompany you, for it is the only way out for me. It will be like Catherine and Heathcliff; though they love one another, his cruelty will destroy her. But I had hoped you would be Hareton, whose love was true."

Duskin stood silent, not knowing what to say.

"I should not have kissed you," she said, "for I have no heart."

The Dayroom

As Carter departed the dining room, he saw, beneath the distant, sanguine lamps, the Transformed sweeping down the transverse corridor in a long line. He stepped back behind the doorway in alarm, and quickly saw how groups branched off at every entry. They were scouring the house; he would not long be safe.

He passed out of the dining room, by way of the butler's corridor, past the cellar, down the men's corridor, and into the kitchen court, but unlike its counterpart at Evenmere, this room had but one entrance. He heard doors opening in the chambers behind him, the din of his pursuers. Several rooms surrounded the kitchen court—the coal house, the housekeeper's room, the scullery, and others, none providing a way of escape.

Thus trapped, he considered the Word of Secret Ways. He had summoned it only with great effort before, and now there was no time. He thought of the false Master he had slain, who had spoken a Word backward. Perhaps, in this house, he could tap into that power as well.

He closed his eyes and concentrated, seeking the way. It was difficult to conceive of the Word in reverse, yet as he mustered the full force of his will, he saw it, deep in the distance. Gradually, it rose, burning not as brass, but ice cold and symmetrical. He feared using this Word, foreign as it was to all he had ever known. He brought it to his lips. *Nideehlat!* It wrenched itself from his mouth, freezing his jaw, burning his lips from its cold. The house shook. Pain gripped his left arm.

He glanced down and tottered in shock. His hand had become a tapering claw, artificial as those of the Transformed. He staggered backward, feeling faint, as if he had been shot.

The boots of his hunters sounded in the men's corridor beyond. Carter searched the walls for a sign of a secret way, but beheld nothing. Nursing his changed hand, he stumbled through the scullery, into the cook's kitchen, where he beheld a faint luminance, not blue but crimson, glowing beside the closet door. He quickly found a concealed latch and entered a thin passage.

The way was completely dark, save for a single pinpoint of light in the distance. He felt his way forward and soon discovered a spy-hole overlooking the kitchen court, where the Transformed passed, guns drawn, soulless and impassive.

Other spy-holes dotted the passage, and Carter made his slow way, finding enemies each time he looked.

He opened and closed his hand, feeling its mechanized stiffness. Though it no longer felt a part of his body, it was still usable. High was the price for using the Words of Power in the False House.

Gradually, he recovered from his shock, and drew forth the shard. It pulled him down the corridor, up a rickety stair, and through a series of passages, all benighted, finally ending on the second floor. A spy-hole showed the way to be clear, and he stepped into a carpeted passage. He had gone only a few feet before footsteps sounded at the turning, and he strode rapidly into a nearby chamber, closing the door behind him.

Voices sounded in the room he had left, accompanied by scufflings. The knob rattled, then turned, while Carter concealed himself behind the door, gun drawn.

"This will do nicely," a voice said. "Let me light the lantern."

A golden glow streamed into the room, and two figures entered. They turned to find themselves facing Carter's revolver.

"Look, Mr. McMurtry, it's Lord Anderson," Phillip Crane said.

"Why so it is, Mr. Crane. Why so it is. Most fortunate since he has a gun. But what has happened to your arm?"

"It's difficult to explain," Carter said, shaking hands with the pair, honestly overjoyed to see friendly faces. "But we've little time. The anarchists are searching the house."

"How well we know," Mr. Crane said. "That's why we were—"

"—looking for a place to hide," Mr. McMurtry continued. "We saw them making their way up to the second floor."

"Then, come," Carter said. "We must find another hidden passage."

Drawn by the shard, Carter led down the hall until he discovered the crimson glow of another secret way. He was thankful to have the architects' lantern as they passed into the narrow corridor.

"What is the plan, Lord Anderson?" Crane asked.

"The shard will lead us to the Cornerstone, where I expect stiff opposition. I wish we could find Duskin and the others."

"Most were captured," McMurtry said. "Mr. Crane and I saw it, though we escaped."

"Were Duskin and Gregory with them? Nooncastle?"

"We saw neither of the cousins, wouldn't you say, Mr. Crane?"

"But we did see Lieutenant Nooncastle, Mr. McMurtry. He was definitely among the captives."

Carter sighed, wondering if the cousins might still be free. But several men went down in the attack of the Chaos-hound . . .

They descended to the first floor, where the passage ended at a spy-hole. Carter glanced through, into the library, and though he could not see the entire chamber, it appeared deserted.

He signaled the architects for silence, then opened the door. The room was indeed empty, the Transformed having apparently already passed through, and lay dark, half-lit, uninviting. Gaudy spirals of bronze replaced the gray dolomite pillars; a mass of shapeless colors supplanted the frond-carpet. Upon impulse, he crossed to the study door of the Book of Forgotten Things. It was unlocked, but when he opened it he shrank back, for an abyss gaped before him, unplumbed depths with sprinkles of light descending forever down. On the overhead skylight, in a ghastly imitation of the stained-glass angel presenting the Book of Forgotten Things to mankind, knelt a man alone, tearing the pages from a tome. Carter shut the door quietly and withdrew.

Neither bookcases nor books stood in the library, save a single thick volume entitled *The History of Man*, all of black leather, shoddily sewn, perched on an oak block serving as a table. When he opened it, its pages were empty.

"A travesty of architecture," Mr. Crane said, rolling his eyes around the room, his voice tinged with bitterness. "The windows are gone, the carved balustrades, the gorgeous lintels and architraves. Is this what they've been building?"

"Apparently so," McMurtry said. "This whole house is an architectural disaster. We've seen nothing of value at all in our whole journey, and we're certainly unlikely to here."

"You are forgetting the stair at Moomuth Kethorvian," Crane said.

"Yes, the stair was good," McMurtry replied. "But this . . ." He waved his hand helplessly. "And it seems endless. How large *is* this house?"

"How large is Evenmere, Mr. McMurtry? Infinite, or so it is said." Crane grinned. "What a gloriously enormous concept. Architecture without end, amen, amen, eh?"

"Not like this, Mr. Crane. Makes you miss Evenmere, doesn't it? The cathedral ceilings, the ballflower decorations, the gabled niches under trefoil arches."

"Yes," Crane said sadly. "I would not wish the whole world to become as this."

The shard drew Carter deeper into the library to another secret way, hidden beneath a twisted version of the gallery. They soon found themselves in another passage, indistinguishable from the first. Their march proved tedious. The passage neither turned nor ended, and still the shard drew Carter on. Finally they stepped from the secret way into a deserted passage ending at white double doors.

"Let me open it, while you stand guard," McMurtry said.

Carter stationed himself to the side as Howard McMurtry drew the door open. Apprehension turned to amazement as Carter stared into a bright hall of tremendous length, with banisters gilded in gold, bronze statues lining tiered galleries, enormous tapestries of birds and bears, and flowing, embroidered curtains.

The shard nearly sprang from his hand. "Gentlemen, be prepared. We are nearing our goal."

As Duskin and Lizbeth cowered behind a door at the top of the stair leading from the basement, they saw the Transformed everywhere, passing thirty paces apart in an endless line.

"We're trapped," Lizbeth whispered, "unless we can find another secret passage."

"Perhaps on the stairwell?" Duskin suggested, hopeful of her powers.

"No," Lizbeth said. "There is nothing there. But there is one across the passage. I'm certain of it."

"We will have to cross in front of the anarchists," Duskin said, "and I have no weapon."

"They're slow. We can make it. I see the button from here."

Duskin drew a deep breath. "Very well. We go the moment the next passes."

Another of the Transformed trailed by, eyes searching, head rotating, emitting gear noises as it walked. As one, Duskin and Lizbeth leapt across the passage, Lizbeth landing on her knees to depress the mechanism in the baseboards. The door sprang open; Duskin stepped between it and the anarchist, and gunfire tore a hole through it. The pair stepped inside, pulling the portal shut behind them, then scurried as fast as the darkness allowed.

Once they were some distance down the passage, they lit the candle once more, and continued on their way for several hours, passing in and out of secret passages, through halls mysterious and gloomy, eventually arriving at places where few of the Transformed were seen. And ever, the thought grew on Duskin that Lizbeth was changing the house as they went, providing secret doors and passages, curving them away from danger.

As they walked through an empty hall, watchful of anarchists, they passed another of the abstract sculptures of Heathcliff that filled the entire house. Lizbeth paused and gaped. Duskin studied the face and saw only staring eyes, with the rest of the features blank, and nothing of his brother, though the resemblance had been clear on all those before. Lizbeth passed on, and together they entered another secret way.

"You look disturbed," Duskin said, once they were behind the safety of the walls.

"I don't understand," she said. "The face is changed. It is no longer Lord Anderson."

"Perhaps this one is different," Duskin said.

"No, they are all the same. Every one."

"How do you know?"

"I just know," she said. "I just know. The eyes frightened me. They seemed so familiar."

"I have a theory," he ventured, seeing she was growing upset. "Perhaps the statue has changed because you have altered your opinion of Carter."

Lizbeth turned to him, her eyes glistening in the candlelight. "You told me he is good, and I want to believe, but can my thoughts transform stone?"

"Perhaps," Duskin said, and related the vision he had seen when Lizbeth was dreaming.

"I see," she said afterward, brow furrowed.

"You do not appear particularly surprised."

She shrugged. "I have understood little in my life."

"No, I suppose not. Have you any explanation for it?"

"Have I been bad?"

Duskin chuckled sympathetically.

"Why do you laugh?" she asked, cheeks reddening. "I have said nothing amusing."

"Forgive me. I haven't come all this way to scold you. You have done nothing wrong. But this manifestation is unique."

"I will try not to do it again."

He put his hand upon her shoulder, but it reminded him of the kiss and he withdrew. "That is not the point. The evidence suggests the anarchists are funneling the Cornerstone's power through you to build this house. We suspected it; the Man in the Dark confirmed it to me. Apparently part of your subconscious mind is involved in the construction, and you have access to that energy. In many ways this *is* your house. I believe you can change the passages at will, and create secret ways when you wish. I think you have done so throughout our journey."

Slowly her face turned crimson, and she turned toward him, eyes suddenly flashing. "Of what do you accuse me? Do you think me some monster?"

"I accuse you of nothing," he said softly, perplexed. "But we could test your abilities, see if you can control them."

"No!" she said, her voice too loud. "I do not know how. I do not!" And she turned from him and would say nothing thereafter.

They sat in silence, he pondering both her willfulness and terrible abilities, searching for words to soothe her, not knowing what to say. At last, it was she who spoke, saying, "I must apologize for my outburst. I have been alone many years, and the book, filled with arguments and controversies, has been my only guide. It was not so at Innman Tor; folk were gentle there. Yet, your words frighten me. You say I am mighty, but I have had no power at all. Still, sometimes at night, when I close my eyes, I see things, as if I were part of a wall, or a piece of furniture. I look out upon all the house. It disturbs me."

"Why?" Duskin asked.

"Because . . . if I have power, I could escape."

"Do you not want to?"

"Yes, but I am afraid."

"Have the anarchists said nothing of this?"

"The Man in the Dark calls me a receptacle. Long ago,

he once said I would become the avatar of Order, but I do not know what an 'avatar' is."

"It is the essence of something. They wish you to become Order Incarnate, Order in the flesh. They want a planned world."

"I thought an avatar was a hawk. I always wondered when I would become one. I used to imagine my feet turning to claws and my arms to wings. Is it better to be Order Incarnate than to be a hawk?"

"No, I am certain it isn't. I would much rather be a hawk. But I don't want you to become either one."

She smiled. "Nor I. But this perplexes me."

Lizbeth continued to lead with unmistakable certainty. They traipsed for hours through the ill-lit manor, and though Duskin soon began to doubt their way, Lizbeth never faltered, drawn by an inner compass he could not fathom. They traveled through a series of interlaced passageways, with intersections every dozen yards. Their footfalls pattered along the marble floors, a telltale sign of their travel, until they came to a stair leading upward to a sliding panel, the opening mechanism, a brass wheel, which hissed with air as it slid aside. They stepped into a lightless hall; their footfalls sent echoes frisking all around, so Duskin knew it to be a large chamber.

"Do you know where we are?" he asked.

"Not exactly. I have never been here before, but it seems right."

Duskin nodded, feeling wholly out of his depth, like a man following the instructions of a little girl playing make-believe. Yet, whatever Lizbeth believed might well be true.

"We should turn to the right," she said, taking his hand,

not bothering to give him time to light a candle, leading as if every step was marked.

After several minutes Duskin detected a faint, white glow streaming from beneath a threshold. They cautiously opened the door and entered a magnificent hall.

Only caution kept Duskin from whistling in amazement. The chamber was large as a cathedral, covered with a sky-blue dome, and radiant with diffused light the color of morning, its source indiscernible. Vines painted around the dome's edge gave the appearance of a forest reaching to the sky; a painted yellow sun looked down from the noon position and a moon peeked above the horizon. Fluffy clouds in the shapes of hearts and cherubs circled the dome. The chamber itself was filled with rag dolls, stuffed tigers, tree houses, sailboats, and hundreds of other things, many oversized, as if part of a giant's toy box. A red wooden wagon, ten feet high, stood nearest.

"I will call this the dayroom," Lizbeth said. "Isn't it wonderful?"

"It's beautiful, especially after so much gloom. But wait, what is the matter?"

Lizbeth looked stricken. Her voice trembled as she spoke. "If I had known, I could have played here all these years. I could have had a happy place."

"The anarchists would never have allowed it." Duskin took her hand. "I doubt they even know of its existence."

As they wandered into the midst of the chamber, they saw many familiar objects as well: an eighth-sized model of both Count Aegis's house and the yellow train engine from Innman Tor, ceramic dolls of kittens, dogs, mice, and Sarah's mare Judith, and miniature stuffed figures of Duskin, Sarah, Old Arny, the Count, and even Lizbeth as a child. And one figure seen in many shapes and sizes, a brooding man Duskin did not know.

"Who is this?" he asked, indicating one of these.

"Why, it's my father. He disappeared long ago." Her features grew cold.

"And you haven't seen him since?"

"No. *'Nay. Cathy,'* the old man would say, *'I cannot love thee; thou'rt worse than thy brother.'*"

They walked in silence a moment, before Duskin said, "Lizbeth, do you realize you made this chamber?"

"I? But I do not understand."

He gazed deep into her eyes. "Look at it! It is all you; all the things within it. Look at the dolls and the wagon, at the hearts etched into the corners. It is like the statues of Sarah, Count Aegis, and myself. Do you think the anarchists carved them? They kept you in darkness because they want the world dark; they gave you *Wuthering Heights* to teach you despair, but in this room, hidden even from them, you have made light."

Lizbeth looked up at the sky-blue dome, her eyes in the light the palest blue, spectral and mysterious, made feverishly huge by her thinness. "I couldn't have made this," she said in a hushed voice, "it is too beautiful and there is no beauty within me."

"How can you say that? Oh, Lizbeth, can't you see? How pretty your eyes are! You *have* made all this—if they had taken your heart, you could not have done so."

"I couldn't have," she said, tears in the corners of her eyes. "I was sent into the darkness because I was bad. They have taken away all the good things. If I had been good, *he* would not have taken me away!"

She began to tremble, all over, a teeth-rattling quaking.

"Who do you mean?"

"I . . ." She put her hands over her face. "The eyes on the statue! If it was not Carter . . ." She gasped as if drowning for air.

Duskin took her hand. "Who was it? Whose features are on the statue?"

She closed her eyes. "I see Carter. I see Carter! But there is another, behind his face! I do not want to look!"

"You must," Duskin said, though he himself was terrified by her passion. He took her by the shoulders. "I am here. Whose face is it?"

She gave an animal cry, between a sigh and a scream; her voice grew desperate. "Papa! It's Papa! He sent me away! He sent me away! Why did he send me away? It was Papa. It was Papa!"

Her breath came in great gasps. She wept then, a deep sobbing unlike anything Duskin had ever heard, a wailing of the soul, the dark, and the deep grief fashioned by isolation and deceit. She threw herself into his arms and cried until exhausted, while all he could do was hold her and stroke her golden hair. Yet, somehow, Duskin thought it a sorrow of healing as well.

When her grief was spent, she withdrew, "You must despise me. I am weak."

"I admire you," Duskin said huskily. "I have never known anyone so strong. Though your own sire betrayed you, you have defied them, here in the darkness. Alone, without help, without hope; you have defied them. They have not broken your spirit."

"But why did he do it? Why did my father give me away? Was I of so little value?"

"No. You mustn't take such a burden upon yourself. We

cannot know his motives. My own mother did terrible deeds. People become corrupt one step, and one act, at a time. Whatever his reasons, whether he was controlled, deluded, or insane, it had nothing to do with who you are. It was not your fault."

She slept a time thereafter, pillowed on the stuffed animals and dolls, while Duskin kept watch. The room gave Duskin his first chance to see her in morning light, and he watched as she slept. Despite being crimson from crying, she was hauntingly pretty—her hair, in all its wildness, haloing her head, glistening gold to her too-thin waist, her chin, pert and defiant beneath a small, delicate mouth that rarely smiled. Her wild spirit allured him most, a restlessness akin to his own, but he did not admit that attraction even to himself; he feared too much her passion, her vulnerability, her strength. He wondered if, posed in a drawing-room chair, daintily sipping tea, her hair neatly coiffed, the fashion of the day upon her, she would still radiate untamed *ferocity*, as if she were a candle and he too close to the flame?

When she awoke, she smiled both sadly and sweetly. "It *is* a beautiful room. *I shall think it a dream tomorrow! I shall not be able to believe that I have seen, and touched, and spoken to you once more.*"

"Have you memorized all of *Wuthering Heights*?" he asked.

"Most of it, though I know my favorite parts best," she said, sitting up. "I have read it over and over, throughout my captivity, and played the roles of every character. It has been my only companion."

"I must confess to never having read it," Duskin said. "I'm certain Sarah has."

Lizbeth looked at him in astonishment. "Never read it? But I thought everyone had." The information seemed to daunt her, for she fell silent, then said, "It is a love story."

"From what I've heard, it seems little like one to me," Duskin said. "Only a tale of vengeance."

"Oh, no. It is indeed a love story, for love is betrayal and pain."

"Do you believe that?"

Lizbeth looked at him, her eyes shifting uneasily. "That is the way the Man in the Dark loves me."

Duskin drew back as if struck. "Are you lovers, then?"

"Lovers?" She laughed. "Oh, no. We are like Cathy and Heathcliff; he treats me as his daughter. He gives me twelve candles. He looks after me."

"And is that the kind of love you want?"

"I . . . it is the way it has been."

"When we return to Evenmere you will be free to choose how to live."

"Could I dwell in my old house in Innman Tor, with Sarah and Count Aegis?"

"Sarah dwells there no longer, but you could live with her in the Inner Chambers."

Lizbeth grew thoughtful. "Would I be allowed a pet mouse?"

Duskin laughed. "We will do better than that. We will get you a puppy."

Her eyes widened with longing. "I have not seen a puppy . . . in a long time."

As they traveled through the chamber, journeying always toward a goal only Lizbeth could sense, she turned to Duskin, and said shyly, "If this chamber came from my mind, do you think me childish?"

"Why would I think that?"

"It is filled with toys—"

"I was thinking, rather, that there must be much gentleness within you, if this is the room of your creation. And I was wondering how my own room would compare."

"It would be even more wonderful," she said, smiling.

"I wonder," Duskin said. "Apparently several generations of my family on my mother's side have been anarchists. Have such associations tainted me? Would my room be filled with anarchist drivel? This is the first time I have had a chance to consider my cousin's revelations."

"Does it hurt? Inside, I mean."

Duskin sighed. "It leaves me aching. Much of my childhood has been a lie. I have been groomed, almost from the beginning, to be an anarchist. Had I grown up anywhere but the Inner Chambers, no doubt I would *be* an anarchist, perhaps one of those who kidnapped you. It sickens me to think it."

"You would never have done that to me," she said confidently. "You are kind, Duskin. You were kind to me on the platform of the train station; you have always been kind. And though you were groomed to be an anarchist, as you say, you are not one."

"Sarah once told me I am restless by nature," he replied. "I believe she was right. Perhaps the anarchists' influence kept me from knowing my true place. My mother must have imparted it early on."

"But you have chosen your own way," she said. "Sometimes the Man in the Dark says things which make me feel good; he tells me I will be a princess, that I will oversee the New Order, that though I will never know love, one day men will bow before me in my cold halls.

Yet, I have not dreamed of the future he would give me; I have dreamed of the Little Palace at Innman Tor. I have dreamed of grass and hills and the stars beneath the true sky. I have dreamed of robins. He has taken everything, but he has not taken that."

Duskin chuckled. "Your spirit gives me strength. Let the anarchists come! I will follow your example and my own course. Ultimately, they are fools, too obsessed to see the truth lying within this room."

"I do not know about that, but they are very cruel. And we must leave this chamber soon. We are to travel down a dark passage, the darkest ever."

"Do you fear it?"

"Yes, but it is the way we must go."

The Hidden Hall

Mr. Hope rose from his desk in the gentleman's chamber as Captain Glis strode smartly into the room. The two men shook hands, and Hope poured tea from a silver service.

"I'll come right to the point, sir," Glis said, "because I know you're anxious. We followed Deep Passage down its entire length until we came to a door cast of a material unlike any I have seen before. Bullets and crowbars were useless against it, so at last, knowing the urgency, I ordered dynamite, first against the door itself, then the wall. Both proved impervious. Whatever the substance of Deep Passage, it is fashioned from materials beyond human engineering. We've tried every conceivable approach. I'm sorry."

Hope shrugged and ran his hands over his face. "It's as I feared. It wouldn't be the first time we've found parts of the house invulnerable to our efforts. I doubt even the

Lightning Sword could breach that door. Do you have any suggestions?"

"Only to send a full force into Shyntawgwin. You know the ramifications."

"Yes," Hope said. "Hundreds will be lost. But how long dare we wait? Howard McMurtry fought for the anarchist cause in the Yellow Room Wars; we must assume Sarah, Enoch, and Chant have walked into a trap. I have tried all diplomatic channels; Shyntawgwin is intransigent; Moomuth Kethorvian, as our agents discovered, is empty. The house is changing more every day."

"We have begun mobilizing our forces," Glis said. "Within two weeks, we can have an army at the borders of Shyntawgwin."

"Two weeks, while we hear nothing from Lord Anderson," Hope said, his eyes feverishly bright. "Very well I suppose the time has come for the brave jaw. Continue your preparations. I've chosen a poor time to become Evenmere's butler, I'm afraid."

Captain Glis rose and the two shook hands again. "I'm not certain there is a good time to be butler of the High House." And then he departed.

Drawn by the shard, Carter led into the opulent hall, Crane and McMurtry behind him. The unnatural silence of a deserted chamber reigned. Tiered galleries rose, row upon row, to the heights—the ceiling was a distant square—and everywhere chandeliers, lanterns, and lamps emitted a clean golden light. Rows of statues, covered in gold, of Sarah, Duskin, Count Aegis, and even Carter, stared from long alcoves. The stairs were inlaid with but-terflies and puppy faces in mother-of-pearl; bronze robins postured on the newel posts. And over all, the ubiquitous thorns.

"It's like something out of the Early Aylyrium era," Mr. Crane said in a low voice. "This is worth the journey, wouldn't you say, Mr. McMurtry?"

"Perhaps, Mr. Crane, depending on how it ends."

They walked around the gallery, slipping between the alcoves, and were half the distance through the enormous hall, when Howard McMurtry suddenly clutched his chest and staggered against the wall.

"Are you well?" Crane asked.

"I'm suddenly out of breath," McMurtry said, "and my chest feels heavy. I have difficulty with my heart some-times. My medicine is in my coat."

Carter helped him sit, and found a jar of white pills in his pocket. McMurtry placed one beneath his tongue and began taking heavy breaths.

"We will wait," Carter said.

"No, Lord Anderson," McMurtry said. "There is no time. You must go on. You as well, Mr. Crane. I'll catch up shortly. Even now the anarchists might be bearing down upon us. I'll be there by the time you find the Cor-nerstone."

"I don't like to leave him," Carter said to Crane.

"He has these spells, occasionally, Lord Anderson. I don't believe there's anything to fear. You'll hide in one of the alcoves, won't you, Mr. McMurtry? Keep yourself safe?"

Reluctantly, driven by necessity, feeling as if he were

deserting a comrade, Carter continued down the gallery, Mr. Crane at his side. They descended a sweeping stair.

"The Cornerstone is here," Carter said softly.

"Where?" Crane asked eagerly.

"There," Carter pointed.

Twenty feet within a wide corridor leading from the end of the hall stood a stone block on a granite pedestal. Beyond, far down the passage, a pair of French doors stood open to the outside, with a wind blowing the gossamer drapery hung over the lintel and only darkness beyond. Something about the look of it made Carter shiver.

"Are you certain that's it?" Crane asked.

"Yes. I sense its power. We have only to take it, and step out of those double doors."

"Then my work, and yours, is done," Crane said, pointing his pistol at Carter's chest. "Please do me the favor of dropping your gun."

"What are you doing?" Carter demanded.

"My duty, sir, as an anarchist," Crane replied. "Steady, Lord Anderson, I warn you! Don't be deceived by my age. I am a crack shot. Drop your weapon, please."

Carter laid his gun on the floor, then stood silent, mind turning furiously.

"When I was a young man I lost my entire family to consumption," Crane said. "It was the beginning of my conversion to the anarchist philosophy. I was the one who first learned of the Cornerstone, over twenty years ago. The Society had planned its seizure ever since. Even when the Bobby stole the Master Keys, it was with this ultimate objective. And it was I who overheard your conversation with Duskin, and used the information to lure your wife, the Lamp-lighter, and the Windkeep to the False House."

"Sarah?" Carter said, stunned.

"Yes. The anarchists are firm believers in turning disadvantage to advantage. When we discovered you were coming to the Outer Darkness we determined to utilize the information. It has worked out well, for you have helped us locate the Cornerstone. Ah, yes, I see the surprise in your eyes. We had indeed lost it, or rather, we had underestimated the abilities of Lizbeth to be a conduit for that power. She is a strong-willed child. Six months ago, the Cornerstone abruptly vanished. The Man in the Dark searched everywhere for it, and then realized she had moved it somehow—not consciously, of course. Then we learned of the shard. I would have killed you and taken it while you slept, except only you can feel its pull.

"Don't look at me that way, Lord Anderson," Crane continued. "I'm not an evil man. Quite the contrary. Someday you'll thank me for this, when we live in a world freed from death and despair."

"You've seen the effects of the Cornerstone," Carter said. "Are those mechanical men on the plain what the anarchists want?"

"It *has* been . . . disturbing," Crane said. "I admit it freely. And the architecture here is dreadful! But that is because most of it is the product of Lizbeth's underdeveloped mind. This hall alone is the exception; it gives me hope for what the world may become."

"What do you plan to do now?" Carter asked.

"We are waiting for the Man in the Dark. Mr. McMurtry and I were followed from the moment we entered the house. My job will be done once the Cornerstone is safe."

"Your job is done, already, I'm afraid, Mr. Crane," a voice said. McMurtry stepped from behind a row of statues, his weapon trained on his friend.

"Mr. McMurtry," Crane said. "How good of you to join us."

"Yes, please drop the gun, Mr. Crane," McMurtry said. "I have no desire to harm you. All these years! And I had only recently begun to suspect you as an anarchist. That's why I feigned trouble with my heart."

"You were always astute," Crane said. "But I have no intention of surrendering. I am a better shot than I pretend, and if you pull the trigger I will kill Lord Anderson before I fall, unless you are a good enough marksman to slay me instantly. His death, though unfortunate, is preferable to our losing the Cornerstone. I am willing to die for this cause, my old companion, and you know I do not lie. But the other anarchists will be here any moment. You haven't a chance, unless you choose to rejoin us. You would be accepted once again."

"I don't want to be accepted, Mr. Crane," McMurtry said, raising his gun. "I gave that up long ago, after the Yellow Room Wars. Yes, that's right, Lord Anderson. I once fought for the anarchist cause. But their doctrine is flawed. They cannot do as they claim."

"We can," Crane said. "We can make the world anew. We can bring my wife and children back, and live in perfect harmony."

Carter stood helpless, Crane's gun upon him, seeking to summon the Word Which Manifests to his lips. Momentarily, he glimpsed it, an ashen spark within his mind, but it faded before he could bring it forth.

"Mr. Crane, I beg you," McMurtry said, voice trembling. "For the sake of our years together, put the gun down. This is your last chance."

"No," Crane replied, brow set, hand firm upon the pistol. "I've always been the optimistic one, wouldn't you say, Mr. McMurtry? I like to believe you won't shoot your lifelong associate. And as I said, you're out of practice with a weapon. Like a leather boot unworn for years, too stiff for service."

McMurtry made no reply, but aimed carefully and pulled the trigger. Lord Anderson jumped at the report, thinking himself shot, but Crane dropped straight to the ground with the barest cry. Rushing to him, Carter found him dead, a single wound in the center of his forehead.

McMurtry dropped the gun from trembling fingers; it clattered to the floor. He hurried to Crane's side, lifted the man's head to his breast, and whispered, "You were wrong, Phillip. I was always an expert marksman. But you had no way of knowing." And then he wept, crooning softly, over and over, "Old friend. Old friend. I have killed my best friend."

Seeing nothing could be done, Carter rose, retrieved his pistol, and approached the Cornerstone. The shard nearly pulled itself from his hand. Except for the numerous inscriptions and the four cherubim shining like brass upon it, it looked no more than ordinary stone, but he paused ten feet away, unable to advance against the immeasurable and terrible power flowing from it, an energy only the Master could perceive, nearly unbearable, the spark of Creation, bespeaking the power of suns, the birth of life, the eternal void between the stars. Nearly, he wanted to worship it; almost, he fled. And he sensed more besides; he knew the purpose of the Cornerstone was being warped, and that it was, indeed, *resisting*, as he had once suspected, though it was, paradoxically, in no sense alive.

He drew deep breath and lifted his hands to seize the stone from its place, closing his eyes as he did so, for though it emitted no light, its power stabbed into his mind, so he could not look upon it.

"That will be quite far enough, Lord Anderson!" a voice called at his back. To his shock, he turned to find Gregory covering him with a rifle, while two of the Transformed stood guarding Mr. McMurtry, who still knelt by his friend.

"Not you, too!" Carter exclaimed, shaken to the core. "Was our company filled with traitors?"

"I am truly sorry," Gregory said, face set. "Duskin at least I hoped would join us freely. I trust he may, yet. I have not enjoyed the role of spy, though it was done for the best of causes. Now, drop your weapons, please. I have no wish to kill you."

Carter laid his pistol and the two Lightning Swords upon the floor, cursing himself for being twice caught unawares. And then he sensed the approach of a powerful and familiar force. His eyes turned to the stair, where the Man in the Dark, swathed in his robes, descended, surrounded by an entourage of the Transformed, including likenesses of Enoch, Chant, Sarah, Nooncastle, and several members of the White Circle Guard. In that terrible instant, Carter realized these were, indeed, his very companions; he struggled for breath; his knees trembled.

"Oh, Sarah!" he groaned, unable to contain himself. "Not you!"

"Yes," the Man in the Dark said in a low, chilling voice. "And the entourage is nearly complete. You have given us victory, Lord Anderson, all in one stroke. If you had not chanced upon Mr. Crane, we would have captured you, then arranged your escape, accompanied by him, to lead us here. The Cornerstone is found, and you, the final piece, have been placed in our hands. We sought to make Duskin Master of the house, but his acquiescence was required and he would not. Now, he is no longer needed. Since you are Master already, once you, too, are changed, the house will have its Master, whether you will or not. The victory is nearly won."

Carter sought to pull his thoughts together, but they swarmed like bees. "I recognize you," he finally said. "I sense your power. Why do you hide behind your shrouds? Show yourself, Lady Order!"

The Man in the Dark laughed a deep rumble. "In Evenmere, you could command me; here you cannot. But I will comply; the time for masks is done."

The Man in the Dark removed his hat, and raven tresses tumbled from beneath it; he drew the swathings from his face, revealing a dual visage: on the left side the features of a middle-aged, intellectual man, on the right the beautiful woman who Carter had once called Anina, her eyes dark, her skin moon-white, her face wholly symmetrical, a perfection unknown to mortal kind. She gave a soft laugh, like tinkling bells, all trace of manliness fallen from her. "It was a game well played, flawless in symmetry."

"And what of the Supreme Anarchist?" Carter asked.

"He foolishly thought to control the forces of Order before understanding the Cornerstone completely. Even from the beginning, when he used his machines to tap my power at Innman Tor, and to strike at you there, he was too ambitious. But he is with me yet, as you can see, though he controls little now. He, rather than Lizbeth, has become the avatar of Order."

Carter glanced at Gregory, who having turned nearly as pale as the Lady herself, said, "So this is why you emptied the house."

"Indeed. Order should be granted to those who first sought it, as a reward for faithful service. So will all of you become, in time. You, sooner than the others, Lord Anderson. The house will have a Master, a Windkeep, and a Lamp-lighter. I will bring all into the timeless precision of Order. Random events will ocase. Time itself will end. All will be beautiful repetition. All will be One. But first, Lizbeth must be found. She is tuned to the Cornerstone; her will, through it, creates Chaos. She is Dreamer, Thorn-maker, Destroyer of Order. She hid the Cornerstone where even I could not find it; her power shields her from my sight. But with the Cornerstone within my possession, she can be destroyed, the power can be rechanneled through me, and the final stage will begin. I will make the cosmos uniform, changeless, and without mind."

"Jormungand said the universe would pass into Eternity if time ends. It will mean utter destruction," Carter said.

"Perhaps. But that, too, will be perfect and beautiful," she replied. "Keep watch upon him," she commanded the transformed White Circle Guard. "And find Lizbeth. I know she is near. I sense her approach."

Lady Order turned from Carter, and stood once more between Sarah and Enoch. Lord Anderson leaned toward Gregory and whispered, "All has gone awry! The plan has failed; the anarchists have lost control. Surely you see it!"

"I have dedicated my life to this cause," Gregory replied passionately, appearing wholly shaken. "In its name I have deceived both Duskin and yourself. Do you think I am proud of that? She promises harmony."

"She will bring only death. This is not the cause you sought. Regardless of her appearance, she is not a person, but Force Incarnate, given physical form by anarchist machinery. She will bring all to Order, regardless of the consequences. Reason means nothing to her, any more than the ocean considers before it drowns a man. Debate is useless. She will pound humanity like surf against the shore. You must help us when the time comes."

Gregory met Carter's gaze with an anguished look, but made no reply.

Lord Anderson turned and surveyed the hall, and suddenly saw, from high in the shadowed ceiling, a pair of enormous eyes looking down.

Lizbeth closed her eyes, thinking of the thorns and the house, and within her mind, found herself staring out from a high ceiling, looking into a great hall. She beheld Carter, and Gregory, and the changed Sarah. *How I wish she were whole again!* Hundreds of the Transformed poured into the room, rank upon rank, lining up before a raven-tressed woman in the garb of the Man in the Dark. With a shock, Lizbeth recognized Lady Order as surely as if the manor had whispered her name, and knew her for the true enemy at last. The revelation stunned her; the Man in the Dark, her tormentor and yet her only guide, had been a sham, a shadow fraud; anguish and relief swirled round her like smoke. For a moment, she thought she might faint, and the vision wavered. Gradually, she caught her breath and it returned.

In the corridor beyond Lady Order stood the French doors, Lizbeth's destination. She had nothing to fear from them now; Carter would not be waiting to stalk her. Before the doors, within the corridor, stood the Cornerstone. She could feel its power channeling through her. Even more, she felt its *call*; it was the source of her strength; she would only grow more powerful as it drew nearer.

She opened her eyes to find Duskin staring expectantly at her. They had left the dayroom and stood in a shadowy alcove of a gloomy corridor.

"I have seen it," she said. "We have only to find a path." She closed her eyes again and envisioned a door, just at Duskin's back, a secret panel with a silver knob, then reached behind him and discovered the cold steel of the mechanism. She laughed in wonder as a portal opened where none had been before, amazed at the certainty she had *made* it appear.

"It is as you said," she told him. "And it was easy."

"You have been building this house for years," Duskin beamed. "Though unaware, you have become well practiced."

As they stepped into the secret way, she told him what she had seen. Then, with the understanding of her newfound abilities, she opened herself, as much as mortal could, to the immeasurable power of the Cornerstone, and recognized for the first time that this vast sprawling manor was her own. It was far larger than she had suspected; the anarchists had kept her secured in a portion of one wing, yet now, every nook, every lock and keyhole, arch and beam, gray stair and stone lane, she knew intimately, and realized, with startling clarity, she had been as much captor as captive, deluded by the lies of the Man in the Dark.

She closed her eyes again, imagining doors and hallways leading to the gilded hall, a creation even finer than the dayroom, and saw all the paths leading to it. Then, she conceived a door, and a secret way, the most direct course, and she spoke the route, and it was so. Doors, stairs, hallways, appeared at her command. She noticed the stunned light in Duskin's eyes, a gleam of wonder and awe. She returned a smile and said, "I told you we would travel down the darkest way of all; darkness may indeed lie at the end of our journey, if Lady Order catches us, but now I can take us quickly through lighted ways."

Together, they walked the False House. She soon brought them to a hidden panel, white and shining, with a pentagonal spy-hole.

"Beyond lies the hallway of the Cornerstone," she said, "and the French doors, which are my sole means of leaving the house. Yet, Lady Order is there and will try to stop me."

"Carter says she is immensely powerful," Duskin said. "Is there no other way out?"

"None. I see it clearly, now, for it is the escape I have made for myself."

"Then we will go together," Duskin said, giving her a brave smile.

Soundlessly, they opened the panel, and leaving it wide, slipped down the hallway, the Cornerstone behind them, the French doors before, the wind flapping on the curtains, the night air cool upon their faces.

Suddenly, an implacable stone wall appeared between them and their goal. They turned, and Lady Order stood beside the Cornerstone, all trace of the Supreme Anarchist gone from her, dressed in silver and ivory, beautiful, serene as a goddess.

"You have come," she said sweetly. "Now will you serve me?"

Power beat down upon Lizbeth, the perfect energies of Order, the splendor of the ticking clock and the wonder of the revolving worlds. For an instant, she thought she would be consumed, but she raised her hand and deflected the Lady's might, though how it was so she did not know.

Lizbeth turned, and with a thought, made a door materialize within the wall. Tugging Duskin's hand, she led through at a run, into a maze of rooms and corridors, all without exits. Glimpses of her objective flashed in the distance, seen through layers of stained glass.

With Duskin still in tow, she ran, making doors where none had existed, causing corridors to open and passages to curve, going ever forward toward the French doors. An abyss appeared, descending forever; she made it a bridge and flew straight on. The ceiling slid downward; she fashioned an archway. The walls pressed toward her, she carved out a tunnel, her mind operating on a level she did not comprehend.

One of the Transformed appeared from around a corner. Duskin slammed him down with his fist and snapped up the creature's gun. They sped on.

Lizbeth, a voice called into her very mind. *Do not run from me. I am Order and Peace and an end to pain. Stay with me within the house, and I will make you as I am, immutable, incomparable, perfect. We will end death and sorrow. All will function upon a marvelous schedule. You see what your powers can do. If you leave the house, you will die, but here you will never die. Give yourself unto me, and I will grant you your dreams.*

But Lizbeth ran all the faster, thinking only of robins and sunlight and the green plain of Innman Tor.

She threw aside a bulwark standing before her, crumbling it with her thoughts, and a horde of the Transformed fell from its heights to lie broken and whirring. She and Duskin stepped over their forms and sped past. Momentarily glimpsing the French doors again, Lizbeth carved a long passage toward them, bracing it with courage, girting it with hope.

The ceiling came crashing, falling upon them; she flung up a shield of onyx and steel.

Three more of the Transformed leapt in their path; she curved all the passage; the walls took the creatures. The floor began tilting, her footing fell from her; both she and Duskin tumbled a distance. As they rose to their feet, she erected a stairway, winding around pillars, back toward the French doors. Their footfalls sent echoes tapping around them; the whir of the Transformed clattered behind.

Duskin fired at two who drew near, and shots ricocheted on every side, chipping the stair, sending marble flying. Lizbeth raised a wall at their backs and the volleys ceased.

They were once more in a corridor, all of her making, with candles and rosebuds on either side. The French doors were nearer and stood straight before them.

For an instant, Gregory appeared from a branching passage, gun in hand, a strange, sad expression on his face, but then he vanished with the rearranging structures.

Lizbeth's eyes were fastened on the French doors as they abruptly withdrew farther and farther back, diminishing in the distance, as the hall grew ever longer, impossibly large.

"No!" she cried. "I won't allow it!" She focused her will, as if climbing a rock shelf with her fingernails, clutching at the French doors, seeking to draw them near. For years, she had feared them; now they were her whole desire. Yet they slipped ever more distant. *Sarah*, she thought, though why she did not know. *If only you could help me.*

Carter watched helplessly under the guard of the Transformed. It was difficult to know what was occurring. Lady Order stood beside the Cornerstone, while her men charged through a single doorway. Occasionally, the walls shifted, and he caught glimpses of Duskin and Lizbeth, fleeing.

Looking down at his changed hand, he pondered the Words of Power, unsure of using them, lest he become one of the Transformed as well. Still, he focused upon the

Word of Hope, seeing it in reverse order at the edge of his mind, waiting for his opportunity.

He glanced at Sarah, and sorrow shook him. As if reading his thoughts, she approached. His guards had moved back, standing implacable, guns aimed at his heart. She paused beside where he sat, and her form abruptly fluctuated, wavering between its mechanical shape and her true form.

"She needs us, Carter. If you can do anything, do it now."

And then, she was one of the Transformed again.

Regardless of the consequences, he had but one recourse. He brought the Word spinning upward into his throat. He spoke it, a cutting, tearing phrase. *Mirrumhar!* Immediately, he felt his legs go numb and knew they had been altered.

The force of the Word of Hope spread outward, and though it did not affect the Transformed, the wall separating Carter from the French doors fell and corridor after corridor vanished.

A breaking noise occurred, like the shattering of glass. The entire passage around Lizbeth splintered in half. The French doors, too, wavered, but Lizbeth reached out and made them whole, though the entire maze of corridors fell into pieces, leaving only the original passage.

Before her stood the double doors of her dream, flung wide, the blowing wind rattling wood and frame, the air pungent with rain. She pushed forward, leaving Duskin behind in her haste, but halfway down the hall, a young woman, an exact duplicate of herself from when she first came to the False House, stepped between her and the doors.

"You mustn't go," the child said.

Lizbeth slowed and approached warily. "Who are you?"

"I'm Lizbeth. The real Lizbeth. The one who belongs in the outside world. You're trying to leave, but you mustn't."

"I will," Lizbeth said, and sought to brush past the stranger, but she blocked the path.

"Do you think you deserve to be loved?" the child said. "Do you think you deserve *him*? After all you've done?"

Lizbeth stood, still as stone, quivering, unable to think, unable to withstand this creature, though she did not know why.

"Your father brought you here for a reason," the girl said quietly. "He brought you here because you've been bad, so bad you can never be loved. You can't even be a real person. Real people don't get punished like this. Real people aren't so bad even their *fathers* don't love them."

Lizbeth felt her face scrunching into a ball; she stood trembling against an assault more terrible than the lash. She wanted to scream her denial, to destroy this child who had stolen her face, but she was too afraid, too certain it was the truth. Her knees shook; she thought she would be sick.

It's like the book! she thought. *It's all like the book. It must end badly. It must all finish in ruin and death. There is never enough love.*

"No," a voice said softly beside her, and she felt once more the touch of Duskin's hand. He had fallen to his knees, as if the little girl had somehow taken his strength. He spoke with effort, as if fighting for every word. "Lizbeth, do not believe her. Sarah, Carter, and the count love you. I could love you as well. I am certain of it. Your eyes have haunted me from the moment we met. You inhabit my dreams. Lizbeth, do not listen to her! Find the way out; it is she who is not real."

The two gazed full upon one another, blue eyes to blue, and Lizbeth listened, the words slipping deep into her soul.

"You *are* my Hareton," she replied softly, tears suddenly clouding her sight.

When she turned back, her tormentor had changed to a younger version of Lady Order, who stared up at Lizbeth with wise eyes, then abruptly vanished.

Lizbeth sought to help Duskin up, but he could scarcely walk. They glanced back to see Gregory striding toward them, with Lady Order far behind.

"Go!" Duskin cried. "My gun is empty, but I will hold them off."

Lizbeth hurried to the doorway, then hesitated, unwilling to leave him, uncertain what to do. She turned toward the opening and gasped in fear, for a figure suddenly stepped into the circle of light beyond the threshold, exactly as in her dreams. But it was not Carter.

"Father!" she cried, staring at the man she had not seen for six years. He looked the same in every way, dressed in a ragged jacket and bowler hat, his face stern, his eyes as impassive as the day he had given her to the anarchists. Seeing him made her heart ache, but she feared him as well.

"Go back," he growled, snarling like a wolf. "Go back."

"I . . . I can't," she said. "I must go on. Oh, help me, Father. Tell me you have returned to help me."

"Go back," he barked again, stepping into the corridor to bar her path.

The rage of all the lonely years filled her, the fury at his merciless desertion. She threw herself at him, pummeling his chest with fierce, impotent blows he blocked with an arm. "You left me! You left me!" she cried. "I was but a child!"

Abruptly his form slid away; his face lowered; his jaws became fangs; his arms, claws. Yellow eyes stared down upon her. She flew back in terror as the gnawling leapt, eight legs churning. He was upon her, the tearing teeth inches from her face, hunting her throat; she shrieked her horror and tried to fight back.

And then the monster's jaws went slack; its eyes dimmed; it dropped upon her, writhing. She tore herself from beneath it, and it lay, bleeding and dying, biting at the air, blood flowing from a wound on the side of its neck. She scarcely escaped its fangs; its claws raked her shoulder.

Gregory stood a few feet from her, his smoking gun still smoldering. He gave Duskin an anguished look and cried to Lizbeth, "Hurry, girl!"

Lady Order stretched out a hand from where she stood, saying, "Those who have given themselves to me cannot repent," and with a cry, quickly cut short, Gregory dissipated into the air, spinning apart like rags in a whirlwind.

Lizbeth was bleeding in several places; she felt the force of Order beating upon her, but she crawled toward the doors. She bypassed the gnawling, which had grown still. *It wasn't Papa,* she thought. *It was never Papa.* It gave her strength, but her vigor withered as she clawed her way to the threshold.

There was nothing beyond save a gaping abyss, an endless fall into a mountainous pit. She looked behind her, and saw Lady Order approaching Duskin, who stood defiantly barring her way.

"Lizbeth, go!" he cried, not knowing what she saw. "Escape! I cannot stop her!"

She looked back at the abyss and knew there was no other way to end the madness. She did not want to die, but it had to end, before Lady Order destroyed Duskin as she had Gregory, and the whole world with him. Only she could make it end.

She closed her eyes. *The book was right. I will not know love, after all.* She stepped into the abyss, screaming as she tumbled endlessly down.

And then, she was no longer falling, but standing dumbfounded on the solid ground of the Onyx Plain, looking through the doors from outside the False House. And at last she understood it all.

I am the house, she thought. *I am the thorns.* And she knew she had always had the power to leave her prison, had she not imprisoned herself. The anarchists had *feared* her! And so they had left her alone. Order herself avoided her, wary of the power of the Cornerstone flowing through her.

She had no time for further consideration, for the Chaos-hound bounded out of the darkness toward her, teeth bared, mouth foaming. "The Mountains of Despair! The End of the House! The Moon in its Darkness! The walls have fallen! My foe stands before me!" Lizbeth raised her hands to ward its attack.

With a mammoth leap, Chaos cleared both her and Duskin to hurl itself upon Order. As the two collided, the air ignited with a blinding flash that shook the house. When Lizbeth could see again, both Chaos and Order were gone.

Upon their disappearance, the Transformed fell to the ground, writhing in pain. Carter's hands and legs burned, as he turned his eyes toward Lizbeth, who stood beyond the French doors. The entire corridor began to splinter.

"It is finished!" Lizbeth cried. And at the words, the Cornerstone glowed with a golden light.

"Carter, destroy it!" Lizbeth cried. "The Cornerstone must be destroyed. I know it now."

"The Cornerstone?" Carter cried, astonished. "I dare not! It is the foundation of all Creation."

"Destroy it!" Lizbeth cried. "Order is not dead. Strike it, before she reappears!"

The mechanical gears and levers serving as Carter's legs scarcely functioned as he retrieved both Lightning Swords lying heaped together on the ground.

"Mr. McMurtry!" he commanded, because there was no one else. "You must assist me."

Howard McMurtry helped Carter make his way to the Cornerstone, where Lord Anderson raised both swords together and struck at the center of the stone. It parted easily beneath the jagged edge.

An enormous cracking scalded the air; the entire house

rumbled in complaint. And suddenly the Transformed were human again.

"This way!" Lizbeth cried. "Hurry! You must escape the house!"

Carter scarcely noticed the return of his own limbs to normal, for Sarah stood whole beside him once more.

"Lord Anderson!" Nooncastle shouted in dismay, eyeing his men, who rubbed their lids as if awakened from slumber. "What are we doing here?"

"We'll explain when we can," Carter replied. "We have to get out. And bring the Cornerstone shards. Is this all the men, Lieutenant?"

"Aye, sir," Nooncastle said. "More than half were lost."

Carter glanced around. Beside the Cornerstone lay the body of a middle-aged gentleman, with a sharp, intellectual face, the Supreme Anarchist revealed at last, slain by the withdrawal of Order from his mortal shell.

Carter took Sarah's arm, and the reunited companions made their way up the corridor, Nooncastle taking charge of the thousands of freed soldiers within the hall, the White Circle Guard bearing the halves of the Cornerstone with them, while the house groaned as if shivering to pieces.

Together they stepped through the French doors into the darkness of the starless Onyx Plain where Lizbeth and Duskin waited together. It took nearly an hour for all the soldiers to quit the manor, and after fleeing some distance from the False House, they stood gazing at its jumbled enormity.

"Look!" Chant said, pointing at the night sky. "Something winged is rising from the attic."

A vast, serpentine bulk rose from the False House, beating the air with massive, leathern strokes.

"Jormungand," Carter murmured. "He said he was once called *dragon*."

As he rose, the monster grew, until his wings overshadowed the whole house. From above, he tore the towers and gables with furious claw strokes; fire poured from his maw to engulf the wooden frame. The roofs ignited all at once, and the flame spread quickly down, the heat driving the companions back.

Explosions erupted from the basements, kindled from unknown fuels, and the whole structure began to slide, tumbling upon itself in a furious destruction. It collapsed with unbelievable speed, the noise of its fall deafening.

With a roar that shook the Onyx Plain, Jormungand turned, wings beating north, toward Evenmere.

As the flames consumed the False House, the companions threw off the last vestiges of their Transformation, an inner haze that thinned and vanished. They looked at one another in gratitude and delight.

Carter touched Sarah's cheek, ran his hands over her shoulders, and abruptly lifted her into the air by the waist. "You're alive!" he shouted.

And suddenly Duskin, and Enoch, and Chant, and Carter, and Sarah, and even Nooncastle, and McMurtry, and the rest of the soldiers were shouting and hugging and clapping one another on the back. But when Sarah turned to Lizbeth, she took her thin hands into her own, and stared into her face, the older a head taller than the younger.

Sarah's voice broke as she said, "Is it really you?"

"Do you still remember me?" Lizbeth asked in a small voice. "I thought you had forgotten."

"Dear, dear Lizbeth!" Sarah said, tears streaming down, reaching to stroke her face and hair. "How could I forget you? No day passed without my thinking of you, praying for you. Oh, Lizbeth! I could never forget you."

And for a time they wept in each other's arms.

At last, they stepped back and looked at one another. Lizbeth wiped her eyes with the back of her hand and asked, "Is it a scientific fact?"

"Like osmosis and steam engines," Sarah said, grinning back.

When Carter came to Lizbeth she grew suddenly shy. He grimaced to see how disheveled and thin she was, and his own voice grew hoarse with emotion.

"You had nothing to do with my kidnapping?" Lizbeth asked.

"I swear it," Carter replied.

"The Man in the Dark lied?"

"About everything."

Lizbeth scooted a pebble with her bare foot. "I'm sorry I taunted you through the bars to the basement."

"It was nothing," Carter said, holding his arms wide.

She hesitated only an instant before bolting into his embrace.

"I love you, child," Carter murmured, stroking her hair.

"I love you, Carter," and she wept once more.

They were interrupted by a final crashing clatter, as the last portions of the False House sank in upon itself, growing smaller as it fell, until it vanished altogether, as if it had been but a dream, leaving only a few scattered flames flickering on the bare rock.

Amazed, the companions wandered over the plain where it had stood, but found no trace.

While all the others were intent upon the house, Lizbeth and Duskin stood apart.

"Will you go back to hunting gnawlings again?" Lizbeth asked, suddenly shy, glancing at him from the corner of her eye.

"No," Duskin said, taking her hand. "I will never again hunt them for sport. Gregory is dead, and I have found something better. I have been frivolous long enough. It is time I gave up boyish things and took up the mantle of a man."

"Did you mean it when you said you could love me?"

"In those last moments before you stepped through the door, I knew it was so. I love you already, Lizbeth."

"And I have loved you forever," she said.

She waited, head upturned, and he took her in his arms and kissed her.

"Look," Sarah said, from her place by Carter's side. The Master of Evenmere turned, and raised his eyebrows in surprise. Then he and his wife exchanged broad smiles.

Chant came and stood beside them. *"And he to her a hero is, And sweeter she than primroses; Their common silence dearer far Than nightingale and mavis are."*

Evenmere

The next few days proved difficult. Thousands of the Transformed had died with the destruction of the False House, and those who survived awoke bewildered, remembering little of their ordeal. Carter and his companions took charge and led them home to Moomuth Kethorvian, much to the dread of the Shyntawgwin people, who found an armed horde filing into their lands from the Outer Darkness. Their leader, Lord Jegged, caught unawares, willingly negotiated a passage, though that, too, nearly proved disastrous—the soldiers of Moomuth soon realized the part the Shyntawgwins had played in their enslavement, and Carter, armed once more with the Words of Power, used all the persuasion of the Master to insure a peaceful journey.

The way grew easier after leaving Moomuth Kethorvian, and with no need to travel in secrecy, the companions soon found themselves safely back in the Inner Chambers. Thereafter, the first duty was the discreet replacement of the Cornerstone in its niche, which caused abundant debate on whether the artisans of Evenmere should attempt to rejoin the two halves, though the fear of causing further harm dissuaded Carter at last.

Nooncastle led the surviving members of the White Circle Guard in setting the two pieces in their place, and Carter, Sarah, Duskin, Lizbeth, Chant, and Enoch came to Innman Tor to observe. Count Aegis was there, and stood beside Sarah, who occasionally helped him push his glasses up over his nose, while Lizbeth continuously hugged him, keeping never more than a foot from his heels. Already, light and love had wrought a change upon her, as if she had grown from a girl to a woman overnight.

The soldiers laid the two halves of the Cornerstone into the hole, then Carter came forward with the shard, and wedged it into its place at the right-hand corner. The three separate parts fused at once with a loud hiss, and smoke rose from the seams. The cherubim and symbols etched upon the stone swirled beneath the smoke as if flying, and as Carter stepped back in surprise, a burst of red and green flame ascended, and within it, for so brief an instant as to provoke uncertainty, a figure stood, clothed in white, ivory hair flowing down to his shoulders, a sword in one hand and a miter in the other. His eyes gleamed, but did not fasten on the surrounding mortals, as if he looked upon distant vistas beyond their understanding, and for this Carter was glad, for the light of his gaze was too terrible to be borne. The earth trembled, as did those assembled, and then he was gone, vanishing to the east. And some said it was an angel, and others, a trick of the light. But Carter dropped to his knees and bowed his head, and his followers did likewise.

"Behold, I lay in Sion a chief Cornerstone, elect, precious: and he that believeth on him shall not be confounded," Chant said softly.

They left the crater at Innman Tor in silence. Later that year, Carter would raise a mound of stones above it, covering the Cornerstone from human sight for all time.

After that, many of the altered halls and corridors in Evenmere became as they had been before, though not all, as if to leave a reminder of what horrors might have been. And three days later, when Carter returned to the Inner Chambers, strange news reached him. He sought Lizbeth, and found her seated in the breakfast nook, drinking tea from a silver cup and staring out at the sun upon the melting snow, its reflection shimmering off her golden hair, which fell in curls across her back. After only a week of decent food, her gauntness was fading, and she greeted him with eyes filled with both sorrow and delight, which never, in all her life, lost their peculiar, haunted quality.

"Good morning," Carter said. "What are you watching?"

She smiled, but it quickly paled into thoughtfulness. "It's all so new. I think everything will always be new for me, every sunrise, every leaf, every touch of a human hand. Do you see how this cup reflects the light? I could watch it for hours! I have missed so much for so long; my childhood has been stolen, and it saddens me. And yet, how else might I appreciate the light, since I have been so long in darkness?" She looked down at her finely beaded bodice and yellow skirt, and her eyes shone. "That I, who thought never to wear a new dress again, should sit here, today, is more than a miracle. It is the answer to all my dreams."

"I have a bit of news," Carter said softly, sitting beside her and taking her hand. "It is good, but strange."

"Tell me," she said eagerly.

"Word came today. Apparently, where the ebony plain and the Outer Darkness stood, a new portion of the house has appeared, complete with rooms and halls, doors and furniture."

Lizbeth sat in silence, before saying, "Is it real?"

"They say so. It appeared a few moments after we replaced the Cornerstone. They haven't investigated it all yet, but they report a special room in the center, the most beautiful of all, a domed chamber, with giant dolls and trains, and stuffed figures of Duskin, Sarah, Count Aegis, and myself."

"Are there windows?" she asked.

"Hundreds of them. And skylights as well. That is one of the things they reported. The sun shines everywhere through glass."

"Is the dark plain gone forever, then?"

"No, it still exists, but it has been pushed back."

Lizbeth looked again at the sun upon the snow. "That's good. But I don't understand."

"Nor do I," Carter said. "Except I believe your sacrifice is the cause, when you stepped unselfishly into the abyss. I thought you should like to know."

Mr. McMurtry remained a week in the Inner Chambers, still morose at Phillip Crane's death, and Carter doubted he would ever recover from the loss of his friend. But one day, he entered the dining room where Lord Anderson sat, and standing brave and stiff before him, said: "Mr. Crane and I worked together at the grand old firm of McMurtry and Crane for forty-two years. He was like my right appendage. And except at the end, I never once suspected him of being an anarchist. He knew of my history, of course, though I confided in no one else. I assume charges will be leveled against me now, for my participation in the Yellow Room Wars. Very well, I have come to tell you I am ready. I have carried the burden of my guilt long enough. It is time it came out."

"Then you have been punished enough," Carter said. "You were a soldier fighting in what you believed a just cause, and the Master has power to pardon. You aided us in the recovery of the Cornerstone; you gave me strength at the end. You are free to go with the blessing of the Inner Chambers. What will you do now?"

McMurtry sighed, gave a thin smile, and raised his eyebrows. "If I am not to go to prison, I think I will retire to Keedin. I have a house there, and will try to finish our book, so I may dedicate it to Mr. Crane. Even though he was an anarchist, I still think I should. But I wonder if I ever *shall* finish it?"

But Mr. McMurtry did complete his book, *The Many-Splendored House*, which is still considered the definitive tome on the architecture of Evenmere, seen on the coffee tables of priests, kings, and prime ministers. Carter fondly kept a copy by his desk all the days of his life.

Later that week, with the dread that always encompassed him at the prospect of meeting Jormungand, Carter ascended the attic stair, lantern in hand, not knowing if he would face a dinosaur, a dragon, or nothing at all. But as he crossed the dusty floor, red eyes unlidded; the reptile's head rose to the ceiling, his form no longer small or faded. A damp, reptilian reek smote Carter; sword teeth glistened diamond points. Lord Anderson caught his breath and stepped forward.

"So! The little Master," the dinosaur boomed. "Come to reminisce on our trials together? We've grown close as brothers, no doubt. Have you brought any more anarchists for lunch, or is there a shortage?"

"I came to inquire about you," Carter said.

Jormungand gave a snort of flame and shook the entire attic with a thump of his leaden tail. "How touching your concern! Wouldn't want to lose the conversational komodo, would we? The gecko soothsayer, monitor medium, revelatory race runner? Never a clairvoyant gila monster around when you need one. How would we get along?"

"The house is my responsibility," Carter said. "You are part of it."

Jormungand blew another blast, singeing the air above Carter's head and catching his hat on fire. He cast it to the ground and stomped out the blaze, then stood shaking in terror beneath the dinosaur's rage.

"Like the pots in the kitchen or a portrait in the picture gallery?" Jormungand roared. "How *dare* you compare me to your meager obligations! You rank me with a davenport when I am the only matter of consequence in the house? That which is essential *is* invisible; thus I remain hidden in the attic. Such mortal temerity!"

The ordeal of the False House had left Carter immeasurably weary, the burning of his hat made him afraid; he grew furious.

"No!" he shouted. "You are *not* the only matter of consequence! I have heard your hopeless babble, your chattering of your own importance, enough! These mortals saved your life! These mortals kept you from ending as a windup toy. You call us nothing; gnats and flies, living and giving birth and dying in endless succession, with neither value nor significance. You call us cursed, declaring our every accomplishment a vanity. And perhaps we *are* cursed, but I say it is the curse of never perceiving the true value of existence, of never fully knowing the wonder of the morning sun, the blue sky, the touch of a lover's hand. Deny it as you will, but I look upon myself and see a man fearfully and wonderfully made. I say the spark of God burns within each one of us. The very existence of this house gives the lie to all your words. I will listen no more; neither will I submit to your hopelessness."

Carter fell silent, breathing heavily, aghast at his own impertinence, while tons of muscle and bone shifted overhead. A fear descended that at last he had given Jormungand liberty and reason to devour him.

An immense roar shook the attic. Carter braced himself, then realized the great beast was . . . laughing.

"Jormungand is amused," he said after a time. "The worm turns on the Worm. But perhaps you are right. Perhaps you and your kind will ascend to your gaudy heaven. Perhaps you will walk with the angels." The dinosaur rumbled his laughter again. "Perhaps the monkeys have a

Maker. If it comforts you, believe it. I do not, for I am *Despair*. I am Futility raging against Darkness. When time ends, as it surely must, so will Jormungand. And if the only significant being in this miserable universe should cease, why should you survive?"

The dinosaur blew flames across the heights of the attic. Smoke roiled from his mouth. "Do you expect me to be grateful you saved my life, especially when by doing so, you spared your own useless skins? If Jormungand had remained changed, if Despair had passed from the earth as the anarchists wished, Hope, too, would have perished. And that, mortal man, no human could bear. But in the spirit of cooperation, I will be touched; you and the child did save me from the fate of a pocket watch. I am forever in your debt; cross my heart. Thank you, oh so much."

Jormungand blew flames again, as if in momentary contemplation, sitting as a man smoking a pipe might rest and reflect. At last, when the silence had grown frightening, he said, "Very well. A present then. A present for the little Master. You desire a child, Carter Anderson. Within the year, you shall have one."

Carter had expected almost anything, but at Jormungand's words, the blood drained from his face. "You monster!" he said softly. "Mocker! This is a trick! A lie! Or will my wife conceive some changeling beast?"

Jormungand laughed again. "So much for faith and hope. Your prayers are answered and you question the source. Or did you disbelieve your own supplications? How like mortals! If I were an archangel or a stork you would be on your knees in gratitude by now. But no! Throw in some teeth and a healthy appetite, and it doesn't fit your preconceptions. Jormungand does not lie. No changeling; no beast; a healthy child. I will not disclose the gender."

"You haven't the power to grant this," Carter said. "You are a destroyer, not a maker."

Jormungand's eyes flickered, the equivalent of a raised eyebrow. "Don't I? Well, perhaps I do and perhaps I don't, but I have the power to see what will occur, and to speak it. And that is my gift to you, the present of the Last Dinosaur."

"Then . . . thank you, Jormungand," Carter said, still filled with doubt. "It is rather unlike you."

"It is *exactly* like me. Do you think this child will bring you joy? It will be a source of sleepless nights, wee rebellions, endless alarms, and constant debate. For the rest of your minuscule years you and your wife will think of, talk of, worry about, and listen to nothing else. It will be your whole obsession. Its victories will be your own; its wounds your anguish. And when you love it most, it will leave you. All the gifts of Jormungand are two-edged. The lives of humans are filled with tiny dooms, and I have just pronounced one for you."

They stood in silence, Carter seeking to absorb the proclamation. Finally, knowing nothing else to say, he replied, "Your destruction of the False House was total. Many lives were lost."

"The destruction of whatever I turn my hand toward is absolute," Jormungand replied. "Every relationship in this world ultimately ends in sorrow; I see to that. It is the nature of the game. Be thankful it took time to free myself from the attic, or you would have died in the house with the others, Master or no. But the anarchists made a fatal mistake in seeking to bridle me, though I admire their audacity, like little scientists removing the oxygen from a room to purify the air. I am a Force and a Power; one does not take the Last Dinosaur from the universe and expect it to continue."

"You say you are Despair," Carter said. "Are you Death as well?"

"I am Jormungand. I have many names but only a single nature. Now, depart from me. Or would you prefer to stay and play a game of Hide and Eat? You hide first, hmmm?"

"No," Carter said. "Thank you . . . thank you for telling me of the child."

"Not at all. I could be mistaken for Father Christmas, except I consumed him in the sixteenth century. The elves were the hors d'oeuvres. But don't tell your children. Mustn't upset the little ones."

As Carter backed away from the behemoth, a gradual happiness descended upon him. Though Jormungand often withheld the truth, he never truly lied, and of all the times he had descended the attic, this once he left whistling.

Spring finally came; the winds died; the snows ceased; trees blossomed around Evenmere, as did the love between Lizbeth and Duskin. Carter, Sarah, and Mr. Hope, having just finished a lunch of beef sirloin with glazed onions, sat on wooden lawn chairs in the yard, beside the stone well, surrounded by immense oaks, hedges, and the short brick wall with bronze statues of angels, longbows drawn, at each of the four corners. Duskin and Lizbeth had wandered away, hand in hand, and were talking together beside the grape arbor.

"Lizbeth laughs now," Sarah said. "She didn't when we first brought her."

"She's a peculiar girl," Mr. Hope said.

"She's extraordinary," Carter replied, "You would agree if you had seen where she lived the last six years. She kept herself sane where many would not."

The three sat silent, listening to the couple's laughter. A throstle landed on one of the angels, hopped down along the fence, and burst into song. Carter finally said, "I nearly despaired on the Onyx Plain, when the Words of Power were stripped from me. Terrified by my circumstances, thinking myself forsaken, I lost all faith. I forgot the throstle's song."

"Easily done in the darkness," Sarah said.

"Yes. Too easily. I learned much about myself. I hope to do better, if peril comes again."

"And so you shall, I suspect," Hope said. "The metal is tested in the forge."

"So I hope," Carter said. "Of course, I don't understand it all. Would God allow his Creation to be destroyed? Gregory, Crane, many of the White Circle Guard, and thousands of those from Moomuth Kethorvian died in the False House. We could have perished as well. The anarchists had lost control of their devices; Lady Order had mastered the Man in the Dark and was about to annihilate the cosmos."

"But she didn't," Sarah said. "So apparently God did not allow it. You and Lizbeth were the instruments preventing it. *When thou passest through the waters, I will be with thee.*"

"Yes," Carter replied. "But I am not fool enough to think the world ends with a 'they lived happily ever after.'"

"Perhaps because we do not know what 'ever after' means," Sarah replied. "In *Phantastes*, MacDonald said, 'A great good is coming—is coming—is coming to thee . . .' I believe it is so; despite the trials and torments the prisoner is finally released from the False House to walk in the light."

Carter rose and placed one hand on the shoulder of his wife, the other on the shoulder of his friend. He watched the bird warbling on the fence, the snails upon the walls of the well, and the sunlight on the new grass. "I know this," he said. "A great good has come to me, in the form of those I love. And if Duskin and Lizbeth can be happy, it is a very great good, indeed."

Sarah smiled at her husband and poured another cup of tea.

About the Author

JAMES STODDARD has had fiction and articles published in such magazines as *Amazing Stories* and *Marion Zimmer Bradley's Fantasy Magazine*. He is an instructor of music recording and engineering at a junior college in Texas and is currently completing his Master's Degree in liberal studies at Oklahoma Univeristy, with an emphasis in archaeology, English, and ancient mythology. *The High House*, his previous novel, received the Compton Crook/Stephen Tall Award for Best First Novel. *The False House* is his second.

717